About the Author

James grew up in Yorkshire and believes h
of fiction was listening to his father's long
stories. A love of the arts was nurtured in his school days and continued through university and beyond. But above all else James has had a lifelong love of history through the ages, which his crowded bookshelves and hundreds of holiday diversions pay witness to.

Historical research work on the two world wars, combined with further battlefield trips to the region, triggered a desire to tell the stories of the ordinary men and women involved at home and on the front lines. Since then, numerous writing courses have followed, as James has worked alongside some of the leading authors in the world to learn the art of combining fact and fiction. This is the second book in the Davison Family Saga, set during World War One, which encapsulates all his interests.

James brings compassion and humour into everything he creates, and a very experienced eye for detail. He has in turn begun tutoring the next generation of aspiring writers, which he finds immensely rewarding. But put simply, he just loves to tell stories. He hopes you feel that, as you read his work. Thank you.

Praise for the author's first book in the series – The Whistle

'Loved every page of this emotive book. Sowerby had me hooked from start to finish, I didn't want the story to end. Can't wait for Will's next adventure, as I am sure it will be just as skilfully crafted.'

'The characters leap out at you as if they are reading the book as well. So vivid and believable. The horror and humour of war are captured perfectly in a story that is well thought out and perfectly executed. I thoroughly enjoyed this book and have recommended it to anyone who will listen.'

'I loved this book and couldn't put it down. James Sowerby's accomplished writing and the level of historical detail make this book about ordinary people in the extraordinary circumstances of WW1 utterly compelling.'

'The Whistle transports you from rural Sussex to the trenches of France. I was completely drawn in to the lives of the characters and I cried, laughed and stood shoulder to shoulder with them, waiting for the whistle'.

'An excellent debut novel from a first-time author. The characters are sensitively written and they become as familiar and lovable as your own family and friends as you follow their story from the slower, more gentile normality of life in a small farming community through to the chaos, confusion, sometimes (surprisingly) banality, and ultimate horrors of the trenches in France.'

'The thing I liked most about this novel is that the narrative is character driven. The Great War backdrop, is one that has been used many times by many great authors but this is different as the action of the war itself is almost secondary to the characters we meet along the way and their very individual experiences... I cannot wait for the next instalment of what I'm sure will become a much-loved saga'

For my Family…

Published by New Generation Publishing in 2021

For historical accuracy to underpin this novel, key events from the First World War are referred to. The majority of names and characters in this book however are entirely fictitious and any similarity to people, events and places past or present is entirely coincidental. Where certain names or locations have been used from 1916-1917, these have been done by kind permission as per the acknowledgements, or due to the fact that the towns in particular remain today. But with that, most of the buildings named are again entirely fictitious.

A CIP catalogue record for this title is available from the British Library

ISBN

Paperback	978-1-80031-498-6
Hardback	978-1-80031-497-9
Ebook	978-1-80031-496-2

Cover design by Lilly Louise Allen, https://lillylouiseallen.com

www.newgeneration-publishing.com

The Post

The Post

James Owen Sowerby

The Post

Prologue. June 1916

The grass felt cool and refreshing beneath his bare feet as he continued to walk forwards, the strands flicking beneath his toes as he brushed them this way and that. The sun was still not clear of the building behind him and he walked in a cold shadow, the early morning moisture adding a chilling exuberance to the sensations shooting up his legs. A firm breeze blew hard against his face now, forcing him to bow his head slightly, but this was a minor irritation compared to the sense of relief he felt being out in the open air once more; after days spent cooped up in the hospital.

Will Davison stood in his hospital issued pyjamas and dressing gown looking out across the ground. He felt the pure dew in the air and breathed in deeply. The cold made his chest constrict however, and his breathing became harder so he paused for a moment before continuing his journey.

He heard a woman shouting for him to come back. The sound forced its way into his thoughts causing him to frown, but Will continued forward regardless. The female voice was soon drowned out by other voices - men shouting at him to return. The voices sounded familiar, scared, urging him back. He knew if he looked round he would waiver, so he broke into a run now, away from safety out across the lawn.

As he ran the lush grass was replaced by an endless black mud that sucked at his every stride and the rain roared in to join the onslaught, lashing his weakened frame. His dressing gown, suddenly sodden, weighed heavily about him and he threw it off just as the first shell landed on the lawn. Will zig zagged away from the explosion, knowing it was his best chance of survival and dropped into a previous shell's crater to get his bearings.

Lieutenant Dunn was no more than thirty yards in front of him but he was not moving, and Will saw the dreaded fog creeping towards the officer like a spider moving in on a wounded prey. But instead of running towards him, instinct pulled him diagonally away from the officer to where the fallen body of Private Castle lay face down in the mud. He turned him over, knowing what he'd see but it was a grisly sight none the less. Maggots and other insects crawled in and out of the bullet holes that covered his comrade's body, feasting on his insides, and he had to fight not to vomit and rolled him back over. He reached down and pulled the mask off Castle's face and looked inside. There was blood on the front, and another large worm wriggled inside and he shook it out before checking to see the mask still worked. Satisfied he sprinted back the way he had come towards the lieutenant.

Dunn was in a bad way and had passed out with the pain. Both his legs were clearly broken and lay at ridiculous angles, and his clothes were tattered and bloody. Will checked him for signs of life and looked back into the fog, relieved that he couldn't see the Germans from here; which he hoped meant they couldn't see him either. The sickly green gas blew forward once more, and as he fitted Castle's mask onto Dunn, the officer jolted awake with a scream. Will put a hand over his mouth to silence him.

"Be quiet sir or you'll have us both killed."

But the lieutenant was delirious and struggled with him violently, pulling at his pajamas and ripping off his breast pocket.

"Stop it sir. I'm here to rescue you," he said, pulling the mask on firmly, "it's Corporal Davison."

It was no good. Dunn began to panic, thrashing about wildly, and ripped Will's air tube from the mask rendering it useless.

"Oh Jesus. You bloody idiot," Will shouted, not caring about protocol, and in his frustration he lashed out at Dunn and knocked him back unconscious.

Will had no option but to rip off his useless mask and throw it aside. The wind groaned now, as if spurred on by the souls of the dead, pushing the devilish fog on and on towards him. Despite the sudden fatigue he felt throughout his body, Will hauled the lieutenant onto his shoulders and with some effort stood up once more.

As he staggered forward a zip like a bee flying past made him jump and almost fall over, and he realised the Germans were still firing at him despite the fog. Another zip and this one hit the bloodied left leg of the lieutenant with a sucking sound.

"Jesus that's close."

Will was near to the safety of his trench, and heard the men there shouting him on. He found fresh impetus in his legs to drive forward. He could see faces now, with outstretched arms beckoning him on, and he allowed himself to believe they would make it. As he approached the lines however, a fresh gust of wind swept the gas on and past the lumbering pair.

Will suddenly realised he was in the green carpet of death. He held his breath and broke into a run, trying to squint in the mist. Just a few yards from the trench, he stumbled and fell, the weight of the lieutenant knocking the air from him momentarily, and he took a deep breath in and instantly regretted it. The searing pain exploded through his lungs as the noxious gases seeped into every pore in his body, making him automatically open his eyes with the shock, and he couldn't help screaming with the effect. As his eyes began to burn as well, watering wildly against the unseen enemy, Will stumbled forward grabbing Dunn by the shoulders and half dragging, half pulling him, forced himself on.

Despite his best efforts he was unable not to breathe, the combination of the pain and the physical effort making his chest heave in short bursts. He felt himself succumbing to this swirling toxic terror. With one last cry out, he hurled himself forward into the trench...

...and fell into the arms of his father.

"Easy lad, I've got you," his dad said, as Will collapsed with exertion and pain. He didn't question why his dad was in the trenches, just allowing strong arms to take hold of him, as his body spasmed violently. As the scene began to fade, the blurred outline of his mum running towards him appeared once again...

The pain made Will shiver violently and with another cry he jolted upright in his makeshift bunk, the sweat pouring off him. He struggled to breathe for a few moments and then his sergeant major was there taking his arm, mopping his head.

"Easy Sergeant, I've got you. Same dream?"

Will nodded, his breathing starting to settle again. He took a swig of the water being offered to him, and raised a hand to show he was okay.

"Sorry Sir. Same bloody nightmare," he muttered, embarrassed to have been exposed in this way. "Just got worse since I was back in France."

Sergeant Major Russell stood up and looked at the exhausted frame of the young sergeant. Luckily the dugout was empty as the other men here were still on duty. He knew full well that Will had been suffering long before they came to France, but he couldn't lose an experienced man on the eve of a big attack.

"I think you need a break Will," he said quietly. "You haven't slept properly in weeks. When this show is over I'll get us all out of the line for a few days. General's briefing in an hour or I'd have let you rest longer."

Will immediately stood up and reached for his tunic. The irony of the demands of duty outweighing rest and recuperation was not lost on him. But he wasn't going to let it show now. He forced a smile onto his face, where sweat still glistened from the horrors of sleep, and turned towards the concerned face of his superior.

"As you always say Sergeant Major, I'll get all the sleep I need when I'm dead. Let's go."

Chapter 1 – Smoke and Mirrors. Four months earlier

The single yellow daffodil stood tall and proud amongst the dark banks of rotting vegetation in the herb garden of Mill Farm. Its perfectly formed cup trumpeted the arrival of an early spring, calling the armies of snowdrops in their bridal gowns to pay homage to it with its golden reveille.

Agnes Davison paused for a long moment smiling at the blast of colour, the newly laid eggs cooling in her wicker basket. It brought a warmth to her heart that the early February morning could not take credit for. As she headed back to the kitchen, her favourite old boots crunched on the frost kissed ground beneath her. Agnes was sure this year was going to be a good one.

She paused with her hand on the kitchen door alerted by a shout from the barn nearby; then turned to take a step in that direction, a slight frown appearing on her previously smiling face. She realised that her husband was simply asserting himself over the cows during milking and the frown vanished as quickly as it had dared to intrude. She wanted to go to him then, the good feeling coursing through her veins perpetuating a need to share the moment. Hearing another shout followed by a curse made her think better of it, and she went inside, not wanting to have her joyful start ruined by some stubborn cows.

As she walked into the kitchen Agnes was amazed to find Fred up and dressed and eating the toast she had left for him. *This is a good day,* she thought, putting the eggs down and giving him a hug. At fourteen, (or *fourteen and a half* as he liked to remind her), Fred was the youngest of her four boys. Recently he had begun working at the local butchers. After an enthusiastic start however, the initial excitement had been worn away by the requirement to get out of bed at six o'clock each morning. Leaving home in the cold dark air to be there in time for the deliveries and cleaning work increased Fred's reluctance, and it became a daily battle to drag him down out of bed.

"This is a pleasant surprise Freddie. Did you fall out of bed?" she teased.

"Not at all," he splurted back with a mouthful of toast. He brushed his wild unkempt brown hair out of his eyes, managing to get jam stuck on some of the strands in his haste to eat. "It's pie day today and I don't want to be late for that!"

Agnes smiled, knowing that after four weeks Fred was being allowed to work in the meat ovens in the back sheds with the baking ladies, where he would grind the mince and bones for sausages and pies. It was a laborious task that he would soon tire of, but the reward was a hot pie at break twice a day. Clearly it was a better motivator than her stern voice, so that was all that mattered. Besides he had cut himself twice in the first week trying to learn how to prepare the carcasses they brought in regularly and she shivered at the thought it could have been much worse.

*At least if he burns himself he can learn to be more careful the next tim*e she mused, as she tried to remove the jam from his hair while he wriggled within her grasp. *Burns can heal, but cut a finger off and that's a lesson for life.* Then she stopped and her mind wandered to the men she had seen coming home on a train once with whole limbs missing. She shook the thought away, not allowing herself to make the natural leap to worrying about her other sons. A sharp sound of a bike bell made her realise that in her daydream Fred had taken the opportunity to scarper outside trailing his coat behind him.

There was a flash of colour past the kitchen window as Fred took off on his bike, shouting to his dad as he did, and she smiled and waved belatedly. Turning back to the kitchen she remembered with a fond smile how only a few weeks past all four of her sons had been there with a house full of music and laughter for New Year's Eve. There was no shortage of guests either. With three boys in uniform it didn't take much to persuade the local girls to accompany their parents, where once they would have given the Davison boys a wide berth.

Yet it didn't go unnoticed to her or Harold that, of their older sons, only David really engaged in any meaningful chatter with the guests. Their eldest James, home for a week's respite, was resplendent in his Guards' officer uniform. He was charming and polite but reserved, while their third boy William kept very much to himself preferring the company of some of his old football friends, who had come from the training camp to be with him. Harold had said to her it was because David had not been to France yet; that there was a noticeable change in the other two. Agnes didn't care. She loved having them home, and wasn't so worried when David and Will went back to their training camp in Witley together. She was just glad that for now at least Will was spared from the lands that had tried so hard to keep him forever.

But James? James was like the daffodil, tall and proud and a natural leader. *Yes, that was how she would think of him. Her strong flower shining bright amongst the darkness.* Though she smiled at this, Agnes needed something to lift her mood up again now. She caught sight of herself in the mirror and saw a tired face looking back at her, and began to pick at her hair dislodging a stray piece of straw in the process. At that moment the reflection captured her husband heading over to the outhouse to clean up, before coming in for breakfast as always.

Agnes smiled. *After all, there had to be some perks to having all the boys out of the house once more.* She hummed to herself as she put the eggs away and took off her old apron. Breakfast could wait.

*

It wasn't frost but thick snow that covered the ground near Béthune as the latest hospital train pulled into the station. It exhaled smoke across the platforms with a deep sigh as it came to a halt, as if the weight of the world was pushing down on its blackened wheels. The funnel puffed heavily from the last mile's exertion, adding thick soot to the choking scene.

Rose Kellett stepped off the last carriage, pushing her way through the usual group of French cleaners. The sounds felt to her like the train was sobbing. She stared at the faces in the group as she moved through them, several of whom held rags to their mouths and noses against the oppressive atmosphere. She had seen many of them time and again on her journeys back and forth to the coast with the wounded soldiers and civilians. As the weeks passed she felt they had become more and more expressionless as the work continued unabated. Emotion and chatter disappeared from them so they appeared as gargoyles on a church roof, and Rose wondered if they had the same opinion of her.

From somewhere a silent signal made them come to life and with reluctant steps they climbed aboard behind her. Rose looked at the blood-stained uniform that hung to her tired bones and did not envy them the job inside. She felt tired and very dirty, and took out a cigarette to stop the tremors getting worse. This had been a harder journey than most with several of her own colleagues amongst the unwilling passengers, after one of the hospitals had taken a direct hit from the long-range guns. She longed for a hot bath and clean clothes, and a large glass of wine, and propped herself against one of the nearby notice boards to strike her match.

"Put that bloody match out! No lighted cigarettes on the platform nurse! You know the bloody rules. Could have the whole place up if the fumes catch fire."

Rose looked up angrily as a military policeman pointed to the nearby fuel canisters by the platform waiting to be moved, and then felt guilty and muttered an apology as she stumbled away, suddenly feeling quite faint. As she staggered by the gate an officer took her arm.

"You should know better than that nurse. Wait until you're outside the station."

"I know, I know," she mumbled trying to move on and then seeing the captain's uniform added "Sir. Sorry Sir."

"That's okay," the captain replied, his voice taking on a more sympathetic tone as he took in her bedraggled demeanour. "You look quite done in. Here let me help you to the bench outside. They won't bother you there."

His voice cut through her exhausted brain now, and as she let him lead her trance like to a seat, she suddenly felt quite safe. The officer helped Rose to a table in the sun, its pure white linen cloth reflecting the life-giving rays. As if by magic a bottle of wine appeared with two glasses, and a jug of ice filled water was already in place with which the captain poured her a glass and waited while she gulped it down.

When Rose placed the glass back with a contented sigh she found the captain already holding a lighted cigarette for her, from his own personal stock, and she took it happily knowing the brand to be far better than her cheap comforters. She inhaled the smoke, and allowed the feeling to wash over her, beginning to feel alive once more.

"Hello Kellett," the captain said, "good to have you back again."

Rose gave her new boyfriend an intimate smile.

"Hello Davison," she replied.

Then, with a furtive glance to ensure no jobsworth MPs were skulking about waiting to pick her up on any lack of professionalism, she leaned over the table and gave him a long smoky kiss. As a group of French soldiers came out of the station they broke apart and Rose took another long pull on the expensive cigarette.

"It's good to be back Jamie," she said, her voice still struggling to contain the emotion of the last forty-eight hours, and James noticed her eyes watering, and knew it was nothing to do with the smoke. He reached forward and squeezed her hand oblivious to the men walking past them, their inquisitive eyes taking in the spectacle of the pristine officer and his dishevelled guest.

Rose let his reassuring eyes bring comfort to her mind for a moment and then pulled her hand away with another sparkling smile and a wink.

"Now stop all this romantic tosh and pour the bloody wine. *Sir.*"

Chapter 2 – No rest for the wicked

They changed trains at Brighton and carried on towards Folkestone. Archie had bought a couple of hard rock cakes in the platform café "to keep them going," feeling slightly guilty that he should make up for eating most of their packed lunch before eleven in the morning. He did love Mrs Davison's sandwiches though. Despite the grey drizzle of the day the two friends chatted and laughed continually as the train huffed on.

Will Davison and Archie Bunden were more football teammates than friends when the war had broken out. But on the day Will joined up on a whim to impress Alice Pevensey, Archie had stood alongside him and they marched to France together. That was in 1914. They shared the dubious honour of both surviving serious wounds, and for that they were considered veterans despite neither being twenty-one yet.

Behind the bravado and the continuous fountain of rock cake crumbs cascading forth onto the carriage floor, the men worked hard to keep a semblance of order in their lives. Each knew the other had been profoundly affected by the war already, though nothing was said out loud; neither of the friends wanting to upset the fragile peace that hung precariously in their minds, by voicing such fears. Yet even as they alighted from the train in Folkestone, the distant thump of the guns in France impacted on their souls, and they pushed on with heavy steps.

It was over half a mile from the station to their destination, but despite the strong coastal winds pushing against them, they seemed to do the journey in a matter of minutes. No doubt the military training and the sense of anticipation helped to speed them along, but mostly it was Archie's stomach.

"They better still be open, I'm starving!"

Will smiled at his friend, shaking his head, and wondered if he was truly better, or simply acting out the part of his former self, for appearances sake, as he was. He had no time to reflect on this further however as Archie continued unabated.

"If they've shut for Winter I might just kick the bleedin' doors in!"

Worryingly the place did appear in darkness as they approached up the final stretch of road, and Will could sense Archie's restless nature building up and feared he might *actually* break the doors down. But as they got to the entrance there were lamps lit inside and it was only the gloom that made it look closed; that and the complete lack of customers. Will looked up at the sign over the door which swayed back and forth in the wind now. '*Maggie's.*'

They were back.

The last time they had been here was the night before they sailed to France in 1914, from their holding camp down the road. That seemed a lifetime ago now, and Will recalled the group of men who had been there with them, some of whom would never come again. A shiver shook his body suddenly. *Just the cold,* he fooled himself.

It had been Archie's idea to come back here before he was due to report to their training camp in Witley. Will had joined him in Brighton on a weekend pass, having already reported to camp. Archie had spent Christmas and the start of the New Year with his new lady friend, a Sister in the military hospital in Brighton, who had treated them both last year. He smiled, knowing how ebullient Archie had been when they met, even more so than usual. Underneath her dour exterior Sister Dent was clearly capable of raising blood pressures as well as calming them.

Will hesitated in the doorway. He felt nervous and would have possibly walked away but Archie was already inside and shouted, "Hello, anyone in?"

Maggie appeared from the kitchens carrying a tray of freshly washed cutlery, her hair pulled back in a tight black ponytail tied with a piece of floral cloth. Her serving apron showing signs of having spent much of the day so far cleaning out the ovens. She frowned at the large bearded man standing in the entrance, stick in hand, and taking a step back to the counter called for Angus.

She needn't have worried. Archie broke into a grin and with a cry of "Aye Aye, there she is, let's have the special then," threw his stick on the floor and strode up to her. The voice didn't match the man in front of her but the familiarity made her smile nervously as she searched for the name, and then she saw the shy blond face of Will come in behind him and as he grinned she shouted out with joy.

Archie gave her a hug and she laughed saying, "Same old Archie," as the name came back to her, thankfully. Will came up then and she gave him a special smile and a deep hug, and felt the thinness beneath the coat. She struggled not to cry seeing the change in the two men that had left so uproariously the last time. She saw this all the time now, as men left and returned, passing through her little world on the way to that foreign hell.

"Welcome back Will," she said with a kiss on the cheek, and he blushed as ever, the young boy still present beneath the surface.

Angus burst into the kitchen with an axe in his hand from where he had been chopping wood outside. The concerned shout from his sister, so unusual for her, and the sound of men's voices had made him dash to the rescue.

"Bloody hell," said Archie taking a step back, "when I ordered the special I didn't realise you had to kill it first! This is going to be some steak."

Archie, Will and Maggie burst out laughing, as Angus looked on confused until she told him to get the oven stoked up and the fire going, as these were old friends returned. She went off to fetch them some beers, seeing the two friends settle at the same table they had sat at last time with their large group of rowdy comrades. Inside she was shocked at the changes in the men and wondered how many of the others were still alive, or would even come back, but decided not to ask if they didn't tell her.

"Busy here ain't it?" Archie said cheekily, as Maggie came up with the drinks and leant against a table nearby with a shake of her head.

"You've not changed," she said, "except for that sheep on your face to keep your warm." Archie grinned boyishly at the remark, stroking it adoringly. He liked this girl.

"Do we get to order then or what?"

"Oh, you said you wanted the special and if I remember rightly you eat like a horse, so Angus is throwing a plateful together for you both." Archie rubbed his hands together with glee at this.

"That's perfect. Besides we are celebrating."

"Oh?"

"Yes lass, it's young William's birthday so it is. Well was. Recently like." Archie sniffed as he always did when stretching the truth while Will raised his eyes apologetically.

"Many happy returns of the day Will," Maggie said taking his hands tenderly and looking at him. "How old are you now?"

"Nineteen miss," he replied shyly. "It was a few days ago now."

"You haven't aged a bit," she said with a broader smile, and Will smiled back. *Not on the outside*, he thought, and looked to change the subject.

"Why is it so quiet Maggie?" he asked wondering at the emptiness himself.

"It's always quiet here in winter when the holidaymakers depart. But with the war on, there have been precious few people coming on holiday this year. We get locals of course who come in for lunch or a cup of tea, but when the weather is bad like today, nobody fancies walking their dogs along the promenade." She smiled again warmly and Will allowed himself to just drift off, gazing dreamily out of the window as Maggie continued. "So, most of our trade has been from the troops passing through, and in the winter months there seems to be far less movement from them too."

"Campaign seasons really," Archie explained. "The weather is so bad out there it's hard to move let alone fight so things just ground to a halt last winter and I guess it's the same this year. Always been the way in war it seems. Funny old thing."

"Yes it is," she replied suddenly thinking about her husband Stuart, as Angus appeared and put a match to the fire in the main café that had clearly been laid in anticipation of any visitors. The paper curled and smoked as the flames licked about it and then the kindling began to crackle as the fire spread quickly through the grate. "Hard to keep the wood dry in this weather," she continued, the small talk easing round the more serious subjects that their presence highlighted.

"Speaking of wood, what's the story with your brother then, the mad axe man over yonder? How did you all end up here?" Archie had not heard the story last time when she had told Will and asked in all innocence. She glanced back at the hulk of her older brother moving back and forth between the room and the kitchen, where delicious smells had started to drift forth, and then leaned in a little.

She told them that Angus, despite his scary appearance, met a Danish girl while he was studying at Edinburgh University for a law degree. Freida was working in the city to improve her English, and took a job as a waitress in a bar Angus frequented with his fellow students.

"Angus used to tease her about the fact she wouldn't learn any English in Scotland, and they hit it off immediately." The friends laughed together, and became hooked on the story. "It was love at first sight like in the story books," she continued, "and when his degree finished, he followed his heart and married Freida. Then despite our parents' objections they moved down to Kent where she had family. Freida believed she could trace her ancestry all the way back to the Danes who invaded Kent in the 9th century!"

Will couldn't imagine the man working behind the counter as an old romantic but Maggie seemed insistent. He listened as she carried on the tale but found himself studying her face more than the words that came out of her perfectly formed mouth. Then guilt overtook him and he focused on the story as Maggie continued, hoping no one saw him blush. Apparently Angus didn't fancy practicing law so they opened this café on a whim, and called it *The Danish Delight,* and despite being so far from home Angus was very happy. Soon after their first baby was born.

"But there were complications during her second child's birth," Maggie told the friends, who were now listening intently, "and while they saved the girl, Freida died two days later." She looked back at the kitchen then, eyes watering. "Angus was bereft." Will found the tears somehow made her look even prettier in the fading light as she carried on the tale.

Frieda's death had been in 1913, and with two little children to manage and the war breaking out the following year, the café had fallen on hard times, and their parents were too old and too far away to help much. Besides they still had a small farm of their own to run to the east of Inverness, between Culloden and the Beauly Firth.

It had seemed natural to Maggie to step in and help as she had told Will before, so when she came down with her husband to see him off to the war, she just stayed. With her Stuart away she rented out their small holding on the parents' farm to a local couple, and then settled here. It also felt closer to the war somehow and thereby closer to Stuart. The café had been run down and the signs fading when she arrived, and as part of the fresh start Angus had insisted on changing the name too. So it became *Maggie's*, as he felt that made people feel more relaxed.

"Angus talked to me about joining up of course," Maggie went on. "He felt the pull like all the men, especially seeing the troops go off. But there was no demand to do it, and with the young ones without their mum he was certainly needed here."

Will watched Angus lifting a crate of empty bottles outside through a back door and saw him in a whole new light. He noticed now the weight of loneliness and grief that clung to his shoulders everywhere he went and regretted his earlier assumptions when they were last here.

"We saw Stuart last year you know," he said unexpectedly. "Just for a few minutes. He's very nice."

"Yes, thanks for bringing that up Will!" Archie replied. "Not the best day of my life!"

"Oh, sorry I didn't mean…"

"Ah that was the day you were injured wasn't it," Maggie chipped in understanding the exchange between the two men immediately. "Yes, Stuart wrote to me about it. And the loss of his friend that day too. Awful."

"It's awful a lot of the time actually," Will said, a sense of sadness coming down on him suddenly.

Maggie patted his knee, and then gave Archie a hug. "Well you are both here now, that's the main thing. Safe and well." She went over to the fire place and poked at the logs to encourage them to burn a little faster. "I had a letter from Stuart recently and he seems to be all over the place, but there has been no fighting for some time now for the Camerons."

"It can be like that, as I said miss," Archie replied smiling again. "Just the shelling and the sniping wears you down after a bit, but you get by." Seeing her look worried now he added, "I'm sure he's okay. Seems a good chap as Will said."

"Yes, he's a darling, but he can be reckless and that's what bothers me," she replied, and Archie and Will exchanged a look, knowing plenty of tales where reckless bravery had led to nothing but death. They fell silent then for a moment; the only sound in the room being the spitting of the logs as the flames dug deep, competing with the constant crashing of the waves outside. Will's guilt returned for admiring her earlier, hearing her talk about her husband, and he chastised himself privately.

Thankfully Angus appeared at that point to break the reflective mood, with two plates steaming with bacon, sausages and eggs and some thick cut liver, and a load of toast on a rack.

"Outstanding," Archie shouted, his spirits instantly soaring. He pulled both plates together and said "What are you having Will?" and they all laughed then. As Angus threw a couple of rough-cut logs on the fire Maggie got up saying she'd leave them in peace to eat, and walked off taking her brother's arm, giving it a squeeze.

*

Later that day as the sun beat a hasty retreat in the West, unable to stem the onslaught of the forces of dark and ice, the four of them sat chatting in a small sitting room at the back. Angus had closed up early when only three retired local residents had come in and spent an hour and a half over one round of tea and two shared slices of cake.

"Not exactly the last of the big spenders are they?" Archie had said loud enough to be overheard, when they had muttered about getting some more hot water for their tea pot to squeeze out a third cup. It had prompted their departure to sympathetic smiles from Maggie.

Now Will and Archie sat as friends not customers, chatting about families and home while the children read to themselves, and coloured on flattened paper that had formed packing for various deliveries over the summer. At some point after a warming supper of home-made carrot soup and some crusty bread, they realised they would not get back to Steyning that night, even if they made Brighton, as the trains would have stopped by then, so they were invited to stay. Will was concerned his Mum might worry with no way of letting her know, and Archie had suggested they make for Brighton and stay in the hospital. Will didn't fancy going back there, even though he struggled with the imposition of staying in such a small place. But Angus insisted, saying "the bairns can bunk in with me so they can."

However, when Archie looked at their room it became pertinently obvious that he would never fit in one of their small cots, and probably not Will either, so Maggie said they could have her double bed if they didn't mind sharing.

"We've been in tighter, colder spots than this lass," he added, though Will was less enamoured knowing his propensity for loud noises after he fell asleep, and not just snoring. But it was settled, and Elsa slept in her room with Maggie, while Hamish shared with his Dad, and the two friends squashed into the small double overlooking the sea. Despite the conditions, after a couple of whiskeys in front of the fire before bed from Angus' favourite personal reserve of the Glen Ord Distillery, Will found sleep easy to come by for once and went off soundly for the first time in a long time.

*

He awoke to the sound of tapping. At first Will was confused about his surroundings and then the long grating snores of his friend lying next to him reminded him where he was. He looked at Archie, contentedly sleeping away, his mouth half open and dribble running into his beard. *He could sleep anywhere that one,* he thought, and raised himself up. The tapping came again and through the gap in the curtains he turned to see a seagull pecking at something on the window ledge outside. As he stood up it looked at him defiantly for a moment, and then stretched its large grey wings and pushed off effortlessly back towards the sea.

He crept quietly down the stairs, carrying his boots, not wanting to wake the children, and then paused by the back door to put them on.

"Up early laddie." Angus' voice made Will jump and he span round. "Och I didnae mean to startle you." Angus looked embarrassed, as if he understood that these men were always on edge, their nerves shot to pieces.

"It's fine," Will said recovering his composure, "I wasn't sure anyone else was up and I just wanted to get some air. And some peace and quiet."

Angus raised his eyes then and smiled. "Aye your mate there can certainly hum a tune when he sleeps. Reminds me of when I tried learning the pipes to please my father. Like a cow in labour 'eh!"

They laughed and Will opened the door to the beach. "Do you know what time it is?"

"It'll be getting on for seven in the morning soon I'd imagine," Angus said looking out of the window as if to reinforce his hunch. "Certainly the back o'six. I'll get a brew on while you're out and some porridge going for your journey."

"Thank you."

As he walked off, Maggie appeared at the bottom of the stairs hurriedly tying up a belt on her dress, the sleep still evident on her face. "I overslept," she mumbled, looking out through one of the large kitchen windows. Seeing the lone figure down by the shore she went to get her coat.

"No lassie. Leave the lad be. Let him work through whatever it is that ails him inside." Her eyes argued with her brother's reasoning and she wanted to go out, but he caught her arm and shook his head. "He'll be needing a hot drink and some breakfast when he gets back, and you can hug him then. His lungs might be better but some wounds run deeper and need longer to heal." She smiled and nodded, letting the coat rest on its peg, as there were shouts from above them. "Sounds like the bairns are awake judging by the noise upstairs, and you can go and wake sleeping beauty for me if you don't mind. That man can sleep through anything it seems."

He smiled at her and she gave him a hug, and with one last look at the solitary form of Will sitting on the shore's edge, she turned and went to the stairs. She had not slept well in Hamish's small cot, the young blond soldier on her mind for much of the night, and she was cross she had finally drifted into sleep and missed him going out. *Oh, it's probably for the best Maggie,* she told herself, as she took the creaking stairs to wake his friend.

*

After an emotional farewell from the café, the journey home was more subdued than their outward one, with both Will and Archie wrapped up in their own personal thoughts and challenges. Maggie was clearly sad to see them go especially as they had all become friends during the brief visit. They promised to try and write, but while she loved seeing the men again, the time spent together just heightened her own anxieties about being separated from her husband. *She couldn't afford to become attached to anyone else,* she told herself, and put a brave face on as they parted.

As the train rattled along back to Brighton, Will turned to Archie.

"You know what? I'm ready to get back to training. It's been too long, and all this socialising is lovely but it feels false somehow don't you think?"

"Oh, I don't know. If they called it off tomorrow I wouldn't lose any sleep over it."

"But that's not going to happen is it Bunny so best get our minds back on the job in hand and get back to it."

"No rest for the wicked 'eh?"

"Something like that."

They smiled at each other, and then looked out of opposite windows, where trees flashed green on either side. Neither friend wanting to show their inner demons to the other.

Chapter 3 – Meat for the Devil

The sound of water fighting determinedly against the icy barriers carried to the men in the trench. The nearby river had been reduced to a mere trickle by the sub-zero temperatures that had gripped the land for days. On the rare occasion the sun did put in an appearance, it drifted lazily across the sky, failing to clear the river's high banks where the dark shadows remained king. Here in the trenches near the town of Ypres, the men of the Coldstream Guards knew this scenario all too well.

As if to emphasise the point their captain stamped his feet to try and revive them, and smashed one of the many stagnant pools of frozen water in the process. It was dreadful here, the only saving grace being that even the rats were not stupid enough to venture out in these conditions. Where January had teased the senses with some warmer unexpected days, February now reminded them all that winter was still in its full power. The hour before dawn was always the coldest to anyone standing duty through the night, and the men's fingers and toes burned with the pain of the Frost Queen's embrace.

Captain James Davison shivered once more and pulled the scarf around his head as tightly as he could possibly manage. Something he had done three or four times in the last half hour already, though his ears still burned. The wind stung his face with its biting breath and made his eyes ache with the strain of trying to look into it. He despaired at the order to 'stand to' from 03:00 that would probably leave most of his company unfit to face whatever the dawn threw at them. Something hit his eyelid and water trickled for a moment across his eye before being whipped away into the darkness. It was snowing again.

Oh great, he thought.

As the sound of the river's strangled gurglings carried to him once more, he allowed his mind to drift to his last period of leave, barely two weeks past…

He was sitting by the river in Béthune with Rose. Despite it being the fourth day of February, the winter sun bathed them in a delicious warm glow, as they drank wine in their regular café and watched the world drift by. Rose, cigarette poised between two fingers, exhaled her smoke seductively and then continued to read poetry to him from one of her favourite collections. He could listen to her all day, and tried hard to focus on her beautiful features. Those deep blue sparkling eyes in a slender face, framed by her flowing golden locks. The way her dark lipsticked mouth moved as she read...

James turned and rested his head against the back of the trench now for a moment's respite from the glacial winds. He tried to dwell on the scene, but saw only the spot covered face of young Lieutenant Pollard waiting for orders staring back at him. He cursed inwardly as the tables vanished in the wind and the poetry stopped. James studied Pollard for a moment, his scarf similarly tied round the top of his head holding the regimental hat tight about him. As he saw Pollard's lips trembling beneath a faint icy moustache, he thought how much like Freddie he seemed now.

"How old are you Lieutenant?"

"Sir?" Pollard answered through chattering teeth. "Oh, N-nineteen last m-month s-sir."

Just a mere boy, he thought to himself. *But then again if we all shaved our moustaches and beards off, perhaps we would all look like young boys.*

"Stay sharp Lieutenant, it'll be light soon and then..." James' voice was cut short by a large explosion some half a mile away on a height they called the Bluff. Despite the distance they all ducked instinctively, and then a second explosion rocked the dark sky and seemed to part the howling wind. James spun round to look and this time the macabre scene was illuminated just for a moment by the blinding flash that rocked the ground. Grim shapes of men and their fortifications being flung into the air projected back to him.

"Mines," he shouted. "Jerry's blown mines under the forward trenches."

The men round about shifted nervously now, the previous battle against the cold forgotten as they began to wonder if anyone was digging underneath them. Even James momentarily felt a different type of chill spread through his bones as he envisaged the ground beneath them erupting and dragging them all down to hell. Whistles sounded then, and the obvious sounds of battle followed. Shouts, screams, cries for help. Rifles and machine guns firing in the dark. But sporadically, James noted, from their side. The mines had done their work well.

As dawn began to peer across the blackened bedspreads of the murky landscape, they could only guess at the struggle going on ahead of them on the Bluff. Fires raged here and there from the explosions, as the battle continued. The men were clearly uneasy, disturbed by the howling of wind and war, but they did not run. They stood waiting for orders. They stood waiting for their captain…

James was in a sunlit room, stockings on the back of a chair…a fire crackling. The smell of cigarettes and half-drunk wine adding to the aromas caressing his senses. The wind was rattling the shutters, desperate to join them, but James was oblivious to anything outside of their little world. He heard Rose laughing on a bed just out of sight in the alcove, and looked down at the envelope she had passed him.

"It's not for now, it's for the fourteenth of February. Valentine's day. I want you to open it wherever you are and think of me my darling. Hopefully the sun will be shining on you as it is now."

"I haven't got you anything," he replied apologetically not looking round.

"I didn't expect you to. These last forty-eight hours have been more than enough. Besides you can make it up to me next time we meet."

He rubbed his hands by the fire and knew she was smiling at him now behind his back. That soft disarming smile, and he turned to see her. But she wasn't there…

Instead his men stood all around, grim faced watching him. Waiting patiently. James tapped his chest almost subconsciously and knew the card was safe within his jacket. The morning was rousing itself now with every passing minute, and it occurred to him then that today was the fourteenth of February. He smiled ironically at the situation and glanced at the snow filled sky. *No sun today my darling I fear*, he thought to himself, and then Lieutenant Pollard heard his company commander quietly say, "Happy Valentine's Day."

Not for the first time Pollard felt confused and somewhat out of his depth in the captain's presence. "Sir?" he ventured tentatively.

James became suddenly aware of his surroundings and his senses snapped to in an instant. The fighting had stopped on the Bluff and he knew instinctively that this was not a good sign. Within moments the foreboding shapes of men moving forward line after line, were silhouetted by the brightening dawn. *No Valentine love from this lot,* he ventured. He took a deep breath in.

"Company will fix bayonets," he stated firmly, and the words brought the trench into life. His order was passed up and down the line by officers and sergeants alike, comforted by the familiarity of their actions at last. Comforted by the presence of their captain.

"Fix...Bayonets!"

There was a shout from his left, and a sergeant appeared to report the enemy were pushing up the communications trenches on that side.

"Lieutenant take a platoon from 'C' company and send them with the sergeant to reinforce Ambrose's company on the left. Keep me informed of the situation there. Everyone else eyes front."

As Pollard detailed the chosen men to move, James checked his new Webley revolver to ensure it worked. His fingers trembled on the deathly cold parts as he cocked and uncocked it, and ensured the six-shot barrel spun freely, before replacing it in its holster once more. *He may need it up close before the day was through*, he thought grimly. As if reading his mind, the Germans advancing ahead of them let out a confident roar, buoyed by their recent success. In the dawn's gloomy light, the sight was unnerving as they surged forward, but the men stood motionless waiting.

James sighed a deep depressing sigh at the stupidity of all this, but there would be time for reflection later. He hoped. Then he raised his arm and brought it down and the guns opened fire. The snow flurries were torn asunder by the hot lead that spat forth from all along the trench, and the first ranks of the enemy likewise melted into the night, never to feel warmth again.

*

Fred blew hard on his fingers trying to inject some warmth into them. He stood in the outside toilet stamping his feet and trying to get some feeling back in his bones but was aware he only had exactly two minutes before going back to work. Gloves were not allowed when handling the frozen carcasses in the deep freezers for fear of contamination and after two hours of hauling the various joints of meat back and forth he was struggling to keep his hands working. Not only that but the men there teased him daily about being weak, so Fred was determined not to give them any more excuses than they needed.

All the men working here were much older than Fred, but that didn't stop them expecting him to 'pull his weight.' Or carry it in this case as they threw another cow flank onto his back the moment he appeared, and he lurched forward on the icy cobbles, towards the chopping shed.

Bernie Blinkhorn, the youngest of the workers, was born with a curvature in the spine that had led to merciless teasing during his brief few years in school. It also meant he avoided being called up into the army, as the Great War dragged on, and more and more men marched to the sound of the drums. Despite his deformity he still faced the scowls of the old men and women in the town, as he shuffled about, who believed he should have gone to war regardless. Bernie bottled it all up inside him and then lashed out at anyone less fortunate than himself.

Fred wanted to tell his parents about the bullying, knowing his dad would deal with it in moments. But he also didn't want to let them down, more aware than ever that his three older brothers were all away to the war. When his brothers left, something inside of him changed, and he felt a need to prove himself in his own way. So, he just focused on working hard, and keeping his head down to try and stay out of trouble.

It was nearly eight o'clock and the yard behind Mullings' butchers was alive with activity. Fred and Bernie had been working with Roger Mullings since six in the morning to get the meat out and prepped ready for the day ahead. Roger's rotund wife Mary, her rosy cheeks glowing more than ever in the early morning frost, was already in the shop with their eldest son John.

The window had to be laid out and dressed by eight thirty in the exact same order every day as their regular customers expected this. Sausages and pies on the left, choice joints of lamb and beef in the middle, and then the fowl on the right depending on the season; which currently was just the usual duck and chicken. Off cuts, mince, tripe and other secondary lines were ranged around the back of the window. Christmas time was an exception when there would be a prime turkey or goose commanding attention in the centre, but otherwise it was the usual pattern.

At fifty-six Roger had worked in this shop for over forty years. His wife had been the daughter of a nearby haberdashers and they had been virtually thrown together at sixteen and lived and breathed the life ever since. Two sons followed – John and Edward, and the business grew. In 1900, Roger's father died suddenly from a heart attack, and he changed the name above the shop from 'Mullings Meats' to 'Mullings and Sons,' which he felt sounded more professional. When Mary's father also died from Tuberculosis two years later, Roger borrowed money from the bank to buy up the failing haberdasher that had deteriorated at the same rate as its owner's health. With an eye for an opportunity he turned it into a cold storage and stockroom area for the main shop.

There was a cobbled alley between the shops that served as a good link between the two areas of the growing business. Roger and Mary had kissed and fumbled about in the dark corners here many a winter's eve when they were young and courting. When Roger was very drunk in the Norfolk Arms, he'd often boast that John was conceived amongst the pots and pans of old Judd's stockroom, but none of this mattered to Fred now as he slithered across the stones once more with a box of pork chops.

Some sixteen years on, the business was thriving. John had stayed in the family line of work, and settled down with children of his own - greedy eyes very much focused on inheriting the wealth. He'd been a sickly child in his early years, plagued by Bronchitis and then being labelled asthmatic by the doctors that had cut short his irregular schooling, and left him exempt from any form of military service. John cared little about that, being content to stay close to home, even renting a small set of rooms above the shop when he was married. Over time his feeble frame had recovered and he grew into manhood secure in his surroundings and his future. Roger was happy to know that the future of the business in Steyning was assured and took comfort from that as he neared retirement.

Edward having the brains of the family was not content to settle. After trying a couple of apprenticeships in Horsham with reputable law firms, he decided to move on and see the world. His wanderlust took him to Portsmouth, and in 1905 Roger and Mary received a short neatly presented letter advising them to their astonishment that Edward was not a lawyer but a sub lieutenant in the Navy. In the years that followed the letters became less neat but were always regular, and by the time war broke out Edward was Lieutenant Commander Mullings on HMS Invincible. Roger and Mary prided themselves on having a pioneering son and the best pies in Sussex.

When Owen Entwhistle signed up for the new Southdown battalions for a handful of shillings and a sore head, and headed off to the training camp near Witley, it left a vacancy for a junior at Mullings. Harold had lost no time in taking young Fred down to meet Roger, and the interview lasted the time it took to buy a steak pie and a pound of mince. Or rather pass them over the counter as Harold was one of Roger's best suppliers of lamb and beef and the partnership worked both ways equally well. Fred's initial enthusiasm at having a 'proper job' of his own however, soon shrunk like his fingers and toes in the dark cold January mornings.

His excitement at potentially being moved to work in the warm confines of the pie ovens did not bring the respite he wanted either. He had hoped the change would give him a break from the constant bullying of the older men. In fact, it brought a terror he had previously paid little attention to even in school.

Girls. Or grown women to be exact.

The ladies working in the ovens every day under the loose management of Mandy Armstrong, were more than able to hold their own with the course habits and language of the butchers. Daily jokes about 'hot sausages,' 'juicy pies' and 'stuffing the birds for display,' were thrown back and forth with no quarter on either side.

While the ladies stuck up for Fred when the men teased him, they also did a lot of teasing of their own. Their favourite was giving him firm cuddles whenever they could trap him against the tray racks or sausage maker, which felt very different to his Mum's affection back home. They would ruffle his hair and try and kiss the top of his head as their stomach-churning breath enveloped him; before he wriggled free and fled with the sound of cackles and jeers echoing off the ovens. He began to have nightmares about the strong buxom women that lurked in the hot hell of Mullings' pie shed, sleeves rolled up and hair pulled back over sweat beaded brows.

By far the worst was Ginny Armstrong, the baking manageress' daughter. Roger had given Mandy a title when she threatened to quit one summer over pay, believing her to be his best worker.

"The baking section doesn't need a supervisor!" Mary had shouted at Roger when he raised the incident with her. "Like having one of those ridiculous automobiles when we have perfectly good trains. Waste of money."

She was right of course, he knew that. The shop was growing and business was good, and Roger and his wife could have managed it all quite well. But he wanted an efficient shop and happy customers above all else, and made the decision to keep the peace.

The important thing was the pie girls were happy and had worked well ever since, with little support. So much so that when Mandy brought her own daughter along one day because they were short, Roger just accepted she was there to stay.

At eighteen Ginny Armstrong was quite simply terrifying. Precocious, loud and a huge flirt to boot, with any and all men, she had a maturity way beyond her years that she had not learnt in school. But while she played up to the older men, she seemed hell bent on making the lives a misery of younger boys like Fred. As Fred trod the cobbled stones each day up to the baking shed, her booming laugh and raucous voice filled his whole body with dread, and it seemed to him as if he was walking into hell. Fred paused now in the meat shed, blowing on his fingers, and recalled the latest traumatic encounter with Ginny Armstrong the day before…

He had been cleaning the pie trays when he heard a clatter behind him and saw that Ginny had dropped a plate of hot pies, taking it out of the oven. If he had done that he would have got a real clout, and for a brief triumphant moment he wallowed in her embarrassment as the ladies turned to chide her. But as she was bending over to pick the pastries up she caught sight of him smiling and immediately went on the offensive.

"What you gawping at boy?" she snarled, stepping over the broken pie shells and ruined meat filling. "'Aving a good look are you?"

"I just turned to see what the noise was," Fred replied timidly trying to get out of the situation.

"You was eyeing up me bosoms that's what you were doing," she continued now, sneering at him and enjoying his discomfort. She turned to the women who now started to smile too, all thought of her mistake disappearing it seemed. "Saw him having a right eyeful as I bent over." As if to exaggerate the point, she pulled apart her white coat and the flimsy dress beneath it to expose her very ample cleavage.

"Here…have another look then."

Fred pushed himself back turning his head away and closing his eyes to try and shut her out of his world.

"That's enough," Mandy said, coming round the side of the oven and tutting at the floor. "Get this cleaned up before Roger hears the racket and comes to see what's going on. Or we'll be seeing it out of our packets come Friday."

Ginny loved making Fred squirm and laughed close to his face, seeming to ignore her mother. He could swear he smelt alcohol on her breath like his grandma had at Christmas time. Was it gin? She had the right name if so. But he didn't have time to remember where he had smelt it before, or laugh at his own jokes as he normally would, as Ginny was still reveling in his discomfort.

"Next time you want a look it will cost ya. That's your last freebie." She laughed loudly again and went out into the yard whistling to have a cigarette. "Come and have a snort with me, Mam," she called, "the boy can clean that up."

Mandy hesitated and then called "Alright Ginny, light me one up. Let's have a cuppa ladies, get the kettle on." She turned to Fred then, still trying to push himself back into the sink where he had been washing up. "Don't just stand there staring then. Get yourself into trouble with girls doing that clearly. Get this cleaned up sharp like, before the boss sees you. Or he'll tan your hide."

Fred burned with anger inside remembering the incident and it took his mind off his freezing bones for a moment. *It was so unfair!* Suddenly he felt a firm cuff round the back of his head.

"Oi squirt, those pigs ain't gonna grow their legs back on and run to the shop themselves to be sold. Stop skiving and start cutting." Bernie laughed as he threw another large pile of meat joints onto the chopping board in the old freezer barn and walked out leaving Fred to chop them up.

Fred watched him go, scraping his feet along the yard. If he had seen him in the street he would have felt sorry for him, as his mum always taught them to care for those less fortunate. But working here, knowing his nature, he stared sullenly hoping he would slip on the ice. Fred wasn't sure how much longer he could do this job, but didn't want to let his parents down and so took his anger out on the joints of dead carcasses piled in front of him. He grabbed the numbing silver trays from the side table and began to load them with meat pieces ready to be taken down to the shop where they would be cleaned and arranged once more.

Having filled several trays up with the choice pieces that would fetch a good price, he took out the large knife and began to hack at the off cuts that would be minced up for sausages, pies and the like. He worked the blade feverishly, with little regard for his already scarred fingers. The memories of Bernie and Ginny driving his hands. As his anger came to the surface he thrust the knife hard into the middle of a beef rump.

*

James pulled on the rifle but the bayonet had stuck fast and he used his boot against the soldier slumped against it to push him back. The fear of being helpless without his rifle made him work harder. He twisted and tugged until with relief he felt the long knife come free with a horrible squelching sound. The German sergeant slumped dead at his feet, his body exhaling a last miserable groan of air. James looked anxiously about at the mass of men struggling on either side of him. He felt the tide might be turning in their favour and was about to call for his sergeant major to organise the reserves, when another German jumped down into the trench next to him.

The man was enormous with a large grey beard covering most of his face, but James had little time to take in his appearance or his rank. His eyes were drawn to the fact he was holding a long wooden club, with dreadful looking spikes worked amateurishly into the end. It was one of many such 'home-made' weapons that both sides carried in the war. Though the army wouldn't approve of them in normal times, here in the hand to hand hell of trench fighting everything could be a weapon, and this one was a particularly vicious example of that. It was made for one purpose. To smash his head in.

As if to emphasise the point, his adversary bashed the rifle aside that James had taken from poor Private Wilks; the former tanner now lying face down in the mud a few yards away, the top of his head shot off. The German snarled and came forward.

A cry of "Look out Sir," came from somewhere to his left. *Sergeant Green,* his mind unhelpfully recalled. Then the man swung the club again and James stumbled backwards almost losing his balance, feeling the *whoosh* of the club as it missed his head by inches. He fumbled for his revolver as the man recovered from his swing and came on again, raising the large club like a mere twig and screaming unintelligibly, spittle snarling out of his mouth. James steadied himself and, with relief, felt the revolver come free from its leather housing. He fired without aiming as there was no time, but the shot seemed to simply graze his enraged opponent. James fired again. *Click.* He pulled the trigger rapidly again, panic rising, and again heard the dreaded *click.* The gun was empty.

He remembered now having to fire several quick shots when the second wave of Germans had overwhelmed the trench despite the murderous fire of their machine guns. They had come on like demons in the dawn dark as if out of the mouth of Hell itself, and now despite their dwindling numbers the battle raged on.

Another wave of Germans now, and they would have to pull back, or remain here forever... None of which mattered in that moment as he threw his Webley at the man in front of him. The German swatted it away like a summer bug, and smiled the evil smile of a predator who knew his prey was helpless. Then he raised the club once more.

James frantically scanned for anything that could help him and spotted the redundant rifle lying near his feet from the dead German he had killed moments earlier. As he lurched down to get it the huge soldier spotted his intentions and stepped forward hefting the club down with an almighty swing as he did so. James knew he wouldn't reach the rifle in time and flinched waiting for the impact of the hideous weapon.

The blow didn't come.

With a roar young Pollard had thrown himself at the German to save his beleaguered captain and now wrestled with him in the blood-soaked trench. James looked up as this blackened beast of a man threw Pollard off and caught him a glancing blow. Pollard was undaunted and, incredibly, came back again. James picked up the rifle now from the floor, checked the working mechanisms and to his delight saw it was loaded. He was about to fire when another German fell dead against him from a struggle on his right and it knocked him over. As he pushed the corpse off, he heard Pollard cry out and this time he had taken the full force of the club and staggered back down the trench and collapsed.

It was James' turn to snarl now, and he fired point blank into the man's stomach. His large belly seemed to just envelop the shot and incredibly he swung the club once more above his head. James noticed blood appear at the corner of the man's mouth as he did so and, sensing victory he rose up striking the man under the chin with the butt of the rifle. He was rewarded with feeling his opponent's wind pipe crush with the blow. The German now made hideous gurgling noises as he dropped the club, but his eyes still widened with anger and he tried to grip James around the throat. He was weakening however, and James pushed back hard, years of manoeuvring the cows back home suddenly finding a purpose, and he shoved him to the ground. As the German struggled on the floor, James coldly reloaded the captured weapon and fired into his face and with a final jerk the man went still.

He felt giddy now, and very tired, and would have sold his soul to the devil for a hot bath and Rose's soft hands on his shoulders. But he knew his duty and, wiping blood and dirt from his eyes, called for his sergeant major and together they reorganised the trench as the remnants of the Germans fell back in disarray.

"Get me a casualty count S'arnt Major, and make sure all the men check their ammo and get a drink if they can. I've no doubt we have a long day ahead so better think about rest parties too."

Sergeant Major Thomas saluted and with a twitch of his enormous black beard, which James took as a sign of support, he strode off down the line. An old campaigner, Oswald Thomas had apparently re-enlisted with the first shots fired in 1914, snapping out of his bored drunken stupor lugging meat about in Smithfield Market in London, to run down to the nearest recruitment office. He had been given his old rank back immediately and James was glad of that now. He noticed the sergeant major's usual booming tone was absent, as he checked and praised the men with quiet words and dark humour. A true professional.

Lieutenant Ambrose appeared and reported that the line had held on the left. Seeing his captain close his eyes momentarily he moved closer.

"Are you all right sir?"

"Yes Lieutenant. I need a casualty report as soon as you can. Is Sergeant Green with you?"

"Here sir."

"Good, I've got the CSM organising the sector and making sure the men stay on alert but rest by sections. Do the same on the left for me will you? Oh, and send a runner to Captain Edwards in 'D' Company on our right. Give him my compliments if he's alive, and get a report from there too."

As the sergeant saluted and walked off, Ambrose spoke again.

"Lieutenant Pollard is dead sir."

James looked round now and then over to where the lifeless form of Pollard lay face down in the trench. He stepped over the German corpses to kneel by his young officer and gently turned him over. He recoiled as he saw the side of his head was completely bashed in. The barbed club had done its job well. James cradled the disfigured face and thought once more about his younger brothers. He looked into the one remaining eye and saw only innocence.

"Organise a burial detail and be gentle with the Lieutenant as you carry him away."

Ambrose saluted and moved off, and James stood up with some difficulty. He lit a cigarette below the trench line, careful not to attract the sniper's scopes that were always out there. He watched as a section of his men lifted Pollard and carried him off beneath a rain sheet. He owed the young man his life but it was a debt he could never repay. There would be letters to write again to broken relatives back home. Pollard, Wilks and others. He felt his chest tighten as he dwelt on the never-ending task. *Still one has to be alive to write letters*, he thought, trying to find some crumb of comfort in this depressing world. And he would ensure he wrote to Rose in the Béthune hospital at the first opportunity.

As the sun breached the trench wall, his darkness continued to linger and he allowed the activity to pass him by, as men moved back and forth upon his earlier orders. James became aware someone was standing next to him and trying to get his attention. He looked round to see one of the orderlies.

"Yes?"

"Beggin' your pardon sir. We got the lines fixed and HQ is on the blower asking for an update sir. Asked if you were okay too like."

James studied Private Bateman from Kentish Town, his north London accent so out of place here in the French countryside. A private demoted twice from corporal for drinking and gambling, and fighting the wrong side of course. He was nevertheless the typical backbone of the Guards' recruits. *Over here he'd share his last drop of water with you, and carry a wounded comrade across No Man's Land without hesitation. In peacetime he'd probably steal your wallet or worse,* he thought half smiling.

"Who is on the line private?" James asked, after taking another long pull on his cigarette.

"A Major Johnson sir. What shall I tell him?"

James dropped his cigarette into the bloodied water beneath his boots and watched it sizzle out. He inhaled deeply, allowing the cold morning air to sting his lungs, invigorating him once more, as he thought about his friend and fellow officer. *Good old Jonners. Still taking time to check on me despite not being at the front anymore.*

Bateman waited nervously, unsure how to read his captain.

"Tell him…tell him this exactly…" James said waving a finger at the orderly. "Captain Davison is still very much alive old boy."

Chapter 4 – Birds of Prey

Sergeant Major Geoffrey Russell watched the men relaxing after their evening duties. His thick moustache twitched into a satisfied smile seeing how many soldiers were taking part in this evening kick about despite the failing light. They had trained hard today. Yet here they were ignoring the chance of a much-needed rest in their bunks after the mess hall emptied; choosing instead to continue to play as they trained, as one large group.

Russell wasn't the only member of the training team to notice this. There was a real bond that existed amongst these so-called *Pals* battalions, which seemed to supersede even the camaderie of the regular troops who had often served together for a number of years. Clearly recruiting whole groups of men from towns and villages, sports teams and work places, men who had often grown up together and been friends for life, added a unique element to their training. It injected in them a desire to work for each other, and ultimately fight for each other and their places of origin. This was something that was impossible for the officers to teach, and to Russell it was a masterstroke of recruiting.

The three Southdown battalions here in Witley were no different. Recruited by Lord Lowther from the villages and towns of Sussex, they were known colloquially as *Lowther's Lambs* and they played as they fought, with a real sense of belonging. As Russell watched he saw one of his own sergeants emerge from a scrum of men with the ball and set off like lightning down the right side of the darkening field. He noted his blond hair dipping in and out of the light beams cast from the windows of the various accommodation blocks as first one, and then a second sliding challenge failed to halt him.

Sergeant Will Davison was one of the new members of the training team hand-picked by Russell himself for this task, who noted from very early on his natural flair for leadership. Combined with his popularity with the men, it instilled a trust to follow him regardless. Will was also a veteran of the war in France like himself, and both had suffered their fair share of danger and death already. Being a veteran also brought with it an unspoken respect amongst the recruits regardless of age, and Will had taken to this new role like a duck to water, with a firm but fair approach.

Here in the evening 'sports' events however, rank and title went out of the window, which was evident by the way the opposition players now attempted to stop Will's progress by any means possible. Amongst the crescendo of noise that echoed from the football pitch one distinctive shout carried to Russell from the far penalty area.

"On me 'ead Sarge!" came the distinctive cry of Archie Bunden as he bludgeoned his way forward through the mass of charging bodies. Will looked up and with pinpoint accuracy floated his cross into the area towards the far post.

"Now or never Bunny," his team mate Danny Boyd cried, making himself a nuisance amongst the opposing defenders despite his diminutive stature, while laughing the whole time as if that excused his persistent fouling.

Archie at over six feet four and muscles to match had little difficulty leaping highest and met the ball full on the forehead, from where it diverted like a bullet several feet over the goal. Archie's momentum took him inexorably forward as he landed, and sent several of the men around him crashing into the goal together with the terrified goalie. Will stood hands on hips observing this melee and with a disappointed shake of the head jogged over to retrieve the ball from where it bounced harmlessly on the parade ground.

"You're supposed to put the ball in the net Bunden you stupid oaf. Nearly knocked me out!" Owen Entwhistle, the goalkeeper, dragged himself up from the human tangle inside the net, not allowing Archie's size to stop his ranting.

"Shut it Ginge. I was fouled so I was," Bunden replied, referring to Owen's wild tangle of red hair; the only part of his Mum's striking Welsh features the goalkeeper had inherited.

"Fouled? You couldn't hit a barn door in the wind Bunden. That's why you don't play up front you big lump of lard."

It was Tommy Landon who now joined in the criticism. He had been caught up in the tangle of arms and legs in the net and was dusting himself down, checking no serious harm had befallen him. In contrast to Owen he was boyishly handsome and was quite particular about his looks, hence adding to his upset.

"Ooof!" he cried as he was sent sprawling back in the mud once more.

"Oh sorry mate, didn't see you there," Bunden said, as he jogged past him with a grin. "You've got a hard head though, I'll give you that," he added rubbing his elbow that had sent Tommy back to the floor. "Might knock a bit of sense into you mind."

Owen helped Tommy up a second time and gave his friend a pat on the shoulder.

"He's a bloody liability that Bunden," Tommy said. "God knows how he ever made Corporal. No brains that I can see."

"You're right there. Might kill half of us before we even get to fight," Owen grumbled rubbing his chest.

"Better get used to the mud boys. You'll be knee deep in it soon enough. And the corporal will be the least of your worries then." Will's voice made the two friends snap round and they nodded embarrassed, as he walked up handing the ball to Owen. "You'll be glad of his experience when we get over there lads. So take the knocks and pay attention. Might learn something, even from someone with no brains."

He smiled then, the easy smile that could diffuse any situation, and the friends smiled back. With a shrug Owen kicked the ball hard down the pitch and the bedlam continued.

"Not very tactical that kick Owen," Will said watching it bounce once and then disappear in the scrum of the opposing area.

"No time for tactics in a game like this Sarge, just a long ball forward and let them get on with it. Safer up that end than here anyway."

"Can't argue with that," Will smiled, noting that despite the fact these men were his friends and teammates from Steyning, they had fallen into using his rank in the camp even in private. *They were good men, reliable,* he mused appreciatively.

As Archie jogged past his sergeant major, he couldn't resist calling out.

"Did you see me leap like a salmon just then sir?"

"Oh indeed I did. And I saw you land like a hippopotamus in labour too laddie. Luckily you shoot better with a rifle than your head."

"The goalposts moved Sergeant Major, I'm sure of it. Swayed in the wind like." Archie gave an impish grin and Russell raised an eyebrow at the remark.

"Just try not to destroy my battalion single handed Bunden before we sail 'eh?"

"I'll try sir, can't promise mind," Archie replied with a laugh and charged off once more.

Russell smiled at his exuberance. It was good to see him fit and well again, and seemingly back to his old self. Archie had been hit by random shelling behind the lines in France, and it was touch and go for some time as to whether he would live, let alone walk again. But thanks to some outstanding surgery and nursing care, here he was larger than life once more. Russell wondered what his mind was like however, and the smile turned to a frown as he pondered the effect going back to France might have on him, and Sergeant Davison for that matter.

"Penny for your thoughts Geoff?"

Russell looked round and saw Nelson Carter approaching him. They had come up through the ranks together, and while not always serving in the same places, they were both now sergeant majors and it was Carter who had requested Russell join him in Witley and help prepare these battalions for France.

Carter was much younger than Russell at twenty-eight, but this didn't affect the obvious bond between the two men. He was intelligent with a quick mind and led by example. Ignoring the trend for beards or moustaches amongst the non-commissioned ranks, Carter's youthful looks made him seem even younger than he was. But those who wondered at his rank on first glance, soon saw in him a quiet determination and discipline that made it clear he had earned those promotions on merit.

"Just wondering about the months ahead Nelson. How these lads will measure up."

"Well I've been impressed with them so far. Tough lot and up for the challenge I'd say. Certainly can't argue with their enthusiasm," he added, nodding at the screaming pack of men attempting to play something that resembled football.

"I hope you're right. Because it's a whole different ball game over there. I've seen plenty of good men in training come unstuck when the reality kicks in."

"I've no doubt of that Geoff. You'd know that more than any of us. But no use speculating about it here. All we can do is get them as ready as possible for when the call comes and then it's in the lap of the gods."

Russell nodded, and as they stood in quiet reflection for a moment they saw Archie grab the ball and start running with it like a rugby player and the game descended into chaos.

"Who's that big idiot again? I can't see in the dark. Is it Peterson?" Carter asked.

"No that's our Corporal Bunden."

"Oh yes. Good God almighty. How did he ever get promoted?"

"That was on my recommendation."

Carter coughed with embarrassment. "Oh, sorry feller. No offence meant but he seems hell bent on injuring half the battalion. Not got German parents has he?"

Russell laughed now and felt himself relax once more.

"They were my thoughts too. But would you rather he was in the opposite trench Nelson?" He slapped him on the shoulder for good measure.

"Good point. I suppose as long as we make sure he's facing forwards we should be fine."

They laughed together as they watched the men come to a natural halt and start to break up into groups and head off to their barracks.

"His experience will help the new lads," Russell added, becoming serious again. "That's why I brought him and Davison on board."

"Oh yes the Sergeant. Now he is a leader. Hell of a shot too. Eyes like a hawk. No wonder he has his sniper's badges."

Russell nodded, knowing full well the extent of Will's ability having seen it up close in France on more than one occasion. He reflected on a battle the previous year when Will had shot a hidden German sniper at over eight hundred yards based purely on instinct. Will had retained his boyish charm however, and it was hard to imagine any of the horrors he had lived through. Russell became aware Carter had paused, clearly waiting for an answer.

"Sorry Nelson, thinking about the men. What were you saying?"

"I was saying, it seems to me we have more than one Davison?"

"Yes, that's right. He's got an older brother here, David. Good lads both of them, and believe it or not there's another one, a Guards officer in France."

"A toff? Crikey. How did that happen?"

"Well he's hardly posh being from a line of farmers, but from the little I've heard he's of the same stock. I'm sure if someone has seen fit to put pips on his shoulders, then he's earnt it."

"Amen to that Geoff."

They turned to go then just as a tall orderly came jogging over and snapped smartly to attention in front of them.

"Ah Peterson, were your ears burning?" Carter asked smiling, returning the salute.

Dillon Peterson was nearly six foot six, and skinny as a rake handle. He had very short cropped black hair that was spiky and stood straight up, and within two minutes of meeting Archie had been designated 'company broom.' He had to endure a host of jokes after that about being 'swept up in the patriotic fervor,' and 'brushing past in the queue' at mealtimes, but he took it all in good part, and as such was another popular recruit. As it turned out, being the son of a lawyer, Dillon's brains were far sharper than his outward appearance suggested, and he was made company orderly for Number One Battalion.

Peterson frowned now at his sergeant major's remark but continued with his message.

"Sorry to disturb Sergeant Major but the Colonel has ordered a briefing for 20:00 hours this evening with all company commanders and NCOs."

"I see Private. Thank you. We are on our way back anyway."

"Any idea what it's about Peterson?" Russell added.

"I believe the Battalions have their marching orders. We are to head to France soon. March I think. The camp has been detailed to Canadian troops coming over to train here on their way to France apparently."

"Thank you, carry on."

As Peterson saluted and disappeared into the darkness at the double, Carter paused and turned to his colleague.

"Well Geoff, it seems like we will see how the lads measure up sooner rather than later 'eh?"

"Yes, it does. We've a busy time ahead if it's true. But if the beds have been rented out to the Canucks then we'll be going whether the men are ready or not."

The two men set off back to the main buildings as night time settled across the camp, stars radiating off each other in the clear dark sky. The near full moon illuminated the area far better than any lamps could do and gave the whole place an eerie perspective. As they walked back in silence save for the echoes of their boots clicking on the hard path, Russell looked up at the sky once more and shivered.

A bad night to be out in No Man's Land, he thought wistfully.

*

At seven in the morning as the men gathered in the mess hall for the battalion briefing, a buzzard circled effortlessly overhead. Its smooth brown plumage glinted in the rising sun as it prepared for another day's hunting. It called a distinctive note to its mate, that to an untrained ear sounded like a cat *meowing,* and its mate answered from the newly constructed nest high up in the oak tree by the firing range.

After a few days of showing off in a dazzling aerial display of swoops and spirals, he had suitably impressed her to stay with him for another year. Buzzards would often mate for life anyway, and this would be the third season these two birds had been together. In time between two and four eggs would appear in the nest and he was out early looking for food; a search that would soon be a constant pressure when the chicks hatched.

Close to the mess hall a mouse sniffed the air nervously. It was late getting back to the hedgerow after another night scrounging scraps in the kitchens. The call from the buzzard above alerted it to the deadly shadow skirting overhead and it froze in the dark under-hang of the wooden building.

The buzzard soared round on the air current once more, wings held in a distinctive shallow 'V' shape, the tail fanned out behind to ease its motion. The eyes never resting, it was well aware that the area below was an abundant source of food. Small mammals and insects frequented the buildings providing rich pickings to the mating pair. Along the shiny black ground where the large rumbling creatures moved, dead carcasses often appeared after one had passed, presumably discarded by the larger predator.

But now the area below was filled with the noise and movement of the two-legged animals that had suddenly gathered here in large numbers. The buzzard swooped lower in case they were converging on something tasty, but they didn't seem to linger, and it allowed the air current to pick it up once more.

The mouse watched the bird of prey circle away and tentatively came forward from its hiding place. It looked about and sniffed the air but all seemed still. Then more of the two-legged things appeared quite close to it and a stone ricocheted past hitting the wooden wall with a loud bang. Startled, the mouse shot forward, and keeping low without looking back, it skirted the edge of the building before making the final dash to the hedgerow. The safety of the burrow's dark hole appeared ahead welcoming the mouse home.

When the strike came it was not from up high where the buzzard was still circling, enjoying the sun's early warmth on its broad back. The little owl had watched the mouse for the last few minutes from its perch in the mouth of the drainpipe by the tool shed. It came in fast and low just above the ground taking the rodent in its right claw within inches of the burrow's entrance. Although barely twice the size of the adult mouse, the owl lifted it effortlessly with a short flurry of its wings and carried it away to a safe place to feast.

As David walked into the mess hall with Danny and Owen, the high-pitched squeak and blur of activity to the right took their eye momentarily.

"Did you see that," David said enthusiastically, "something just took a mouse."

"What was it, an eagle?" Tommy replied stopping short so the men behind bumped into him.

"You daft sod, eagles are huge," Danny scoffed.

"Could be a chick."

"Oh right yes, seen lots of eagles here have you while we've been training?"

"Small bird of prey," David said, being more sympathetic.

"Oh, like a sparrow?" Tommy replied.

Both men stared at him then.

"A bloody sparrow?" Danny said.

"Oh yeh, deadly killers those," Owen chipped in, as he passed by picking up on the last snippet of conversation. "Maybe we should train some and send 'em over to fight Jerry." He walked on into the hall laughing and telling someone what Tommy had said.

"It was an owl I'm sure of it," David said authoritatively.

"Hurry up you men!" The voice of Sergeant Major Russell made the small trio double up into the hall.

"Owls are nocturnal aren't they?" Danny said as they took their seats at the back.

"Not always. Little owls hunt by day," David replied.

Danny raised his eyes in a show of interest and then whispered, "Of course it could have been a killer sparrow." The two men laughed as Tommy blushed, and a few rows in front another group of men with Owen grinned and then Archie turned and made bird signs back at Tommy. It would be a long day for him.

*

Will had joined the other non-commissioned officers at the back of the hall. As he saw his brother relaxed and joking with his peers he felt a pang of jealousy. It was not so long ago he was sitting in a similar place with his enlisted comrades joking and chatting, and making fun of the sergeants. Now he was a sergeant and had to stay apart from that, to set an example. But there was more too. David was his brother, and although it was great to be in the same battalion, it felt different here somehow.

Yes, I am jealous, he conceded to himself, *and angry. Why was he so angry inside?* Will knew really. They had all been so very close growing up. It was an inevitable anger that the war was changing everything, and he felt powerless to stop it. All he could do was try and live through it and hope they all came out the other side.

He frowned now just as David happened to glance over to him. David saw the look on his brother's face and frowned too. The carefree laughter of a moment ago dissipating in a second. They held each other's gaze for a moment and Will gave an almost imperceptible shake of the head, warning his brother to behave. David took the look as a sign of disapproval anyway and looked away, muttering to his friends to pipe down. In that moment Will hated the fact he was a leader, his mind a cloud of contrasting thoughts. He wanted them just to have fun, to muck about like they used to on the farm. He just wanted to be a younger brother again.

David seemed to intuitively read his younger brother's thoughts and looked at him again. As Will raised his eyes from the floor David stuck his tongue out at him behind his hand and smiled. Will had to work hard to suppress a laugh and gave a mock stern look back at his brother, but the moment had been perfect, and he felt better instantly.

Russell called the company to order and the Commanding Officer marched in to the front of the assembled South Down battalions. They were joined by the men of the Hampshire regiment too that made up the full Brigade. The hall was packed with expectant faces and the smell of men pressed together made the humid atmosphere oppressive and added to the growing sense of tension that the widespread banter had lightly disguised. The smell brought back other memories to Will, of men huddled together in dugouts hour after hour during the shelling, and crowded stinking trenches. He looked over to where the unmistakable hulking form of Archie was perched near the front on a chair too small for him. He saw his head was bowed and knew that Archie felt it too. He knew the dread was rife within him.

Much of what the CO said to the men went past Will unheard as he battled with his own thoughts and demons. He had heard a similar speech in Folkestone before they set sail for France in 1914, from their doomed Colonel Bradshaw. Bradshaw's words had not stirred him as a fresh-faced recruit, as much as he felt they should, and did little to quell the darkness within him now. Often he felt perhaps there was something wrong with him, and certainly knew he was in a minority here.

Or perhaps it was everyone else that was deluded, he pondered and then shook that image away. As a sergeant the men would look to him now and Will tried not to let his concerns show. As he focused in again on the new colonel's words there was cheering in the hall as he fired the men up, turning fear into bravery with patriotic rhetoric.

Lieutenant Colonel Harman Grisewood, from Bognor had been with the battalion since May 1915 when he had been appointed by Lord Lowther to take over the formal training of the newly raised battalions. Popular with the men, his easy manner made the task of rallying his troops at times like this quite simple for all but the hardened veterans in the room. Of which Will now ranked among that number. Will was also aware through the mess news that Grisewood had already lost one brother to illness in the war and yet here he was undaunted, urging the men on to France and victory. In the end it was impossible not to feel the old stirrings of national pride cramped in this wooden hall with the cheering men, and he allowed himself to be swept along with it and shouted with the rest. They would need all the courage they could muster in the months ahead.

Chapter 5 – The gathering storm

"What do you mean he's not come back?" Will said to his sergeant major, a look of disbelief on his face.

"He had the weekend off to go and see his Mum. She was unwell he said. He was supposed to be back by last night," Russell answered, continuing the discreet update to his new training sergeant.

"Perhaps she's taken a turn for the worse?"

"Maybe so. I'm not sure though, he hasn't been the same since we got our marching orders." He watched the reaction in the young man opposite and saw that he had noticed it too. "He's your friend, what do you think lad?"

Will's mind was flying all over the place. He wanted to believe that Archie was with his Mum, even if it meant she was unwell, but something told him otherwise.

"I don't know," was all he could think to say.

"Well we march on Friday, right after the passing out parade, so if he's not back by Thursday I will have no choice but to report him missing and send out the MPs. You know that won't go well, even away from the front."

"I'll find him," Will said suddenly, the image of Archie being marched before a court martial by burly policemen suddenly clear in his mind.

"Think you can lad?"

"I have an idea where he might be."

"And I'm guessing that's not at his mother's. Am I right?"

"Possibly not Sergeant Major."

Russell mulled it over.

"You've got forty-eight hours Will. I'll get the word out you are on errands for last minute supplies before we march. But you know this place, tongues will soon start to wag. And don't disappear yourself either!"

"I'll be back sir, I promise. We both will."

"Ok lad. You know you can call me Geoff when we are off duty right? Now you're in the sergeant's mess and all?"

"Thank you Sergeant Major."

Russell smiled now at the polite young man in front of him. Still only nineteen, but already a veteran and decorated with the Distinguished Conduct Medal for his bravery in France. *So much like me when I was younger.*

"Go. And if anyone asks you...Bunden's Mum is very ill and he will be sailing with us Friday regardless. Understood?"

Will nodded and walked out. He closed the door behind him and let out a deep sigh.

Oh Bunny, you've really gone and done it now mate.

As he left the building the sun was sinking fast below the horizon and a twilight glow sparkled across the camp. Russell had caught him after the evening meal to raise his concerns. Will wanted to leave straight away but knew he was better to go prepared. He hoped his hunch was right and set off back to his barrack hut to pack his kit before getting an early night. He would be on the first train he could get out of Witley in the morning before reveille was even sounding.

Heading to Brighton.

*

Staff Nurse Teresa Halliday sat a short way from the field hospital and watched the swallows dip and swerve in the late afternoon sun. The break in rain had brought the insects out near the swollen brook and the birds feasted on the wing as they swooped and swirled in seemingly chaotic patterns. Teresa knew, like everything here, that beneath the apparent chaos there was always a plan. Of course, finding out who actually knew the plan in this army was as tricky as the latest operations she had performed with Colonel Hamilton throughout the morning.

She smiled to herself and untied the faded pattern head scarf she used to keep her hair back. As the long black locks fell free about her face Teresa stooped down to dip the scarf in the brook. She dabbed the ice-cold water on her neck and across her brow, allowing the drops to run tantalisingly down her face and neck and onto her blouse. She gasped a little as some ran onto her stomach, and then lay back enjoying the precious few minutes of respite in her favourite spot. She would be called back soon enough.

Teresa now allowed her thoughts to focus on Will, and when she might see him again. There had been no letter since the New Year but then the post was as chaotic as everything else these days. With the latest spring offensive, the hospitals were overrun once more, and they were desperately short of nurses and supplies. As much as she missed Will, a trainload of medicine and help would be just as welcome a sight.

Teresa frowned now, pondering the question she had turned over in her mind a thousand times since Will was taken back to England. Remembering how he left France, his body wrecked by the gas attack in the trenches, a part of her hoped Will might never come back to this hell hole. She still feared for his mental state as much as anything else when he did return.

What can you do anyway Halliday? she thought. *No point worrying. He's probably found another nurse to look after him now, or some Baroness. Maybe that Alice has changed her mind and snatched him up.*

This wasn't helping her relax and she sighed and chided herself. Despite the freshening wind, and damp ground, Teresa decided a few minutes sleep wouldn't hurt. She'd been working since just after midnight when the latest casualties came in. *How long was that? Hours and days all merging...* she closed her eyes.

"Ah, there you are Staff."

A female voice broke into Teresa's shallow slumber and brought her back from her desperate descent into sleep.

"Oh, hello Rose," she murmured through half open eyes.

Away from the confines of the army rule book, Teresa dispensed with all that rank and discipline nonsense whenever she could.

"You sent for me?" Rose continued. "I'm sorry Staff, it's been manic as you know and I had to get over to the supply depot and try and steal some more bandages and what not."

"You can call me Teresa here, Rose. The birds won't squeal on us. Or squawk I guess," she added offering a brief smile as she sat up.

Rose smiled and said "thank you," and perched on a broken stone wall near the brook.

"So, you've turned to stealing now?" Teresa asked gradually pulling herself round.

"Had to. Some jumped up clerk at the depot said we'd had our allocation for the week and there was nothing he could do."

"And yet you managed to get some things?"

"I found a new Lieutenant, and used my charms on him."

Teresa raised an inquisitive eyebrow. "And what would the Captain think about that?"

"Oh, nothing like that. Just a smile, and a shared cigarette and my big lost baby eyes." She widened her eyes and looked as bashful as she could and Teresa laughed.

"Men are such pushovers," Teresa said, and took a cigarette from Rose who had already lit up. She wondered when she had started smoking herself, and couldn't for the life of her remember.

"I can assure you James has nothing to worry about. Besides you told me you shout downwards and you flirt upwards." Rose smiled broadly, taking another pull on the cigarette that made her eyes sting.

Teresa grinned at her reliable colleague. They had grown closer since they discovered they shared a common bond with the Davison brothers, but more so because whenever their work got really intense, Rose never flinched, and stood shoulder to shoulder with her.

"Absolutely Rose. I'd never make love to anyone less than a Colonel to get what I needed." She winked as Rose came and sat on the floor by her. "Speaking of which what did you manage to acquire anyway, from the new officer."

"I got several cartons of morphine, half a dozen bandage boxes, and no end of ties and splints. Oh, and even found a bottle of the Colonel's favourite rum, which I gave him earlier. I think he smiled, hard to tell under the beard." She pulled a face to mimic his stern appearance.

"Well done you. Those baby eyes worked a treat. And what about the poor nurses. Did you get anything for the little people while there?" Teresa asked expectedly.

"Well you're smoking some of it, and you'll find the tea and biscuit supplies look a lot healthier. Not to mention a nice dash of gin to go in it."

"Hoorah!"

There was a shout from the tents and Teresa knew they were looking for them.

"Rose, before we get dragged back, I just wanted to let you know I heard from Major Johnson up at HQ last night, but with going straight into the onslaught of work, I haven't had a moment to catch you."

"What old jolly Jonners?"

"Yes, the very same. Anyway, he said the Guards have been in action all week. James' brigade." Rose's demeanour changed in a moment. "But before you hear that yourself, or we get any of the worst cases dumped on us, he said to let you know he'd heard from James himself. He was fine, and even passed on a message for you."

Rose leant forward now looking at Teresa, trying to read her face.

"He said Happy Valentine's Day Kellett. That's all." She saw the anxiety in her friend's face. It was underneath the surface every day in this place. She looked away to be polite and watched the birds swooping madly this way and that again. *That pretty much summed up their lives,* she thought.

The shouts from the tents came again, their names clear now. It was Colonel Hamilton's voice. It would be another emergency. *Weren't they all?* Teresa thought.

Rose jumped up and squashed the remains of the cigarette out under a muddy, booted heel. "Well I should bloody well think so too. I was beginning to wonder if he'd forgotten me, with all this gallivanting about in the trenches. Not like there's a war on or anything now is it?"

"Quite right nurse," Teresa said standing up and linking her arm in Rose's and giving her a quick squeeze. "Be sure to tell him off next time you see him."

They smiled at each other and walked back along the bank where the deepening gloom of the tent interiors pulled them away from the life-giving sun. It was getting colder now quite quickly, but Teresa knew as she walked arm in arm with Rose that her friend wasn't trembling because she was cold.

*

Will stepped out into Trafalgar Street from Brighton station as the sun emerged once more from behind the smoke slated rooftops ahead of him. His body shuddered with the change in temperature, the warmth of the train carriage left behind; and he pulled the army great coat about him, pushing his hands deeper in its pockets. He set off to walk through Victoria Gardens towards the military hospital. It wasn't yet seven in the morning and his tired mind struggled to catch up with the speed his physical body adopted now to push on.

After a restless couple of hours of sleep Will had walked down to Witley station from the camp in the dead of night expecting everywhere to be locked up. However, freight trains were still passing like ghosts through the landscape and he persuaded a guard to let him hop on one with him, in exchange for some cigarettes. His luck held and he switched to the first mail train of the day at Dorking and travelled down the main lines to Brighton.

As he came out onto the promenade the wind grabbed him without a care and shoved him roughly forwards. He held onto the rail above the sea wall and watched the storm-tossed waves charge up the pebbled beach, howling with every fresh endeavour. Will lifted his collar high against his neck, but the wind simply flattened it again, and he relented and just stood for a moment transfixed by the wild montage in front of him.

A seagull cried overhead; the sound whipped away in a moment as it flapped hopelessly against the gale. It hung for a second and then allowed itself to be carried away back across the crashing surf. Will recalled another gull that had trailed him once before in Brighton and half smiled wondering if it was the same one. That particular outing had breathed new life into his soul after he returned wounded and broken from France. It helped him to move on from Alice, in a way he hadn't realised he needed to, and to prepare for the next chapter in his life.

Alice was the daughter of Lord and Lady Pevensey, and his first and only love so far. On reflection Will came to accept it had been no more than a brief dalliance with someone well outside his reach socially. But it had felt serious to him at the time and the pain on learning she was engaged to an officer was very real, and affected him badly. She had written of course, wanting to *stay friends* as his dear friend Albert said girls always did. That letter was gone now, cast into the very sea where he now stood. And with it his love for Alice. Though he still wondered how he might feel if he ever saw her again.

Perhaps he was not meant to find love, like poor Bert now buried in some corner of a field in France. It didn't matter, war was not the place for love, he told himself, as the rain rattled against his face once more.

He pushed on into the wind and passing a bench, his face now changed to a smile at a different memory. He pictured his dear friend Archie sitting there eating cakes and shouting at him on the beach. The roar of his laugh now echoed in the sea and he reached out and stroked the back of the seat fondly. A couple passed by, propelled by the storm, the man's coat like a kite as he held it behind his sweetheart to try and protect her from the worst of the rain. Will nodded and the man frowned seeing him patting the bench, but then nodded back and hurried past allowing the natural elements to quicken their stride. The memory of Archie reminded him why he was here and he returned to the task in hand; the scattered remnants of the torn letter from Alice once more buried at sea.

It was raining. Will hadn't realised until he saw it accompany the young couple. He had thought it was the sea spray that lashed about here with careless abandon, but now he looked up into the dark maelstrom and let it fall onto his face as if seeking agreement. He took his regimental hat out of an inside pocket and considered putting it on, having been reluctant to announce his status so blatantly when he left the train. *Won't last five seconds in this lot,* he thought to himself. *More likely be blown to France before I am. Wet anyway now. May as well just plod on.*

His mind made up, Will set off along the front determinedly once more. The large grey walls of the military hospital loomed in the distance like a ship far out to sea. He fought his way towards it, determined to salvage one passenger from its cargo of lost souls.

*

Fred pushed his way up the icy cobbles towards the meat shed. The wind howled down the narrow passageway here, chilling him to the bones, as if he was not cold enough. He longed for the end of the day and the chance to get home and a hot bath in front of the fire. As he passed the store shed there was a loud crash but he carried on believing it to be the wind roaring through the open windows. *I'm not getting blamed if anything has blown down,* he thought ruefully.

Then voices came to him as the wind paused for a moment, deciding which way to blow next. He stopped, thinking he heard a girl laughing, and then there was a shout. Curiosity got the better of him and he went inside.

"Hello?" Fred called hesitatingly as his eyes adjusted to the dim interior, but there was no reply and he tentatively moved in a little further. He felt nervous suddenly and pulled on the light switch hanging down in the centre of the first room, and there was an almighty clatter from round the corner that made him jump out of his skin. Fred looked round into the back room and came face to face with John fumbling frantically with his clothing.

"Oh er…sorry…" Fred said startled and began to move backwards.

"What you doing here?" John shouted, clearly scared as much as angry.

It was then Fred noticed Ginny on the floor behind him, she was sitting against a box grinning but as he spotted her, her face became spiteful.

"Oh look, it's the little runt here to have a gawp again. Been spying on us 'ave ya? Listenin' through the keyhole?"

"No I haven't," Fred protested, "I heard a noise outside, and a shout, and…"

"Li-ar!" Ginny retorted, kneeling forward and her dress now fell open revealing an ample cleavage, and she grinned pulling it together.

"He's always snooping around that one, and gawping...you should sack 'im babe."

"Quiet Ginny," John said sharply, the tone making her recoil with a frown. He grabbed Fred now by the collar and pulled him closer. "What did you see here? Tell me."

Fred was terrified and started to stammer. "Hon-Honestly, sir, I…I…thought something was wrong. I was on my way back to the meat shed and…"

"Listen to 'im. What a load of tosh. Calling you 'sir' to wheedle out of it. Give 'im a good hiding to keep his mouth shut then let's carry on." Ginny winked and wriggled her shoulders at John, who was momentarily thrown.

"I won't say anything."

John looked between the two of them, and Fred could see his mind was whirring not sure what to do. He felt the grip on his collar loosen so took the chance to run and pulled back hard, slamming straight into the immaculate checked tweed suit of Roger Mullings.

"What the bloody hell is going on here then!"

*

Will paused on the lawn of the hospital. Broken memories swirled about his mind as if the storm itself had entered his head. He saw the shadow of a barefooted man staggering across the lawn in pyjamas, bent double under an invisible weight. A ghost pain returned to plague his body and he clutched his chest automatically. The wind howled through the nearby trees, and in the dank dark of their interior he heard voices crying out to him, wounded and in pain.

He took a few steps towards the soaking canopy, branches drooping to the ground like broken limbs, his mind tormented once more. *He shouldn't have come back here. What was he thinking? If he wants to run away let him. God knows he wished he had the strength to do that.* Will knelt on the lawn, oblivious to the wet, needing to focus, the piteous voices shrieking in the wind. He punched the ground angrily.

No! He had to do this. They would find Archie. They always did. He owed it to his friend to try.

In that moment the wind finally relented, the rain unsupported slowing to a light drizzle. Will breathed deeply and slowly, controlling the anxiety that had suddenly risen at this return to the past. The shadows cleared and he saw a nurse walking along the drive to the front entrance. He rose and shook his rain-soaked coat to free the excess water, the action designed to do the same thing with the haunting images that fought now to re-enter his conscious mind. Satisfied he was in control once more, he set off after her.

*

Polly Jenkins was thinking about the next shift, and wondered if the badly burned Royal Flying Corps Officer was still alive. They were becoming numb now to the range and state of injuries that came to them in the hospital, the attachments of the early months worn down by the steady flow of broken and burned bodies, and regular deaths.

But Pilot Officer Brown affected them all. His attempts at humour and humble gratitude amidst rasping breaths, seemed to trigger the anger and despair in them all once more. Especially when they found the family portrait in his ragged jacket pocket of the handsome blonde officer standing with parents and siblings. His father was in uniform too. An officer it was clear from the picture, although it was impossible to tell which regiment. Oswald Brown was not yet eighteen, and now the face was half burned away, the body broken and his right leg amputated in France to give him a chance of life. *Life! What life was there for him now? Better to die in France surely than...*

Polly stopped on the steps and shook her head. The doctor was confident he would live. "They could do wonders these days," he had told them. *Today would be a long day*, she thought. Not least because the young officer appeared to her in her dreams, asking for a dance politely and then raising the burned shrivelled limbs to invite her onto the floor. She had woken with a start. Her roommate alerted by Polly's shouts, lit the lamps, half scared to death herself.

Sleep had been fitful after that and Polly felt exhausted before she even started her shift. She shivered at the thought of ghosts and looked out across the lawn, as the wind mercifully dropped finally, the brightening sky offering hope. Her mind was probably still debating the existence of ghosts when she saw the dark looming shape of Will walking unexpectedly across the lawn, and she screamed before she could stop herself.

*

Sister Elsie Dent had just finished her final rounds of the night before heading home. She had been on her feet for the last eight hours and was so tired she was sure the moment she sat down sleep would engulf her. The first night shift was always the hardest as the body clock adjusted to this unnatural routine. But the lure of a hot bath first was difficult to ignore.

She passed on her notes to Sister Mertonshaw, with the usual customary exchange between two colleagues who barely saw each other outside of these passing moments, and who had never bonded since their induction week at Brighton. Ignoring the usual internal disgruntlement that followed any reflection on those terse few days, Elsie allowed her thoughts to return to her young beau once more. She smiled knowing his warm strong arms would be waiting to embrace her the moment she walked in. No matter what time she came home, night or day he seemed to anticipate her arrival. *Perhaps he would join her in the bath.*

She allowed her smile to return again, the night having elicited only the fixed stare required to get the job done.

"Home time at last," Elsie said, and then Polly's scream echoed off the highly polished floors.

*

Archie snoozed contentedly in front of the fire. He had fallen asleep in the parlour last night, unable to settle in the small back bedroom without her. A crack of thunder outside made him jolt awake, as the storm refused to wane. He shivered and felt uneasy momentarily until he remembered where he was. The fire had stayed smoldering away throughout the night, and he roused himself now to poke it into life, knowing how much his Elsie would love it when she got back. As it crackled and spat fresh sparks onto the hearth Archie was delighted to hear the front gate click. He chucked a log quickly into the rejuvenated flames dancing about the grate, and bounded to the door.

"Welcome home darling!" he shouted, his smile beaming through the wild sleep-crushed beard. Then the glow dropped from his face in an instant when it was Will's image that loomed up in front of him, the worried form of Elsie loitering behind.

"Oh, Bloody hell," he exclaimed, stepping back from the shock.

"Hello Bunny," Will said calmly. "Shall we go inside?"

Chapter 6 – Rum and true religion

Agnes used a cloth to take the kettle from the rack above the fire where it was whistling away as loudly as the trains that ran through Steyning every day. The steam merged with the smoke and followed it reluctantly up into the chimney and away.

"Noisy thing," she muttered to herself, placing it carefully on the table, and proceeded to make a pot for the men. Harold was outside repairing a partly collapsed wall that had succumbed to the recent storm. There was a young lad from Tulip farm helping him, the youngest of the Harris brood, probably not much older than her Freddie. Harold's dad had also agreed to come over to lend some moral support, but as Agnes watched them through the window, it seemed Arthur was doing nothing more than chatting and smoking his pipe. *That will irritate Hal*, she thought. *No doubt regaling him with railways tales as ever. Just as well it's time for a break.*

She called out to them from the back door and set about laying out some mugs, and took the rolls out of the stove where they had been warming. She put a dish of raspberry jam from the remains of last summer's crops out alongside it. Arthur had certainly had his fill of breakfast from her, but Harold had been in a rush to get on and simply grabbed some fruit, so she was keen to ensure he didn't go hungry. *Raspberry jam was his favourite.*

As the men trooped in she heard the farm gate go and the distinctive high-pitched voice of Freddie called out to his father. She frowned wondering why he was back so early but got on with pouring the tea.

"There she is, our wonderful cook, slaving over a hot stove as ever. Smells wonderful Agnes. Doesn't it Norman, my lad?" Arthur waved his pipe at the newly laid table, and then popped it in his mouth again. He took a couple of strides towards the table rubbing his hands gleefully.

"It does smell lovely Mrs Davison," the young Norman Harris replied bashfully.

"Well lovely or not, if you don't leave your boots by the door and wash your hands, you can just turn round and go out again!"

"Oh, so that's why you were frowning 'eh?" Arthur held up his hands in a show of submission. "Right come on lad let's beat a retreat and sort ourselves out."

Norman blushed and tried to do both things at the same time, tucking a boot under his arm while grabbing the soap, and succeeded only in falling from the sink while hopping about on one foot.

It wasn't why she was frowning but Agnes was happy to let it be seen as such, and now smiled as Harold and Fred came in together, Freddie chirping away non-stop to his dad. Harold looked at the prone figure of young Harris, struggling on the ground, and lifted him up one-handed as easily as a new-born lamb.

"Why are you not at work Fred?" Agnes asked, concerned.

"Mullings are taking some stock over to Horsham mart lass, and they've given him the rest of the day off," Harold said, answering for his son.

"And John said he would pay me for the whole day for working so hard recently!" Freddie announced triumphantly.

"Really?" Agnes said, raising an eye and looking at Harold who just shrugged kicking his boots off in the corner.

"Well someone's making a good impression," said Arthur, ruffling Freddie's hair. Agnes set another plate at the table for Fred as they all began to settle down. Harold reached over for a piece of bread unable to resist the warm aroma anymore.

"Hands Harold," Agnes chided, and he raised his eyes seeing his dad grinning at him. Then he cheekily dipped the bread in the jam pot and took a bite before retreating to the sink. Agnes frowned again but he winked at her and she shook her head and moved round the table fussing over the men.

"I'm pleased you are doing so well Freddie," she said, as she finally sat down herself.

"Expect nothing less from a Davison," Harold added, between mouthfuls of warm bread. He was famished after the stone work having worked relentlessly since getting up. The impending departure of their boys to France, announced in a letter home from David, had set him off on a frenzy of work. It was as if he had to get everything repaired and straightened out on the farm before they went. Deep down Harold knew he was just using the work to stop his mind from wandering; dark thoughts that disturbed his sleep, and had him out working before the cock crowed of late. He was pleased with the company today and smiled as he ate, joining in the idle chatter around his hearth.

Only Fred knew the real reason he was being rewarded at work. As Norman spoke about the new litter of piglets on their farm, he stuffed the food down happily, reflecting on the recent upturn in fortunes for him…

When Roger Mullings had exploded on the scene in the store room, Fred had kept quiet except to say he heard a commotion and found Ginny had slipped on the floor and John was trying to help her. John quickly picked up the thread explaining he'd sent Ginny to get some more jars of pickled eggs and when she hadn't come back he came to look for her and found her here in pain. Roger was no fool and had sent Ginny and Fred out before taking John to one side and giving him a piece of his mind.

"You're not too old for a wallop John, if I thought it would do any good. But I haven't built up this business and my reputation to see it dashed to bits in the store shed. I'll deal with this for you, then we'll say no more about it."

John nodded shame faced. "What about the kid?" he asked.

"Fred? He's a Davison and clearly loyal to you. A trait inherited from his father no doubt, who isn't a man to cross let me tell you lad. So, I suggest you just keep an eye on him. He'll be an asset one day mark my word."

Roger was ruthless when the business was at stake, and by the end of the week he had said cuts were needed with the war on and had paid the gloating Ginny off. She left with a flourish of tears, and when her mum stepped in with an ultimatum, he told her he couldn't afford a supervisor either and she could go back to the same pay as the others or look elsewhere. They were both gone before the day was out. From that moment on Mullings Butchers became a happy place to work once more.

John had said nothing to Fred after the incident, but the day after Mandy and Ginny Armstrong left cursing the lot of them, Bernie had scolded Fred for dropping a pan in the yard. As Bernie went to strike him, John appeared out of nowhere and caught his arm. He beckoned Fred away with a nod of his head and then pushed Bernie into one of the sheds. Fred didn't look back and Bernie never raised his voice to him again.

Sally came in from her kennel, skirting the adults at the table, and quietly nuzzled up to Fred's leg, bringing him back to the here and now. She pushed against him affectionately until he sneaked her a piece of bread, and then was off, circling round by the fire before settling down to chew. Fred took another big bite of jam-soaked bread and stretched out in front of the fire, feeling its warmth creep up his legs. *Today was a great day,* he thought.

*

James struggled with the tin of bully beef; his hands still numb from the cold outside. The rusty tin opener was half broken and he had to work hard to prize any kind of opening to get his knife in. He squatted on an old crate in the officer's dugout, having finally been given some respite from the front-line fighting, when Captain Edwards had taken charge for the next few hours. He had reports to write, and some letters home to fallen soldiers, and he stared now at the blank paper on the old table in front of him. A small brazier sizzled in the corner where the corporal had worked hard to get it alight in the winter chill. But the heat it gave out did little to change the temperature in this mud lined shelter, and ice still clung to the boards and the roof. And to his heart.

James needed to eat before he could focus on anything else. Such as there was. Tins of congealed meat, some hard tack biscuits that even the rats avoided, and of course 'P and A' jam by the bucket load. Plum and apple seemed to be the only fruit grown in England these days if their supplies were anything to go by. When he got his last parcel from home with different flavoured jams in it, their value was such he had swapped it for no end of cigarettes, gin and chocolate. There was only so much you could eat of the army jam, and frankly the crates they came in were more popular for furniture, storage and shelves. He put his feet on one now, having finally cracked the beef tin, and leaned back. He was so tired he couldn't even remember the last time he'd had hot food, but the cold chewy contents were welcome nonetheless.

A fresh blast of cold air signalled the arrival of the army chaplain, and his cheery demeanour seemed to lift the temperature in the dugout instantly.

"Ah young Davison. Enjoying the army's finest delicacies, I see."

James remembered suddenly that the chaplain was promoted to major at Christmas after yet another mention in dispatches for caring for wounded men under fire. He sprang to his feet, sending the 'P and A' crate spinning away.

"Oh sit down Captain. Please don't disturb yourself on my account. Jerry will do that soon enough without you leaping about for me." He picked up the crate and set it right as James obliged and sat back down again.

Major, (the Reverend), Ernest Wyman had already won the Military Medal in the early stages of the war, and continued to distinguish himself both behind the lines and at the front. He was tremendously popular with all the ranks, and despite wearing the insignia of the Coldstream Guards, had endeared himself to a number of other regiments too in this region, including the Royal Sussex to the north.

"It's James isn't it?"

"Yes sir, I mean Reverend."

Ernest laughed. "Call me whatever you want young man. At least when the General is not here. Which I daresay isn't that often." He raised an eye at James but James knew better than to answer any leading questions even with the chaplain.

Ernest smiled and patted his shoulder. "Reverend is just fine. All this Captain and Major business gets too much even for me. Now talk to me about this morning. Tough business I hear?"

James started to give a military style briefing about the events of the previous few hours, learning from experience to leave emotion and specific detail out of it. Ernest studied the young officer in front of him, seeing the strain in his eyes, and hearing the sorrow in his voice. He waited calmly until James had stopped speaking.

"Thank you James. And what about you and your fellow officers? How are you all bearing up?

"We are all fine thank you Reverend. Just one officer lost and one wounded. Hopefully replacements on the way."

"And the men still in good spirits?"

"Always Reverend. The men are grand sir. Nothing a hot meal and some relaxation wouldn't fix in an instant."

"And not much chance of that looking at your meagre feast."

"No Reverend. Can't really have fires going in the forward trench, and even this brazier would take all day to heat something…" James looked wistfully at it, wishing he was somewhere else, and Ernest smiled sympathetically, understanding.

"Not got a roast chicken in your bag have you by any chance Reverend?" James suddenly said with a smile, snapping out of his melancholy.

Ernest laughed and took off the small shoulder bag he was carrying. "Afraid not James, just my bible and a few bits and pieces. But I do have a flask of rum."

James sat straight up. "Rum sir? Isn't it wine you need for communion?"

"Why yes of course, but sometimes the Lord's work needs a little boost and I believe this to be just the right moment." He winked conspiratorially and took out a small corked ornate jug. Opening it, Ernest sniffed deeply and passed it to James. "Have a good swig Captain you've earned it."

James looked amazed but took a drink nonetheless, and then coughed as the rich contents coursed down his throat.

"Wow, that hits the spot," he said croakily. "Where did you find this?"

"Family stocks sent up at Christmas, praise the Lord. Still got a couple of bottles for emergencies left. Doesn't last long working with the wounded and all that."

It was Ernest's turn to betray a moment of sadness, before smiling once more and patting James on the leg as he stood up. "Now I must continue my rounds. Bless you Captain, and all your lads. You've done a fine job today. I dare say there is more to come."

James stood up too, handing the bottle back reluctantly, and then they spontaneously shook hands. "Thank you Reverend. Your words mean a lot to everyone. And you continue to surprise us," he added, gesturing at the shoulder bag.

Ernest paused at the entrance and looked back. "Well I believe it was Lord Byron who wrote, *'There's naught, no doubt, so much the spirit calms as rum and true religion.'* I pray I may embody those fine words as I go forward in my life."

James smiled. "Amen to that sir."

Ernest nodded and left with the same icy blast that had driven him in.

*

When Elsie returned from her second night shift she found Will and Archie sitting in the front parlour. It was obvious from their appearance they had been up half the night debating Archie's absence.

She felt exhausted emotionally and physically. She had barely managed any sleep the day before, too worried about the implications of Will's appearance and his ultimatums to Archie. When she was finally persuaded to rest she had woken to the sound of raised voices and Archie storming out. Will had pleaded with her to make him see reason, and she had pleaded with him to leave them alone. To tell them he couldn't find him, that he was lost, dead even. But she knew Will couldn't lie.

"If I go back empty handed they will come for him Elsie, and I won't be able to help him then."

Will's words went round and round her head all night. Archie had returned of course and the two men had partly reconciled but there was no escaping the fact he must return or face the consequences. Elsie knew what the right thing to do was, but she couldn't bear to lose someone else. Less than two years ago she had been engaged to another soldier and he had jilted her on their wedding day. Simply sending a note to tell her *'He didn't want to be married with war on the horizon, and having to worry about people at home.'*

Elsie had made it right in her head, and defended his actions to her family, but the note had been cold and inside she realised he hadn't loved her after all. She had closed down then emotionally and thrown herself into her work, and would have stayed that way for ever had the wounded Archie not exploded into her life. *She loved him for that, as he clearly loved her to take such drastic action to be with her. And yet…*

"Can I get you some tea?" It was her answer to everything.

"Oh hey lass, I didn't hear you come in. How are you?" Archie came over to her in an instant and gave her a big hug. She saw the fire was unlit over his big broad shoulders, and realised it must have been a difficult night here too.

"Have you been cold without a fire?"

"Oh sorry, I barely noticed the thing wasn't lit. Been a mild night anyway." He started to poke at it now vaguely attempting to get it going. She moved across the room and touched his arm.

"That's okay. Leave it be for now, and I'll make us a cuppa."

"Slept in a lot worse 'eh Will?"

Will had got up when Elsie came in and had been standing awkwardly to one side. He simply nodded at his friend's remark. Elsie turned to Will now as she headed out to the kitchen.

"How are you William? Did you manage some sleep?"

"A little," he mumbled, lying. "I have to be off this morning. I'm due back at the camp today."

His words stopped her in her tracks and she flashed a scared look at Archie who hung his head. She realised Will was in his coat and had clearly been waiting for her return. She glanced briefly back in the hallway, expecting to see Archie's army bag packed and ready. But there was nothing except the small side table her mother had given her, and the vase with the flowers Archie picked only a few days ago, wilting now in the gloomy interior.

"Archie isn't coming back with me Elsie, don't worry." Will said, guessing her reactions. "He's agreed to join me later…wants to sort a few things out here with you first. Isn't that right Bunny?" He looked at Archie who nodded as he continued. "I'll cover for him until he gets back. It will be fine. There's plenty of time."

Will looked at his shoes as he spoke the last words, unable to meet her eyes, and she knew at once he was lying. He wouldn't have come all this way, and pleaded so earnestly if it wasn't urgent.

Seeing she wasn't convinced; Archie took up the mantle. "Don't worry yourself Elsie lass. I've talked it through with Will and we have a plan. He's going to see if he can get me onto their recruitment team. Go round the county drumming up recruits. You know I can talk people into anything when I put my mind to it."

"Is that true William?" She said suddenly, a vague glimmer of hope flickering inside her. "Will they let him do that?"

"They might. No harm in asking. I'll write and let you know when I get back and speak to the CSM."

"What if they don't?"

"Then we cross that bridge when it comes along lass." Archie said, letting Will off the hook. "But in the meantime, I get to stay here with you, and that's what matters 'eh?"

Elsie smiled weakly but said nothing, and then touched Will on the arm and went through to the kitchen to put the kettle on the hob. She grabbed it tightly and clutched it to herself, hearing the voices of the two men in the room next door, and found herself shaking now with the emotion of it all. Will shouted goodbye and she moved to the door still holding the kettle, forcing a smile.

"Take care William. Let's hope we all meet under better circumstances one day. Somewhere miles away from herc…" Her voice trailed off and Will snapped into action to break the moment.

"Thank you Elsie," he said, flashing his boyish smile once more. He reached out his hand to his friend and Archie took it with a firm grip. With a last look at them both, Will nodded and stepped out into the morning brightness and strode away.

Archie closed the door and turned to look at Elsie. She had slumped against the door frame and was still visibly shaking.

"We need to talk lass," he said softly and moved up to her taking her arms. He took the kettle and placed it on the side table and then she began to weep, in long slow aching sobs, that pierced his soul.

"I can't…bear to…lose you…Archie," she said, crying into his shoulder.

"Hey now stop that. I'm not going anywhere. Not without you that's for sure. If Will can't swing it for me with the CSM, then we will just take off lass and move away."

She stopped crying then and pulled back. "Move away where?"

"Ireland. I've a cousin in Dublin or thereabouts. Not seen him since we were little mind. My Dad and my uncle used to meet up every summer with all of us in tow. I'm sure we could go there though. My uncle always said we'd all be welcome any time after my Dad died."

"Go on the run you mean? I can't just leave my work here Archie. I'm needed. You know they would find us eventually."

He looked at her then and she could see the desperation in his eyes. The internal conflict. Elsie softened, not wanting to lose him whatever that meant.

"If you ask me I will come with you. Even if it means leaving my post here. But we'd always be looking over our shoulders. What sort of a life is that?"

"Not in Ireland. There's a war on don't forget. Too much on their minds to chase after one man. They'd soon forget."

"Would you forget Archie?"

He pulled her in close and dropped his head, placing his face against her still moist cheek. Archie could feel her heart pounding and kissed her tenderly on the top of the head. As he looked up he found himself looking straight into the mirror above the fire, his reflection simply reinforcing what he didn't want to admit. *She was right of course; she was always right. It was why he loved her so very much. But how could he ask her to live with him, if he could never live with himself?*

"Let's have no more talk of running away. Get that kettle on lass and let's forget about this bloody war for one night. Tomorrow's another day 'eh?"

Chapter 7 – Over the hills and far away

"Are we boring you Sergeant?"

Will realised the captain and sergeant major were looking straight at him and he must have missed a question. He struggled to remember the last thing he had heard them discussing, while thoughts about Archie raged inside him.

He was standing to attention in front of the company captain while Archie's continued absence was discussed with Sergeant Major Russell. Despite Russell's sympathetic approach to the situation, he was duty bound to report Archie's absence following Will's failed trip, and within a couple of hours an inquest was being held. Any attempts to stall the captain had failed and Will found himself reflecting on another time when he had stood before a board of inquiry to give evidence on behalf of a friend who was also charged with desertion. On that occasion they were saved by the intervention of his brother James' friend and fellow officer, Harry Johnson. *Although poor old Ernie Isaacs later took his own life, despite being sent home,* he recalled now, as he responded.

"No sir, sorry sir."

"Perhaps we are wasting our time here Sergeant, discussing this man if you are not interested enough in his whereabouts to pay attention."

"No sir. I was just considering whether Corporal Bunden would run away sir. I don't believe he would."

Will was relieved something in his sub conscious had picked up part of what the captain was asking, and he noticed the CSM smile out of the corner of his eye. The captain was momentarily thrown by Will picking up on the thread of their discussions but pressed on regardless.

"Well I disagree. In my experience once a man's nerve breaks he always runs. In fact, I would be very surprised if he's not already over the hills and far away by now. Probably legged it the moment the Sergeant here walked away."

"He's no coward sir," Russell said, irritated by the remarks.

"Oh really? So what do I say to the Colonel then about his continued absence? That he's just having a holiday and will be along later?"

"I was with him in France sir. I've no doubt being wounded so badly has shaken him. It would shake anyone who's been over there and lived through that. But I don't believe his nerve has gone."

The captain looked Russell straight in the eye. The jibe about not having been to France was not lost on him, and years of being put down brought an ice-cold look to his eyes.

Captain Horatio Brooks was an Eton educated officer. His grandfather had been a colonel in India but was killed during the Indian Rebellion of 1857. His grandmother had been one of the few Europeans to survive capture, with her young children, but the experience had been enough to put Horatio's father off army service for life. Instead Sir Reginald Brooks had made his way in industry, ably supported by his mother's influence however, who gamely played the heroic widow with a variety of rich suitors, to ensure her children profited. The resulting spoils meant they now owned a large estate in Kent close to Tunbridge Wells; which Horatio saw fit to tell anyone who would listen had been given the prefix 'Royal' only a few years before the war.

Horatio was not close to his parents, and despised the stories surrounding his grandmother's 'activities', which had blighted his early days at Eton. He therefore ignored the obvious path into the Brooks' business, and instead focused on his grandfather's illustrious career, and soon joined the military cadets, keen to follow in his footsteps. An outstanding sportsman, the focus helped Horatio ward off the bullies and in time, while he made no real friends, the taunting stopped. Of course, it only increased the tensions with his father, and when war broke out he didn't even write to tell his parents he was going.

But Horatio was born to army life and passed out from Sandhurst as one of the top cadets. He was distraught not to be able to join the Queen's Own Royal West Kent Regiment of his birthplace, which itself had been formed from an amalgamation of regiments including his grandfather's beloved 97th Regiment of Foot. He was however offered a commission with the neighbouring Royal Sussex, with the promise of fast promotion and so it proved being already a captain at twenty-four. Horatio felt no loyalty to the regiment though, which he deemed to be inferior to the Kents, and even less so to the newly raised Southdown Battalions that he regarded as little more than local militia.

He was determined to make a name for himself regardless, so that when the time came he would be able to transfer to his rightful heritage. He had a reputation as a fearful martinet with the men, and as before in his schooldays had no close allies amongst his fellow officers. A stickler for discipline and regulations, in a training camp with inexperienced soldiers, he was therefore looked upon favourably by those on high. Despite the colonel being of a far more caring disposition, he was also extremely busy, and Brooks was allowed a lot of freedom to run the camp as he saw fit. The captain was not known for being sympathetic…

"That may be Sergeant Major but rules are rules, and we can't have our soldiers breaking them as and when they see fit. Regardless of what they may or may not have been through." Russell went to speak again but Brooks stopped him with a raised hand. "In my eyes he's a deserter and should be treated accordingly. But given you both seem to think so highly of him I am happy to let a formal inquiry decide what's to be done and allow him to speak his piece of course. That's if he hasn't run off. To that end I've contacted Aldershot to send the military police down to get him"

"Already sir?" Will couldn't help his astonishment that even before they discussed what to do, the captain had already acted.

"Yes Sergeant. Time is of the essence. We march tomorrow and I don't want this hanging over us while we travel. The MPs can deal with it now."

Will knew the captain didn't want this on his record. He didn't care about the regiment's reputation. He also knew if no one was here to support Archie he was as good as dead.

"But sir, if we are gone, who will speak up for him at the inquest?"

"You can both write statements on his behalf that will be taken into account. As far as I am concerned that will be the end of the matter for us. And I don't want to know it's affecting your ability to lead over there either Sergeant Davison. Am I clear?"

"Yes sir."

"Good. Dismissed."

Will looked at Russell but he gave a brief shake of the head and Will saluted and marched out. After he was gone Russell stood up.

"Something else you wanted to add Sergeant Major?"

"I mentioned he's living with a nurse now sir. From the hospital where he was treated. I hope the MPs will be sensitive to the situation sir? You know how they can be." He tried a half smile.

"I'm aware of where the deserter is loitering Sergeant Major. Doesn't reflect well on our nursing colleagues either does it?"

Russell didn't speak.

"Yes well. You may think me over zealous but I'm not a monster either, and the last thing we need is this getting out into the public domain. I have advised the policemen to act with discretion."

"Thank you sir."

“Though if reports about this corporal are to be believed he may not come quietly, and if that’s the case well then on his head be it. Let’s hope he sees sense ‘eh?”

“Indeed sir. Will there be anything else?”

“No, carry on Sergeant Major. I’ve got a thousand tasks to sort out before we march, especially with the Canadian troops arriving here this week. You have a parade to organise and I expect it to pass off without further incident.”

“Sir. Yes sir.”

*

Agnes paused as they turned into the main street in Witley. The wall of noise that greeted them from the assembled crowds made her hesitate. Her mind registered the sound of music somewhere ahead as the local band entertained the crowd and she felt her body begin to tremble once more. Harold realised his wife was no longer walking with them and turned back.

“Aggie lass. What’s the matter? We’ll be late if we don’t hurry. Taken long enough to get here as it is.”

She looked at him with tear filled eyes as he moved in close.

“I never thought this day would come. It was always there in the background, like a cold shadow, but somehow I hoped it would all be over before they had to go back. Now David as well and I…”

Her voice faltered and Harold took her gloved hands and squeezed them.

“You’re shaking again. Come on now. We both knew this might happen while this blasted war trundled on. The lads will be fine. Better that they are together too. Who knows, they might even get posted near James’ lot. Then God help old ‘Jerry’ I say.”

He could see she wasn’t convinced. But he was saved any further discussion by Freddie’s excited shouts to “come on,” and he led her forward with a reassuring hug. They had been through this in 1914 when Will had suddenly signed up. It had been different with James as they had not watched him go, but Will had marched with the Royal Sussex in full pomp and ceremony. As she allowed herself to be urged along, Agnes felt like she was being drawn into a recurring nightmare.

Everywhere there were excited faces. Families, friends and local people gathered to cheer off the latest regiments marching to war. Only a handful of wives and families stood silently amongst the masses; families whose men had been to war before, understanding all too well like Agnes the horrors that lay ahead.

Harold spotted the Entwhistles standing near the old Stagecoach Inn, or rather the unmistakable flowing flame-red hair of Gwendolyn which would stand out in any crowd. Her husband Alfie stood next to her and seeing Harold, he smiled and waved. Close by was Tommy Landon's mum, Caroline. Tommy's dad had been a fisherman when they lived in East Wittering near the sea. He had been lost in the great storm of 1907, although no trace of the boat was ever found, and Old Gettings in the Star Inn reckoned he had more than likely run off with Sally Sheldon from the bakery there. *How he knew these things was anyone's guess*, Harold mused as he manoeuvred his family through the gathering masses to where their friends stood.

The three parents had managed to get a really good view and were working hard to keep it, and Alfie Entwhistle was pleased to see friendly reinforcements arrive, especially given Harold's hulking frame.

"Alright Harry lad? Big day at last then. Should be quite the show."

"No doubt Alfie," Harold replied as they shook hands. He nodded politely to the two women who smiled back, the anxiety clear on their faces despite the revelry going on around them. They had spoken to Agnes many times since her boys had gone to war, and were under no illusions that this was not quite the grand adventure that it felt like in 1914. It was hard however not to be swept up in the patriotic fervour that gripped the town on this bright March morning, and Harold was relieved to see Agnes smiling and chatting with the other mums. Freddie pushed to the side of the main road with Caroline's youngest boy, Nigel, who was clutching a bag of hot chestnuts and Harold smiled seeing his son burn his mouth on one.

"Hello Mr Davison."

He turned to see the piercing green eyes of Brenda Entwhistle smiling up at him, and tipped his cap to her.

"Hello young Bren. How are you? Looking forward to seeing your brother march off?"

"Very much so. We are all really proud of him. And I'm not so young anymore. I'm working at the factory now."

"Is that so? How time flies past. Seems like yesterday you and Fred were at school together."

"Fred? I'm seventeen Mr Davison. I left three years ago." She laughed in a teasing way, that was almost attractive and Harold was momentarily thrown. "I used to walk to school with Will, not Freddie."

"Oh right. And are you enjoying being at work then?"

"It's alright. Bit slow really. I bet you are proud of your sons going off to fight."

"Yes very." Although Harold's tone was not convincing, Brenda didn't notice. She was on a fact-finding mission and continued her questions.

"I saw Will when he was home at Christmas. Very handsome in uniform. Is he a sergeant now? My Dad said he is."

"Yes, that's right."

"Has he got a girlfriend?"

"What? Er, no. That is, I don't think so," he replied, now clearly flustered and looking around.

"Oh, that's a shame," Brenda said with a smile that said she felt anything but upset at the news. She opened her mouth to speak again but was thwarted by her dad's appearance holding two mugs of warm cider.

"There you go Harry. Get that down you. Is my lass bothering you?"

"What? Oh no, not at all." He blew on the steaming liquid and risked a sip, feeling its effects instantly warm his throat.

"Away with you girl, and chat to the mums. I need to ask Mr Davison a thing or two about these new automobiles that seem to be all the fashion at the moment. Men's talk."

Brenda frowned and was about to protest, but at that moment an officer rode past on a large black mare, and she walked off to see where he was riding to. Harold raised an eye at Alfie as if to say "Well?" but Alfie just smiled and took a big swig of his drink.

"Oh, I don't care about those things. Toys for the Toffs. They won't last. Horse and cart still be going strong long after they've all been turned to scrap. I just wanted some male company for a change. Get a few drinks down us before I get dragged off."

Harold smiled. He was happy not to chat. His mind was full of thoughts about the past and the future. About his boys and the war. Despite his continued optimism they would all be alright, he felt something inside that he hadn't felt for many years. Fear. It unsettled him and as he looked at Agnes and smiled to reassure her, he also silently prayed it would all be over soon.

*

Lieutenant Colonel Grisewood rode up to the waiting ranks of men, resplendent on his black charger. He dismounted and moved to speak to a group of officers standing nearby enjoying the first sherry of the day.

Grisewood accepted his gratefully, taking the glass delicately between thumb and finger as if at a summer ball, the other hand holding his baton behind his back.

"Won't be long now then," Will said to the men standing next to him, noticing the event. Some of the men grumbled about the officers having a drink, but it didn't bother Will at all. He cared little for drink, and was just keen to get on with the parade and do something to take his mind off the last few days. Everywhere the NCOs started to gather the men, knowing the time to march off was approaching.

David was standing in the row next to his brother, and took the moment to lean into him without needing to observe rank.

"Cheer up brother. Don't mind them. Some of these lads would grumble if they had nothing to grumble about. You know the army as well as most these days Will."

Will turned and managed a smile. "Oh I know. They'd be grumbling whatever job they were doing. I'm not bothered. Just want to stop standing around and get on."

"Yes, I know what you mean. Lots of young ladies lining the road up ahead. I'm keen to put on a good show." He winked and Will shook his head.

"If you can fight as well as you can woo the girls you might just pass muster, David."

"What? I'm the new record holder for the assault course don't forget. Whose record did I beat? Oh yes…" He grinned as he continued. "Got my first stripe as well. Will be catching you up soon *Sergeant*."

Will smiled warmly now. "Yes, I meant to say well done. I heard you got a promotion while I was away. Well done David." He was about to say more but noticed the sergeant major walking over and instead told the men to prepare.

Close by the Salvation Army band was still playing away to entertain the crowds with hymns interspersed with other well-known tunes. Will had been impressed with their enthusiastic playing, and earlier many of the men had joined their families in singing some of the hymns, as their own excitement began to grow. That is until Danny Boyd began offering different lyrics for 'All things bright and beautiful,' and the men had to be hastily called to order by the officers, as the laughter and banter spread through the battalions.

The band began playing 'Over the hills and far away,' an old military folk song adopted by many regiments as a marching tune, and this time the men simply nodded or hummed to the lyrics. Will looked across to his sergeant major and raised his eyes. Russell understood the significance of the words, following the confrontation with their captain, and simply shrugged his shoulders and nodded back. There was no hiding Archie's disappearance from the barrack rooms, and gossip was rife by now. He was such a larger than life character that his absence could not be covered up, but despite rumours of desertion or indeed a breakdown, he was still sorely missed by many of the men.

Before Will could dwell further on Archie's absence however, the officers suddenly gave the signal to form up. Will smiled and nodded at David, as if to say "this is it." Then his demeanour changed and he began barking out orders with the other sergeants, and the men obeyed like clockwork, whether friends or relatives, young or old. Obeying the orders as they were told to do, without question.

As the lines were formed in moments, Will looked at his brother staring straight ahead. Despite David's seniority in years, Will suddenly felt very protective towards him. *Top of the class on the assault course yes,* he thought, *but logs don't shoot back.*

Chapter 8 – Death with two sugars

An excited buzz spread through the crowd as the Salvation Army band stopped playing and marched off. There was generous applause for a moment but soon all eyes turned to the end of the street. A momentary lull drifted up the road as necks strained to get the first glimpse of the local battalions. They couldn't see the men yet but the military band had gathered at the top of the high street and it was enough to make the families start jostling for better vantage points. Harold and Alfie stood firm and the crowd swayed back and forth around them like waves on a rock.

Colonel Grisewood mounted his horse and walked it calmly to the front of the assembled men. The other officers marched smartly to their respective positions at the head of each company. Captain Brooks took his place in front of Will's number one company with an almost theatrical flourish, and Will heard one of the older soldiers behind him whisper "Gawd almighty." He looked round and saw Lance Corporal Perkins' ragged-tooth smile flashing at him; the men nearby smirking in support. Now was not the time for jokes though, even if he agreed with the implied derision of their officer. Now was the time to follow orders and respect the rank.

"Silence men. Wait for the orders." He spoke in a quiet tone that still commanded respect and the lines went still. Any support for Perkins instantly gone from the men round about him.

Grisewood looked back and nodded to the men assembled behind him. Serenely confident on his favourite horse. He inspired and calmed the men in that single gesture.

"When you're ready Sergeant Major. Bring them along."

Russell nodded. It took all his army service training not to smile. He respected and liked the new CO in equal measure; two things that did not necessarily go together where leadership was concerned. Officers and NCOs were often respected for how they led, but not always liked for it! He turned to face the waiting battalions with a sharp snap of his highly polished boots, and imperceptibly took a deep breath in.

"Parade…

…Parade…'Shun!"

Over eighteen hundred pairs of boots snapped to attention in a heartbeat. Rifles slammed into the left shoulders as one. The voice of Sergeant Major Russell reverberated off the nearby buildings and seemed to ignite the waiting crowds like a firework going off. Instantly his order was answered by the Drum Major of the Royal Sussex regimental band.

"Band…Band ready!"

The band drew themselves up, bagpipes and drums at the front, and the commands made the crowd begin to shout out.

"Come on the Sussex!" A man cried near Harold.

"God bless the Southdowns," a younger female voice answered from across the street, and there was instant applause from round about.

Agnes looked at Harold as if wondering whether they should shout something but he just smiled calmly at her and she turned back to look down the road. The time for cheering would come soon enough.

"God save the King!" an old man cried out from behind them. A number of heads turned and several people echoed the words. Harold noted the man was wearing medals of some previous campaign on a dirty grey coat. He realised being at the back of the crowd the man couldn't possibly see, and considered leaving his position to fight his way through to bring him forward. Then he noticed he was blind and was holding onto a woman of similar age, and felt a lump in his throat. He struggled with what to do but Russell's voice crashed into the waiting crowds once more and there was another surge forward, and the old couple were lost from sight. It took Harold all of his strength not to be pushed onto the street and the men linked arms with the women to form a tight semi-circle, with the children in front.

"Parade will move to the front in fours. By the right…quick march!"

The pipes and drums at the front immediately roared into life with an explosion of noise, the brass instruments behind soon in support. Company by company the Southdowns set off, orders shouted down the road to step off in pursuit of their commanding officer and leading ranks. Russell stepped up and down the first few lines ensuring they were straight and then fell in step with Will's number one company.

As the first ranks appeared into view the crowds began cheering and waving madly. The noise was extraordinary, and far louder than Will had experienced when he marched through Steyning in 1914. He glanced briefly at David who was beaming from ear to ear as he marched. The Southdowns were immaculately turned out and hundreds of arms and legs swung in unison, as if they were wound up toy soldiers.

As they approached the place where the Davisons stood with their friends, Agnes spotted Will and David and cried out to her boys. By luck they had picked the side their sons were on, and sure enough Owen and Tommy were in the rank behind. Russell spotted the cheering faces in the crowd and remembered the kindness shown by Agnes to his family when they visited their farm late last year. He also never forgot that Will's actions in France probably saved his life. Captain Brooks had now marched some ten yards ahead of the leading company to ensure he was in full view of the crowds. *Oh, what the hell*, Russell thought, deciding it was worth the risk.

"Number one company." He screamed, to make himself heard. "Eyes…left!"

A hundred heads swung left, ninety-six of which had no idea why, but followed the order without question. Russell snapped up a salute to the small party as they passed and Will smacked his right hand hard across his rifle in a similar show of respect. Brooks marched on immersed in the crowds, nodding left and right.

Agnes recognised the sergeant major now and clasped her hands to her chest. Tears of joy flowed freely down her cheeks as her boys marched past. David was still smiling broadly, and Will gave a small nod as they went by. Next to her Caroline and Gwen were waving madly, while Alfie was cheering at the top of his lungs, cap in hand.

Harold nodded at his boys and they both saw him, their young eyes burning with patriotic zeal. *My lads.* The lump in his throat returned, and his large barrel chest threatened to burst with pride. As the cry for "Eyes front" snapped all the faces away again, Harold dropped his head and wept.

*

Elsie awoke to the sound of loud bangs on the front door. For a moment she thought she was dreaming. As her senses returned she realised it was already daylight and began to panic she may have slept in. The constant switching of shifts from day to night made her attempts at any kind of quality sleep hard enough without worrying about Archie on top. She sat up and realised that once more she had fallen asleep in the chair by the fire and was still dressed. Late or not she wasn't going into work in a crumpled uniform so they would have to wait.

The knock on the door came again. Louder this time and she thought she heard a shout. Whichever nurse it was clearly didn't understand manners or indeed her status. She may have slept in but she was still the senior sister and as she walked to the door, ignoring the mirror, she composed herself to tell them so. *Go on the offensive Elsie,* she thought. She unlocked the door and pulled it open firmly, her face fixed determinedly. But the sight of the two burly military policemen in her front garden, with another waiting by a truck, made her resolve crumble in a moment, and she struggled not to instantly cry again.

"Sister Elsie Dent?"

She nodded.

"I'm Sergeant Kilpatrick ma'am. Military Police from Aldershot. With respects ma'am, we've come to arrest Corporal Bunden. I have a warrant for him, and believe he is here with you."

The sergeant was mindful of the words of his captain, who had told him it was a sensitive case, and to be polite with the nurse who was not to be touched, even if she became emotional. He was also extremely mindful of the fact that despite him being six foot four and well built, he was advised that Corporal Bunden was not a man to come quietly unless he had a mind too. Sergeant Kilpatrick had therefore brought back up.

"I'd be grateful ma'am if you could just ask him to come out of his own regard. We don't want any trouble now. I've got two of my lads round the back as well so he's nowhere to go."

Elsie studied the thick set sergeant and gave a half smile making him tense expecting an outburst.

"You're Irish aren't you Sergeant?"

"Ma'am?"

"Where are you from?"

"Kildare ma'am originally. Though I don't see the significance."

"It's just a little ironic. It doesn't matter Sergeant you wouldn't understand."

He was momentarily confused, then fell back into his training. "As I said ma'am we don't want any trouble, but if he won't come out, we will have no option but to come in and get him." Kilpatrick looked round and with a nod the other police officers now moved forward, and the man by the truck motioned to someone unseen by the side of the house.

"There won't be any trouble Sergeant. Archie…" she shook her head, "I mean Corporal Bunden is not here. He's gone."

"Gone? Gone where?" Kilpatrick said, dropping the formalities suddenly concerned his target had escaped them. He glanced about as if expecting to see their intended prisoner running across the hospital lawns.

"Well he talked about going to Ireland to visit his family." She saw the point now register with the man in front of her who frowned trying to process what that meant. "But if I know my Corporal Bunden he will hand himself in before too long, so you could have saved yourself the bother Sergeant."

Elsie frowned herself then, the memory of waking to find him gone still raw inside her heart.

"I will need to search the house to make sure. Then I will have to ask you some questions if he has indeed gone."

Elsie bristled at the insinuation she was lying. "I'm late for work Sergeant; there are injured servicemen and staff waiting for my help."

"I'm just following orders ma'am," Kilpatrick answered, becoming suspicious again instantly. Elsie realised being rude or obstructive wouldn't do her or Archie any good at all, and now forced a smile.

"Of course you are. I'm sorry. Please come in and look round, and then how about a cup of tea for you and your men. I can put the kettle on while I get myself ready for work, and you can ask me what you need to while we have a drink. More civilised than out here."

One of the policemen came round from the back of the house where they had clearly searched the neighbouring gardens and outbuildings and gave a shake of his head. Kilpatrick knew already his man had gone, and it was obvious the nurse wasn't lying. He had a nose for these things, and decided he may as well make the most of the situation. At least then he could report back they were civil as instructed, while he waited for fresh orders to chase down the deserter.

"Thank you ma'am that's very kind. Two sugars for me." He beckoned her inside with a polite smile of his own. "After you, please ma'am." Then he turned back to the other soldiers. "You two in here with me. Make sure it's clean. Corporal have a wander over to the hospital and see if you can find out anymore there about our man. Gibson, stay by the truck with Smith, and keep your eyes peeled."

*

Over by the hospital main entrance Polly watched this incident unfurl at a distance having come out to fetch the Sister. Sister Dent had never been late since Polly had come to work there, even recently with all the issues following Sergeant Davison's appearance hot on the heels of Archie.

After a while she saw some of the policemen move inside with Sister, and one of them start to walk towards the main building. *Well they won't find anything out here that's for sure. I hope they don't find Archie ever either*, she thought to herself, pondering what to do now. It wasn't that she was against the police; she knew they were just doing their job, but she knew what Archie meant to Sister too. What he had meant to all of them, both last year and since his return. In truth they were protective of all the young men that came here. They had suffered enough without being made to go back.

She thought then of Pilot Officer Brown who had died suddenly yesterday. The doctor was so sure he would live, and yet on realising he would never fly again the young pilot had just given up it seemed. Just another death here, but it hit them all hard once more, and especially the doctor, who took it upon himself to write to his parents.

Now they had policemen running about the lawns. It was all just too much, Polly thought angrily, and found herself feeling tearful again. She looked over to Sister's house and wondered what she must be feeling. The policeman came nearer and called out "Miss," which brought her back to the current predicament.

Hmm 'Miss' indeed, she thought. *Dr Harrison will know what to do.* And without waiting for Corporal Lamb, she turned and went back inside heading to the doctor's office.

*

"I have some news that might interest you Captain."

James looked up from the table where he was studying a map of the front line as the handsome major walked into the room. The Guards were moving to a new area and he had been detailed to HQ to get a briefing for the battalion from the intelligence officer. Major Harry Johnson had been working in headquarters for several months now since his last promotion, and specifically asked for James so they could spend a bit of time together.

Harry and James had a close friendship that went back further than 1914, as James was working in Harry's family business in London when war broke out. They joined up together and served in France with the Coldstream Guards for the first year before Harry's transfer behind the lines. It didn't affect the bond between them however, and James was still nursing the hangover from their initial 'briefing' of the previous evening.

"Does it involve Rose?" James asked his senior officer with a smile.

"Afraid not old boy, bit closer to home than that. Besides you've just spent some leave with her haven't you? So, it's time you got back to the trenches for a rest."

James grinned at his friend, an image of Rose walking by the river floating deliciously across his mind. Then he saw Harry was holding a piece of paper and asked, "So what is it this time Jonners?" his tone relaxed without any other officer present. "Does the Kaiser want to play a cricket match to resolve the war?"

"I bloody wish. With my spin bowling and your dab hand with a bat, reckon we could skittle them out in no time, and knock the runs off before a nice spot of tea. I must make a note to write to him and ask."

James laughed and then raised an inquisitive eye, nodding at the paper.

"No this is a family matter James. I've just seen on the listings that the Southdown battalions are sailing this week from Southampton. Got a posting up north somewhere first, away from the main stuff. Ease them in gently I suppose as they are mostly new chaps."

He handed the note marked 'confidential' to his friend, and poured a mug of tea for them both. He replaced the pot on the makeshift hob, where it hissed as it reacted to the heat again. Harry watched James' face intently as his friend spoke up.

"Landing at Le Havre, then being billeted up near Merville," James commented, as if reading out loud to himself. He went to find a relevant map, but Harry was one step ahead of him, and answered his friend's chain of thought.

"It's quite close to where the Sussex have been all along. Back in their old stamping grounds near Estaires. More than likely bump into some of the old timers. I've got a section map here." He rolled out a yellow stained trench map and used his tea to hold one side down.

"Will would like that I'm sure," James replied, as he traced the names of the area with his finger. Harry saw the frowns and moved to lighten the atmosphere.

"Which as you jolly well know is near the regimental field station at Béthune, where Rose and your brother's squeeze Teresa are based. So you should both be pleased."

"I don't think they are together Harry," James replied frowning.

"Well gives you an opportunity to kill two birds with one stone though 'eh, if little brother is back in the region." He smiled broadly under his thick moustache, his face wonderfully charming when he did so, as many a lady would agree.

"I suppose it does. Though I don't want anything happening to either of them just so I can get up there."

"Ah of course. I forgot you have another brother coming over too."

"Yes, David."

"How old is he?"

"He will be twenty-one in April."

"Is he an officer like you?"

"No just an ordinary rank and filer."

"Bet that's a bit odd for him with his younger brother a Sergeant now."

"Yes, I suppose it is. Never really thought that much about it to be honest. But now you mention it Jonners, he'll be regretting picking on him when he was younger."

They laughed together and Harry dropped a spot of rum in his friend's cup and did likewise with his own. The map rolled up with a 'whack' as he picked up his cup again and drummed his fingers against it.

"But on a practical level there's every chance the Southdowns will pass through the Somme region you are deploying to on the way there, so you may get a chance for a quick *hello*."

James looked up excitedly.

"*May,* I said. I will see what we can do for you. Seeing as the General and my uncle are in the same club back home in Mayfair, I can always call in the odd favour as long as it's not taken advantage of." Harry took a swig of his tea and then became more pensive. "The scuttlebutt here is there's a big push on the way in the new campaigning season though, so you may find weekends in Arras or any other jolly japes are on hold for a bit. Frenchies are having a rough time of it. Around a town called Verdun. They are pressing our government to get involved and pick up the slack. Get Jerry off their back. Usual whines." He raised his eyes. "All confidential for now though, strictly between us."

"There's always a big push on somewhere, I'm used to it," James replied with disinterest.

"I know but this sounds like a bona fide rumour for once."

"I understand Jonners. So long as my brothers are away from the action I don't care frankly."

"That's the spirit Captain," Harry said and clapped him on the shoulder. "Now how about another tea? We had fresh rations in this morning so I can afford to give you two sugars today."

"I thought it was sweeter than normal. Just assumed it was because the tea bag hadn't been used several times before and dropped in the mud!"

"Hardly James. Only the finest Indian blend for the Guards don't you know, and two large lumps for good measure." Harry smiled as he stirred the cups, handing one back to James. "I always find I can face imminent death far better with a good cup of tea inside me."

Chapter 9 – Three's a crowd

The men of the Southdown battalions travelled by rail to Southampton, with three special trains being put on to move them there. The majority of the officers went ahead in cars but the non-commissioned officers were instructed to travel with the men and ensure they conducted themselves properly at all times. Sergeant Major Carter took the lead train to ensure all was in order in Southampton when the men arrived. Will's number one company with Sergeant Major Russell were one of the last to leave, with Captain Brooks insisting Russell carried out all the last-minute checks. If Brooks had known his sergeant major better, he would have known it was a redundant order, and Russell personally paced every yard of the camp before handing over to the Canadian Infantry's advance party.

At Witley station the remaining men squashed onto the train headed south. Will managed to get a seat by the window at the back of the train, alongside David and Danny. The other men were scattered all about and Will noticed the sergeant major jump on the driver's plate in the engine at the last moment. Whenever they went round a slow right curve he could see him at the front, looking out over the green quilted landscape, apparently loving being up there.

The men were in high spirits and Danny was making a lot of them laugh with some ribald tales of his exploits in the factory before the war. He could take a simple story and stretch it beyond recognition but the men loved this and Will smiled with the rest. In truth he was struggling to focus. As the time for embarkation grew closer, the dark shadows of his past fought to get into his conscious mind more and more. And since the failed trip to Brighton the nightmares had returned to haunt his rest. The memories that the hospital awoke in him meant that, every morning since, he woke up soaked in sweat, and began to dread sleeping.

Trains were not his favourite mode of transport either and it clearly showed as David suddenly put a caring hand on his arm, and he jumped.

"Easy Will," he said quietly so that no one questioned the informality. Not that they would here, surrounded by loyal friends. But even so David knew Will was a stickler for these things so always stepped carefully on matters of army protocol.

"You don't look great. Are you ill?"

"Just a bit tired after all the preparations. Hot in here too. Travelling making me uneasy I guess."

David knew full well that Will was rarely sick but made a show of opening a couple of the train windows. Some of the men complained about the smoke coming in from the engine but David just looked them square in the eye.

"There's more smoke in here than there is out there," he said taking his seat again, noticing most of the grumbles were from men puffing away on pipes and cigarettes. "The Sergeant wants to be able to breathe."

"Oh, it's fresh air he's wanting then is it?" Owen chipped in. "Well he needs to move away from Danny then boyo. All the hot air that man is blowing like, probably upsetting his constitution look you."

The men looked at Will but saw he was smiling and the laughter and banter broke out again. Danny smiled too, happy to be the brunt of the jokes he so often dished out, and stuck two fingers up at Owen for good measure.

"Yes, that's right," Owen shouted. "They were Welsh bowmen at Agincourt and you do well to remember it boyo. What with us going back to France now. No doubt you will be needing us to help you again Englishman."

Someone threw a pie at Owen at this point and a scuffle broke out. Will was glad of the distraction and let the men have their fun, but couldn't shake the darkness that swirled about him. He tried to focus on things passing by… *A farmer ploughing his field; a hovering buzzard disturbed by the train's passing flapped angrily away down a hedgerow; an older couple riding their bikes gaily along a lane, laughing in the late morning sun. The lady waving to the driver and the sergeant major waving back.* But still the screams and faces of the wounded and the dead reflected back to him from the window.

Then suddenly Will noticed the train was slowing down as they came into a station. He focused in and saw the first sign to pass by on the platform which read 'Havant,' and recalled they were getting off here to join a passenger train. When he was commanding his sections the demons went away, and he immediately leapt up.

"Right settle down men. We are in Havant. I don't want the locals thinking we are a bunch of undisciplined louts." Someone muttered "He's talking to you Owen," and he saw Owen's fiery red hair spin round, but Will shouted louder to stop things spilling over again. "That's enough of that. Sort yourselves out and grab your kit. We change here for Southampton. And remember this is a passenger train now, so watch your manners, or I'll remember when we get on the front line and you will find yourself on guard duty for a long time."

With that the men stood up and began getting their kit together and making their way to the doors to get off. David was reminded once again that his little brother was not so little anymore, and not for the first time felt glad to have him around for what lay ahead.

"When you are outside move to the back of the platform so you are not in anyone's way and form up by sections. Clear?"

"Yes Sergeant," they echoed back.

*

Will stood on the platform amongst the ranks of uniformed men, waiting for the eleven forty-five to Southampton to arrive. A guard shouted "All aboard" from the opposite platform and he looked across at the ageing man in the ill-fitting black uniform. "Last call for Brighton," he called now, waving his green flag. Will had to fight a sudden urge to run across the tracks and board the train. Not only was it going to Brighton, where he thought Archie might still be, but he unexpectedly felt an overwhelming urge to travel on from there to Folkestone and go to 'Maggie's' café.

There had been a brief correspondence in Witley after their stay, but he had not found time to reply. Of course, the letter was just very nice and polite. Nothing to suggest they were close friends or that he could just turn up in a crisis, even if it was a café. He had no idea if her husband was alive or dead, but she was married and he had to be careful not to overstep the mark. *But there had definitely been a connection* his mind whispered, and he wished now he had kept in touch.

Maggie would understand; she'd know what to say, I know she would, Will thought to himself. The chance of being able to speak to someone about what he had been through, to talk about the nightmares without being seen as weak, or worse a liability, made him feel giddy suddenly. He felt hope rising within him that someone might carry the cross on his back even for a few hours and bring him peace. Will found himself by the platform's edge now, and trembled with the emotion churning away inside at the prospect of just running across and leaping on the train. Of running away from the darkness, and letting himself be carried away from the war.

"Look out lad, train's coming in. Can't lose you before we even get over there."

The voice of Sergeant Major Russell cut through the turmoil in Will's mind, and he felt a firm hand on his pack, easing him back.

"Sorry sir was miles away."

"Course you were lad. We'd all like to be there with you too I'm sure. And one day we will be when this war is over."

Russell seemed to understand Will's angst without anything being said, and Will turned now and nodded at his sergeant major, returning to the reality of the present. The Southampton train roared into the station with a loud shrill whistle blast and the platform burst into life.

"He'll turn up you know, one way or another."

"Sir?"

"Bunden. I saw you looking at the Brighton train, probably set you worrying again about him. Am I right?"

"Yes Sergeant Major, it's just that..."

"Never mind that Will. Train's here. Get your boys aboard and let's get on."

"Sir."

Will nodded and watched Russell snap into his everyday role, shouting and cajoling the men onto the train, and speaking quietly to the officers present. He couldn't remember the sergeant major ever calling him *Will* before, and felt an overwhelming sense of relief that he would be with them in France once more. Will looked around and saw dozens of faces from his section looking at him waiting for orders. He noticed a number of civilians too who must have been concerned by his precarious position on the platform edge as the train came in. One bearded man standing near the station tea shop entrance some distance away appeared to be frowning disapprovingly at him over the top of his newspaper. Will suddenly felt like a little boy again.

He chastised himself internally. *What an idiot. Hundreds of troops probably pass through the café every month and I was just another in a long line. Why would she like me any more than the rest? You fool Will, what were you thinking?* Will snapped into action; his safety net whenever he was in danger of letting his emotions boil over.

"Well don't just stand there staring like a bunch of monkeys in the zoo. You heard the Sergeant Major. Get your backsides on the train. Move it."

Whatever the men were thinking dispersed in a moment and they pushed and shoved their way into the train in seconds. As Will jumped on behind them, Russell watched him from further down the platform and gave a satisfied nod that normal service was resumed. *He liked this lad a lot,* he thought as he signalled to the driver and climbed on the train. *Probably too much, but he was going to do his damndest to try and get him home again in one piece.*

As the guard on the platform flagged for the train to move, the man with the newspaper threw it onto the bench near him and scratched briefly at his beard. He was less than impressed seeing all these soldiers invade the station, hour after hour, to be carted off to certain death. *Perhaps better that the sergeant had jumped*, he thought, misunderstanding Will's intentions, and shook his head as the train slowly began to move away.

*

The conditions in the onward train to Southampton were even worse than the previous train, being a mixture of soldiers and sailors heading to the front, and family members following them blindly. There were a number of local people too, and Will noticed the mood on the train was upbeat despite the fact the war was clearly not going to be over anytime soon.

It was a train comprised of individual compartments in each carriage with long corridors running down one side, that were soon so full of soldiers that it was impossible really to move along the train. Will got a seat in one of the compartments when they left the station, the men giving up their place to the sergeant; but as the local people crowded in, he likewise stood up for a young lady carrying a small child. However, as the corridors filled up, people spilled over into the compartments and it became very congested.

Will suddenly had a flash back to the hospital train he had been evacuated from France in, and had to push his way out. Panic gripped him and for once his normal manners were tossed aside in his need for air and space. He fought down the corridor past the mums with clinging children; the weeping lovers sharing these last hours together, and the smoking soldiers shouting and swearing, until he found a space at the back of the train in the doorway. As the train slowly climbed up along the coastal tracks, Will pushed his face against a rattling window, and allowed the air to flow over him from the cracks around the door.

A farmer's field of half-grown crops dragged past slowly in the smoke. *Spring cabbages or cauliflowers*, Will's farming brain advised him. He watched Brimstone and Red Admiral butterflies chasing their mates around the field, enjoying the early spring warmth, lost in the moment. Will envied the simplicity of their lives, however short. Someone started singing 'Keep the home fires burning' in one of the compartments and the off-key notes invaded Will's thoughts, as a number of the soldiers joined in. It triggered a memory of the Christmas truce in 1914, and he felt anger now build within him. He watched local people pick up the song with smiling faces, and he fought the urge to scream at these nameless people. He wanted to tell them what it was really like. How there was no such thing as a noble sacrifice out there in the bloody mud of the trenches. But he caught himself and looked away. Will closed his eyes and tried to block out the other noises inside his head, as the train rattled on. Then they passed through a tunnel, and the shriek of the whistle echoing in the darkness became too much.

As they came out into the light once more, he forced open the carriage door and stepped out onto the plate between the carriages. He paused for a moment looking at the tracks whizzing past below in a blur and then stepped purposely forward onto the opposite plate. He worried the door would be locked and he would have to go back but it turned easily in his grip, and he moved inside. He found himself in the short guard truck, but there was no one here. He took a deep breath relishing the solitude but was aware the guard would return at some point and moved on. Crossing the plates into the next carriage, the silence made him stop short.

This carriage appeared completely empty, and for a split second he wondered if he was actually asleep and this was a dream. He glanced back through the door window and sure enough through the far door could see the crowded corridor he had just left, people swaying and swinging their arms, mouthing silently along to a new tune. Will turned and started forward down the corridor, noticing the first compartment had several people in it but was not full. A man in a crisp white tunic came out of one of the compartments in the middle of the new carriage carrying a tray. He frowned at Will and then turned and walked away, pausing at the end of the carriage to look back again before disappearing.

Will noticed a row of empty seats in the next compartment and quickly slid open the door and stepped inside. He continued to look down the corridor in case the man returned, and assumed he must be a porter of some kind. He was unaware the compartment was occupied, so when a female voice behind him said, "Hello William," he jumped, banging into the door that had started to slide shut as the train curved sharply to the left.

Alice Pevensey was standing by a table raised between the seats, where she was pouring tea from an ornate china pot into matching cups. At the sound of the door opening she had paused and now delicately set down the teapot.

"This is a surprise. We seem to keep bumping into each other unexpectedly."

"Alice," Will mouthed almost silently in shock, his thoughts exploding inside him.

She smiled, that heart flipping smile that he had tried so hard to forget, and he found himself completely lost for words. Alice looked at Will and then briefly at the corridor where he was staring when he came in. She noticed he was pale and sweating.

"Is anything the matter William? Are you okay?"

Will recovered slightly and said, "Yes I was just…what are you doing here?"

Alice was about to speak again when a male voice behind her asked, "Do you know this man Alice?"

Will was even more thrown by this, having failed to notice anyone else in the carriage, and more so when Alice stepped back to reveal an officer sitting with a newspaper on his lap, tapping a cigar into an ashtray built into his chair arm.

"George this is William, he's a…an old family friend."

"I see. Are you lost Sergeant? This is First Class you know," the officer replied, appearing to dismiss what Alice had just said.

"My apologies sir. I didn't realise this was First Class. The carriage I was in was overcrowded and so I was just looking to see if there was space further back to move some of the men along and give the families some room."

Will seemed much more able to think on his feet speaking to an officer than he did with Alice, but the explanation and his conciliatory tone seemed to soften the man.

"Yes, good idea not to upset the locals too much, though they have to accept there's a war on what? Everyone has to make sacrifices."

Will surveyed the freshly served afternoon tea on the table, complete with sandwiches and cakes, and the luxurious surroundings of this large carriage. *Not everyone,* he thought, and simply nodded. Alice noticed an awkward pause developing and smiled again.

"William this is my husband, George. He's just been made a first Lieutenant with the Sussex Yeomanry. We are on our way to Southampton before he sails to Egypt. A delayed honeymoon really as he's been busy in the London war office since we married."

Will didn't hear anything after the word *husband* and looked at her for a moment, and noticed her blush momentarily and look down. He realised he must be staring and pulled himself together.

"May I offer my congratulations sir. To you both of course. It's a pleasure to see you again Alice." He did a half bow and then wondered why, but the officer was already scanning the papers again as if he wasn't there.

"Will is with the Royal Sussex, George," Alice added, trying to make small talk and move the conversation on.

"I see," was all he answered with a very cursory glance in Will's direction. Then added, "Tea will be getting cold Mrs. Wilson," without looking up, and Will took that as his cue to leave. He was probably being too sensitive but felt like the man had emphasised the words *Mrs. Wilson* on purpose.

"Would you like a cup William?" Alice said suddenly which caused both the men to stare at her. Will noticed the flash of anger in the officer's eyes and knew discretion was the better part of valour here.

"That's very kind but I must get on and see about my men."

"Quite right," Wilson said, as Will moved to the door.

"I understand." She passed the cup of tea to her husband and took two light steps to the doorway. "Do give my regards to your family won't you. All well I trust?"

"Quite well thank you Alice. One of my brothers is here with me. We sail back to France tomorrow." He noticed a hint of concern around her beautifully painted eyes, and then added, "and James is a Captain now with the Guards."

"That's lovely," she replied but he hadn't said it to impress her, and noticed her husband's eyes flick up at the sentence.

"I'm sorry to intrude, my very best wishes again," Will said.

Alice laid a delicate hand on the side of the door, and for one moment he thought she was going to touch his face. She didn't but that brief moment felt like hours and then he nodded again and went back the way he had come. Will stopped on the plates between the carriages, watching the ground rush by beneath mirroring his emotions. Then he leaned over the side and threw up, the pain in his chest exacerbated by the motion. He leaned back against the carriage, and as he swayed with the emotion he grabbed the rail to stop himself from falling. Angry thoughts now bombarded his mind and Will chastised himself for being so affected by Alice's appearance. He stepped forward and slammed open the next door before moving on.

Sometimes it's better to be lost in a crowd after all, he thought.

*

Alice sat down pretending to fuss over an invisible mark on her dress. She was aware George was looking at her, while relighting his cigar.

"Bit odd you being friends with a ranker, darling."

"Oh, acquaintances more than friends. His father did some work on the estate for a while and sometimes he brought one or two of his sons. Will was always very friendly," she lied smoothly.

"I see." George's face remained expressionless.

"Nothing like that, don't be silly. He was always very polite."

"As indeed they should be. Seemed a reasonable enough sort. Good Sergeant am sure, but not very socially aware loitering about in here. Fancy not knowing its First Class. Just as well his sort aren't in charge what?"

"Quite right George," Alice said although her mind was elsewhere in that moment.

"All in the breeding, isn't that right darling?"

Alice felt herself flustered inside, and inclined to speak up on Will's behalf. Her father was supporting his close friend Lord Lowther with raising the Southdown battalions, and through working with him she was aware of the officers and NCOs involved, and their past. She knew now that Will had been wounded in France and decorated for bravery and was quietly following his progress. Before she could reply however, the door slid open once again, and a tall bearded man stood in the doorway. The man from the station.

Alice and George looked up, both slightly concerned by the large frame of the man that now filled the entrance. He was in a suit that struggled to contain his muscular frame, and carried an umbrella and a suitcase with him. A bowler hat perched on his wild dark hair, like an egg on a nest, which he now tipped towards Alice and took off.

"Please excuse the intrusion, I believed this area to be vacant. Dashed train is very full today."

His accent was a little odd but etiquette dictated an answer and Alice looked at George.

"That's quite alright, are you looking for a First-Class seat?" George asked warily.

"Of course, Sir. What other way is there to travel?" He smiled unnervingly through his heavy beard.

George was thrown by this, but the man put him at ease by continuing. "Where are my manners? Allow me to introduce myself. I am Brigadier Barrington-Smythe, 14th Hussars." He held out a hand to George who instantly pushed his cigar in the ashtray and shot to his feet, knocking the table and spilling a little tea into the saucer of the nearest cup.

"George Wilson, Sussex Yeomanry, Lieutenant. You are welcome to sit here sir if you can't find a space."

The brigadier gripped George's hand firmly shaking it several times and nodded, before turning to Alice. George started to introduce his wife, but the brigadier had already taken her hand. He raised it to his lips, giving it the lightest of kisses on the knuckle.

"Your servant Ma'am."

She nodded politely, but was also quite flustered inside, and reached for her fan from her bag. The sudden appearance of Will and now this ebullient stranger made her start to feel faint. She opened it and wafted it slowly as the brigadier sat down next to her, staring at George.

"Do sit down man. No ceremony here. I'm not in uniform. Had a spot of leave, shooting on the estates." He waved a hand airily as if it was tiresome. "Where are you headed?"

"Egypt sir. With the Yeomanry. My brigade are just back from Gallipoli and I am being sent to join them there."

"Gallipoli 'eh? Did you serve there?"

"No. I was at the war offices in London last year."

"I see," the brigadier replied, his face as unreadable as George's had been with Will moments earlier, and it unnerved the younger lieutenant. "Dashed bad business what. Lucky to have missed it perhaps, or rather have been there with the regiment?"

He raised a questioning eye at George who struggled with what was the right answer. "Just joined too late to get there sir, but looking forward to doing my bit now."

"Good show. That's the spirit. Give it to the blasted Hun eh?"

"Indeed sir," George said visibly relaxing, having apparently said the right thing, though he was still unnerved by the officer's domineering presence.

"Was that one of your men I saw leaving as I approached?"

"What? Oh no. He's a Sergeant from the Sussex. Trying to find a seat but obviously took a wrong turn here." The brigadier smiled politely. "Worked on my wife's estate before the war. A Sergeant Williams I think. Isn't that right darling?"

Alice didn't answer directly and the brigadier spoke up.

"Quite the coincidence then. Did you offer him a seat?"

"Sorry?"

"You said he was looking for a seat, and your wife knew him."

"Yes, but this is First Class. And they were not friends. He was just one of the labourers or something."

Alice interjected, not wanting them to have appeared impolite. “He didn’t want to stay. He was busy with his men. His name is Sergeant Davison.”

The brigadier turned to Alice and smiled, before noticing her using the fan.

“Are you unwell Ma’am?”

“Just a little hot, thank you”

“Some water perhaps?”

She nodded, and he reached out and poured some for her from a silver jug before George could do it himself.

“Forgive me barging in like this. You will forgive me won’t you?”

Alice took a light sip and nodded.

“I do have a tendency to run on sometimes. So, are you being the faithful military wife and following the drum to Egypt too then?”

“Alice is accompanying me to Southampton. My wife and I are having a honeymoon before I sail,” George answered for her.

The brigadier didn’t even look at George but reacted to his words taking Alice’s hands once again.

“See what did I say? How improper of me. Will you accept my apology? I’m sorry I didn’t catch your name?”

“Alice,” she said quickly, before George could answer for her again.

“Will you accept my apology Alice?”

She smiled sweetly at him and he took her hand and kissed it again, before standing up. George immediately stood up too.

“Thank you. I will take my leave. Two’s company and three’s a crowd and all that. Especially on a honeymoon.” He glanced at Alice and she politely averted her gaze. “Well good luck on your grand adventures. Together, and separately,” he added, looking directly at George.

“Thank you Brigadier,” George replied.

He slid the door open and stepped out closing it firmly behind him. They watched him replace his hat and stride off, and then George collapsed in the seat, unsure what to make of the recent turn of events. They sat in silence as the train rolled on.

*

Sergeant Major Russell knew the train was becoming overcrowded. From his position at the very back he could see that more people were trying to get on the train with every stop. He decided that some of the men would have to get off at the next station and wait for a following train, providing they would still get to Southampton in time to board the boat. He was making his way to the guard carriage to ask about timings when he heard someone say "Thank you Brigadier," and saw a tall bearded man exit a compartment in First Class.

Instantly he had stood to attention, but seeing the man was not in uniform he followed him through into the guard carriage. The guard was still absent. *Probably stuck further up the train*, Russell thought to himself. He had seen the guard using the platform at the last stop to move between carriages.

As there were just the two of them in this truck, he called out.

"Excuse me sir." The man in the bowler hat appeared not to notice so he tried again.

"Brigadier. May I have a word?"

This time the man paused just as he reached the far door, and turned round. In the gloomy interior Russell noticed the officer looking his uniform up and down.

"Yes, Sergeant Major. May I be of assistance?"

"Certainly sir," Russell said politely. Then he walked right up to the officer and shouted in his face. "First you can take that stupid hat orf your 'ead. And then you can tell me what the bleedin' 'ell you are doing on my train swanning around like you're in 'Ide bleedin' park, calling yourself a bloody brigadier and speaking posh. Corporal Bloody Bunden."

"Well I…"

"Shut up…Do you have any idea of the trouble you've caused? Well?"

"Sergeant Major, I…"

"Shut up…What's in the suitcase?"

"My uniform, Sergeant Major."

"Right get it on and sit tight here and stay out of sight until we stop and I come back for you. Understood?"

"Sir."

"In all my days. If there wasn't a war on I'd shoot you myself. Does Sergeant Davison know you're back?"

"Not yet sir. Will told me you were all travelling down today so I just hid out nearby until I saw the battalions start to arrive, and then jumped on the last train when I saw you."

Russell shook his head looking at the man now slouched in front of him. His mood softened. "Well I don't know how I'm going to square this with the Captain, but I'm glad you saw sense and returned. Sergeant Davison said you would. Just as well you have such loyal friends." Archie nodded and Russell smiled then. "Where on earth did you get those clothes?"

"In a local pub last night sir. Got talking to a travelling salesman down from London like. He was about my size and build and I only had my uniform under my coat and stuck out like a sore thumb. So, I helped him back to his digs like and put him to bed." He grinned broadly then, teeth flashing white in the dark carriage.

"And when he wakes this morning he will be minus one suit and a hat, and not remember what happened?"

"Something like that sir. Can't be too careful at night. Some dodgy people about."

"Get changed Bunden and wait here." Russell opened the door and the noise and wind rushed into the space as the train gathered speed downhill. He turned back then frowning. "One last thing. What were you doing in that First-Class compartment?"

"Oh, just having a spot of tea with my fellow officers."

Russell didn't know whether to laugh or cry. By rights he should throw the book at him. In fact, he felt like throwing Archie off the train, he was so exasperated with him. But there was something about this soldier he couldn't help liking. Perhaps he saw a little of himself in this man when he was younger. Russell never knew his father, but his mother was one of the 'camp followers' so there were always men around. By the time he joined up at fourteen he was as cheeky and streetwise as any kid, and never far from a fight. The army straightened him out of course, but not before he had his fair share of punishments. *Would he have bunked off for a girl? Maybe.* He thought of his Ginny then. *When they were younger they were daft for each other.*

He looked at Archie. *Big daft lump. But no coward. He proved that by coming back. At least no more scared than the rest of us.* He shook his head once more.

"Bunden the day they make you Brigadier, I'll eat that bloody hat of yours."

Chapter 10 – Blood, sweat and tears

Colonel Hamilton put the bloody saw back onto the trolley, and tried to rinse his hands in the basin of dark red liquid nearby before wiping them briefly on a rag tucked into his apron strings. The rag, like his hands, was caked in blood, and he called for Rose to wipe his brow briefly where the sweat from the amputation ran crimson streaks down his face.

Teresa worked furiously to tie off the ends of the severed blood vessels above the knee while another nurse applied pressure on the new wound. Private Bell had long since passed out from the pain but the orderly continued to hold his shoulders down just in case. The recent intense bombardment had scored several direct hits on the forward lines near Festubert, leaving dozens of seriously wounded men, and that was before the attacks that followed. Hamilton knew he would only have a few hours before the next wave of casualties reached them and worked through the night once more, with his team, to try and clear these wounded men first.

He stepped back in to help, shouting orders as he did so.

"Orderly you're not doing anything there. Get rid of this limb then record the man's details and go and get some more fresh bandages. Find Jenkins and start mopping these floors. He's probably shirking outside somewhere. Go!"

The orderly picked up the recently detached lower limb as if it belonged to a shop room dummy, and carried it off towards the furnace area. His departure finally signalled the end of that particular night's work, and Hamilton's tone softened as he looked at Rose.

"Nurse, get these tables cleaned up again, then grab five minutes fresh air. Am sure you need a cigarette." He smiled. Rose noticed he had blood on his teeth. "When you've had it, do the rounds for me again with one of the other nurses. Usual checks. Breathing, bleeding, infection. Find me when you're done and update me."

Rose turned and began picking up instruments off the tables that had been well used that night. Hamilton raised the pad soaked in Bell's blood. He examined the freshly hewn stump without a flinch, and grunted in approval. Then he glanced at Teresa, standing sweating by the side of

Private Bell, and raised an eyebrow inquisitively. She felt his pulse and looked at him, nodding to confirm the man was alive.

"Well done Staff. What would I do without you?" Teresa smiled as the orderly returned with fresh bandages for the wound. He turned to a junior nurse who was helping and his expression hardened. "Right nurse. Simpson isn't it? Dress it off for us, then have him moved carefully to bed fifty-six. Orderlies will help. I'm going to clean up and have a cup of tea, before the next batch of customers arrive."

Just as the colonel was about to ask Teresa if she wanted to join him, Nurse Simpson vomited all over the floor.

"Bloody marvellous," Hamilton said enraged, and Simpson began to cry as she crouched down with a cloth to try and clean it up.

"It's her first week sir," Teresa said jumping in. "Rough week to start. I'll sort this out and come and report when we are done. Maybe put a spot of rum in that tea." She winked and diffused the anger in a second.

"Oh right, oh right. I'll leave it with you Staff."

He walked off, checking a couple of the men as he did, nodding at his own handiwork. There had been fourteen amputations in all. Five arms, seven legs and two feet, and so far only four men had died. Two due to the severity of their wounds, and the others from shock. Though he had no doubt, with better facilities and more supplies, he could have saved more. Not least because the last four were done with no morphine for the pain. *Poor bastards,* Hamilton thought as he walked outside towards his tent.

Teresa put a sympathetic arm on Simpson's shoulder and told her to go and take a break, and come back when she felt better. She had been sick all over her shoes and looked fit to drop, tears running freely down her grimy face. In truth Teresa was just as tired but was used to drawing on reserves of energy when the pressure was on. At least she didn't have to march and fight when exhausted as the men often did. Still if she was too tired to work then she would make mistakes, and behind the lines or not, mistakes here were just as fatal as on the front line.

Teresa set about expertly dressing the wound while Rose worked silently alongside her scrubbing down the two operating tables. They were both too tired to talk, and worked in silence while one of the orderlies cleaned up the remains of Simpson's breakfast from the floor. When Teresa had finished she then helped the lone orderly to get Private Bell to a bed, noting the more senior Jenkins had vanished again when the going got tough. As she turned away from the groaning soldier, she saw Rose heading for the exit.

She was going to leave her be when a motorcycle courier appeared at the opposite entrance and called her name.

"Staff Sergeant Halliday?"

Teresa put a finger to her lips gesturing to the men as she moved through the tent towards him. She ushered him outside and frowned, her short temper not improved by this new intruder disturbing her patients.

The courier removed his goggles and gave a wince of embarrassment. He had incredibly striking blue eyes that immediately made her think of Will.

"Sorry about that. Private Evans from HQ. Are you Halliday?" he asked falling back into business mode.

"I am Staff Sergeant Halliday yes," Teresa replied, in no mood for any familiarity with strangers whatever the circumstances.

"Telegram from HQ Staff. From Major Johnson, Intelligence. Shall I wait for a reply?"

She opened it slowly, unsure exactly why her hands were shaking. *Can't be bad news,* she thought, *must be more tired than I realised.* She pulled the contents out and scanned the piece of paper.

"No reply," she said and gave the briefest of smiles. The courier hid the shining eyes once more and walked off to where his bike was leaning against a shed. Teresa read the note again.

Hello Staff. Stop. Thought you would want to know the Southdown family are visiting Le Havre this weekend. Stop. No more details currently. Stop. J hopes to meet up with W and D for big family reunion! Stop. J sends his love to you know who. Stop. Can't say where they are heading for on next outing. Stop. Let's just say, old habits resumed. Stop. W hopes to catch up soon. Stop. Stay safe. Jonners. Stop.

Harry has been in intelligence too long, she thought to herself smiling. *'Old habits resumed' can only mean one thing. Will's battalions were heading back to their original trench area surely?* Teresa knew the Royal Sussex were still near Estaires, but had seen no real action this year to date as far as she was aware. *Unlike the poor Guards and the Devon and Dorset brigades near them,* she sighed looking across the overflowing hospital hut.

But there was no doubting the fact the news had picked her up a bit and she instantly felt less tired. She fancied some tea with rum herself now, and walked quickly in the direction of the colonel's tent. *Funny how the courier made her think of Will and then low and behold he was back in France*, she mused, as she picked her way across the rutted tracks. Her shoes were long since ruined by the persistent mud that got in everything here, but she still endeavoured to avoid sinking up to her knees whenever possible.

As she skirted another huge puddle, she spotted Rose, half propped up on a supply crate. Rose waved the cigarette packet feebly in her direction. *Hmm. A celebratory cigarette was in order first,* she decided, and changed direction to join her friend, waving the telegram as she went.

*

Agnes saw Harold come towards the kitchen for his lunch, whistling as he did so, and she decided now was as good a time as any. Despite the emotion of recent events, farming life continued to dictate their days. But with Fred now working every day at Mullings, Agnes felt she needed to do more. As busy as she was on the farm, since watching the Southdowns march off, the pull to do something for the troops overseas grew steadily inside her.

Harold came into the kitchen kicking his boots off in the corner as always and began scrubbing his hands in the sink.

"Got your favourite homemade soup on the stove today Hal," Agnes said.

"Oh yes?" he replied, looking over while continuing to wash.

"Yes, leek and potato, and I have fresh bread too."

"We have been busy today, and not even my birthday." Harold smiled, and then pulled her in close for a hug.

She smiled and gave him a quick peck on the cheek easing him away. "You'll get me covered in muck, now go and sit down."

"You don't always mind that," he said, giving her a pat on the bottom with a cheeky grin.

"Well the bread will burn so stop that nonsense. Besides I want to chat to you about something."

"I see," he muttered raising an eyebrow and reluctantly sitting down. Though his face lit up when she ladled some soup in a bowl for him and the mouth-watering smell mixed with the fresh bread to tantalise his senses.

Agnes watched him break a chunk of bread off and dip it heavily in the soup, blowing it before shoving it whole in his mouth. He didn't look up so she just took a deep breath. "There's talk of a new group forming in the town. It's called the Women's Institute, Hal. It apparently started over in Singleton and they now want to open up groups all over the county."

He looked up briefly. "Any tea love?"

She went to pour some, feeling nervous and a little frustrated. But as she set it down she continued. “It apparently started in Canada and has now been launched over here.”

Harold took a swig of tea and looked at her. “I see. And whose idea is this?”

“I can’t remember who started it over here, a Lady somebody I think, but do you remember John Harris from the Agricultural Society that came to speak once as guest of honour, at Steyning Fete?” Harold frowned and then nodded briefly. “Well he is apparently supporting the idea to do what they are doing in Canada.”

“So, a man is launching a women’s event?” He laughed then and went back to his soup.

“It’s more of a club than an event I think,” Agnes said, her hands trembling now with nerves. “He’s just helping it get started I think but Caroline Landon wants to set up a branch here. To support the war effort, and…”

“Was that what you two were gossiping about during the parade then?”

“She mentioned it there yes, but we didn’t have time to chat much about it at the time. But then I saw her again at the market yesterday. They are going to ask Celia Goodman to be an honorary chair I think, though she may not do it.”

Harold wiped the soup from round his mouth on his sleeve and frowned again. “I thought you couldn’t stand that woman.”

“Well she’s alright in small doses. The thing is…”

He started slurping the remains of his soup and she could feel her courage start to desert her.

“Is there anymore love?” he asked handing the bowl to her, before picking up a paper from the table. She ladled some more in his bowl, but paused before putting it down which made him look up. He raised an eye as if to question why she wasn’t serving him.

“The thing is I have said I will join too. I want to do my bit for the war.”

“I see. And what is it then, this *institute*? Just another group of women, knitting for victory or something?”

“No Harold. It’s to help send food parcels to the troops and things. Organise supplies. Raise funds. It’s all still quite new. A bit like the Red Cross do, but for wives and mums to feel a part of something.”

“You are a part of something. You’re a mum to three boys fighting in France, and we have our hands full growing crops and raising livestock here. We give a lot to the community for this war already.” He dropped his head and began eating his soup again, and Agnes felt her anxiety grow. She began to feel teary and gripped the back of the chair.

"Hal." He didn't look up. "It's not enough for me. I have to do something else. It won't affect the running of the farm I promise. I want to do this. For our boys. For all our boys. Please Hal."

He finished the soup and took a long swig of his tea and stood up. She tensed waiting for an outburst.

"Will I have to get my own meals?"

Inside she cried with relief. "No silly, it will only be occasionally in the evenings or the odd daytime meeting. Not even sure if we will meet every week. I will make it work." She realised she was speaking too quickly now and paused.

"Aye go on then. But if it takes you away from here too much, I'll stop it."

Agnes moved over to him by the door. She gave him a kiss and stroked his face. Then smiled the smile that never failed to move him as he pulled his boots back on. "It won't love I promise."

"Hmm, and don't think I'm going soft either. Now let me get on woman."

He opened the door and strode off up the yard, pulling out his cigarettes as he did so. Agnes paused in the doorway and let the early afternoon sunshine bathe her skin in a wonderful spring glow. She felt a rush of emotions then, and now her eyes welled up with real tears as she realised just how worried she had been about asking Harold for permission to join the institute. Yet at the same time she felt excited about doing something different in her daily routine, and she brushed the *ridiculous tears* away.

But more than that, she felt something else. It wasn't that she was unhappy with her daily life, despite her worries for her boys. She was certainly busy enough too with the farm and church work, and caring for Freddie. But this was different. This gave her a purpose. It made her feel very alive in that moment and she sang as she cleared up in the kitchen.

*

The troop ship lurched suddenly as another coal-black wave smashed against the bow with relentless fury. Will was deep in thought and seemed one of the few men on the upper deck who didn't care about the crossing. He watched his brother clinging to the side rail and moved over to him.

"How are you feeling David?" With the storm raging about the boat, he dispensed with the formalities of rank, as anyone within earshot was too sick to care.

"That's my fourth time so far, I'm obviously not good on water. If you don't count the rowing boats in Hove park." David gave a weak smile trying not to be sick again.

"Over half way there already the Sergeant Major reckons, so soon be back on dry land mate. Looks a bit brighter ahead too so may calm down in a bit."

The ship lurched again and one of the men behind lost his footing and slid from one side of the deck to the other where he promptly hauled himself on the rail and continued to throw up in one motion. David raised his eyes at Will who shrugged sympathetically and then patted him on the back.

"I wanted to tell you something Will," David said weakly. "Now seems as good a time as ever." Will moved round so David could see him without having to turn too much.

"What is it Dave?"

"I've asked to be trained as a medic when we get there. Want to do something other than just ordinary soldiering. Though seems a bit ironic now with me being sick and all." He managed a smile.

"Well luckily we aren't in the Navy mate," Will said trying to lift his spirits. "Does that mean you will be leaving the Southdowns? You're a good soldier they would miss you."

"No don't worry. I can stay attached, just gives me something extra to do like. You've got your sharp shooting, I wanted to try my hand at this."

"I see," said Will, worried now. "You know that means you will be in the thick of things even if the battalion doesn't fight that much? Orderlies and stretcher bearers often have to go out under fire, even for other men."

"Yes, I do. And it doesn't bother me. I've seen my share of blood and guts on the farm."

"The farm isn't the front line."

"I'm not scared Will."

"I know that Dave. Just worried is all. You told Mum and Dad you doing this?"

"No thought best leave it be for a while. Maybe later on."

"Yes, probably for the best."

David now lurched over the side again as his body tried to retch despite being emptied of its contents some time ago. He looked at Will when the feeling started to subside. "Frankly I'd run naked at the enemy if I could just get off this damn boat."

Will laughed then. "Well if I get shot I will be comforted by the sight of my brother running free as nature intended to rescue me!"

David managed a laugh just as Archie appeared from the door to the upper stairway, munching on a sandwich. He clearly didn't suffer from seasickness. He waved seeing Will and strode steadily over to him, unaffected by the roll of the sea.

"Alright lads" he shouted, waving the half-eaten sandwich at them, as more food was whipped away from his beard. He tried to take another bite but had to grab a side rail as the ship pitched once more at a frightening angle.

"Bit choppy 'eh?" He continued eating which caused several of them to instantly tip their heads over the side and be sick once more, including David. Will ushered his friend away with a shake of his head.

"Don't know what's up with 'em Sarge. Loads of grub down in the hold too, as no one's eating it. Cooky said to ask about."

"Don't think he will have any takers up here Bunny," Will replied smiling, "and I'm not sure asking them is going to help their current predicament either."

"Oh right," Archie said begrudgingly. "Their loss. Anyway, I noticed you disappeared after the briefing so thought I'd better come and see you're okay."

"Yes, I just needed time out. How did it go with the Colonel?"

"Oh, he never appeared. Won't speak to the likes of me Will. I mean Sarge. Captain Brooks passed on his comments with the Sergeant Major like."

"You don't have to worry about rank up here Bunny. What did they say then?"

"Well Brooks wasn't at all happy to see me again, but the Sergeant Major had already put his tenpenneth in and told the Colonel that back home I'd just be confined to barracks for going AWOL and given punishment duties. Seems the Colonel agreed and said as they needed every man they could muster I wasn't about to be confined anywhere, which I thought was funny as we are stuck on a ship."

Will raised his eyes. "Go on."

"So, I will be given extra duties when we get there and my behaviour will be monitored. And if I run off in France I will more than likely be shot. Which again is a bit daft given…"

"Yes, right well see that you do behave. And remember what happened to poor Triffitt and his mate. You were lucky to be spared that, but I won't forget their faces in a hurry."

Will stared now at the raging sea, recalling the fact he was part of a firing squad that shot two men for cowardice the last time he was in France, even though they were scapegoats for an officer's own failings. Archie took the moment to change subjects.

"What about that Alice then?"

"What?" Will was thrown and snapped out of his dark memory.

"I know that's why you are up here sulking about on the top deck. What did she say after all this time?"

"Not a lot really. I think we were both just as shocked to see each other. She was on her honeymoon with her new husband. And I'm not sulking."

"Yeh right course you're not. I can't believe she's married that toff. Seemed a right pompous arse…"

"Yeh well was never gonna marry me was she? And god knows what you thought you were doing pretending to be an officer."

"Just keeping an eye on you. Making sure you didn't do anything stupid."

"That's rich coming from you Archie. It was weird seeing her again though. Not easy with her husband being there but she did sort of seem pleased to see me."

Archie looked at Will and could tell he hadn't got her out of his system quite yet. He didn't like the effect she had on him, especially as they were heading back to France.

"Don't go there mate. I had enough of you fawning about the last time we came here, and for what? It's her loss, so get Princess Pevensey out of your head and let's get on with winning this war. Unless you get shot of course, in which case I can highly recommend nursing care."

"What are you like Bunny? I don't intend to get shot or *fawn about* as you put it. Besides…as you were, Captain Brooks is here. Attention!"

Will and Archie managed to stand straight and tried to salute but slipped partly on the deck in doing so. The rest of the men up there could barely turn round, but a couple attempted to feebly stand.

"At ease men don't worry," Brooks shouted into the snarling gale, though he smiled perceptibly at their misfortunes. "I was told you were here Bunden."

"Sir?"

"Just wanted you to know that whatever the Colonel has said, you're not off the hook in my book. And whether the Sergeant Major thinks you are a good soldier or not you will have to start from scratch with me. Until I see you prove yourself. Is that clear Corporal Bunden?"

"Sir, yes sir."

"Good, I'll find you plenty of fatigues to do when we're not busy with Jerry don't you worry. You'll be sweating day and night in my company lad. Make you think twice about running away again. And if you try it over there you won't get off a second time. Understood?"

Archie simply nodded but Will spoke up, though he had to shout into the wind, the words being snatched away over his shoulders before they had barely passed his lips.

"I will keep a close watch on him sir, don't you worry."

"Good. Well then I will leave you to it. Just remember I've got my eye on…"

Before he could finish the sentence another wave hit the side of the ship and Brooks was sent skidding along the floor to the stairway entrance. Will and Archie stood open mouthed as the officer struggled on the sea-soaked surface. Finally, he dragged himself up and angrily threw the door open, before pulling himself inside.

"I didn't quite catch that," Archie said with a grin, cupping his ear in the direction of the stairs. "What was he keeping his eye on Sergeant? Should have been watching the sea I think."

The two friends looked at each other and laughed then. As Archie strolled away, Will felt the warm smiling image of Alice return to linger in his mind. Her clear blue eyes piercing his soul as they walked together by a stream. He shook his head a couple of times until the memory was broken up in the wind like a puff of cigarette smoke. Then he walked back to where David hung limp over the starboard rail.

No looking back now.

Chapter 11 – Back to the beginning

The trucks pulled up in the centre of the village of Festubert. The men of the Southdown battalions fell out into the rough stone area and formed up surveying the damaged surroundings with a sense of foreboding. Much of the village had been destroyed in fighting the previous year, and everywhere there was evidence of the conflict. As they spread out, details jumped out at the men, amongst the piles of spent shells and pieces of kit strewn about.

A bicycle was propped against a wicker fence as if the occupant was inside having tea. Except there was nothing left of the house the fence fronted, except a great crater of rubble. One of the men found half a pair of glasses and a crushed felt hat, and put them on. The men laughed as he clowned about with them, easing the tension that gnawed away inside them all. Then another one found their owner's head nearby, the other half of the wire frame still clinging to the skeletal remains. The nose socket widened where a bullet had clearly gone clean through the person's face rendering his spectacles in half. The hat was dropped to the ground.

Archie picked up a child's doll from the middle of the street and laid it carefully on a broken wall; before one of the men found the wheels of a pram in a nearby garden, and no one voiced the conclusion they came to. In moments the laughter ebbed away, as life did here from the very foundations of the village.

Will detailed small groups of men to check the surrounding area for any signs of enemy activity, keen to get them active to stop their minds wandering. Even here behind the lines, there could be traps left behind, and it was common knowledge that snipers could stay hidden and wait, long after a battle had moved on. The sergeant major spotted him take the initiative and shouted at the other NCOs to follow suit.

Will picked a handful of men from his own company including David, and walked up to the front of the church not far from the centre. He paused momentarily, marvelling at the detailed architecture of the ornate doorway and tower above. In another time and place he would have felt at peace here, but today his senses were on full alert. He signalled the men with him to fan out either side of the building slowly, and told David to keep his rifle trained on the tower above for any signs of movement. Slowly, carefully, he pushed the door open and moved inside, looking everywhere for anything that would trigger death. Wires, boxes, even a pile of prayer books could cover a trap.

Once inside however he realised the threat was probably non-existent. The church was almost totally destroyed behind its splendid medieval front and he found himself looking at the other men with him staring over the chest high walls of the aisles. *No need to go climbing through the rubble for the sake of it,* he thought, *even God isn't waiting about in here.* He beckoned the men to carry on with their sweep of the buildings and turned to leave. A robin flew over the rubble and settled on the font that now lay on its side, the baptismal bowl cracked in two. It pecked at something out of sight and then looked at Will, head to one side.

The sudden flash of colour in the deathly pale interior seemed to challenge his previous thought. Will felt guilty and turned back as he was about to leave. He wasn't sure what he felt about God currently; there would be time for that debate later if he survived hell's time on earth. But if nothing else he wanted the comfort of hoping that the good men and women that were already lost, were being cared for somewhere. Moreover, he certainly didn't want to upset any 'powers that be' that might be watching his progress.

Will paused and bowed his head towards where he guessed the altar would have stood, then strode out to where David was waiting for him and together they moved on up the street. The robin chirped a brief thank you behind them, and took off, rising and falling across the ruins.

The patrols soon established the shattered remains of the village were no longer in German hands, although incredibly in some of the houses on the outskirts, local French people still tried to eke out a terrified existence. One of the battalion officers, Captain Steven Fennell, instructed some of the men and their medics to visit each family in turn and see if they needed any help. He spoke reasonable French and was able to reassure them at least that they meant no harm, and most importantly that the fighting was now further away.

Fennell had been a professional soldier for only five years before the war broke out but had received a well-deserved captaincy upon transferring to the Southdowns. Not a product of the usual private schools, his parents did run a successful merchant company, which ensured he at least had a grammar school education. Despite some obvious challenges, their son had gained his commission in a territorial regiment and may have lingered there unfulfilled, but for the war. Now in the midst of a global conflict, his personal attributes, and kind hearted nature, flourished under the harshest of spotlights, and ensured his natural leadership qualities were no longer ignored.

Captain Brooks sniffed with disdain as the men handed over some of their precious medicines and food to the locals. This improvised action was not in their *Trench Orders* handbook, and he felt uncomfortable doing anything that wasn't clearly laid out for them. He was relieved to see a courier appear on a motorcycle from a base camp in Béthune, that would hopefully get them on the move again rather than loiter about here. He took the dispatch and called the sergeant majors to him. Russell and Carter doubled over to where he was standing, map stretched out on a wall.

"Sergeant Major. We are to rest here for another hour at the most and then move on to the forward lines near a place called Neuve-Chappelle and meet up with the Royal Sussex. Now looking at the map it would appear…"

"Beggin' your pardon sir but I know where it is." Russell interrupted his officer uncharacteristically. The town's name giving a frame to the uncomfortable memories that had been stirring in him since they arrived. Brooks looked up slightly taken aback, as did Carter wondering how their officer would respond.

"We served here in fourteen and fifteen sir. I know this area well, though it's not as pretty as last time I saw it."

"Hmm I daresay it isn't. Well then you can join me with the lead companies and show the way Sergeant Major, though best check the map just in case it's changed more than you remember I suggest."

"Yes sir."

"Inform the other officers we are to move within the hour. Carter you are to remain here and bring up the remainder of the battalions and the logistics corps. Make sure you liaise with the Colonel. We'll all rendezvous at NC."

"Sir!" The two CSMs saluted as one.

"Oh, and better go and tell Captain Fennell to wrap up his mission of mercy too. We may need those supplies before long."

"Right away sir." Russell glanced at Carter, as he marched off, who raised his eyes to him, before disappearing in the opposite direction barking orders. Russell was irked by the tone of his captain's remarks and the obvious lack of faith in his previous experience here. On the other hand, part of him also agreed that they might need all the supplies they had if things got as bad as last time, regardless of the locals' plight. The men needed to remain an effective fighting unit and with so few experienced men in the battalions, they couldn't afford to be short of kit. He spotted

Captain Fennell handing out chocolate to two small children in a small single storey house up ahead. The captain was very popular, but he would also need to be tough in the months ahead. Whereas Brooks was quite the opposite.

Russell sighed at the difference in their personalities. There was enough to worry about without internal conflict as well. He spotted Archie now chatting together with a number of the men, brewing up tea and laughing casually over shared cigarettes. *At least Brooks accepted the colonel's decision on Bunden*, he thought to himself now. *Whether he liked it or not, it was only a company punishment matter not a court martial. If it wasn't for the war he'd just be washing toilet floors for a month, for being absent without leave. Not thrown against a wall and shot. Hopefully now we are here Brooks will realise we need all the veterans we can get.*

He pulled out his own cigarette and lit it, giving himself time to clear his thoughts. He knew underlying everything was the fact they were returning to the region where he was nearly killed. "This bloody war," he muttered out loud to no one in particular, blowing smoke into the hazy sky. *Now was not the time for weakness.*

"Corporal Bunden!"

"Yes, Sergeant Major." Archie ran over instantly and stood to attention.

"When you have finished mingling with the other officers," he paused for the effect of his jibe to sink in, "then start rounding up the men and tell the NCOs we are leaving in an hour."

"Sir."

"So I want everyone ready to march in thirty minutes just in case." Archie started to open his mouth to protest but then thought better of it and stayed silent.

"And find Sergeant Davison and send him to me."

"Yes sir."

*

Will stopped the courier as he was about to leave and smiled, offering him a cigarette he had taken from one of the men. The courier looked round briefly then nodded and took it, lighting up with his own matches.

"Did I hear you've come from base camp?"

"Yes Sergeant why? Want a lift back?" The courier's eyes glinted under his goggles, as he took another drag on the cigarette.

"I bloody wish. And is the base camp still near Béthune?"

"Near it? It's in it. Know someone there do you Sarge?"

"Got a friend in the medical camp yes, if they are still attached to base."

"Yes, big set up there now. One of the largest aid posts for the region with so much going on. Moved 'em all into proper buildings too. Looks like we will be here a while don't it?" Will nodded. "Supplies and nurses coming in daily. The lads there are loving it. Big push coming they say."

"That's what they say. Just never the direction we are meant to push."

"Haha. True enough. Well I best be off. Appreciate the fag mate." He flicked the stub into the road and it bounced over a discarded empty magazine.

Will let the informality go as he needed a favour. "Here's another one for your journey and a note for a Staff Sergeant Halliday in the hospital if they are still there."

"Halliday? She's still in the hospital."

"Are you sure?"

"Oh, very sure Sarge. Delivered a note to her just the other day. Good looking girl, dark hair, curves that go on and on…"

"That's enough of that. She's a Staff Sergeant to you. And you might need her services one day Private."

"I truly hope so Sarge!" He laughed and roared the engine into life and spun away before Will could challenge him.

Will frowned wondering who the other note was from, unaware that Harry had sent it. He felt ridiculous that he was jealous and kicked a stone down the road in the direction of the disappearing courier. Will felt anger rising and struggled to control it. *Let's face it Davison you've not been the same since the train journey. In fact, come to think of it, the last couple of weeks starting with Archie's disappearance,* he reflected.

Will hadn't slept well for a fortnight now, which wasn't helping, and was struggling not to be irritable with the men. On the boat over he deliberately distanced himself from the rest, except during battalion briefings and training, saying he was busy with planning for when they landed. Seeing James briefly on the road up to Festubert had certainly raised his spirits momentarily, but his brother knew him too well, and had been quick to notice something was up. He'd passed it off as "pre-match nerves," which James seemed to accept, yet inside Will knew full well seeing Alice again had thrown him completely. *Last thing I need now is to be thinking about girls. Only got to look at Bunden to see what trouble they cause.*

"Don't know what you're frowning at Will, but I can probably trump it. Sergeant Major wants you." Archie smiled as he walked up, and then paused when he saw Will's face.

"Speak of the devil," Will muttered.

"Oh oh."

Will looked around in case anyone was in earshot. "It's Sergeant when we are out here Corporal. Unless we are alone in the middle of nowhere, which is hardly likely now is it? And only then if I'm not angry with you, which again will be very rare the way things are going."

"Sorry Will," he answered automatically, then grinned at his stupidity.

Will shook his head in despair. "Anyway, I think you have a lot more to be worried about from the Sergeant Major than me Corporal. Know what he wants?"

"Orders to move out within the hour, so we have to get formed up in thirty minutes. Sergeant."

"Sounds like standard army logic," Will answered ruefully. "Still I'm happy to get cracking. This place gives me the creeps."

"It's not that Will…I mean Sergeant. It's just that I overheard one of the young lieutenants talking about where we was heading like, when the Sergeant Major collared me."

"And?"

"Noove chapel."

Will frowned, then said "Neuve-Chappelle?"

"That's the fella. After all we've been through we end up right back where we started 'eh?"

"Yes. Terrific."

"See I said I could trump whatever it is that's bothering you."

"There's a long list and I haven't got time to go through it now."

"You can talk to me you know."

Will paused for a moment, grateful for his friend's support, and considered taking a few moments to talk about how worried he'd been about his friend. And of course, seeing Alice. Then he shook his head and smiled. He had written it all in a note for Teresa, well what he thought he could get away with, and hoped next time he saw her they could talk it through. Until then there was a war to fight.

"Thanks Bunny. Some other time perhaps. Besides as my Grandma often says, *'When you're lost, best thing to do is retrace your steps back to the beginning and start again.'* So, this is as good a place as any to get back in the war I guess."

"If you say so *Sergeant*."

"I do. *Corporal.* So let's get cracking."

Chapter 12 – Sausage on a stick

Unteroffizer Hans Liebsteiner felt the cold water's embrace begin to caress his legs from the ankles up. Despite the additional clothing they always wore when out here, eventually nature found a way to infest their bodies with its deadly charms. Whether it was snow and frost, or rain and mud, the outcome was the same. Even in summer the heat could make the ground burn as if hell itself was pulling at you. Hans preferred the winter months though. For the most part it kept the flies and rats at bay, and the days short. Perfect for a sniper.

They had been out here over two days now, and as night fell, he struggled to stop his body trembling with the cold. He looked at his friend lying next to him. At least the weather would not bother him again. *Poor Klaus.* He lay dead, the top of his head blown clean off. Even that hadn't brought the flies back, despite the day's warmth. Klaus lay where he fell, eyes wide with shock. Hans had heard the familiar scurry of rats though, and knew he would have to leave his friend to their grisly attentions once he left. Besides Klaus could not feel the infected bites, and his last act for his comrade was to potentially flush out his assailant.

Hans and Klaus had worked this sector successfully for four months now. Unlike the teams further south in the Second army who sat behind protected steel-proof loopholes in concrete bunkers and shot the French at will with little risk. They read about them all the time in pamphlets from the communications officers proclaiming their heroics. *Let them have their glory and their medals.*

Hans prided himself on hunting in the old way. Staying in one place and studying every inch of the opposing trenches. The changing landscapes, blown this way and that by the bombs, the effects of the seasons, and of course the different English regiments that came and went. Though they never changed their daily routines. *The English and their rules.* Just sometimes some were cleverer than others. It mattered little.

Klaus Mitzver, and Hans had grown up in neighbouring villages in the Black Forest and hunted together with their fathers. When war broke out they volunteered without hesitation and very soon proved themselves to be crack shots despite their youth. For the last year they had worked in the

Neuve-Chappelle sector to deadly effect. Between them they had over fifty confirmed kills, and probably the same number of wounded. *The lucky ones. Or maybe not,* he reflected, knowing the damage his beloved Gewehr.98 rifle could do at such distances. *Better to be dead perhaps.*

Moving just his eyes Hans studied his dead comrade again for a moment, and thought of their families back home. His mother would be heart broken. Not to mention Lisl. He had told Klaus not to marry before they left but would he listen? *So much for love.* He closed his eyes for a moment to try and calm himself.

Hans was angry too. The stalemate in this sector meant both sides became too relaxed. Despite not charging about at each other, casualties still mounted from the shellings and snipers, when normal caution was worn down with boredom. Both sides engaged in macabre trench sports. Willing the opposing soldiers to fire at presented targets or shouting at each other trying to provoke them into action. Into doing anything except sitting about on their asses freezing all day.

He hated the unprofessionalism of it all. The rivalry almost bordered on camaraderie, and was not the face of the army he joined in 1914. Together with Klaus they endeavoured to spoil such antics at every chance, and remind their comrades sitting in the trenches that this was a war, not a game. *A war that they had to win.* During the recent exchanges Hans saw one particular English officer start to regularly glance over the parapet. Waving various objects from underwear to food, and even a German helmet. They could see his thick moustache and the pips on his uniformed shoulders gleaming in the sun.

Sometimes his trench shot at the objects, but mostly they just jeered and waved their own captured items. More than once the officer had lingered just a little too long and Hans wanted to shoot him, to stop this childish behaviour. Yet dear Klaus said it was *unsporting* as it was *too easy*. So they agreed if he popped up again before they 'stood down,' then this time Hans could shoot him. *For being stupid.* He smiled briefly recalling the exchange, their quiet laughter while they debated his fate. It was the last words they had exchanged.

The English officer duly popped up at first light, waving what looked like a large sausage on a stick. Something they often ate at home with fried potatoes in a stew. *He could almost smell it.* Often in the summer his mother would roast them on sticks over an open fire in the field behind their house. As he watched the man waving it about, he pictured himself then as a young boy chasing his sister around the field, using the emptied stick to taunt her. The sun dazzled off her wavy blond hair as she giggled and dodged him easily with her long slender legs...

Just for a moment the officer risked a glance to the German trench whooping as he did. The cries broke the memory and Hans fired instinctively. The sausage fell from view as the man gave one last shout. Within seconds the echo of his shot seemed to reverberate from the shell holes roundabout, and there was a small thud next to him. Hans spun round to see Klaus simply fall forward on the edge of their pit. Within seconds a second shot took the helmet and the top of his head off, pushing him onto his back with the force, where he had lain all day ever since.

Stupid! To be careless after all this time. Of course they would have their own snipers out. Klaus must have looked up for a moment watching Hans' shot. Now his friend was gone, and young Lisl was a widow at nineteen.

An angry tirade followed the death of the British officer, with wild exchanges of fire. Some grenades were thrown, presumably in grief. It was too far to hit the German trench but they fell all around Hans making him press himself further into the unforgiving mud. At some point the sniper must have signalled he had killed Klaus, because cheering broke out in the English lines and they waved the German helmet about again. *That was their mistake*, he thought.

Up until that moment he couldn't be sure where the shot had come from, perhaps even from the enemy trench itself. For all he knew the sniper might have moved too, under cover of the fire from the trench. But the delayed cheers meant the man was not in the trench. Now he knew for sure he was not alone, out here in No Man's Land. Somewhere in this pock holed hell, someone just like him watched and waited. Except he wasn't like him. For Hans now held the edge over his opposite number.

His own trench called out to him several times but he made no move to reassure them. He wanted the English to believe Klaus was operating alone and the danger was past. That was his edge. Their sniper was waiting for dark to move back to his lines, his task complete. His mind would be on a warm drink and some dry clothes. Hans was waiting for dark to kill the sniper and complete his mission. His mind was on nothing else.

German shells fell then on the English lines, probably in response to his supposed demise, and in the hour-long barrage Hans took time to assess the area ahead that was ingrained in his mind. Barely moving his head, he scanned left and right. There was nothing different except in one spot. By the old wire post away to his right, a tattered testament to the former front line, rocks were stacked up around it, as if they had been thrown there by a shell. Yet something about the way they lay told Hans they were too precise, and more likely placed there to cover a sight or rifle muzzle.

He could see nothing more from here only daring the briefest of glances. Nor could he risk using his scope for fear the sun would catch it. So, throughout the day he lay flat below the rim of his hole, cleaning and reloading his rifle inch by painstaking inch. As the hours passed and the sun moved quickly overhead towards its evening repose, Hans sipped water to keep his mind sharp and his eyes clear.

He would only have one shot. Then he would have to move because they would surely open up again. If he missed, the Englishman may get him, and even if he was successful the chances of getting back were slim. He would have to leave Klaus. The thought made his pain rise, and he dismissed it. Now was not the time for tears. *Tears would affect his aim.*

The sun started to sink rapidly over the western horizon. Dark clouds rushing to envelope the light, as shadows grew across the ground. Hans wriggled his fingers and toes trying to get some circulation in his body without making any noise. His legs now felt like blocks of ice from the knees down and he worried that when the time came to act, his muscles may fail him and his feet refuse to move. He pushed the thoughts aside, relying on his training. Relying on his instincts to fire his body into life once more.

A starling flitted across the ground in front. It landed briefly and pecked at something before darting on, keeping low, as if it too had learned how to survive here over the past few months. *Is there anything left here worth eating?* Hans wondered. Then he almost jolted when the bird veered sharply away from the old post. *I knew it,* he told himself, though now was not the time for self-congratulations.

There was a barely perceptible noise as Hans now peered intently at the closest hole to the wire post. Yet when the movement came it was already two holes away to the left and he was caught out by the speed at which the English soldier was moving in the darkening light. *There must be a lower section somewhere connecting the holes nearest the British side of No Man's Land for him to get so far unseen.* He was close to safety now but Hans knew patience was the key. He also had luck on his side as the sun setting in the west silhouetted the trench lines ahead of him; while he knew they would already be straining to see into the blackness where he lay.

Hans raised his rifle slowly, sliding it out over the lip of the hole. Every tiny sound seemed to magnify tenfold in his imagination. He heard a clicking sound from the direction of where the Englishman was now waiting, and sure enough a similar sound echoed back from the trench.

He's letting them know he's coming back. At that moment he saw a steel helmet rise ever so slightly above the line of the shell hole the man was in. A year ago, he would have shot it and in so doing achieved nothing but an empty helmet. Now he simply waited. *He's not doing that for me. He's checking my sentries aren't awake before he makes his move. He doesn't know I'm here.*

As these excited thoughts went through his mind, Hans aimed along his sight, guessing the direction the man would take to the trench. Then with impressive dexterity and hardly any sound, he saw the man appear and roll over the edge of the hole into the adjacent one in a matter of moments and then be still again. He had rolled right in the centre of Hans' sights but he did not take the shot. He watched and waited, his body taut, all thought of cold or discomfort now banished.

Now the helmet raised again. Then by some unseen signal the man threw his rifle over the last lip and Hans saw the dark shape of an arm reach up and catch it. Again, a pause, and then his helmet went over, followed by a bag of some kind. Each time caught silently. Each time a pause. No words came forth in the stillness. *He's good this Englishman. He's very good.* It was almost totally dark and Hans knew that if he waited significantly longer the chance would be gone, and he would have to start his own cat and mouse manoeuvre back to his lines. He took another breath and held it, trying not to blink into the sight.

Then the man was up and throwing himself over the last mound of earth into the trench. Hans fired, and as he did so he moved like lightning, knowing he was too exposed this time to stay put and wait for things to die down. He moved two holes in the time it took the Englishman to fall into the trench, and then flattened out against the side, hoping it had not filled too much with water since he last used it.

The shot and the cry that followed was enough to distract the waiting British soldiers from his move, but they were fully alert and as he slid into the second hole a flare went up and machine guns started in seconds. His own trench responded and then British artillery fired in a number of rounds, which no doubt sent his comrades deep into their bunkers. For half an hour firing followed flares until in time he heard the order to *"Cease fire."* Nothing was aimed at him though and he knew the British believed the shot to have come from the trench. He would rest for an hour and then zig zag back to the lines himself. His work done.

*

In the British front line trench all hell broke loose in that half hour, following the single shot, as medics fought desperately to save their sniper's life. Ollie Harris of the Royal Sussex had trained as a sharp shooter like Will the previous year. Though his ability was not quite in the same league, in the months that followed Will's departure, he became a highly respected member of the battalion with over fifteen confirmed kills. But he was no match for Hans' cold-blooded expertise, and the shot that took him through the lower back rising into his left lung took his life, and he passed away gasping for breath on the rotten filthy boardwalk of 'E' company's trench section.

Sergeant Cedrick Longworthy stood looking down at the dead body of his friend as a couple of men prepared to take him away. Following Captain Barclay's demise earlier in the day, Harris' actions in taking out the sniper had raised morale considerably and they were ready to give him a rousing reception on his return. Now his death brought the mood crashing down once again, and Longworthy could sense the men were keen to be replaced and move on from this cursed spot.

He lit a cigarette and walked away, deep in thought, his large bushy moustache twitching as he mouthed silently to himself. Something caught his boot and he looked down to see the outline of a rat scuttling along the trench floor. He realised it was carrying part of the sausage their doomed Captain had waved that morning. Longworthy swung his boot at it and grunted with satisfaction as he felt it connect hard, the rat being hurled against the far wall with a desperate squeal. Striding forward, he brought all his anger to bear as he crushed its head under his heel. He stopped then and glanced out into the black unclaimed land between the trenches.

"Enjoy your moment of glory with your mates Fritz. There won't be any more when our Davison gets here."

Chapter 13 – Potatoes

The men of the Southdown battalions marched four abreast into the main camp behind the front lines near Neuve-Chappelle. Their hearty singing caused the activity in the camp to pause momentarily, and a number of comments were thrown about the fact their enthusiasm would soon wane when they reached the trenches. In stark contrast to the wild cheers and bands that had sent them on their way, here at the front the reception was quite the opposite. Everywhere the men looked they were met with everything from anger and disdain to tired indifference, and the singing soon died away as they halted in a large wide muddy square.

A number of the experienced NCOs stepped forward from the ranks, medals gleaming, challenging the hecklers to continue their barracking. It had the desired effect and any interest in the newcomers dispersed as quickly as it arose. The officers were greeted by a young lieutenant who asked them to report to the senior colonel in one of the nearby houses, long since evacuated by its owners. Captain Fennell handed the CSMs a sheet of paper each then instructed Russell to take over with a quick salute and a smile. He then strode after the other departing officers as they followed Colonel Grisewood to the HQ building nearby.

Russell and Carter walked to one side by a barn and studied the divisional orders briefly. The Southdowns were now attached to the 39th Division of the army as part of the 116th Brigade of which their three battalions made up a part.

"Looks like you've got the 12th then Nelson. I've got the 13th."

"Unlucky for some Geoff?" Carter asked with a raise of his eye.

"Don't believe in all that superstitious nonsense, Nelson, you know that. If it's unlucky for anyone it will be the Hun when our lads get stuck into them."

"Can't argue with that," Carter replied, "who's got the 11th?"

"Sergeant Major Billings. New man already here with the 2nd battalion of the Sussex. Been here since the off so they should be in good hands once he gets to know them."

"They'll grumble whatever. It's the army way."

They laughed then before noticing a thousand pairs of eyes were looking at them.

"Alright I'll dismiss 'em and then the Sergeants can break down who goes where. It's all in here anyway."

"All yours Geoff," Carter smiled, and stepped back out into the square before snapping to attention, which caused the men to fidget now waiting for the next command.

Russell looked around the area and saw that a number of men supposedly dealing with supplies were using the distraction of the Southdown's arrival for a crafty cigarette break. These were not Sussex men though, but judging by their cap badges he ascertained they were from the Royal East Kent Regiment, known colloquially as 'The Buffs.' He was also well aware the camaraderie of his own men had waned considerably while he'd been chatting, and now the familiar sound of muffled shells falling somewhere up ahead, added a morbid beat to the scene.

Russell laid his pack carefully by a low wall and took out his pacing stick, tucking it neatly under one arm before stepping forward into the middle of the area and coming to attention.

"Battalions…Stand at…Ease! I have here our divisional orders where you have all been formally assigned to our three battalions. You may not be in the one originally posted in England due to necessity. When you're dismissed, get a drink and check your kit. The Sergeants will advise you in time of which battalion you are now in. But no wandering off now. That means you Bunden." Archie grinned with pride being signalled out in this way, until the sergeant major held his gaze. "Sergeants keep the men ready to move when the officers return. Battalion…wait for it…Dismissed."

As the men broke up into groups all around the square, Russell turned his attention to the other men who were supposed to be working.

"Alright you lot. Where the 'ell do you think you are? At the bleedin' zoo? Stood around gawping like a load of monkeys. No one told you to stop working did they? So get sweatin'." There was a scramble of noise as the men scattered in all directions to resume their tasks, and Russell nodded with satisfaction. As he looked around he saw Captain Fennell approaching, and snapped a salute up.

"S'arnt Major. Colonel's got orders to move the men forward to our trenches this afternoon so they arrive in the evening, hopefully as it goes dark. Apparently there's a regular enemy barrage around four so we will aim to get in after that."

"Sir." Russell looked at the men, many inexperienced, and his concern probably showed on his face.

"Best thing we can do is get them up there and settled in as soon as possible. More we delay it, the more nervous they might become, so good to get going soon, what?"

"Yes sir, absolutely. We will be ready."

"I know we can count on you and the other experienced men. Now the Colonel's organised some hot food for the battalion over there, in the canteen hut. Got a good couple of hours at least so I suggest they eat their fill and take time to relax. Maybe drop a note home 'eh? That sort of thing."

"I'll see to it sir. I'll get 'em fed by companies."

"Right. The other officers and I are dining with the CO and some of the Sussex officers. There's a Major Brown here who's been involved from the off. He's going to lead us up to his lines. It's his mob we're relieving, and pretty damned glad they are too by the sounds of it. They are getting some well-deserved rest out of the front lines before being moved south. He's suggested you send a forward patrol ahead just in case. We are behind the lines here, but the trench lines are very fluid in this sector, and just in case some stray Jerry patrol happens into our back garden, worth having a section out in front."

"Sensible approach sir. I'll pick some willing volunteers."

Fennell smiled. "Quite right. Although one of your lads is on punishment duties apparently. Corporal Bunden? Captain Brooks insists he goes along regardless."

"Understood sir. Walk will do him good am sure. I'll send Sergeant Davison along to lead it. He's been here before. Knows the area and has his wits about him. If I let Bunden lead he's liable to head in the wrong direction."

"Think he's going to scarper again Sergeant Major?"

"No sir, he's just not the sharpest tool in the shed."

Captain Fennell laughed now. "Well he's not alone in that. Anyway, I'll send a runner when it's time to push off. Get the men rested up." They saluted each other again then, but as Fennell turned to go he called back. "And Sergeant Major. That includes you. I'll need my best men fighting fit when we get up there."

Russell nodded and then moved off to pass the orders on. He spotted an old wooden bench propped against a farm wall a hundred yards to the right of where they stood, and decided to bag that for himself once everything was sorted. *Captain's not daft. I'll drop my Emmie a note. Just in case.*

*

"Cor blimey. If we move any slower war will be over by the time we get fed."

There was a grumbling of agreement from the long line of men filing into the canteen to get their meal before heading off. Inevitably despite the best efforts of the sergeants to keep things orderly, slow service coupled with the leading men taking more than their fair share soon led to the companies bunching up. Tommy Landon was making his feelings known as 'A' company finally got inside the building and approached the tables where the food was being dished out.

"You're not wrong there boyo, not that I'd mind like," Owen replied. "I'd happily stay here if it meant we missed sitting in the mud getting shot at day after day."

"What and miss all the fun Welshy? After all that training." Archie's booming voice carried over the lot of them and they all turned to see his bearded face grinning as he slowly made his way up the outside of the line.

"Hey there's a queue Bunden," one of the men called out despite being half his size.

"Course there is, for privates and people daft enough to stand in it. Besides I'm here to look after the Sergeant."

Archie nodded to Will as he joined him near the front. Will stood patiently waiting his turn, not willing to pull rank to jump the queue. He nodded and smiled back at Archie, as the cooks appeared once more with fresh tubs of steaming hot stew and warm bread.

"I'm in the 11th battalion," said Archie. "Did we all get the same?"

"Not me. I'm assigned to the 13th. Most of the lads we know are. Tommy, Danny, Owen. How did you get the 11th?"

"God knows that's typical that is. I bet Brooks stitched me up."

"You get the new CSM then from the Sussex regulars."

"Yeh terrific. Am I supposed to be pleased by that?"

"Just saying Bunny."

Archie started asking men round about what battalion they were in as David walked back down the line from the front with a plate full of stew.

"Oi Davison. How did you get to the front so quick?" Archie shouted, indignantly. "Using your brother to pull food favours now?" Will raised his eyes as David laughed.

"I just happened to be near the door when we broke up, and we got in first as I'm off to see the medical officer."

"Why? You sick?"

David paused, concerned his food was getting cold, but Will chipped in. "He's going to transfer to the medics Bunny."

"Oh? We not good enough for you now 'eh, is that it? This day just gets better and better!"

"I'm going to be a battlefield medic Archie," David replied. "So still with the Southdowns. I'm posted to the 11th."

"Oh, you're in luck. You'll be with Archie. He was just grumbling he didn't know anyone." David gave Will a look that said *Oh terrific*, but Archie was no longer listening. His mind had moved back to focus on the food, or lack of it, and the smell from David's plate wasn't helping.

"I will catch you later Will," David said, "I'm going to sit with some of the new lads and get to know them."

"Good idea…"

Watching David walk confidently off made Will feel like the younger brother again in that moment. Despite him being less experienced in the army, his brother clearly didn't need to be with Will except to follow orders. Of course, he was glad about that, and they were still brothers, but somehow that made him feel lonely. He was going to say more to David to prolong their chat when Archie grabbed his arm.

"How is it 'A' company is one of the last to be fed anyway Sarge?" Archie demanded, eyeing the food ahead with anticipation. "Last I checked the letter *A* was first in the alphabet."

"Well the first will be last and the last first, as they say Corporal," Will replied, shaking his head as he reached for a plate to get his ration.

"And which bleedin' idiot said that then?"

"Jesus," Will answered with a laugh.

As Archie pondered what to say in return there was a sudden surge from behind as the aroma of the food carried to the waiting men. Someone from 'B' company banged into the back of Archie and he turned round and splayed his huge hand across the man's forehead and pushed him back. Half a dozen men fell down like dominos in the queue. Archie now joined Will in being served, taking advantage of the chaos.

"Well it's now or never lads," Danny muttered skipping between two of the fallen men and a number of the Steyning group followed suit. Tommy hesitated but Owen and Danny pushed him forward and the friends watched eagerly as food was spooned onto their plates, ignoring the clamour of protests from the floor.

Archie was already heading off with Will and called back. "Watch out for the potatoes Tom. They'll hurt your eyes."

"Hurt my eyes?" Tommy replied. "How's that Corp?"

"They'll hurt your eyes trying to spot 'em. There ain't any!"

The men laughed then as Tommy began moaning again.

"How come there's no tatties cook? We got Irish regiments here ain't we?"

The cook paused, holding his ladle menacingly near Tommy's head, and for a moment Danny tensed ready to step in. Then the cook sighed and poured a pile of stew on Danny's plate as he replied.

"For your information private, just because we have Irish soldiers here, doesn't mean they all turn up with a sack of potatoes over their shoulders. Just like the Scots lads don't turn up riding Haggis."

"I happen to know on good authority most of our potatoes come from Scotland anyway. Keeping us going in England." A rather posh sounding private had spoken up from behind the group and they all turned to stare at him including the cook.

"And who the bleedin' hell asked your opinion Filbert," Danny replied.

"And I happen to know on good authority we are in France now, so the fact there are potatoes in England or Scotland is neither here nor there, my good man," Tommy chipped in, mimicking Filbert's accent and making his friends laugh.

"There's no Scottish potatoes in Steyning mate," Danny said, taking the chance of a distraction to grab a second chunk of bread for the stew. "Back home we eat our own potatoes, home grown on our farms."

"Here, here," his friends responded.

"Oi. Shake a leg up there. What's the bleedin' hold up?" someone cried from down the line.

Owen stuck two fingers up at the voice, and then pushed Tommy forward. "Come on hurry up, you daft Englishman."

"I bet the ruddy officers are having potatoes, served on silver plates," Tommy grumbled as he got his food. "How can there be no bleedin' tatties?"

"Well it may have escaped your notice sonny," the cook said as he started serving the men behind, "but there's a war on."

Tommy moved off with his friends, then turned to Owen. "Can you ride Haggis then?"

Owen shook his head. "Tommy, people like you make me proud to be Welsh."

The group laughed and went to sit on some old crates.

Will and Archie were already perched on a low wall, the pale blue sky of a spring afternoon masking the dark days to come. The sun was warm on their faces and they could have been back home by Mill stream. The noise from the canteen continued behind them but in that moment it seemed a million miles away.

"This is the life Will. Hot sun, hot food, and a place to rest my weary bones." Archie sunk to the floor, his back against the wall, taking care not to spill his food. He knew full well it was important to enjoy these rare breaks whenever the opportunity arose, and closed his eyes for a moment as Will ate quietly next to him. A shadow came across Archie's face and he opened his eyes ready to complain about whoever was blocking out the sun's rays.

"Ah just the men I was looking for," Sergeant Major Russell said, as he walked up to them with a grin that always meant trouble.

"Bugger," said Archie.

*

Agnes walked out of the Red Cross tent by Steyning station and adjusted her hat in the afternoon sun. She had spent a couple of hours serving teas to raise money for the war effort, and there was a steady trade from the farmers opposite where they were set up. It was auction mart day, and the noise from man and beast still reverberated behind her, as she crossed the bluebell-carpeted village green heading home. She smiled to herself at the notion that it was hard to tell which was which without looking, grunts and brays all merging together; then felt instantly guilty as she passed the church.

Today had been particularly interesting for two reasons. First, two train loads of soldiers had passed through on the way to the front, while Agnes was working there, and she galvanised the ladies to run up and down the platform offering cakes and drinks. As the first train waited in the station, puffing steam slowly like an old man on his pipe, Squire Goodman had arrived with his sister-in-law Celia. Celia was Chair of the parish committee and the local operatic society, and most of the ladies were scared of her, regardless of the fact she was also married into the Squire's family. Celia made it quite clear she disliked Agnes. Partly because James had completed his education and got a very good job in London, which was unheard of for a working-class boy. But also, because he had then got a commission, and like her own husband Theodore, was now a serving officer in France.

The ladies had all frozen in fear expecting to be chastised for giving all the cakes away for free, and Agnes braced herself for the backlash. It didn't come.

Instead the squire just smiled and said, "Well done ladies. Supporting the troops at home as well as overseas I see."

"It was Agnes' idea sir," Gladys Nightingale squeaked up, who looked and sounded like a mouse. Celia glowered, and Agnes wondered if the tiny church organist was saying it to praise her or disassociate herself from Celia's wrath.

"Splendid Mrs Davison. Quite right too. I'll pay for this lot," the Squire added with a wave of his hand, and took a currant bun from a nearby tray and walked off eating it with an appreciative nod. They watched him drop a load of coins into their collecting tin at the tent entrance, and Caroline gave them a 'thumbs up' as he left with a big grin. Agnes felt a warm glow inside.

Caroline was also behind her second interesting outcome of the day and she reflected on that now as she turned into the high street. It seemed the Women's Institute was firmly established in Singleton in Sussex under the patronage of a Lady Denman. Even more excitingly for Agnes, Caroline told her that they were due to officially open a number of other branches that year and were hoping to include Steyning or Storrington. Regardless of that fact, women were being encouraged to support the movement anyway and work unofficially in the meantime to grow crops and organise food parcels for the troops overseas. Her head was spinning with lots of ways she could help with the farm, when Fred cycled up to her on his bike and jumped off.

"Hello Mum."

"Hey Freddie. Have you finished work for the day?"

"Yes, and John gave me a string of sausages for me tea!"

"For *my* tea Freddie." She took the sausages and smiled, putting them in her bag as he pulled a face at her. "Well that's very nice of him. We shall *all* enjoy them. You must be doing well."

"Have you had a nice day mum?"

"Well yes, as a matter of fact it's been very interesting. Shall I tell you about it as we walk home?"

"Maybe later Mum. I promised Harry I'd do some pond dipping with him when I was finished. I'm off over there now."

"Oh, I see," Agnes said feeling deflated suddenly. "Well don't be late for tea!"

"I won't. What's for tea tonight?"

"Potato stew."

"Oh yummy. See you later. Love you."

With that he shot off across the road on his bike and disappeared towards Dog Lane and was gone. Agnes half waved but he never looked back. She stared after him for a moment and sighed, before turning back towards home. *Oh well. Back to the grindstone Agnes.*

*

Will's forward patrol moved patiently along the tree lined track, the late afternoon sun prompting shadows to dance around their feet through the sparkling foliage overhead. As well as Archie who was volunteered by Captain Brooks, Will chose men he could rely on to work together. Consequently Danny, Owen, Tommy and with some concern David, made up his six-man patrol that were probably about half an hour in front of the battalions following on.

While there was no reason to suspect the Germans had broken through in this sector, Will was also aware that a small party might be allowed to pass by without incident in order to attack the large force behind. So they moved as slowly and quietly as possible, constantly pausing to check tree lines, and hedges and anything that might hide a raiding party. At the same time they didn't want to stumble head first into a new German forward line if indeed an attack had been successful.

As they reached the end of the track, the old farm lane opened out into a wide field of crops that continued up a slow incline for some distance. The woods on either side were well over half a mile away and at this distance it was impossible to detect anything significant. Nor could Will risk sending men in both directions, when his orders were to press forward and make contact with the rear lines of the Royal Sussex. He paused, signalling the men to take cover, and took out the binoculars the sergeant major had given him before he left.

"And whatever happens to you, I want those back in one piece Davison. Mean more to me than you do."

The words made him smile now remembering the exchange between himself and his CSM. He knew it wasn't the case and was Russell's way of telling him to take care. Will brought his thoughts back into the moment and focused on the horizon ahead, scouring the ridge. He continued to sweep the binoculars round in both directions scanning the tree lines on either side. He was known for having terrific eyesight but even he could detect nothing here. *They could hide an army in those woods and I wouldn't see it without going in.*

He contemplated walking round the edge of the field in one direction and checking one side but that would only deal with one half of the problem. A pheasant broke cover about one hundred yards to his left and he froze watching the spot where it emerged from. The pheasant flew chaotically away across the broken ground and then settled again further up the hill with a loud cry. Will recalled seeing another pheasant break cover like this the last time he was in France and on that occasion it had been disturbed by a sniper. He stared hard through the binoculars but could see nothing that would conceal anyone. He frowned, unsure what to do, as David moved up by his side.

"Owen said he can hear the battalions moving up behind us. He went back to try and see them, but on a clear day like this, sound is carrying further so they could be a mile back still."

The news made Will's mind up and he gave the orders to move forward. They would follow the main track across the field straight ahead. Then he decided to play it doubly safe and turned to David.

"Private Davison I want you to wait here for the battalion's arrival and if we haven't come back before then, tell them where we went and to be careful of the woods on either side. What time is it now?"

David looked at his younger brother and a smile passed his lips being addressed so formally. He was still getting used to it despite the weeks in training but he was aware that in the army he followed orders regardless of who was giving them. He took out the pocket watch their grandfather had given him, that had seen much service on the railways, and clicked it open.

"Five minutes past five Sergeant."

"Ok. Make sure you let them know how long we have been gone when they arrive. I'll lead off and the others will follow in pairs at one minute intervals just in case. You time it for me."

"Ok Sergeant. And…be careful yeh?"

Will nodded and patted his brother on the arm, and then paused and gave him the binoculars. "Use these to keep an eye on our progress and two eyes on the woods! At least when the CSM gets here you can deliver them in one piece. You see anything out of the ordinary fire two shots in the air then find cover. Understood?"

"Yes Sergeant."

"Ok then." Without further delay he moved up to where the other four were waiting. "I'll start first and lead the way then you four come in pairs at one minute intervals. Davison will time you and keep an eye on our tails as we cross."

They all nodded and Archie looked back to where David was scanning the tree-lines either side through the binoculars. He looked at Will then and realised he was keeping him safe in case it all kicked off crossing the field.

"Danny you follow with Tommy. Then Owen you and Archie come last. That way we have at least one brain between each pair."

The men smiled at him then. The bond between them growing every day. As David moved forward to join the group, Will set off slowly at a half crouch into the field. As they watched him move further away the tension grew in the group of friends. The second hand seemed to be moving painfully slowly and Will looked horribly exposed now. All five men were watching the woods either side. At last David tapped Danny on the shoulder and him and Tommy moved off.

Archie needed to do something to break his own anxiety. He looked at David.

"You're a farmer. What sort of crops are these like?" he whispered, too loud for Owen's liking who "shushed" him.

David looked at the broad green plants, and only now noticed the number of white butterflies dancing around them in a joyful feeding frenzy. He gently examined a leaf on the nearest one.

"These are potatoes Bunny. Charlotte's I think."

Owen laughed suddenly. "There's an irony and no mistake look you. You wait 'til we tell Tommy after all his fussing in the mess hall earlier."

Archie smiled feebly but it didn't help the knot in his stomach. "I wish Charlotte had grown trees instead of bloody vegetables. Far too exposed out here."

"Time to get going lads," David said and gave them a nudge. "Sooner you get over there sooner we can relax. Good luck."

"See you soon boyo," Owen said, and his red head turned and followed the huge bulk of Archie skittering across the broken ground.

By now Will was half way up the field heading to the high ridge, but still unable to see what was on the other side of it. He paused and looked around and then back down to where he could see the others faithfully following his orders. He looked at the trees on either side, dark and foreboding, and wished he had kept hold of the binoculars. *Not that they would have done much good. Can't see through trees.* He tried to reassure himself that if someone was hiding there they would have shot by now. The friends were fully exposed. *Shoot the front and back man first, then the others would be doomed. No cover here. That's what I'd do.*

Will realised he was the front man of course and shivered at his own melancholy. He moved off again, and then heard the familiar spine-tingling whine of a shell. A terrifying noise buried in his subconscious for a year, which now triggered his whole body into life. He screamed at the men behind him.

“Incoming! Get down. Down!”

Will hurled himself flat amongst the dry rutted ground and the flourishing plants. The shells however landed repeatedly in threes and fours on the other side of the ridge for what was probably only a few minutes, but seemed like hours to the cowering men. After a short while Will risked a glance up and saw they were quite safe here as long as they stayed still. Caution told him to keep scanning the trees as well in case anyone was using the bombardment to move. All was still on this side of the ridge. He shouted to Danny to pass the word back to Archie to wait for his sign before moving again, and to try and signal David they were okay. *So much for every day at four*, he thought to himself. *Just as well we waited at the end of the track or we would have been over the ridge when the shelling started.*

As the last salvo died away he raised himself to his knees and listened intently, and then motioned for the men to get up and move on again. They had barely gone a few yards when there was a ‘whine’ overhead, and he just had time to shout “look out,” before the shell landed behind him. He felt the force from the blast but it was too far away to knock him off his feet, yet he still dived down again. Will’s first thoughts were that someone had ‘spotted’ them from somewhere, possibly the trees, and had honed the guns in on them. But as the silence returned again he realised it was clearly a stray shell fired from the final salvo that had overshot its target. He raised himself up again and called back.

“Everyone ok? Sound off.”

“Boyd.”

“Bunden.”

“Entwhistle.”

Silence.

“Landon. Shout up.” Will heard Danny call and felt the familiar cold knot of fear wrap itself around his spine.

“Tommy. Tommy.” Danny was up and moving to his right now and then Will spotted the crater and could see a helmet nearby. Then he heard him cry out.

“I’m hit. I’m hit.”

Least he’s not dead, Will thought as he dashed back. He saw Archie and Owen charging forward too but motioned to them to spread out and keep their eyes on the trees. When he got to where Danny was kneeling by Tommy he expected the worst.

“My back. It’s my back Sarge. Can’t feel my legs.”

Danny looked up at Will clearly frightened unsure where to begin. “I can’t see any obvious wound. He’s half buried.” Tommy was stuck fast from the waist down and covered in the potato plants so it was hard to see how badly he was hurt.

"Let's get him dug out, quick."

Then realising time was of the essence he called the other two over to help. *If anyone was in those woods we'd be dead by now,* he told himself. As Archie and Owen raced up he spoke to them trying to keep his voice calm.

"Get your spades out and get him dug out. But gentle like, we don't know what state his legs are in."

The other three exchanged glances as Will comforted Tommy and gave him a sip of water from his canteen.

"Tell me where it hurts Tom. Where's the worst pain."

"Got hit on the back Will, felt loads of thuds, but now it just feels numb. Can't move my legs."

"Your legs are trapped under the earth from the explosion. Sounds like shrapnel but I can't see anything on your back." He carefully started to lift all the plants off him as he whispered to Danny. "Easy now. His back could be broken."

As they gradually uncovered his legs Will started to check all round Tommy's kitbag for wounds or puncture holes.

"I can't see anything. Can you move?"

Tommy gradually brought his legs free of the earth and moved onto all fours.

"Careful laddie," Owen said caringly.

Then Tommy turned round and sat up. "I…I think I'm alright lads he said," with a half-hearted smile. The four friends looked at him in a mixture of bewilderment and concern. For a moment there was just silence between them, then Archie spoke up.

"Felt a few blows on the back did you?"

"Yes Archie, then the earth fell on me and I think I must have been knocked out."

Archie held up a large group of white objects obscured by the dirt, in his two spade like hands.

"You were hit by bloody potatoes you daft sod," and threw them at him.

"Jesus bloody Christ, Landon," Danny said. "Scared the pants off me."

"All of us," said Will and then stood up and gave the thumbs up to David, who was noticeably standing concerned on the edge of the clearing below. "Let's get going c'mon. May as well stick together now."

Owen helped him up and handed him his rifle and helmet. Then he grinned.

"Nearly got mashed up there boyo."

Danny laughed and said "Yes mate. We thought you'd had your chips then."

Will looked back as the laughter continued and added, "You might think twice about demanding potatoes in future Private. Be careful what you wish for!"

"Yes indeed Tommy lad. The Lord moves in mysterious ways you know," Owen added chirpily.

Behind them Archie was deep in thought. Unusually for him the opportunity to jump in with both feet and tease a fellow soldier went unnoticed. He was thinking of the shells. And how the last time one dropped; he had been blown to bits.

Chapter 14 - Home sweet home

Will led the group cautiously forward towards the top of the field. As they went over the rise they all stopped dead at the sight that greeted them. There was an old boundary wall for the field just in front of them that was no more than rubble for most of its length due to the shelling, punctuated at intervals by shell craters where the wall had ceased to exist. Beyond that however was what really caused the friends to pull up short. For there, laid out in a patchwork of textbook planning, was an entire trench system no more than four hundred yards from where they stood now. From the advantage of their high ground they could see the reserve and front lines clearly, with the communications trenches zig zagging between them.

It reminded Will of a game his grandfather used to bring out years ago when they visited them, with snakes and ladders on, running this way and that as the trenches did now. He wondered if somewhere in headquarters the generals did something similar with their armies in the same way on cardboard maps marked into squares. *I wonder if that's all we are,* Will mused, *just pieces on a board being moved this way and that.* Then a voice shouted out and they all jumped.

"Halt who goes there?" A soldier appeared behind a section of the wall; his rifle pointed directly at them.

The men initially raised their weapons instinctively and Danny even ducked, but Will was alert to the uniform and the English accent, and calmed the men down. Gesturing at them to lower their rifles he replied, "Advance party of the Southdown Battalions, Royal Sussex Regiment."

A second man appeared then from behind the wall and beckoned them forward. "This way you lot, we'll take you to the operations dug out."

As the men moved towards the wall, Will could see the second soldier was a corporal and by the look of him much older than the initial man. The corporal ordered the other man away as they scrambled over the broken boundary.

"Lightfoot. Shift yourself down to the sergeant and tell him our relief's here. All five of 'em. Either we are really short of men back home or these lads are tremendous shots!" He turned back to Will then. "Just a bit of humour Sarge. I'm Corporal Swift. I trust there are more of you on the way?" He raised an eyebrow hopefully.

"Yes Corporal. We've got three battalions marching up, less than a mile away. I'm Sergeant Davison. I left one of my lads in the woods back there to bring them on. We nearly walked right into that bombardment."

"Oh right. Yes, a bit late tonight. I think Jerry must have been napping. Not lose anyone did you?"

"No Corporal, but I should tell Dave…I mean Private Davison that all's well."

"Your brother is he Sarge?" Will nodded. "Leave it with me." He walked off a few paces and detailed a man to double back down the hill, then turned smiling.

"Right well this way. Mind your step lads." He paused and looked towards an old stone trough where Will suddenly noticed a machine gun team, facing down the field. "And you lot don't get trigger happy. We're expecting Sussex lads along soon. But make sure you challenge 'em nonetheless."

With that he turned and squished ahead down through the sodden ground and into an entrance in the reserve trench. The difference in the two sides of the hill was like night and day Will thought. *Nothing growing on this side at all. Just mud. The same soulless deadly mud.*

They followed the corporal along the trench line but the first thing that struck Will was the differences in the trench make up from when he was last in France. The boardwalks appeared permanent and the sides of the trenches here were solidly made and fully boarded up from ground to top. Here and there concrete bunkers interspersed the wooden walkways. Will glanced into one as they passed and steps descended into darkness, as if going down to hell itself. *It wouldn't surprise me if they did,* he thought.

The trenches here were much wider too and men passed easily without having to stand to one side. Moreover, every fifty yards or so there would be a dog leg in the line and the trench would change direction at right angles before back again in the original direction, and here especially the walls were often made of stone. Owen asked the question they were probably all thinking.

"We were taught trenches ran in straight lines Corporal. Why are these zig zags built into them? Must slow you down moving back and forth."

The Corporal shouted over his shoulder without looking back. "One direct shell burst in a trench can cause casualties a hundred yards either side. These walls contain the blast to a much shorter area. And, if the front lines get overrun, Jerry can't fire down the lines and kill more than a few men in one section."

It made perfect sense and they all nodded appreciatively as the corporal stopped suddenly and looked at them. "We learned it from the Hun when we took some of their trenches in Fifteen. Clever buggers they are. They built their trenches for the long haul, while we built 'em as if we were camping for a weekend. Took the top brass a while to catch up but we got there in the end. You'll find 'em all like this now. Anyway, here we are. Sergeant!"

They had stopped outside a large dugout with 'RSR' carved into a wooden support beam over the doorway. As the men looked at each other and reflected on what they had just been told, a sergeant appeared with Private Lightfoot who had challenged them earlier, and nodded at the corporal. "Alright Bill thanks, get yourselves a quick cuppa then get back on the hill and wait for the main group. Major Brown's coming up with 'em so make sure the lads are tip top."

"Sarge."

As the pair left the sergeant looked at them, stroking his thick bushy moustache, then he looked at Will and his eyes widened with disbelief.

"Well stone the crows. Davison!"

"Ced!" The two men hugged instantly while the rest of the group stood awkwardly to one side for a moment, but then Archie pushed through and grabbed Ced too.

"Longworthy you old bugger. How did you make Sergeant?"

"Good god almighty. Bunden! How did you make Corporal more like? We all hoped you were dead." He grinned broadly under his moustache.

"In your dreams Longworthy. Someone has to come and run the show."

"I think I'd rather have the Generals. And it's Sergeant Longworthy to you. Who are the rest of your rabble then?"

"Oh, sorry Ced," Will answered, "these are some friends of mine from Steyning who joined up when the Southdowns were formed. All from my football team! That's Danny Boyd. This joker is Tommy Landon, and the carrot top is Owen Entwhistle." They nodded and shook hands with Ced. "And my brother David is here too. Left him behind to wait for the main column." Ced raised his eyes and was about to comment when Archie interrupted.

"Owen sounds local but he's a Welshman so watch your sheep." They laughed as Owen flicked a finger in Archie's direction.

"That explains the red hair then. Well don't worry we have all sorts here. You're all welcome lads," and they felt relaxed in his company at once. Ced then called out to a man nearby. "Nightingale. Take these four to the kitchens and get them some scran. We can sort your billeting out when the main party get here. I'll try and find you a room with a sea view." They laughed again as he continued. "Put your kit in the Sergeant's bunk here for now Will, and then you better come with me to the officer's dugout to report."

They were about to go when Archie's booming voice stopped them.

"Nightingale. I don't believe it." The others frowned for a moment. "It's Bertie Bloody Nightingale. Gladys' lad."

"Oh yes he's a Steyning lad too that's right. Came up just last week with some replacements."

"What you doing here Nightingale? Acting duty telegraph pole or what?"

Bertie blushed as the men stared at him. He had signed up originally in 1914 with Archie and Will and many others, but had failed basic training and since then was on the reserve list. But in 1916 with the call for more troops and the raising of so many new battalions, all the reservists had been put into active service and Bertie was sent overseas with the rest.

Bertie was six foot six tall, but skinny as a bean pole like his diminutive mother, the church organist in Steyning. He was also terribly clumsy and when he first started training he had failed on so many things, and appeared so daft, that Archie nicknamed him *company tree.* Bertie was in essence just a gentle giant and very shy and nervous. He should never have been a soldier, but in wartime personalities and abilities were pushed to one side to satisfy national demands. Unfortunately for Bertie, the effects of the shelling on Archie's nerves had now worn off and he was back to his belligerent best.

"Good to see you again Bertie," Will said and shook his hand, as Ced motioned to him to move the men along.

"Off you go lad."

"Y-yes Sergeant Longworthy, sir."

As they walked off Archie came up alongside him. "So, tell me Private Plank, what they using you for then? Floorboards or roof supports?"

"I d-don't understand A-archie," Bertie replied.

"It's C-c-corporal now, N-n-Nightingale my lad."

"Go easy on the boy Arch," Danny said.

"Alright Boyd. Just wondering what area of the regiment you've *branched* out into is all Nightingale?" Tommy laughed and Owen raised his eyes.

"I d-don't understand Corporal."

"Oh never mind. Just take us to the restaurant and we'll call it quits."

Bertie looked even more confused. "Restaurant? I d-don't know where that is."

"Saints preserve us. Are all the new recruits like you?" Bertie blushed and looked down.

Danny stepped in. "Where can we get some grub lad? Where do we eat?"

"Oh." His face lit up excitedly as he finally had a question he could answer. "Just over there in that concrete dug out. They cook it all underground now."

"Thanks lad," Danny replied with a smile trying to put him at ease. As the four men walked off, Archie patted Bertie on the back. "Hey that's given me an idea. Maybe you should volunteer for the tunnellers. You know. Back to your *roots*." He laughed and walked off.

*

Ced had stayed outside the dugout with Will watching the men walk off. He shook his head disconsolately now. "That lad Nightingale is not alone you know. It doesn't bode well."

"What do you mean Ced?"

"The new recruits coming up. Hardly any basic training and most of them like Nightingale. Nice lads but not cut out for soldiering. Your lot may be locally raised but at least you've had a decent amount of time preparing. Some of these lads have had four weeks at best."

"That's not good." Will agreed then added, "But we were all green as grass when we came over in 1914 and relied on the experienced heads to show us the way."

"That's true Will but in 1914 there were a lot of experienced men to go around. Now the new troops outnumber us about twenty to one! And if there is going to be a major offensive well…" He let the words hang in the air, not wanting to voice the natural conclusion.

"Who else is here that I know?" Will asked.

"Hmm," Ced pondered. "Well Major Brown is 1st battalion commander on seniority. You saw him on the way up. He's been here since the start."

"Yes, I remember him from when we first came to France in 1914."

"Ok, well Major D'Arcy was the 2nd battalion CO for a while but when they had some new officers arrive, he got moved to us due to casualties. They needed more experience here. As I said we are stretched thin. He's back as a company commander for now though, but I don't think he's too happy about it. Straight guy but less experienced than Brown. Other company commander is Captain Wittering. Now he's a proper officer. You know them both right?"

"Yes I do. Must have done something right as they put me up for my DCM."

"Did they indeed, always were a bloody teacher's pet." Ced smiled, as Will looked on awkwardly.

"Not with Dunn I wasn't!"

"Yeh that's true and no mistake!"

"What about the lads. Are any of the old gang still here?"

Ced's smile faded then. "You remember Harris? Sniper like you?"

"Yes, I do. Good shot too."

"Yeh he was, did really well, even better after you left!" He raised an eye at Will then paused looking at his feet. "Got taken out by a sniper he was trailing two days ago. Bastard got a captain the same day too. We thought he'd bagged him which made it worse, but turned out they were working in pairs."

"They often do."

"Maybe. Anyway, Ollie got one. The other got him. Whether he works alone or not, they say this Jerry can't be touched. He's a ghost of a former soldier out for revenge or something the men reckon. Rumour has it he's killed dozens of our blokes. For all I know could be loads of 'em out there but you know what it's like here. Superstitious bastards." Despite sounding as if he wasn't party to any ghost stories, Ced lowered his voice nonetheless. "Got everyone spooked, Will. Even some of the officers. Saying he can't be killed. Calling him the *Phantom*. When we heard you were coming we thought maybe…"

"Well been a while since I shot anything moving Ced. But if I see him, we'll put that name to the test 'eh?"

Ced smiled and patted Will on the arm.

"Who else?"

"Barry Jones is here." Will frowned trying to recall the face. "You know, Franko."

"Oh yes. Another of Archie's splendid nicknames."

"Indeed."

Barry Jones was from Sussex like the rest of the men, but having a large square forehead and wide neck had earnt him the nickname of Frankenstein within an hour of meeting Archie. And *Franko* stuck thereafter.

"Oh, and Paul Lifton is in 'C' company still. You know 'Preacher Paul.'"

"Yes. God bless him! Not many then."

"No lad. But anyway, never mind that, tell me all about you. I got your letter saying you were with this lot now and yet I never thought you would be daft enough to do it."

"Like you say, Ced, they needed experienced men." Will smiled, trying to mask the volcano of emotions that had been erupting inside him ever since he saw the trench lines once more.

"Am sure you could have worked some home-based ticket?"

"Never thought about it really once I was better. Was offered this posting by Sergeant Major Russell and…"

"Don't tell me Russell is here too."

"Ok I won't."

"Oh great, the news just gets better and better. And there was me pleased to see you! But seriously Will, you came back, to a place like this?" He looked around spreading his arms out wide. "Why?"

"Just couldn't stay away I guess."

Ced looked seriously at his old friend. "After all you've been through Will? Why would you?"

"Unfinished business maybe, I don't know. In truth I wasn't sure how I'd feel and now that I'm here I still don't and yet…" Ced raised an eye. "Being back has a familiarity to it that is comforting in some way. Crazy I know."

His friend smiled, understanding the macabre comment. "Maybe. Maybe not lad. I hear a lot of men find it hard to settle when they are wounded and sent back. Or even on leave. Survive here long enough and it starts to feel like home. This war is going to leave its mark on a generation long after it's over I shouldn't wonder."

"Sergeant Longworthy."

The new voice made them both turn round. A man towered above them, standing a few steps in front of a dozen or so soldiers with faces blacked out.

"Oh speak of the devil. Private Jones. You remember Will?"

"Blimey, back from the dead and no mistake. And Sergeant too."

Will laughed. "I'll take that as a '*pleased to see me'* Franko."

"Yes I am Will."

"It's Sergeant Davison now, Franko," Ced reminded him.

"Sorry Will. Sergeant. It is good to see you though." They shook hands while the dark shadowy men behind looked on trying to work out who the new sergeant was; their eyes blinking like torches in a tunnel.

Ced raised his eyes. "What do you want Franko?"

"Sergeant Lovel's compliments sir. Platoon ready to go out."

"Understood. Where is he?"

"Briefing the forward posts Sarge. I had to get the men and join him there."

"Ok. Kit all squared away? Mufflers on?" They all nodded now, as Will noticed for the first time the sun was already melting into the muddy horizon. "Does the Lieutenant know?"

"Not yet sarge."

"I'll tell him then, as we are heading over there shortly. Be careful out there and make sure you say hello to Siegfried on the way out."

"Yes Sergeant."

They moved off and Will raised an eye quizzically. Ced pointed to a spot in the trench wall behind him. He turned and was momentarily shocked to see a skeletal arm sticking out of the side of the trench. Above it on a makeshift wooden shelf, a skull was perched upon which a German pointed helmet sat proudly. There was even a scarf around the neck that drooped down over the wooden plank. Will watched as the men all filed by one at a time either shaking the hand or nodding at the macabre trophy. As the last man passed by into the gloom, they heard him mutter, "See you later Siegfried. Don't wait up."

Will turned and looked at Ced shaking his head.

"As I said Will, superstitious bunch." He rubbed his hands together now against the cool evening air. "Well let's get in here and have a brew up. You can tell me all the news. Welcome home lad."

Will gave a sarcastic laugh as Ced went in the dugout. He glanced back at the wire topped trench behind him, the sky darkening rapidly beyond as if indicating the impending doom to come. The thought of the night patrol stirred something inside of him. Deep rooted. Unsettling. Yet familiar all the same.

"Yep. Home sweet home," he muttered.

Chapter 15 – Old Haunts

Teresa couldn't stop smiling as she watched the kettle finally come to the boil on the old metal stove in the hospital kitchen. She felt Will's note crinkle in her pocket and smiled remembering how she was reading it for the tenth time when he walked into the office area, large as life. She still found it hard to believe he was here again in person, and was overwhelmed with how excited she was to see him. So much so that she had virtually had to run off and make tea to compose herself. *After hugging him to death first of course.*

She looked at him through the gap in the doorway, where he stood chatting to Rose. In one way he seemed very different from the wounded boy that had been evacuated last year, suffering from gas and burns. A sergeant now, and no doubt a very capable leader, he seemed incredibly mature for his age. But in his eyes the young blond lad still lingered, if you knew where to look, and she hoped he would never lose that vulnerability.

Teresa became aware the kettle was whistling loudly and took it off the stove with a cloth. A few moments later she came out with two mugs of tea.

"Oh, that's subtle," said Rose pulling a face.

"I left some in the pot in the kitchen nurse," Teresa replied, flicking her eyes behind her. "I know you have a lot of reports to catch up on before the next rounds."

"Oh of course Staff. Lots…" she said with a knowing look, and then smiled warmly at Will. "It's lovely to finally meet you - standing up." Will grinned and blushed slightly. "You have a look of James you know. I think it's the eyes. Is he well?"

"Last time I saw him he was as dashing as ever."

"He certainly is that. Though he's rubbish at keeping in touch."

"I think it's a family trait." Teresa said handing the tea to Will with a mock frown.

"Oi."

"Well take care Sergeant and I hope to see you again soon. Outside of the hospital." Rose winked as she walked off and Will could see how James would be smitten with her. He turned back to Teresa to see her staring at him while blowing her tea to cool it in a way that made his heart beat faster.

"Hello you," she said, and they both smiled then. "So, to what do I owe this honour?"

"I'm here with one of our Captains for a briefing. Don't know what it's about yet. All a bit hush hush apparently. We had only been up at the front a few days when I was called here."

"Oh, so it's just coincidence then Sergeant. Not a special trip to see me."

"Teresa, I didn't mean…"

"I'm just teasing you. Still the same Will underneath those stripes I see."

"Sorry. It is lovely to see you. I was excited when I heard I was coming to the camp. I can't believe how much it has changed."

"I know proper buildings with running water and sanitation. A half decent hospital at last. Although of course the fact they have built a permanent base doesn't bode well that the war will end anytime soon."

"Yes true. Double edged sword I guess." He looked around before continuing. "You do make good tea. It seems just like yesterday I was sitting here. Although it's much nicer now."

"Felt a lot bloody longer for those of us stuck over here I can tell you," she replied with a short laugh. "And not sure *nice* is the right description, but it is good to see you." She moved and sat next to him then and took his hand. "I got your note. You said you wanted a chat. So am all ears. Tell me everything that has gone on Will."

The next hour passed in the blink of an eye, and Will felt he talked more than he had ever spoken to anyone. He felt so relaxed in Teresa's company and realised just how much he had missed her. Everything fell out in a jumble of memories and nightmares. The journey back to England. The hospital. The dark days at home. The recovery process with Archie. His family and friends. The new battalions and Archie's love life. And of course, Alice. All of which Teresa listened to intently, apart from breaking off for fresh tea and cakes, making just the right comments at the right intervals.

At some point while they chatted Will realised he was in love. He wasn't sure if it was the way she looked or the way she spoke, but something inside of him just felt whole again the moment he saw Teresa. He thought about Alice then, especially having seen her again, but that had been different. They spent so little time together that they didn't really have the chance to get to know each other in a way he had with Teresa. He was blown away with Alice's beauty, and flattered by the attention, but he always felt 'out of his depth' somehow with her. Moreover, deep down he expected to be let down.

Will struggled with that thought, feeling guilty that he didn't really know Alice. For a moment on the train there was a sense that she married out of expectation rather than love, because her status demanded it, and was just as lost as he was. He wondered if she longed to be an ordinary girl, away from all the riches and trappings of her life, or if she was too attached to it now to change. *He would never know.* As he watched Teresa sign off a medical report for one of the junior nurses, one thing was for sure, he loved being with this woman. She had no airs and graces. She just made him feel special in a way he could not put into words. But as she turned to come back to him, he knew he had to say something before he left. Panic gripped him in a way he never felt in the trenches and he blushed terribly, and wondered for a moment if he might faint.

"Are you alright Will? You look very hot. Shall we get some air?"

Will nodded. *Outside would be good, away from distractions,* he thought. "Just a bit run down," he mumbled as she led the way outside.

"Let's have a look at you." She felt his head and then took his wrist lightly in her hand and checked his pulse. He was sure it would be racing. "Hmm you are quite hot. I can check you over properly if you want?"

She meant nothing by it but he blushed again, looking at his feet as Teresa laughed. Out of nowhere a dog had appeared, and he was momentarily startled seeing it there. It pushed against his leg and he took the moment to compose himself.

"Oh hello. What's your name?" He ruffled the dog's ears and it let out a contented grumble. "Boy or girl?" It was hard to tell under the shaggy mop of muddy fur.

"He hasn't got a name yet. Started hanging about the camp a couple of weeks ago but no one's been to claim him. I guess he's just another orphan in this war."

"Collie cross looks like. Black and tan I'd wager under all this mud. Probably from a farm roundabout, though you might be right about not having a home anymore. We will have to get you cleaned up a bit 'eh?"

The dog now whacked the ground with its tail excitedly showering them both in wet muddy splashes.

"Oh, thanks Will. You can have him if you like."

"Can't have a dog at the front sadly. Though I'd like to. Reminds me a bit of our Sal around the eyes. I miss my dog."

"Well if he stays around here I'll get one of the orderlies to get him cleaned up. He's clearly scrounging food from somewhere as he's not starving. But we can hold onto him, until you are ready to adopt him if that pleases you." Will's smile answered the question and she raised her eyes. "Though what the Colonel will say I don't know."

"Thanks Teresa. I'll call him Bert. Albert would have liked that."

"Yes. He would." She touched his arm then, knowing Will was thinking about his friend who was killed the last time he was in France. He looked at her, a deep intensity to his stare, as if he had something very important to say and she took half a step back.

"Look Teresa. I need to tell you something."

"Oh?" She frowned now, looking concerned. "You know you can chat to me about anything Will. I won't judge."

"That's just the thing. You never do, and I love that I feel so comfortable chatting to you. I can't remember ever chatting this much."

"Thank you. I'll take that as a compliment." She smiled then and he plucked up the courage to look her in the eyes and smile back.

"The thing is…" He struggled with the right words.

"Ssh." She put her fingers to her lips. "Enough words." Teresa's face changed, and the world seemed to freeze. In that moment he knew she felt exactly the same. She took his hands then and squeezed them and gently pulled him towards her.

"Here they are!" Rose called out loudly and they sprang apart as if an electric current had passed through them.

"Ah Davison. Good show. HQ waiting for the briefing so we have to go. Everything ok?"

"Er, yes sir," Will stuttered, looking wide eyed.

"It was very stuffy in there and I needed a cigarette," Teresa said with a disarming smile that deflected the mood instantly.

"Quite right Staff. Get your breaks where you can. Captain Fennell at your service." He saluted politely and then, nodding at Rose, walked off round the outside of the building. The two nurses curtsied, then looked at Will as he made to follow, both of them expecting him to say something.

"I'll try and call back after if I have time. Was lovely to see you again."

"You too Will. Take care of yourself won't you."

"Of course I will."

"I miss you too," Rose teased.

Will hesitated then, embarrassed, looking sorry, and then the captain paused half way along the side of the hospital building and let out a polite cough.

"I'm just teasing," Rose said smiling.

"You better go," Teresa added, nodding at the captain.

"Yes," said Will, then suddenly he took two steps back to her and kissed her softly on the cheek, and for a moment squeezed her side, looking right in her eyes.

She looked flustered briefly, then her eyes smiled and she whispered, "I know."

Will grinned and marched off after the captain.

*

They paced in silence towards the HQ building, where two soldiers saluted the captain as they passed, coming to attention on the top of the steps by the entrance. Inside they were ushered by a clerk towards a meeting room on the first floor, with open double doors, through which they could see several officers were sitting around a large oval table. Fennell stopped Will briefly as they approached.

"The man at the head of the table is General Worthing. Not entirely sure what this is about but someone has asked for you, so let's just see what it is 'eh and if it gets sticky let me do the talking." He smiled reassuringly.

Will nodded, happy to follow his officer's lead, the emotions of the last hour clashing with the nerves of the meeting that grew with every step, and he began to feel faint again.

"Oh, and Davison."

"Sir?"

"My sister's a nurse too, back home in England. Top girl. You can't go wrong there." Will looked stunned as the captain grinned even wider and beckoned him forward.

As they entered the room, Will recognised Major Bluffington-Sykes sitting at one end of the table where a clerk was writing some notes down. The major was laughing and joking with another officer who had his back turned to them looking out of the window.

"Ah Captain Fennell. Right on time. Take a seat then, and let's get started. There's sherry on the side if you fancy a tot. You have Davison with you I see?"

"Yes sir."

Will saluted, terrified, and the general nodded back. At the sound of his name Bluffington-Sykes looked up and also nodded curtly at Will. Will realised then that even the clerk was a lieutenant, and he was the only one there not commissioned. He tried to smile back at the major attempting to feel at ease, but he looked away. The last time he had seen Marshall Bluffington-Sykes was at the court martial for one of his friends, Ernie Isaacs, who was tried for cowardice having suffered a breakdown. He had been saved by the last-minute intervention of his brother's friend, Harry Johnson.

"Well let's crack on with item five on the agenda gentlemen," the general said, taking a monocle out of his breast pocket and glancing at the paper in front of him. "This bloody sniping business. Bad for morale and all that what?"

"Bad for your health too sir," a colonel said, sitting to the general's right, and a couple of the other officers laughed.

"What? Oh quite," Worthing commented with the briefest of smiles. "Anyway, we have a chap here from HQ intelligence who will tell us all about it, and his plan more importantly to sort it out. Which I'm guessing involves you, young man," he continued, looking sternly at Will.

General Worthing was completely bald but had thick grey sideburns that ran like river tributaries down each side of his face, into the large unkempt estuary of a beard that hung several inches below his chin. His eyebrows were so bushy they almost covered his eyes when he frowned, which made his whole appearance very unsettling quite apart from his well-documented fearsome temper.

Will had no idea what was going on, and as it was impossible to judge the general's mood, he just tried to keep his expression neutral and nodded, hoping that was the right answer. The general seemed happy with this and turned to the officer standing by the window.

"Johnson. The floor is yours," and with a dazzling smile, Major Harry Johnson stepped up to the table.

*

Rose and Teresa stood in silence for a minute watching the two men march off.

"Shall I buy a hat then?" Rose said, to break the silence.

"What? Oh shut your face Rose, you're a one to talk."

"Hey we could have a double wedding how about that?

"Right. Like that's going to happen. It's hard enough getting any work done round here as it is with you swooning about, without any more fuss."

"So, you don't like him at all then?"

"I didn't say that Rose," she said with a mischievous grin.

"Will was telling me he has another brother here with him, up at the front."

"Yes he said."

"So, if we introduce him to one of the lasses we can split the costs three ways."

"Ha Ha, trust you Rose. Who said I want to be related to you anyway?"

"Yes, there's a sobering thought. There's always the Captain. He certainly caused a stir walking through here. You can always trade up. Bag yourself a Captain like me."

"He was quite the picture. I do wonder if the Sussex pick men just on looks alone."

"See." Rose grinned, and tossed Teresa a cigarette.

"You're trouble with a capital T, Kellett. I think I can manage just fine without your help."

"Suit yourself."

"I will indeed," but inside Teresa's heart still pounded against her chest. "I think medicinal brandy is in order nurse."

"Now that's an order I will never dispute Staff!" They laughed then and linked arms walking back inside.

*

"So, to conclude General, we need this so called 'Phantom' taken out and I believe the Sergeant there is capable of doing it." Harry leaned back in his seat as the officers looked about at each other. He caught Will's eye and nodded.

"Thank you Johnson," Worthing replied. "Thoughts gentlemen?"

"Seems a lot of fuss over a handful of deaths Major." It was the colonel who Will didn't know, that spoke up first. "There are snipers up and down the lines; I don't see why this one is any different frankly."

"The casualties are one thing Colonel Hargreaves. Compared to open warfare they are insignificant, granted, but the effect on morale is entirely different. The fact we've heard about it back at base camp from numerous sources suggests this is becoming an issue, and we need to stop it causing real panic. One only has to look at Verdun."

The colonel raised an eyebrow questioningly at Harry's reply.

"Good point Jonners," Bluffington-Sykes intervened, "The French are deserting in droves due to poor morale. Once one lot cracked they're folding like cards. Morale is as important on the front as bullets these days." There were noises of ascent around the table.

Colonel Hargreaves snorted and walked over to the side table. “I hardly think we can compare French morale to our own British standards gentlemen,” he said, refilling his sherry as he did so. “Hardly made of the same stock what?”

The general cleared his throat which no one was able to interpret as agreeing or disagreeing.

“Respectfully sir, given their casualty rates, lack of reinforcements and supplies, I am surprised they haven’t cracked sooner. I don’t think it’s a question of courage.”

The colonel looked coldly at Harry over his narrow-rimmed spectacles, saying nothing, and simply sipped his sherry as he returned to the table. The general now spoke up again.

“Which is precisely why we are about to launch a new front, to aid our beleaguered allies is it not? Though I very much doubt the wisdom in it, given our own precarious situation in many sectors. Still not our job to play politics. I’ll have enough of that when I retire I daresay.” He smiled and several of the officers humoured him by smiling back. “But for now, someone else is making the policies and it’s our job to carry them through. And we can’t do that with our men scared of their own shadows.”

The colonel went to protest again but the general raised a hand and continued. “Even worse if the French get wind of the fact there’s a phantom sniper destroying British troops. Makes us look bad, and might just set the rest of those damned Frenchies galloping back to Paris leaving us surrounded. Hmm?”

“Quite right sir,” Bluffington-Sykes said, “don’t you agree Colonel?”

“General has a point about the French,” Hargreaves replied begrudgingly, and nodded to the general as if to acknowledge it. “We don’t want to be blamed for their failures. So, what about the Sergeant here then? Tell us about him.” Hargreaves was keen to try and move the conversation on, and focus on someone else. “Can he sort this out quickly?”

“I think Sergeant Davison is quite capable of speaking for himself, but from what I’ve heard he’s the best shot in his battalion.” Harry looked at Captain Fennell who leant forward and continued.

“General Worthing sir. Not just his battalion. Sergeant Davison is widely held by his own officers and NCOs to be the best shot in the whole of the Sussex. He’s a decorated veteran and I’m sure he would rise to the challenge, am I right Sergeant?”

The room went quiet and all eyes turned to look at Will. There was a mixture of support and doubt in the pairs of eyes that now surveyed him. Will saw Worthing take out his monocle and raise an eyebrow expectedly.

He cleared his throat, taking a sip of water in front of himself to gather his thoughts.

"General. I don't believe in ghosts. But I do understand the effect of morale on the lads, I mean the troops, that an experienced sniper can cause. This particular one, if it is the same man, shot a friend of mine Corporal Harris, an experienced sniper himself, just two days ago. He's clearly very good and I think he's a lone wolf which makes it harder to stop."

"Are we supposed to understand what that means?" The colonel said irritably.

"Sorry sir. I mean he probably isn't under any restrictions and will work alone. Free from any unit. German snipers tend to be attached to an area not a unit so they learn it inch by inch, which gives them the edge over us."

"Are you saying he's a better shot than you Sergeant?"

"No sir I just mean…"

"I understand what he means General," Fennell interjected. "Our snipers are attached to their regiments and if the regiment moves so do they. This means every few weeks a new group has to settle in and learn the area. Whereas Jerry leaves his men in place and that way they understand the terrain better."

"The Captain is quite right," Harry said in support.

"Well that's easily changed. Detail this man to stay in this sector until it's done, even if his battalion moves out. Is that clear? And that includes him being excused any patrol duties. He focuses solely on this so-called *Phantom*."

"Sir, with respect I am happy to do my usual duties as well. I don't want to be given special privileges."

"I think we have just established this is vital to the war effort in this sector, so the last thing we need is you getting shot on some dumb fool night patrol Davison."

Will blushed but Harry came to his rescue again. "No one doubts your willingness to fight Sergeant. You've proved that many times already. And I don't think anyone can accuse you of shirking if you are going to be lying out in No Man's Land for days on end with someone trying to kill you."

"Quite right Jonners," Marshall said, forgetting the protocol in his willingness to add support.

"Good, that's settled then. Unless there are any further questions, you can go Captain Fennell. I suggest we have a short break for lunch. I've ordered some additional luxuries as it was Easter Sunday just gone and I believe the Pastor will be joining us for some prayers. Seemed appropriate?" The officers nodded as much in anticipation of the lunch as the prayers. "Good-oh. Then we'll move onto item six, which I believe is the issue with the cavalry. Is that right Colonel?"

"Yes sir, and the proposed use of these new-fangled monstrosities called *Tanks*." Several of the other officers raised their eyes at this.

"Right. I read your report and…" The general paused, noticing Will and the captain were in discussion.

"Is there something else Captain? Otherwise I said you can go and take your man with you. The clerk will sort the orders today."

"Sir we do have one more question." He looked at Will.

"General, it's just that normally on a particular mission like this, we would work in pairs. Jerry always does. One spots and one shoots sir. Then you rotate to keep fresh, especially if you are working out of the trench for hours on end."

"I see and do you have someone in mind?"

"No sir, I'd have said Harris but…"

"But he's dead. Dashed inconvenient what?" Hargreaves said smiling coldly.

"I'm sure we would all have hoped he succeeded Colonel," the general said. "So, is there anyone else? This is frankly a battalion matter isn't it?" He looked at his pocket watch, clearly eager for lunch now and not wanting to be delayed by the detail.

"Actually sir, there is someone that might just fit the bill." Harry spoke up now. "You recall the young lad we spoke about earlier from Luxembourg?"

The general frowned and then said, "What that Wagner chap?"

"Yes sir, Joseph Wagner. He's apparently a crack shot too, like our sergeant here. Escaped the clutches of Jerry when they invaded and got picked up by one of our patrols at Christmas, in fourteen, wanting to enlist. They passed him onto the French where he was attached for several months until I came across his file citing the fact he had shot over twenty Germans, or so they claimed."

"Name like Wagner, how do we know he's not a spy?" Colonel Hargreaves added. "Might just shoot our lad in the back first chance he gets."

"We debriefed him thoroughly in case he was a spy, sir, and I'm satisfied his story checks out. He's very young too. Only eighteen. He's done pretty well for us as an interpreter, particularly decoding some of the Jerry transmissions. I'm not keen to let him go but seems to me he might be just the right fit for the job."

"Well if you're convinced Johnson that's good enough for me. I have my doubts about the numbers, given his age, and especially as the French are prone to exaggerate all their triumphs; but frankly I don't care who you use as long as you get it done. Anything else?"

It was a rhetorical question and Harry shook his head, as did Captain Fennell. They all stood together then and replacing their hats, saluted and walked out. As they walked down the corridor a number of servants walked in the opposite direction pushing trolley loads of freshly cooked meats, fish, and bowls of fruit as well as a large quantity of wine and spirits.

I doubt the lads will be having quite the same thing at the front, Will thought. Then it dawned on him that Easter had come and gone during their movements without him even realising it. Such a big thing at home, and he knew there were a lot of services held at the front still. But if you were marching or fighting, you just had to hope God would understand and say your prayers for forgiveness when you stopped to draw breath. *If indeed you did still draw breath.* Will was sure his Mum would have put in a good word for him regardless, and felt a strong yearning to be home enjoying a slice of her delicious Simnel cake by the fire.

"I assume you want to stay for lunch Major? Don't walk out on our account."

"That's okay Steven; I'm rather particular about whose company I dine in. Prone to lose my appetite if I stay there." Harry smiled and the captain nodded. "Besides I have young Joe with me and I think it's time you and him became acquainted Will."

"I take it you two know each other then?" Fennell asked looking at Will.

"Oh yes. Well actually his older brother is a dear friend of mine. Guards officer down on the Somme."

"An officer?" Fennell looked at Will. "You continue to surprise me Sergeant!"

Will looked at them both unsure what to say, but then Bluffington-Sykes popped out of the meeting room for a moment, speaking in hushed tones.

"Are you deserting me Jonners?"

"'Fraid so Bluffers old boy. Despite the spread. Work to do and all that. Catch up later for a tot though?"

"Absolutely old man. Will need it by then. Once the General hits the sauce these meetings are liable to go on for hours. He fell asleep in one once and we all had to sit around for an hour waiting for him to wake up and continue!"

Harry grinned, then motioned over his shoulder with his eyes to where Will stood pretending not to hear.

"Hmm right. Best get back." Marshall raised his voice slightly. "And good luck to you Davison. Blag the blighter won't you?"

"Do my best sir."

"Splendid." With that he hurried back to the room.

Harry turned back to them then. "Right gentlemen. Let's go and meet young Wagner."

Chapter 16 – Boxes, books and bandages

Harry Johnson led the way to the small spiral staircase at the back of the old library building that was now serving as the logistics base for the Second Army Division in this sector. Here and there along the walls of the ground floor several tall bookcases remained, now full of files and reports for incidents and demands across the region. Will wondered where the original books were now housed, if anywhere at all, given there was a hole in the roof where a shell had apparently landed in last year's fighting, taking the front porch with it. The front of the building was now shored up with a make shift wooden wall and a sand bagged entrance.

Harry must have read Will's mind and paused by the stairs.

"This library apparently housed manuscripts going back to the 11th century. Medieval books carefully copied by the monks in the region, and all sorts of tithe scrolls documenting the comings and goings of the people in the area for generations. Explains the wonderful carvings on the walls outside. Those that haven't been shot off of course."

The three men stopped and stared at the bustle of military activity in this two storey building, sharing a moment of due deference. As if they all expected a monk to suddenly appear carrying a weighty tome and tell the soldiers to "shush."

"Miraculously it was hit by two huge shells, the first of which crashed through the roof but didn't go off," Harry continued. "The second one did explode, and threatened to send the whole place up in flames, but the impact of the first shell caused the porch and the upstairs balcony to collapse, and they smothered most of the blast."

"Quite a miracle indeed. Unless you were enjoying the view from the upstairs balcony with a brandy of course," Captain Fennell quipped.

"Quite," said Harry, now proceeding up the spiral staircase with a broad smile. "Anyway, this way."

"What happened to all the books and stuff sir?" Will asked as they unwound at the top of the stone steps and walked along the upper corridor.

"Good question. Rumour has it some sharp eyed Frenchies smuggled them away but they are blaming Jerry of course, and if the Mayor knows anything he's playing dumb. They weren't here when the support companies moved in that's for certain."

"No doubt someone's library will be very impressive after this is all over," Fennell remarked with a raise of his eyes.

Harry paused with his hand on an ornate brass handled door. "If they live to enjoy it that is! Come in."

They walked into an ante room off the main corridor which contained a wooden table with two carved high-backed chairs either side of an oval window with a rapidly decaying frame. There were a number of papers on the table, and nearby a second smaller table had the remains of some refreshments scattered across them. A brightly decorated jug of water and some pieces of fruit surrounded a plate where crumbs suggested something tastier had been devoured first. In the corner was an ornate chaise lounge sofa which was very much in keeping with the historic tone of the house; but seemed absurd somehow to Will in the middle of the mud and bullets. As they entered, a young boy, who had been sitting on the chaise lounge, jumped to his feet and stood awkwardly facing the three men.

"Gentlemen this is Joseph Wagner, our volunteer from Luxembourg. Joe, this is Captain Fennell of the Royal Sussex Regiment, Southdown battalions, and this is the man I was telling you about. Our own renowned sniper, Sergeant Davison."

The captain and Will paused for a moment both thrown by how youthful this boy looked. His records stated he was eighteen and apparently a crack shot, but in any other time or place he could have passed for fourteen at most. He reminded Will more of Fred than any of the eighteen year old soldiers he knew in his company. A bob of brown hair surrounded an oval, slightly plumpish face, and the civilian clothing made him look anything but a soldier. What struck Will the most though were his eyes. Hazel green eyes, bright and clear, with a sharpness about them that belied his age. In his eyes Will saw the experience, saw the troubled past, saw the man.

"Captain Fennell at your service. You will be attached to my company in the 12th Sussex, and we will sort you out a uniform and whatnot." He looked at Harry questioning the boy's appearance. "But you will be working outside the normal boundaries as it were, with the Sergeant here." He put out his hand and Joe shook it.

"Thank you Captain. I will do my best to follow your orders as you see fit."

His English surprised them both, and Harry smiled seeing the same effects on them that Joe had had on him when they first met.

"Joe did have French kit, Steven, but seemed appropriate to get him into something more suited given his transfer to your lot," Harry now advised, picking up on the earlier unspoken question. "I am sure you can furnish him with what he needs from stores. He may need a rifle too so perhaps Davison can sort that with him." He looked at Will now, and he stepped forward as the captain nodded in agreement.

"Hello Joe. Good to meet you." They shook hands too. "There are a number of spare rifles down at the stores I'm told, so I'm sure we can find you something you like."

Joe smiled in appreciation then spoke up. "Actually, I have father's rifle with me. I prefer to use if possible. Is that okay?" Will still felt uneasy about the boys' youthful appearance, made even more pronounced by his high-pitched voice as if he hadn't even reached puberty. Something didn't quite fit in his mind but orders were orders, and if Harry Johnson vouched for him then that was good enough.

"Yes of course it is," Will said, making his face as neutral as he could.

"Well I'm sure you two will be able to catch up properly over the next few days. Let's face it you are going to be spending a lot of time together so best get cracking," Harry remarked. "I'll leave them with you Steven."

Will was clearly still looking thrown by Joe's appearance because he spoke up then.

"Perhaps we will sort the problem out quickly, and the Sergeant will not have to, what is it you say, baby sit me for too long?"

Will felt embarrassed his worries had clearly been read by the boy, as the officers shared a laugh.

"That's the spirit," Captain Fennell said jovially, "though you're welcome here Joe. And I fear you may have a lot more work ahead of you." He reached for the door when there was an urgent knock on it.

"Come in."

An orderly appeared. "Beggin' your pardon sir. Urgent message for Major Johnson."

"Thanks Philips." Harry took the note as the others hesitated by the door. Will used the moment to reach out to Joe, and spoke quietly as Harry read the dispatch.

"I'm Will, but once we get you kitted out you better call me Sergeant like the rest." He smiled and he could sense Joe relax. "But the Captain is right; we need all the specialist help we can get in this war. I've got a couple of lads younger than you in my platoon but most of them are buried under beards and dirt, and it's always a surprise to see what normal people should look like at your age. I didn't mean to stare."

"I understand Sergeant. I am used to it. If you had seen me last year by Verdun you would not have given two looks in my direction I think."

"Is it as bad there as they say?"

Joe was going to answer when Harry spoke up. "Troubling news I'm afraid gentlemen so I best inform the General straight away. I suggest you get going before the proverbial starts flying about." He raised his eyes.

"What's going on Harry," Fennell asked concerned.

"Ireland," he replied, the cheery disposition for once missing. "Seems the rebels have risen up against British rule in Dublin over Easter and grabbed control of the city. Taken advantage of the focus being on France no doubt, and the lack of troops probably. Reports of fighting in the streets no less."

"Bloody hell," Fennell said, then looked slightly sheepish remembering the others in the room. "Is it spreading?"

"Don't know yet but I'm ordered back to base, and to let the General know to be on alert. It's going to ruin his apple pie."

"Alert? Over here? We won't be called back surely?"

"No, nothing like that. I'm sure there's enough local troops to handle it. But we do have a large number of Irish regiments with us and within their ranks there will be those with strong feelings for and against British rule, given a spark. So we need to make sure this doesn't spread here as much as there. Get back to the front Captain and get these lads to work."

His formal tone snapped Fennell out of his initial shock and he shook Harry's hand and walked out. Joe followed; and as Will went to leave, Harry touched his arm.

"Watch yourself out there Will. From all the reports I have this *Phantom* is no ghost, but what we do know is that he's bloody good at what he does. And that's kill people. Looks like I've got other things to focus on now, but I'll still keep one eye on what's happening here and if I can help at all, just ask." He patted Will on the shoulder.

Seeing the other two were out of ear shot, Will smiled and said, "Thanks Jonners. Say hello to James."

Harry laughed. "You Davisons are all the same. No respect for your betters. Now go and get the bastard."

*

James watched the sun setting from the entrance to the barn. The stunning combination of reds and oranges spread across the sky like dabs on an artist's palette, waiting for their master to conjure them into something permanently beautiful. *Nothing seems to last long here, no matter how wonderful*, James reflected, and tried to commit this sky to memory, before the darkness came again to smudge it. He thought then of the top fields at home, and the many skies he'd seen sitting by the standing stones. Sadness tugged at his sleeve, demanding to be let in, but was pushed back in an instant when Rose slipped her hand in his.

"Hello Captain, penny for your thoughts," she said, smiling warmly, and the sun burst within him again.

He smiled without answering immediately, instinct making him look about the barn, but everywhere the men were just busy inside their own personal worlds. Rose had been careful to ensure no one was watching, so he took her in his arms holding her tight, as if the very act of doing so would ensure she stayed there forever.

"Someone's missed me I see. I should think so too." She grinned mischievously and then they kissed briefly, aware of their surroundings.

The Guards had been in action for three days in a row, and in response to a request for more immediate and substantial medical treatment near the front Colonel Hamilton had come up himself to view the facilities. James' commanding officer, Colonel Fanshaw had impressed on HQ how many men they were losing en route to the main dressing stations for want of simple treatments at the front lines. Gangrene, blood poisoning, and just loss of blood were all taking their toll through a lack of adequate medicines and bandages. More galling was that many casualties were dying from broken bones due to a lack of proper stretchers. Men were carried across No Man's Land and longer distances over broken terrain, either over their comrades' backs or on makeshift crates or blankets strung on poles that jarred the breaks terribly and caused further injuries that quickly became fatal.

The helplessness of it was beginning to wear on them all. Within minutes of being there Hamilton agreed, and sent back for a medical team to come and work with him for a few days and bring an urgent requisition of supplies.

The subsequent sight of a consignment of thirty stretchers being unloaded at the dressing station caused the local medical officer to weep. Hamilton uncharacteristically put an arm round him and led the medic gently to one side, appreciating the appalling conditions he was being asked to work in. James had been watching this discreetly from the side of the tent, when he saw Rose walk in with three other nurses to assist the current wounded. When Hamilton sent back for volunteers she had been on the truck almost before the request had been read out.

James had then endured a frustrating stint at the front, for eight hours, organising the defences and listening parties in case of further attacks. But finally he was able to get some downtime, and moved back to the reserve area where the exhausted men rested in barns and under canvas, as rain threatened in the night sky once more. Here surrounded by his soldiers he got to catch up with Rose at last, and while they would have no privacy, the mere sight of her alone was enough to make him feel human again.

He laid his coat on some of the damp straw in one of the animal stalls and they sat sharing a cigarette together, careful not to let the sparks fall onto the floor.

"You shouldn't have come up here you know, it's too dangerous."

"Oh stuff and nonsense. I'm just as likely to get blown up back at base as I am here with Jerry's long range guns these days. Not to mention their airplanes dropping presents randomly on any target they see. We've had more than one dressing station bombed despite the red crosses on the roof."

"Bastards. Where's the honour in that?" He shook his head and she made a disgruntled snort.

"I don't see much honour anywhere Jamie." He thought about that for a moment, something that he had imagined many times before. Dying heroically. He dreaded just wasting away in No Man's Land somewhere, never to be found again, and shivered spontaneously. *Not me, I'm going out all guns blazing,* he thought, then realised she was looking at him puzzled. He moved closer smelling her warmth.

"Even so the chances of you being hurt are far greater here," he continued, ignoring his own demons.

"Would you rather I hadn't come?"

"No of course not, I love seeing you." He squeezed her free hand tightly. "But if anything were to happen to you I'd never forgive myself."

"Oh and I suppose you think I don't worry a jot about you at the front day after day, and just get on with daily life as if I'm back in England?"

He frowned then, concerned about the worry he was causing her. Rose laid a hand gently on his battle-weary face and stroked it softly. "Look Jamie my love, we both know the score here. It's war, and people die every day. You can either dwell on it or live life to the full while you can, and give thanks to God at the end of every day that it wasn't your turn. We see precious little of each other as it is, so let's not spend it worrying about what might be, and focus on what is."

James nodded in agreement and put out his cigarette on the stone wall next to him.

"And right now, what I am focusing on is the fact I haven't had a decent kiss in weeks," Rose continued with a cheeky pout of her lips, and James laughed.

A young female head appeared at just that moment over the top of the stall.

"Ah there you are Rose. Colonel is asking for us all to get back to the dressing station. He wants to get a number of the wounded men ready to be moved back with the trucks under cover of darkness. I'm going back with Sal. I said you would probably be happy to stay another day." The nurse grinned now as Rose nodded. "See you in a jiffy then."

"I'll be there shortly Henny," Rose said at the disappearing face, and then looked at James with a resigned smile. "No rest for the wicked."

"In that case I'm surprised you get any rest at all nurse," James said with a wink, and pulled her to him. "Now about that missing kiss…"

Chapter 17 – In the name of the father

Captain Fennell popped his head into Will's dugout without warning. "Good morning gentlemen," he said, smiling into the gloomy interior and doing his best not to react to the overpowering human odour that greeted him from the dozen inhabitants within. He pulled the makeshift door open fully, and taking a deep breath from the outside air stepped inside; beckoning the soldier with him to do likewise.

"Stand up," was all Will could think to shout in the moment, and chaos ensued as the men spilled out of bunks and chairs. Fennell smiled and put up his hands to tell them to relax.

"That's fine. Relax gentlemen. This is Private Joseph Wagner who I briefed the NCOs about last night. Volunteer from Luxembourg. He's a crack shot and God knows we always need more of those." He looked at Will knowing he would look after him. "I'll leave him with you Sergeant. Make him welcome and get his kit squared away somewhere. When he's settled in find the Sergeant Major and get your briefing. Time we put jerry on the back foot what?"

"Yes sir. Of course, sir."

Fennell walked out and Joseph looked nervously at the mud stained faces around the dugout.

"I am…Joe." He tried a smile but no one moved.

"Wagner? That's German isn't it?" Archie said suspiciously, and there were some murmurings of discontent from the group.

"It is common in Luxembourg."

"Not sure that answers the question. Are you on the right side Jerry?"

"I am not German, I'm…"

"We heard you the first time boyo. Wherever the hell luxelburger is," Owen added looking equally distrustful.

"Luxembourg. It's squashed between France, Belgium and Germany. Was overrun in the first few weeks of the war," Ced answered, not that Archie was interested in where it actually was. "It's been occupied by Jerry ever since," he added unhelpfully, which caused all the men to now look at Joe.

"Doesn't matter where it is," Will said sensing the tension growing in the room. "He can bunk over there with you Danny. And I expect him to be made to feel at home or you will have me to answer to."

"Great," was all Danny said then looking at Joe. "Stick your kit underneath that pit. There's not much room so watch your head. And you better not snore louder than the Corporal there, wherever the hell you come from." Will pushed him forward but Joe paused half way across the room and turned to look at the stony faces eyeing him suspiciously.

"It's true the German army is in our country. They came in large numbers one night. They said they just move through to France but they stay. We had no real army. No chance. What could our government do?" No one spoke and all he saw was suspicion in the eyes around him. "My father was mayor of small town in north where I am from. He protested and they took him. My older brother too. To labour camp they said. We have heard nothing since." Some of the men looked at each other now but Archie was unconvinced.

"How come you speak English so good, Herr Wagner?" he asked in a mock German tone.

"My mother is school teacher back home. She taught me and my brother. Wanted us to be teachers too but the war has stopped that." His voice wavered now with emotion and seemed even higher pitched than normal.

"So, what you doing here then young 'un," Danny asked sitting down now and lighting a cigarette.

"My father taught us to shoot. When they were taken I wanted to fight. I left home and travelled across country until I came across an English base."

"Don't look old enough to shave, never mind shoot. Your mum had the right idea kid. Lots of us not doing what we wanted to here." Danny smiled now and Ced came over.

"Well that's fine by me sonny, I'm Ced. Or Corporal Longworthy when the brass are about. Let me introduce you to the lads."

Will sighed with relief but then Archie moved over to speak to him. "What if he's a spy Will?"

"I hardly think they would bother…" Will paused, and looked at his friend and understood the concerns. He changed his tone. "I don't think so Bunny. HQ is pretty tight on this and he's been well vetted. You can never say never I guess, with countries supporting both sides, but let's give the young lad the benefit of the doubt eh?"

He noticed then that Tommy had sneaked into the dugout following the Captain's departure and was loitering at the back while the discussions about Joe went on. "And as for you Private. I didn't put you outside on watch to record the flora and fauna. Next time you see an officer coming, you bloody well give us a head's up. Got it?"

"Sarge." Was all Tommy could say feeling suitably sheepish. He had been enjoying a brew with some of the men in the next dugout and the captain had flashed past with Wagner in tow before he could react.

"Right well we won't say any more about it." He looked at Archie now, still scowling at Wagner. "I don't think we have to worry about spies in the camp Corporal. If they try to watch the likes of Landon here they will end up more confused than the rest of us."

Archie smiled then and the men laughed. "I'm going to check along the lines then report to the Sergeant Major. Make sure your kits are sorted out. We start patrols again from tonight, and the word is we are going out in strength so get your minds back on what's important, in case our company is picked." Without waiting for an answer, he pushed out through the makeshift door leaving the tension in the room.

Someone muttered "Bloody well bound to be us, always is," and there were noises of ascent from the gloomy edges of the hole, as most of the men forgot about Joe and just went back to their daily routines.

Owen saw Joe now take out his rifle from a long cover and begin to check it. It was not like anything he had seen before, and had a very long scope that he laid on the bunk next to it.

"What sort of rifle is that then boyo?"

"A Mauser. It was my father's."

A number of men gathered round now to look at it.

"So, you've shot twenty Germans is it?" Owen continued. "You don't look old enough."

"Twenty-four I think, being exact," Joe replied, without looking up from what he was doing. He said it like he was answering a question in school.

"How old are you lad?" Ced asked.

"I was eighteen last month."

Danny let out a low whistle.

"Our Sergeant said they have nicknamed you the *ice man*, because you never miss. Is that right?"

Someone muttered, "Nobody's that good. Especially at his age. Bet he's making it up."

"Will said it's true," Danny answered. "Is it? Joe?"

Joe just shrugged and looked up. “I don’t think about missing when I shoot.”

The men all paused at this comment and the room became solemn once more. Then Archie spoke up from where he was standing near the door, a cigarette in the corner of his mouth.

“Ice man. Hah! Looks about twelve. More like Jack Frost.”

The men laughed.

“My name is not Jack, it is Joe.”

“Look sunshine if I say it’s Jack Frost, then Jack Frost it is right?”

“If Bunny gives you a nickname that’s the end of the matter boyo.” Owen confirmed.

Joe frowned.

“Could be a lot worse Frosty trust me,” Danny added, and the men now visibly relaxed and went back to sorting their kit. “Sort your kit out young ‘un and we’ll have a brew up.”

Tommy piped up. “How can he be Jack Frost and Sunshine? That wouldn’t work Archie.”

“Stone me Landon. If you get any more intelligent you will be taken to HQ. How can we compete with brains like these lads?” The men laughed out loud now.

Tommy looked pleased and said “Thanks Corp,” which made the men laugh even more.

“Here,” Archie threw his boots at Tommy. “There’s your prize for coming top of the idiots test. Clean those.”

*

Major Rupert Brown of the Royal Sussex Regiment, sat at the desk in his dugout looking at a copy of Moby Dick, by Herman Melville. He moved his thumb over the title words on the frayed cover as if trying to imbibe the very words within through his action. As he flicked through the book, he noticed a number of the pages were quite worn from a combination of being read many times over, and the lack of anywhere decent to keep it. He sighed, and longed in that moment to be back home in Arundel, sitting in the library with his hounds for company; or watching them bound along the river banks in the shadow of the great medieval castle. He looked at the wooden walls surrounding his seat, keeping back the dirt, a far cry from the light, high-ceilinged rooms of their town house. Above all else he wanted to be back with his family, before the nightly terrors of his dreams, and the horrors that each new dawn seemed to bring. Back before this accursed war.

Rupert read the letter from his wife again, itself tatty and torn from being passed from pillar to post in order to reach him. A letter advising him of the death of their only beloved son Oswald, several weeks ago now, 'peacefully in his sleep.' *Peacefully? With half his body burnt and broken?* The funeral already done and dusted and his son's life ended tragically early…*While he marched up and down this stupid patch of ground. And for what?*

He shook his head at the irony of the fact his son wanted to be a pilot, after hearing from him how horrible it was for the men to be cooped up in little dugouts like ready-made coffins. *And now that's where he was anyway. Never to come out again.*

Angry tears fell onto the letter and Rupert wiped them away with the bandages he had taken off his wounded arm, and laid the note aside. He opened the book to where his son had signed it, and remembered the day in 1914 when they came to see him off to war at the station. The bands. The cheers. The laughter. He glanced down…

To Father. As you embark on this great adventure of your own, take the first book you read to me, and keep it safe until you return. May the Lord guide your arm and keep your aim true as you hunt the big white bloated whale - the Kaiser! Fondest regards. Ossie.

A lump formed in his throat, as Rupert glanced underneath where his son had signed the book anew, at his own faded words from when he first purchased it.

To our little soldier, Oswald. On the occasion of your tenth birthday. March 15th, 1908. May the Lord guide you on your path in life and always bring you safely home to port. Your loving parents xx

He snapped the book shut. "Orderly!"

Corporal Day appeared immediately and frowned seeing the streaks of wet across his officer's normally granite-like face. To the men of the 1st battalion Major Brown was a hard taskmaster, firm but fair, but never known for humour or warmth. He had made himself that way after the first few bitter months in 1914, when the early defeats made it obvious this would not be the short war the politicians had promised.

Rupert had made a private pledge to put his home and hearth in the ornamental box with the treasured possessions from his wife and son, given to him when he boarded the train at Arundel station on a gloriously sunny day in 1914. As time passed the box was opened less and less and until today it had not been opened in 1916 at all. *Survive at all costs and then go home and let his old life out once more.* That was his mantra. But fate delighted in disappointment, and now that dream was gone.

"Advise Captain Wittering I want to go out on the reconnaissance operation tonight. Jerry's been probing us for days so chances are we might run into trouble and I think we need as much experience as we can get."

"Yes sir. Beggin' your pardon sir, but how's the arm?"

Rupert glanced briefly at the scars on his right arm where the barbed wire had torn into it last month after they were surprised on a night march. Some of the lacerations were still healing, and one even weeped blood from the force with which he had pulled the bandages off. Now he focused on it, the pain and stiffness returned and with it his anger.

He still blamed himself for the loss of life in the brief skirmish that had followed the sudden flare, illuminating his men like frightened rabbits. *Just hiding there waiting for us. No rules anymore. A different kind of war, and one he didn't like.* He recalled diving for cover and becoming impaled on their own wire, and would have been killed or captured for sure but for the bravery of two of his men coming back to drag him to safety. He rubbed the arm gently now reflecting on how they had literally had to tear him off the wire to save him, and the agony that followed. Of course, there was no blame attached, but he would not make the same mistake again. *He would not make any mistakes again.*

"It's fine thank you Corporal. Now get along to the Captain and tell him to prepare." As the man saluted and left, he took the beautiful ink pen from the box, engraved with his initials. Then picked up the last of the notepaper his wife had sent him at Christmas, and wiping the table, he placed it down carefully and began to write…

'My darling girl…'

*

Two days later Sergeant Major Russell called the men together to advise them of the new orders. The Southdowns were to stay in the front lines and take over the main holding role, while the rest of the Sussex regiments and Hampshires would go with the second army corps as it moved south to the region known as the Somme.

They gathered behind the lines in the main square at their rear base. It was little more than a large area of flattened earth that was used for storing supplies most of the time, but currently was virtually empty with so much kit already packed off south with the departing battalions. Now the men from the Southdown battalions stood in large groups around the square, or sat on the banks that surrounded three sides of it. Interspersed with them were the men from the 1st and 2nd battalions of the Royal Sussex regiment too; Will's former comrades.

Will couldn't help but marvel at the determined army of bluebells that carpeted the banks where the men sat, despite the awful conditions that surrounded them. The colourful flowers were a symbol of hopeful continuity for those that stopped to look. *No doubt many of them would be trampled underfoot by the gathered crowds,* Will thought, *as they were themselves when they went over the top.* Yet the flowers would come back again and again, and their ability to regenerate, unlike the soldiers, added to the sadness that settled across the square on this May Day morning.

Russell had found himself a large crate to stand on, to ensure he could be seen by as many of the men as possible. He didn't need to make his voice carry however; he could do that well enough without props. Billings and Carter stood either side of him, resplendent in their sergeant major uniforms, the red sashes on display across their chests in a rare moment of parade ground splendour, before the need to adjust to the conditions kicked in. Behind him a number of officers were gathered from all the Sussex regiments, including Captains Brooks and Fennell and their CO Colonel Grisewood.

Will stood with a number of his friends from back home, ranks mingled easily, as Ced and Franko pushed their way into the group too. He looked round and saw David and smiled. Further back Danny was standing with Joe and chatting casually to him. They exchanged a nod and Will felt pleased that Danny had taken the young lad under his wing, remembering his initial hours in the dugout. *In time, home and status mattered little out here. It was just about survival.* Then the booming voice of the sergeant major cut through all the quiet chatter and the whole place was silent in a moment.

A starling flew overhead calling for its flock and Russell looked at it briefly. It veered away suddenly to disappear over the nearby blue bank, as if the mere look of the CSM was enough to scare it off. *He certainly had that effect on me once upon a time,* Will thought to himself. He raised his head to focus on what Russell was saying, although he had already been briefed on the orders that morning, and his mind began drifting to Teresa and what she might be doing at that moment. The sound of a new voice however made him snap back into the here and now. It was Colonel Grisewood.

"…so, for those of our fellow Sussex men who are moving to new quarters and new adventures we wish them well and may God keep you safe in the weeks and months ahead."

There were a number of polite appreciative murmurings at this point, and a couple of the officers even said "Amen." Archie leaned into the group and said, "Quarters? Since when has a mud pit no bigger than the dens we used to build as kids become quarters? Hardly the bleedin' Ritz now is it?" There was some muffled laughter.

"Settle down," Will said quietly without looking round, unsure as to who might be listening. Then risked a sideways glance to Archie and a quick raise of the eyes that said *I know*. Archie shook his head as the colonel continued.

"I know you men of the Southdowns will be anxious to get properly stuck into the Hun. Our time will come gentlemen, mark my words, and I am sure when it does you will do your King and country proud." Owen let out a disgruntled noise at this, but Will let it pass. "Not to mention your county. The Sussex have already achieved great success in their endeavours to date, at great cost," Grisewood continued, "and we will continue to do so until we emerge victorious from this bloody conflict."

The reference to their losses noticeably changed the mood in a heartbeat, especially among the hardened veterans of the campaign, many of whom Will noticed looking down at the ground now. Sure enough the colonel picked up on it.

"I wish I could bring you all home safely, I truly do, but I cannot promise that. I can promise I will do everything in my power to ensure we are fully prepared for whatever lies ahead of us. And more than that, I know with great certainty that we fight on the side of God, and on the side of righteousness, and will carry on until the bitter end if need be. But whatever the cost we shall not flinch from doing our duty. Am I right?"

The Southdown men cheered in agreement, some more heartily than others, and then he raised his arms for calm once more.

"It grieves me however to bring you news of a noble sacrifice from amongst our officer corps. Last night men from the Sussex while out on a reconnaissance patrol in an area to the south of here, met with stiff German resistance in the low woods. As always the Sussex reacted magnificently and were able to bring back information about the German front lines vital to our war efforts. Sadly however, during the fighting, Major Rupert Brown was mortally wounded while carrying out a rear-guard action to enable the majority of the men to withdraw safely. Two other soldiers died with him, and our thoughts and prayers go out to their families at this time. Major

Brown's actions exemplify the spirit of the Sussex regiment and are an example to us all. May they rest in peace."

There was a pause then as a local chaplain stepped up calling for the men to pray, in French. Colonel Grisewood impressed many of his own regiment by translating the words fluently and the men removed their caps and bowed their heads as the chaplain continued. Will saw some of the old Sussex regiment murmuring amongst themselves until an NCO lashed out at one with his cane. He glanced away as they sullenly looked down. More worryingly he saw some of his own company looking at Joe now with barely disguised anger. The initial fragile acceptance of the foreigner amongst their number severely strained by any casualties they suffered.

Will knew he needed to get out with Joe and show them whose side he was on sooner rather than later. It ran deeper than that though. He realised in that moment that he needed to work with Joe to prove to himself he was no German sympathiser. Despite all his words to the contrary, Archie's concerns mirrored his own initial scepticism and he was angry at himself for feeling that way. Even considering the lad's background and youthful looks, something about Joe just didn't add up.

The chaplain now made the sign of the cross as he gave out the blessing. "Au nom du père et du fils et du saint esprit, Amen," then waited patiently while Grisewood translated for the assembled ranks.

"In the name of the Father, and of the Son and of the Holy Ghost, Amen." Several of the officers crossed themselves as the chaplain walked sedately away. "As a final point of order," Grisewood added, "our own Captain Brooks will be going south with the 1st battalion as their Acting Major until a replacement is found. We wish him well." Brooks nodded solemnly. "Carry on Sergeant Major."

The voice of the CSM cut through the emotion in the square and the men were dismissed. Some to prepare to leave, others to dig in and wait. Tommy piped up as always. "Cor that's a stroke of luck Archie. You said old Brooksy had it in for you and now he's off."

"Yeh that's right Tommy lad. I scared him off more like."

The men laughed as they walked back up the line to their dugouts, but Owen chipped in. "Won't be long before Bunny upsets some other toff though Tommy, mark my words. He can't help himself now can he?" The men chorused in agreement and Archie looked back.

"If you ain't got anything useful to say then shut your cake-hole Welshy."

Owen wasn't intimidated but decided not to push his luck any further, and the group walked on in silence. As they reached the zigzag line up to the front trench Archie spoke again. He had obviously been thinking about something.

"You know it's funny, but my old lass Elsie said they had a Brown in the hospital before I left, young pilot like. Badly shot up. Wonder if he was any relation."

"Did he survive Arch?" Will asked stopping to look back.

"No idea. Had a lot on me plate at the time funnily enough. But I can write our Els and ask 'er if you like?" Will and Ced exchanged knowing looks but said nothing.

"No matter now. Let's crack on lads."

Chapter 18 – Mind your head

"I'm just saying that's what I heard Will," Ced continued as the two men stood near the dugout door, their voices lowered so as not to be overheard. "Which is probably why some of his company reacted the way you said they did."

Will shook his head looking out into the night sky. "You know how these stories can get exaggerated Ced. It was dark and they were fighting for their lives. You and I both know what that's like. Easy to say what you like afterwards, especially when people can't defend themselves. Don't forget Lieutenant Dunn after the battle in the woods blaming everyone but himself."

"Who can forget that bastard? But that's just the point. You risked your neck for him, after everything he'd done to you. That's all I'm saying. The men will try and help the officers when the chips are down." Will beckoned him to lower his voice still further. "Will, the lads over in number two company said Brown could have pulled back with the rest but instead charged the Jerries single handed. Lost his head they said. Went berserk. They're good lads. No reason to lie."

Will reflected on it for a moment, looking round to ensure no one was listening. "Maybe he did, maybe he didn't, we will never know. Could happen to any of us I guess."

"Yeh but he lost two good men with him, trying to save his bloody life. They said his orderly wouldn't leave him and another corporal went to try and drag him to safety and they both got chopped."

Will put a hand up to calm his friend. "Look Ced. It's just the bloody war. Perhaps this Brown that Archie mentioned was a relation, might be just coincidence. Maybe he lost his head, maybe not. For all we know the Colonel was stating what happened and someone needed to hold them back. Doesn't change the fact he's dead. Too much going on here to fret over individual events."

Ced let out a deep sigh. "You're right mate. I best be off. Nightingale, Franko. Get your packs time to go."

"You too Wagner," Will said, "It's time we were off to prepare." He looked to where Joe sat alone. Once more talk of British casualties had left the men unsure how to act around him, and they just avoided eye contact or conversation. But Danny slapped him on the back now, and said "Get it done boy, now or never."

Will turned back to Ced. The two old friends smiled now and Ced held out his hand. "'til we meet again?"

"Look after yourself Longworthy."

"And you Davison."

"Cor blimey," Archie said, interrupting the pair as they shook hands. "When you two have finished kissing goodbye, I'd like to propose a toast, especially as the group is all breaking up. Ced and his mates scampering down south to avoid the real fighting. Will off to sit in the sun with Frosty, and me to whip the 11th into shape!"

There was the usual amount of abuse hurled back in his direction which he ignored as ever, handing round some brandy that the men poured into their drinking cups. Will noted with satisfaction the mood was very buoyant in that moment despite the break-up of the group, and felt his sadness at Ced's departure disappear as Archie held his cup aloft.

"To Sussex men old and new. Sons of the Downs."

"Sons of the Downs," the men chorused. Nightingale stood up and whacked his head on the lamp hanging from one of the beams, causing him to spill his drink.

"God help you Ced with this one," Archie said. "If the Jerries capture him we'll win the war for sure. He'll bloody terrify them." The men laughed and then all shook hands.

"You're not wrong there Corp," Owen chipped in, "but that leaves a two-way race for village idiot between you and Tommy like. I'd call that a tie boyo."

Before Archie could react, Danny burst into song spontaneously singing a new county hymn the men had learnt…

"Oh Sussex, Sussex by the Sea!
Good old Sussex by the Sea!
You may tell them all we stand or fall,
For Sussex by the Sea."

As most of the men now joined in, Sergeant Major Russell appeared in the doorway.

"What the bleedin' 'ell is this 'orrible racket? Didn't see church meeting in standing orders today for number six dugout."

"Sorry S'arnt Major we were just…"

"Shut up Longworthy. Ought to know better. Why don't you just put a sign up to Jerry saying 'Please drop your shells here?'"

Some of the men smiled despite the CSM's face.

"You're right Sergeant Major. We were just saying goodbye to the lads moving off. Sharing a spot of brandy and such." Will held up the bottle to Russell.

"Spot of brandy is it? Well then, don't mind if I do." He took a deep swig and Will winked at Ced behind his back. "But get yourselves moving now. Davison you and the lad are to come with me. And let's just leave it at handshakes shall we?"

"Yes sir," the men chorused.

"Nice spot of brandy that." Russell walked off down to the next dugout.

"Oh you're welcome," Archie said begrudgingly looking at the empty bottle.

"Right c'mon you pair," Ced called and moved out into the trench followed by the lumbering figure of Franko and then Nightingale. As he walked out of the dugout Nightingale hit his head on the top of the door frame and stumbled forwards against the trench wall. He banged into the ghostly figure of Siegfried, knocking his helmet off onto the shelf.

"God help us," Archie exclaimed. "Can you mind your head for once? Even Franko knows when to duck. You could have the whole place down on us."

Ced shook his head and waved at Will once more before walking off.

Nightingale said, "Sorry Archie. So long fellows..." and then stumbled again as he stood up, falling face first on the board walk. The muddy water splashed up either side of him, and as they watched Siegfried's jaw fell open as if in laughter. All the men laughed out loud and Archie pushed through the group beaming from ear to ear.

"Mary, mother of God. Would you like me to carry you to the Somme? Here..." He dropped the German spiked helmet next to him and added, "put that on, even Siegfried realises you need it more than him."

Ced stopped and looked back exasperated while Franko roared with laughing next to him. "Get up! Come on," Ced called, "we haven't got all day."

Nightingale didn't move.

"Think he's too embarrassed," Tommy said, and some of them laughed again.

"Think he's hurt?" Owen asked Will, looking down at the prone figure of their comrade.

"Only his pride," someone muttered.

"Knocked himself out more like to save us all a job," Archie countered.

Will had been leaning on the door frame the whole time and now stepped forward. "Archie get him up before he drowns in the sewage. Easy like."

With a sigh, Archie leant down and pulled him up backwards. "C'mon you big lump. No shame. Just get up and get going."

Joe appeared by Will's side. "I heard something," he said.

Will looked round and frowned seeing the concern in Joe's eyes as the young lad scanned the area beyond the trench.

"Get him up now," Will said more urgently and a couple of men now bent down to help pick him up and they sat him against the trench wall. Ced was already moving back up to them as Will stooped forward. Muddy water ran off Nightingale's face and onto his neck and, as they watched, it joined a darker pool that mingled and swirled down into the folds of his uniform.

"He's out cold," Archie said.

"Cold is right," said Will feeling his pulse. "He's dead."

*

Hans Liebsteiner slipped out of the shell hole he had been lying in since yesterday morning. Then waited, listening for any sound of movement from the British trench. None came, so he carefully undid the scope of his rifle and folded it into his pack. Silently he picked his way across the hole, careful to ensure no loose stones dislodged and rolled into the stagnant pools at the bottom. A simple splash out here could mean life or death for him. He slithered slowly into another dip working his way back towards the safety of his lines. There to relax and prepare for the next hunt.

The soldier's mistake was a bonus for him, and his mood was now giddy with the thrill of the kill. It had been a barren period since he shot the British sniper with these men clearly learning from their mistakes. Hans had lain in the hole overnight without any success, and hoped the new troops, that appeared to be moving in, would become careless again as each new group seemed to. He was about to return to his own lines, dejectedly, when the sound of singing had made him pause.

At first he thought to use the noise to cover his movements in case anyone was listening. But then the melody reminded him of the songs they used to sing when hunting in the Black Forest, and he found himself reminiscing about home once more, and of course dear Klaus. As he watched the trench almost in a day dream, he had seen the soldier stumble against the wall and just for a few moments the side of his head was visible. Instincts had done the rest. He knew the man was dead.

Regardless he wouldn't get a second shot, so while the men of the Sussex laughed and joked around the prone body of their fallen comrade, Hans slipped silently away.

Sniping was just like hunting and fishing he told himself. Sometimes you were successful and sometimes not, but always if you waited long enough, another opportunity would come along. There would be no disgrace in returning to his dugout this time.

*

"Can't see anything moving out there." Ced pulled down the trench telescope the men used to look over into No Man's Land and handed it back to Will. "Wherever it came from he's long gone I reckon."

Will nodded and handed the piece of kit to Joe who seemed to marvel at the simplistic box design that had saved so many lives. Just two mirrors placed at angles at the top and bottom of the box, allowed you to look through it over the top of the trench without ever having to pop your head up.

Just then Sergeant Major Russell appeared with a second man and walked straight up to Will for a briefing. Noticing the telescope, he took it and passed it to his companion while Will gave him the basic facts of Nightingale's death.

"I see. Thank you Sergeant." Turning to the new man he said, "See anything?" The man shook his head but continued to look without turning round. "Right. Longworthy you get off with Private Jones and catch up with your mates. Most of your battalion is already away down the line. Davison, detail two men to get this body back to the mortuary and have him tagged. Then you and Wagner need to get about your business."

"Yes sir" Ced and Will said, almost in unison, and then shook hands one last time. Will nodded to Tommy and Owen standing nearby. "You heard the CSM lads. Get Nightingale back to base and sort out his details for next of kin."

Tommy whispered to Owen. "Think it's cursed?" nodding at Siegfried's skull.

"Don't be daft boyo. No such thing. He was just unlucky. Only thing cursed round here is the whole bloody country look you. Now shift yourself."

"So long fellow," Tommy said sadly, mimicking Bertie's last words.

As the friends picked up Bertie's bedraggled corpse, Will looked at Russell. "His mother played the organ at our church Sergeant Major. I'll try and get a note off to my mum to let her know."

"Its sad lad, I know, but that will have to wait. Captain's heard of the shooting and wants you out tonight. And every night thereafter if need be. Once HQ hear of another incident they will want good news." He punched Will on the arm. "Take what you need. And get the bastard."

"Yes sir."

"Oh, I almost forgot. This is Sergeant Picton." He beckoned to the thick set man who had been standing patiently to one side while the orders were carried out. "Some of you may know him already from 'D' Company. He's taking over this section for the next few days while we reorganise. So many changes at the moment we are just all going to have to muck in until we get the command structure stabilised again. Any questions?"

The men knew better than to ask anything unless it was urgent, and Russell wasn't known for long speeches so he grunted and moved off down the trench. Picton narrowed his eyes and looked at the remaining men. He was short but well-built and was almost square shaped as a result. He had the trade mark thick moustache that most sergeants had, unlike Will, but when he removed his hat to adjust the lining they saw he was quite bald. He replaced it and peered at them again, surveying the area. His eyes were very dark, like coal, and it reminded Will of the snowman they used to build at home. Will was aware of Hubert Picton from company briefings and stepped forward now to break the awkward silence.

"All yours then Sarge" he said, offering a hand. "Appreciate the help. We need to get going." As ever his manner diffused any potential awkwardness and Will saw the moustache twitch upwards slightly in the faintest of smiles.

"Indeed. Good luck to you feller. Rest of you get back about your business. I'm going to check up the line and let them know the good news. Then we can settle into the business of proper soldiering can't we?"

As he walked off, Will was tempted to react to the obvious jibe but let it go. He knew Picton was a stickler for discipline, and he also knew him for his reputation for enjoying a drink. The latter often leading to the former after a heavy night out, and needing someone to shout at. *But the men were used to that by now*, he told himself and picked up his kit and rifle. Danny stepped forward.

"I'll drop a note home Will, and try and soften the blow. You just focus on the job in hand. That's all any of us can do. Just keep on keeping on."

"Thanks Danny." As they shook hands, Archie stepped over to him.

"Seems a bag of laughs that one," he said with a movement of his eyes in the direction of the departing *snowman*. "Still not like we ain't been there before."

"My thoughts entirely," Will replied. "Just try and keep your head down, literally 'eh Bunny."

"Oh, don't you worry." Archie said, then noticed Joe standing to one side looking down at the ground. He shuffled from foot to foot clearly struggling with what to say to the young lad.

"Oi Frosty." Joe's worried face looked up slowly at the towering corporal in front of him. "Give 'em hell for me 'eh?" He slapped him on the shoulder then and Joe visibly had to take a step back to stop himself going flying.

"Thank you Corporal. I will try."

Archie grunted satisfied, then with a nod to Will went back into the dugout with the other men.

Will smiled at Joe. "Well think you made a breakthrough there. I've never known him to be so gushy." He laughed at his own joke but Joe just frowned.

"What is gushy please?"

"Something you don't normally associate with the army lad. Now let's get going. I want to be ready to go out as soon as it's dark and we have a lot of preparation to do before then." He nodded to the trench wall then. "And mind your head."

Without waiting for an answer Will marched purposefully off along the boardwalk, mud and water lapping around his boots. Had he looked down he would have seen a small red trickle of blood mixed in with the murky grime, making its way down the slightly undulating slope in the trench to the next junction. It spun round in a frantic whirlpool made by the passing strides of the two men, before slowly moving on dispersing as it went into the water that carried it. Gone in the blink of an eye. Just like its former owner.

*

Agnes and Harold walked up to St Andrew's church with the reluctant Freddie in tow, who as ever was doing everything possible to delay his entry into the church. It was a routine they seemed to go through every week, and they took it in turns to deal with it. Sometimes Agnes took time out to explain to Fred the importance of going to church, and sometimes Harold dragged him inside.

This week however they were running late after one of the cows had actually managed to get through a gap in the hedge by the road and wander off. If it hadn't been for the persistent barking of Sally they would have gone to church blissfully unaware, while Emmie pottered off towards town, munching anything she could find on the way. Luckily she had been attracted to Mrs Earp's tulips and casually clopped into the front garden to help herself. Harold and Fred rounded her up with a sense of relief and an apologetic shrug to the open-mouthed Mrs Earp, and returned Emmie to her rightful place.

Consequently, they were now unusually late, which Agnes hated given she sang in the choir and liked to be early to help. But more so because of the wrath of Celia Goodman, sister in law of the Squire and choir mistress among many other self-appointed titles. *She will love the opportunity to practice her best frown on me,* Agnes thought, as she dashed up the path to the door.

The Reverend Arthur Congreve-Pridgeon, was at the door as ever, smiling to welcome all comers, early or late, and reached out a hand to Agnes as she approached. She shook it briefly and with a flurry of garbled explanations and apologies rushed past. Harold, following on behind, due to Freddie's final attempts to avoid the purgatory of religious attendance, noticed that the station master, Walter Miller, was also standing at the door. He also noticed the reverend's failed attempt to halt Agnes, and the fact his customary smile had been replaced by a frown on seeing his wife.

"Good morning Vicar. Everything alright?" Harold asked with a raise of his eye. Walter took a couple of steps forward before Arthur could speak.

"Could I have a quick word Harold?"

"Of course, Walter, what's up?" Harold's senses were now heightened and he felt a sense of dread rising within him and worked to calm it. Walter Miller was also the telegram officer for the town, and over the last eighteen months, his visits had become more and more unwelcome. It was an unenviable task.

"Fred go inside and wait in the pew. I will be there shortly." He looked at the two men again, as Fred slouched inside.

"Not good news I'm afraid Mr Davison," the Reverend said, "but better that Walter explains it, I need to go in." He shook Harold's hand and then the two men were left alone for the moment, as the church bells dropped to a single peal.

"Something about my boys Walter?" Harold felt cold.

"God no Harold, nothing like that. Sorry. Didn't mean to startle you. It's just I got a telegram yesterday. It's Gladys."

"Nightingale? The organist? What's up?" He was overcome with a sense of relief for his boys and realised now he needed to focus on the problem in hand. As he did so he noticed the organ wasn't playing as usual but instead there was the sound of tinned piano music. *That's odd.* "Is she sick?"

"No Harold. Her lad's been killed. In France. Few days ago. Poor Bertie."

"Oh, the poor woman. He's only just gone over too."

"Yes, I know. I think the reverend wanted to catch Agnes to have a word but you were late and…"

"Aye I know. Bloody cow got out. Anyway, I'll tell Aggie."

"I'd appreciate that. Everything else alright?"

"As good as can be expected given the circumstances," Harold replied. "You heard from your lads recently?"

"Not for a bit. But they never were great talkers. I expect they're just busy soldiering over there. Still things like this bring it all a bit closer to home…"

His voice trailed off; the obvious worry evident in his face. Harold gave him a pat on the arm. "They'll all be fine Walter, I'm sure of it. Bertie was just unlucky. I better get inside and catch my Aggie."

"Yes, course. Off you go. And thanks Hal."

Harold nodded and Walter watched him go in. He took his bicycle from the wall and walked down the south path towards the station. He wanted to go on believing everything was fine, but there was a nagging doubt inside of him that wouldn't go away.

*

As Harold walked into the church the first thing that got his attention was the sight of the vicar's wife playing the small piano to one side of the main aisle. This was a very unusual sight being generally used only for Sunday school singing or practice. He naturally looked to the organ where Gladys would normally be playing a welcoming musical ensemble with a gusto that belied her slight frame, but the chair was markedly empty. He moved over to join Freddie in their usual pew at the back, where his son was kicking a prayer mat back and forth.

"Where's your mum lad?" The sombre depth to his voice was enough to make Fred stop what he was doing and look round.

"She's gone to the vesty. Said she couldn't wait. Mrs Landon came and dragged her off. Said something to her."

"It's called the vestry. What did she say?"

Fred frowned and then shrugged. "I can't remember."

Harold raised his eyes, and then as much to himself muttered, "I need to try and catch her."

But at that point the reverend appeared at the front of the church and nodded to his wife to cease playing. Louise smiled and paused. Pushing her shoulder length blonde hair behind one ear, she quietly changed the sheet music in front of her.

Too late, Harold thought.

"Good morning to you all."

"Good morning," the congregation echoed back.

"The Lord be with you."

"And also with you."

"Let us begin today by singing the processional hymn 'Praise my soul the king of heaven,' which can be found on page ninety two in your hymn books." He nodded to his wife and she began the introduction.

The door to the vestry opened and the senior choir master appeared carrying the golden cross aloft.

"Praise, my soul, the King of Heaven;
To His feet thy tribute bring..."

As the congregation burst into song the choir processed out up the side aisle towards the back of the church, Celia Goodman leading them as ever. Most of the people were focused on the hymn, some reading the words intently staring at their book, while others raised their eyes to heaven, joyful faces staring upwards.

"Ransomed, healed, restored, forgiven,
Who like thee His praise should sing..."

Harold wasn't singing. He was watching, concerned, for his wife to appear, and wondering if he could catch her as she came round the back of the church. *Perhaps if she was at the back of the line.* He checked his jacket pockets. *If only he had some paper on him to scribble a note. He always had paper. Damn and blast it.*

"Praise Him, praise Him,
Praise Him, praise Him..."

Then he saw Agnes; not walking with everyone else, but sitting in the vestry, the inconsolable sobbing figure of Gladys Nightingale collapsed in her arms. As did everyone else sitting on that side of the church through the wide-open doors of the rear room. Those that didn't picked up on the heart wrenching wails that echoed now from the empty room, and the singing stumbled.

"Praise the...everlasting...King."

The choir now hesitated at the back of the church, but the Reverend nodded to his wife to keep playing and waved them forward. He burst forth into the second verse and the singing picked up again in sections, with some people whispering to each other or trying to see what was going on.

"Stay here lad," Harold said and stepped out of their rear pew and moved past the choir heading in the opposite direction, some of whom glanced at him as he passed. Caroline Landon gave him a sympathetic smile, and then he stepped down the side aisle briskly to the vestry and moved inside, closing the doors behind him.

Agnes' eyes were red as she looked up. "Oh Hal," she said, seeing him come in, and then began to cry herself.

"Now then lass. Let's get Gladys home."

Chapter 19 – Sinking feeling

May passed quickly into June without any further incident of note for the Southdown battalions. The perpetual cycle of patrols, sentry duties and trench repairs became almost monotonous. Were it not for the daily shelling that occurred and the occasional risk of sniper fire, the men could very well have been on exercise on the Downs.

For Will and Joe however the lack of any significant action was not something to be welcomed. Since the incident with Bertie Nightingale, they had been unable to track down the phantom sniper, and yet casualties continued to mount. It was as if he could appear and disappear at will without leaving any trace.

They lay together now, in a small rutted track that had at one time been a lane meandering peacefully between two small hamlets, following the course of a local stream. Will wondered who had walked along here in times of peace. *Workers going back and forth to the fields perhaps. Lovers courting to the sounds of birds, and the rippling stream.* Now the stream was gone; multiple breaches in its banks draining the water that came through here, the incessant shelling merging track and brook together into one unholy mess of twisted roots and blackened earth. The nearest hamlet was nothing more than a few burnt out shells of people's lives. *Too open to use as cover.*

Instead they lay under the roots of an old oak tree, thrown high on the sunken remains of the road. The dark broken stumps pointed accusing fingers at the men behind them. Joe was focused on the task in hand, and now gestured forward slowly to a section of the German trench.

"Two officers on the left, close to the wire end."

Will followed his colleague's finger and saw the two helmets appear and disappear again. They were moving slowly down their trench, the tops of the helmets in line with the trench top. *Not stopping, not rising enough. Not enough for a shot.*

"I see them. Follow them while I watch the sides."

The two men took it in turns to watch a target while the other one watched their backs. They were on edge the whole time, and never knowing where the German snipers were, it would be fatal for them both to become fixated with one person or place. They moved here during the night, crawling painstakingly slowly, inch by inch to conceal the smallest of sounds.

They had picked this place the previous week when deciding where to go next. *Never the same place twice.* Here they would stay for up to two days waiting for a suitable target but hoping more than anything to see their ghostly opposite number. Before he spotted them.

Joe tapped Will's leg. "They stopped."

Will looked round. Sure enough, twenty yards from where he last saw them the two officers had stopped to smoke a pipe. Amazingly right in the place where there was a small gap in the sandbags. Too small almost to be noticed, but to sharp eyes using the best rifle scopes, such a gap was magnified fifty times. It was a killing shot. They both knew it and Will nodded at Joe.

"They are both in view," Joe whispered. "We could take both. Perhaps they are senior commandants."

Will considered this for a moment, watching the smoke drift lazily away from their communal pipe. Then dismissed the thought.

"If we both fire they will know there are two of us," he hissed, "and we lose the edge. They might send more men out or move our man for good somewhere else. He has to think he's in charge."

Joe shrugged and looked again. "Left or right?"

Will looked through his scope at the officers. They would move soon and it needed a snap decision. A snap decision that meant one life ended and another spared. A daft school rhyme chanted in the playground years ago came into his head. *Eeny, meeny, miny, moe...*he shook it away. *No time. Left, say left.* He was about to speak when a voice suddenly shouted from the German trench and both Will and Joe jumped as it seemed so close. Joe almost fired, and Will put a hand on his shoulder to steady him.

"Hey Tommies. Good morning to you. How are you?"

The English was good but heavily accented.

"They see us," whispered Joe, clearly worried.

"No. They are just shouting to our trench, trying to provoke us. Perhaps trying to flush someone out for their own sniper. Stay sharp."

They both looked in different directions, looking for any sign of movement. Anything different. The voice continued.

"We know you are going to attack. It will do no good. We are ready. We are prepared. You will all die. Why not surrender now and save yourselves?"

"Piss off Jerry," someone shouted from the trench behind and Will smiled. There were insults shouted back now, and whistles, and Will risked a glance back and saw 'Siegfried' being waved in the air on a stick.

"We have Tommies here too," the German countered, and now a steel helmet of a British soldier appeared being waved back and forth. Will looked back through his scope and saw amazingly that the officers hadn't moved. Instead they were clearly laughing and shouting things to their colleagues. He moved the scope along the line but couldn't see the German who was shouting the insults. His view was blocked by one of the very roots that was hiding their presence.

"Can you see the man who is shouting Joe."

"Yes. A little."

"Enough?"

"Yes."

"Take the shot."

"What about the officers?"

"Ignore them. If you shoot the man shouting, it will affect their morale."

Joe nodded. Will looked at him focusing in on his target. It was a difficult shot into the wind, at over four hundred yards, and through the sandbagged protection. Inside he almost felt relief that he did not have to choose which officer should die. Yet he knew that someone was going to die. *Someone's father, husband, son. He couldn't think like that. They wouldn't.*

Crack!

The helmet on the stick fell. Will saw the two officers shouting, clearly scared, and then both duck down. He looked at Joe. He had withdrawn his rifle and slipped back immediately, removing the scope to keep it clean. *Ready to move quickly if needed. Good lad.* Will saw the trench periscopes come up along the German line and slid down next to Joe. They looked at each other and Will nodded. He saw the sweat on his friend's face. Saw the tension.

They lay still, not making any sound. Knowing the area was being scanned, dreading the sound of shells being sent in. None came. After a while their breathing slowed.

"Have a drink, quietly," Will whispered. "We will head back at dusk."

*

Hans Liebsteiner looked at the flurry of activity in his trench from the safety of the shallow hole that he had been lying in for most of the day. The grey green cloak he nestled under completely masked his presence and was well worth the effort in creating it. Beneath him the damp loose earth sucked at his prone body and he felt himself sinking into the mud as many men had done, never to be found again.

But Hans was not scared. He was happy to let it pull him down. The more he merged with the earth, the harder it was for anyone to find him. He couldn't see the British sniper from where he was lying, but he knew the general area the shot must have come from to hit their soldier at that angle. He nodded approvingly.

At last. Someone worthy of my talents, he thought to himself. *Let the games begin.*

*

Freddie skidded into the centre of town on his bike whizzing in and out of the tree lined street, as he liked to do in the mornings, before most people were up and about. The increased hours of daylight meant these rides were not only easier to see, but warmer too than his winter journeys, and he made the most of them before the hard day's work began in earnest. Today he was pretending he was a pilot in the skies, flying his double-winged biplane in and out of the clouds shooting down a horde of German bombers. As the last one span out of control, spiralling down to the earth in flames, he 'landed' opposite *Mullings and Sons*, the butcher's shop, and dismounted from the cockpit. The place was in darkness.

Frowning, and with the sky battle gone from his thoughts, Fred crossed the street to where the shop was all shut up. The gates to the yard were similarly locked. Upstairs the curtains were pulled to with no light visible within. For a moment he pondered what day it was, but he knew it was Monday, so there was no reason not to be open. *Maybe I got here too early*, he thought then, but remembered just as quickly that the Mullings all lived on the premises so there were always lights on.

He was about to knock on the main door, when he saw a sign in the window. *That's new.* He laid his bike on the floor and walked up to it, rubbing a bit of early morning dew from the glass to see better. It was written on a simple piece of card and now he noticed the shop had a black drape across the whole window so you could see nothing inside at all. He put a hand on the glass to cover the glare from the sun rising behind him and read the note.

Mullings and Sons regret to inform you that we will be closed for the foreseeable future. We would like to thank everyone for the kind words expressed so far following the death of our son, Edward, and would ask that our privacy is respected during this time of mourning. We will advise all our regular customers when we intend to reopen.

Fred read it twice in case he had missed anything and then stood there wondering what to do.

"They're shut lad. Can't you read?"

He spun round and saw the milkman walking along the row of shops opposite with some empty bottles in his hands. It was Ethan Blizedale, who spent his mornings delivering milk and his afternoons in the Star Inn. Divorced long ago he was rumoured to have a son, but neither his ex-wife or the boy lived locally now. Blizedale was also the town crier and Fred remembered his mum saying once he did it just to 'stick his nose into everything.'

"Ideas above his station that one," his mum had said more than once in the kitchen, but Fred didn't really understand which station she was referring to.

"I work here. Didn't realise they were shut."

"Well they are. Been shut since Friday. Gone down south to Portsmouth I think."

"I was half day Friday." Fred called back though not sure why he needed to explain that he hadn't heard.

Ethan ignored him, picking up another empty bottle before walking over to the milk cart where his horse stood patiently sniffing the road. He seemed to limp from side to side as he walked and it made Fred smile, and reminded him of an old clown he had seen once, who did a similar walk to make people laugh. It worked then as it did now.

Fred lifted up his bike and was about to cycle off when he thought his mum would probably ask more questions. He walked over to the cart where Ethan was sorting some milk bottles out between crates.

"Excuse me Mr Blizedale but do you know how he died? My Mum will ask and…"

"It's young Davison isn't it?"

"Yes sir."

"Your dad still selling his milk to Curtings?"

"I don't know sir."

Ethan frowned at him, and then muttered something under his breath that Fred only half caught.

"…alright for some taking orders away, while rest of us try and get by."

Fred tried a different tack. "I like working at Mullings. Do you know anything else? I would like to be told."

"I know everything sonny. I'm the town crier aren't I?" He got on the front of the cart and picked up the reins.

Fred was wondering whether to give up and cycle off when Ethan turned to him. "I ain't one for gossip, but as you at least have some respect for my position, I can tell you a little. There was a big sea battle recently. Heard it all at the weekend when I was meeting my customers."

In the pub, Fred thought.

"Place called Jutland, know where that is?"

Fred shook his head.

"In the North Sea. Know where that is?"

Fred shook his head again.

"What do they learn you at school these days?"

"Sorry Mr Blizedale, will you please tell me where Jutland is?"

"Never mind that. I'm telling you what happened, and this is not to be blabbed around mind you, so I'm doing you a big favour."

Fred didn't know whether to look grateful or serious, so did neither and just nodded.

"From what I know the navy took a beating but they won't tell you that official like. Calling it a draw Mr Gettings told me. Lot of ships lost. One of them was the Invincible. Went down with all hands, including Edward Mullings. Not so invincible after all." Ethan looked at Mullings shop as if suddenly aware his voice might carry even though no one was home. "Anyway, you best be off home now. Mind you keep that to yerself young lad. And tell your dad he needs to sell his milk local."

Ethan cracked the reins and the horse moved off. "Get along Sunshine. Move yerself lass."

Fred was still thinking about what was said and went to shout "thanks," but Ethan was already down the road. He jumped on his bike and set off for home, excited about the prospect of being able to play instead. Not only that, but he had some news that he could trade for sweets and favours with his friends and that made him feel very powerful indeed. His 'plane' kicked into life and 'Captain Davison' was up into the skies hunting for the enemy once more.

*

Agnes lifted the kettle off the stove and set it on the table. Harold continued with his breakfast, taking a piece of bread and wiping some egg off his plate, before popping it in his mouth as he pushed the plate forward.

"Tea lass." He held up his mug without looking at her.

She poured him a cup before sitting at the table again, and then looked at Harold shaking her head.

"I'll go down there later. Find out what's going on."

"Don't be in the Star all day Hal."

"Don't be daft lass. Too much to do. Besides may as well ask the cows as old Gettings. I'll go and see if Roger's there despite what Freddie said. If not I'll ask about."

"It was all in darkness when I was there Dad. Mr Blizedale said they'd all gone away."

Harold merely huffed and took a swig of his tea.

"I'm meeting Caroline later to do another stint in the Red Cross tent at the station. She's got some news on the Women's Institute too."

"You still doing that today? What about the lad here?"

They both looked at Fred then who was sitting patiently at the table, not really listening and hoping to be allowed to get down. He'd been stuck here since returning early with the news.

"Yes, I'm needed. Fred will be fine. And besides I can pop into the vicarage and see what they know. Louise is bound to be home even if the reverend isn't."

"I suppose that makes sense. We can leave you some chores anyway Fred my lad. Can't have you sat idle." Fred raised his eyes. "Oi, less of that."

"Those poor parents." There was silence in the kitchen for a moment.

"I know lass. War's touching us all in one way or another." He finished his tea and went to leave. "What did Blizedale say again about the milk?"

"Said you should sell it local or something dad."

"Did he indeed? Well maybe he should pay me what Curtings do and I might. Not like Upper Beeding is exactly on the moon anyway. And we all know he adds a few pence on his orders when he feels like it."

"Now then Hal. None of that. Not today. And don't get into a fight again if you meet him in the pub."

Hal raised his hands in submission with a grin, and said "I never start anything lass."

"Hmmm. Well anyway he's not worth it and there's more important things going on in the world than that."

Agnes got up and began fussing over things at the sink, her mind a whirr of emotions. She tried not to think of Gladys Nightingale or the Mullings, and more so her boys in France. But the image Freddie described to them of the shop bathed in darkness played on her mind; and she wondered how many more houses would display black drapes before this war was over.

Harold motioned to Fred to get up. "You can help me move the lambs up the field as you're here Fred. Go get Sal out and meet me at the gate. I'll catch you later lass."

Agnes nodded, not wanting to show the tear slowly moving down her face, and dabbed it away with her shawl, as the door shut behind them. She smiled and waved at Fred through the window watching him walking off whistling across the yard. Safe in the knowledge she was alone, she clutched her hand to her stomach as the awful sinking feeling lurched within her again.

*

Sergeant Major Russell moved along the trench talking to each company in turn and advising them of the new orders. He came to 'A' company at the end of the line, and nodded to Sergeant Picton before calling the men from a number of dugouts together.

"Gentlemen, good news."

The men looked on warily as 'good news' in the army normally meant the opposite.

"We are all getting a week off the front line. Hot food, hot baths, and even some time for sport and relaxation. How does that sound?"

"Bloody brilliant," said Tommy.

"Just a week is it?" asked Owen with a glint. "Was hoping for a proper holiday look you. We always have three weeks when we go home to Wales."

There was a smattering of laughter and Russell smiled.

"Well seeing as we're not in Wales, it's the best I can do for now Private Entwhistle, but if the news I'm being told is anything to go by, we could all be heading home by Christmas. Big things afoot lads mark my words."

Some of the men cheered now and looked at each other excitedly, but Danny piped up, "I think that's been said before Sergeant Major. What's the catch?"

Russell looked at Danny deciding whether to pull up Private Boyd in front of everyone, but decided not to undermine the good mood. "No catch Private, spot of light training required and some manoeuvres but nothing too strenuous. Right then. We are out of here at six am sharp, so get yourselves sorted and ready to go. Sergeant Picton."

"Yes sir."

"Rotate the men through the night and tell them not to be too jumpy. The 2nd battalion OBLI are moving up to replace us."

"Very good sir." At that moment Russell noticed the dishevelled figures of Will and Joe making their way up the trench back to their area, and he turned back to the sergeant.

"Make sure Sergeant Davison and Wagner get a good rest and then get their kit squared away with the rest. Leave 'em off the roster. There's a briefing for NCOs at seven pm tonight so I'll tell Davison what's going on, and see you both there." He nodded to the group and moved off.

Picton turned to the assembled men. "Right you heard the CSM. Get away and get everything you need, and don't leave anything important. Which means your rifles and your helmets, not your smokes. Duty parties as rostered until we hand over. Carry on."

The men drifted away and Tommy looked at Danny. "Who are the OBLI Dan?"

"Oxfordshire and Buckinghamshire Light Infantry."

"Cor that's a mouthful ain't it? No wonder they shorten it."

"They do it cause you can't spell boyo," Owen quipped as he walked past them back into their dugout. "What you frowning at Danny? Not like you to be sad, especially when we're getting out of here."

"Yeh I know. Just all sounds too cosy to me. Something's been brewing for a while now and I don't like it. Especially when the officers and Sergeant Majors start being nice."

"No pleasing some people. Hot baths and hot food is fine by me, whatever they have planned. I fancy myself sleeping under a tree by a stream somewhere, food all laid out."

"Count me in," said Tommy, and a number of men agreed, the happiness spreading through the group.

"Yeh maybe, but I've got a horrible sinking feeling that what they have planned isn't the kind of picnic you boys are imagining."

Chapter 20 – Going over old ground

The grass felt cool and refreshing beneath his bare feet as he continued to walk forwards, the strands flicking beneath his toes as he brushed them this way and that. The sun was still not clear of the building behind him and he walked in a cold shadow, the early morning moisture adding a chilling exuberance to the sensations shooting up his legs. A firm breeze blew hard against his face now, forcing him to bow his head slightly, but this was a minor irritation compared to the sense of relief he felt being out in the open air once more; after days spent cooped up in the hospital.

Will Davison stood in his hospital issued pyjamas and dressing gown looking out across the ground. He felt the pure dew in the air and breathed in deeply. The cold air made his chest constrict however, and his breathing became harder so he paused for a moment before continuing his journey.

He heard a woman shouting for him to come back. The sound forced its way into his thoughts causing him to frown, but Will continued forward regardless. The female voice was soon drowned out by other voices - men shouting at him to return. The voices sounded familiar, scared, urging him back. He knew if he looked round he would waiver, so he broke into a run now, away from safety out across the lawn.

As he ran, the lush grass was replaced by an endless black mud that sucked at his every stride and the rain roared in to join the onslaught, lashing his weakened frame. His dressing gown, suddenly sodden, weighed heavily about him and he threw it off just as the first shell landed on the lawn. Will zig zagged away from the explosion, knowing it was his best chance of survival and dropped into a previous shell's crater to get his bearings.

Lieutenant Dunn was no more than thirty yards in front of him but he was not moving, and Will saw the dreaded fog creeping towards the officer like a spider moving in on a wounded prey. But instead of running towards him, instinct pulled him diagonally away from the officer to where the fallen body of Private Castle lay face down in the mud. He turned him over, knowing what he'd see but it was a grisly sight none the less. Maggots and other insects crawled in and out of the bullet holes that covered his comrade's body, feasting on his insides, and he had to fight not to vomit and rolled him back over. He reached down and pulled the mask off Castle's face and looked inside. There was blood on the front, and another large worm wriggled inside and he shook it out before checking to see the mask still worked. Satisfied he sprinted back the way he had come towards the lieutenant.

Dunn was in a bad way and had passed out with the pain. Both his legs were clearly broken and lay at ridiculous angles, and his clothes were tattered and bloody. Will checked him for signs of life and looked back into the fog, relieved that he couldn't see the Germans from here; which he hoped meant they couldn't see him either. The sickly green gas blew forward once more, and as he fitted Castle's mask onto Dunn, the officer jolted awake with a scream. Will put a hand over his mouth to silence him.

"Be quiet sir or you'll have us both killed."

But the lieutenant was delirious and struggled with him violently, pulling at his pyjamas and ripping off his breast pocket.

"Stop it sir. I'm here to rescue you," he said, pulling the mask on firmly, "it's Corporal Davison."

It was no good. Dunn began to panic, thrashing about wildly, and ripped Will's air tube from the mask rendering it useless.

"Oh Jesus. You bloody idiot," Will shouted, not caring about protocol, and in his frustration he lashed out at Dunn and knocked him back unconscious.

Will had no option but to rip off his useless mask and throw it aside. The wind groaned now, as if spurred on by the souls of the dead, pushing the devilish fog on and on towards him. Despite the sudden fatigue he felt throughout his body, Will hauled the lieutenant onto his shoulders and with some effort stood up once more.

As he staggered forward a zip like a bee flying past made him jump and almost fall over, and he realised the Germans were still firing at him despite the fog. Another zip and this one hit the bloodied left leg of the lieutenant with a sucking sound.

"Jesus that's close."

Will was close to the safety of his trench, and heard the men there shouting him on. He found fresh impetus in his legs to drive forward. He could see faces now, with outstretched arms beckoning him on, and he allowed himself to believe they would make it. As he approached the lines however, a fresh gust of wind swept the gas on and past the lumbering pair.

Will suddenly realised he was in the green carpet of death. He held his breath and broke into a run, trying to squint in the mist. Just a few yards from the trench, he stumbled and fell, the weight of the lieutenant knocking the air from him momentarily, and he took a deep breath in and instantly regretted it. The searing pain exploded through his lungs as the noxious gases seeped into every pore in his body, making him automatically open his eyes with the shock, and he couldn't help screaming with the effect. As his eyes began to burn as well, watering wildly against the unseen enemy, Will stumbled forward grabbing Dunn by the shoulders and half dragging, half pulling him, forced himself on.

Despite his best efforts he was unable not to breathe, the combination of the pain and the physical effort making his chest heave in short bursts. He felt himself succumbing to this swirling toxic terror. With one last cry out, he hurled himself forward into the trench...

...and fell into the arms of his father.

"Easy lad, I've got you," his dad said, as Will collapsed with exertion and pain. He didn't question why his dad was in the trenches, just allowing strong arms to take hold of him, as his body spasmed violently. As the scene began to fade, the blurred outline of his mum running towards him appeared once again...

The pain made Will shiver violently and with another cry he jolted upright in his makeshift bunk, the sweat pouring off him. He struggled to breathe for a few moments and then his sergeant major was there taking his arm, mopping his head.

"Easy Sergeant, I've got you. Same dream?"

Will nodded, his breathing starting to settle again. He took a swig of the water being offered to him, and raised a hand to show he was okay.

"Sorry Sir. Same bloody nightmare," he muttered, embarrassed to have been exposed in this way. "Just got worse since I was back in France."

Sergeant Major Russell stood up and looked at the exhausted frame of the young sergeant. Luckily the dugout was empty as the other men here were still on duty. He knew full well that Will had been suffering long before they came to France, but he couldn't lose an experienced man on the eve of a big attack.

"I think you need a break Will," he said quietly. "You haven't slept properly in weeks. When this show is over I'll get us all out of the line for a few days. General's briefing in an hour or I'd have let you rest longer."

Will immediately stood up and reached for his tunic. The irony of the demands of duty outweighing rest and recuperation was not lost on him. But he wasn't going to let it show now. He forced a smile onto his face, where sweat still glistened from the horrors of sleep, and turned towards the concerned face of his superior.

"As you always say Sergeant Major, I'll get all the sleep I need when I'm dead. Let's go."

*

Outside Will saw the familiar hulk of Archie heading to the briefing and quickened his pace to catch up.

"Jesus Will, you look like shit."

"It's Sergeant here amongst the men Corporal. How many times…"

Archie took his friend's arm and stopped him for a moment as the soldiers streamed passed. "I'm sorry Sergeant. But you do look proper awful like," he added, leaning in so as not to be over-heard.

"Just a bad dream is all, but the bloody Sergeant Major came in and heard me."

"Russell? What did he say?"

"Said I needed some proper rest but we had to get to the briefing." Will smiled at the irony. Then he noticed the sergeant major emerge from the dugout and motioned to Archie to move along.

"Russell likes you Will. He won't say anything if that's your worry. You need to go and see your nurse. Get some proper rest." Archie continued as they walked down the trench amongst the lines of jostling men.

"It's real action I need. Not sleep," Will replied irritably. "Sick of crawling about in No Man's Land with just a kid for company."

"Real action? That's what I said. Go and see your nurse," Archie replied with a wink, breaking into a big grin.

Will shook his head but couldn't help smiling at the quip and pushed the man mountain of a friend forward with a playful shove. "Just get moving Bunden. General's waiting."

*

General Worthing stood in front of the assembled Southdown battalions and rubbed his monocle on his sleeve before replacing it to study the paper in his hand. It was a theatrical gesture really as he was well aware of the contents and indeed the information that he could pass on during his speech, but it gave him comfort to hold it. The men were told to 'stand easy' and the main square became silent, save for the occasional bird song from behind the buildings, the sweet sounds from another world entirely.

"Men, I have here some news that I know will be of great interest to you..."

Archie whispered, "It's a pay rise," and the men round about tried hard not to laugh.

"I have in my hand new orders for the Division. But more than that I have news of a new offensive that is to take place soon. An offensive that will change the whole course of the war in our favour. You will understand that I can't give you precise details, suffice to say that it will be a huge undertaking between a number of the allied nations." The General looked up, and all eyes now stared expectedly at him. "What I can tell you is that the 116th Brigade of the 39th Division has been selected to carry out diversionary actions to confuse the Germans as to where the main attack will come from. Within the brigade that honour falls to you men, of the Southdown battalions."

He paused to let his words sink in. In a world where noise was a constant companion, you could hear a pin drop now. "Before the main attacks you will go over the top against a weakened part of the German line and capture it, and in so doing draw their attention away from our main force for as long as possible."

"There goes the picnic," Danny muttered.

"I appreciate despite being a limited action, this will not be easy men, and there may be casualties. But you will be well supported and I have no doubt that you will be successful. Every gain you make will drain more and more men and resources away from the real fighting so do not think for one minute that your role is merely a side show. Our planes and spotters have spent many hours flying over your target area, photographing it and mapping it out for you to study and learn. More than that, the Logistics Corps have built a replica of the German defences here in the fields behind me for your Officers and NCOs to drill you in, until you know it inside out."

"And there goes the holiday," Owen added glumly, and there were a few nods from round about.

As the general carried on his speech, Russell moved over to Will, and stood next to him. He spoke quietly so as not to be overheard.

"You will hear all this again in detail over the next few days. For now, you need to know we are bringing you and Wagner in until this show is over Sergeant. Too risky to have you out there at the moment." He saw that Will looked disappointed but continued. "Officer's call. And I agree. You did great recently. I saw that shot Wagner took. Top notch. That's why we can't risk it, either of you, especially with a bombardment coming."

Will knew he was right and sighed reluctantly. His shoulders felt heavy with the weight of expectation and weariness, and he pulled himself up, so as not to appear weak.

"We will get him Sergeant Major."

"Of that Sergeant I have no doubt." He patted Will on the shoulder. There was an outbreak of cheering then as the general finished his rousing speech. Russell waited for it to die down before he added. "It's not guts these boys lack, but experience. That's what bothers me. All these new battalions coming over like ours. 'Kitchener's new army' they are calling it. All very well but over there the Kaiser's mob is waiting and they are anything but new." He flicked a finger in the direction of No Man's Land and Will could see the anxiety in his worn-out face. "That's why men like you will be vital when we go over Will," Russell continued. "Now get back to your battalion and let's get on with the job in hand."

"Yes, Sergeant Major."

Will watched Russell walk off, clearly deep in thought. It was only the second or third time he'd used his Christian name so it was clearly important. He looked round at the excited faces on every side of him now, and knew exactly what his sergeant major meant. So much hope. So little understanding.

*

Major Harry Johnson studied the pile of papers on his desk and made a decision. "Orderly."

The door opened instantly and a young acne marked face appeared at the door. "Sir?"

"Irwin. Get me Major Bluffington-Sykes on the phone, over at Divisional base. And find out where the 1st and 2nd battalions are heading to will you? I know they are being moved again. See if you can locate Colonel Fanshaw. He'll have a finger on the pulse."

Irwin nodded and disappeared.

Harry's desk was a myriad of operational orders for the huge operation ahead, and many other pieces of counter intelligence on German troop movements and numbers. Not to mention the various 'urgent' reports and instructions following the violent riots in Dublin, despite order now being restored there. It had been a costly and hugely political event that the British government could well do without he was sure. *Not what I'm paid for here though, Harry old fruit,* he thought with a raise of his eyes. So, he ignored them all and picked up the single page notification of the diversionary attack scheduled for the 30th June, led by the Southdown battalions. *One day before the big push.* As if to echo his thoughts the thunder of the guns reached him again now and he looked out of the window in the direction of the deadly noise.

Even here several miles from the front they sounded loud. *What must it be like to be standing next to them, or worse on the receiving end?* Harry reflected on the fact the General's staff had indicated they were going to fire two million shells at the Germans over the next week prior to the main attacks. *Do we even have that many shells? How many is that every day, or hour?* His mind tried to do the maths, but he simply reflected on the fact that it must be impossible to live through that. *They wanted to gain ten miles in the first day, the top brass said. We might not stop until we run out of bullets more like! Unless they don't destroy the defences, but then how deep would someone have to be underground not to be hit?*

Harry shook his head. No use speculating now about that, he had more pressing matters in hand. Namely the Southdowns. They needed support companies of pioneers and other troops including machine gun detachments, and were sorely pressed for any given the demands further south. Harry reflected on his promise to Captain Fennell and to James' brother. *No news on that blasted sniper yet sadly. Could do with a morale boost this week.*

There was a knock and the unfortunately spotty faced Irwin reappeared once more. Harry waved him in.

"Beggin' pardon sir. I couldn't locate the colonel but his orderly told me the brigade is marching down towards *Albert* as support to the first waves of attack. Leaving this week."

"Ok find me a courier. I want to get a message to an officer there before they go. Then while you're at it I will send you on an errand to Field Hospital number three." Irwin's face lit up.

"Yes, you can stay for tea," Harry said, knowing Teresa and her ladies mothered him the last time he was there. "But make sure the messages go out first."

"Yes sir. Oh sir I almost forgot. I've got Division on the line. Shall I patch it through?"

"Yes, at once." Harry tapped a pencil on the desk as Irwin vanished once more, thinking through a number of options. He looked at the note on the Southdowns and frowned. Just then the phone rang and made him jump.

"Major Johnson speaking. Ah Bluffers old chap. How the devil are you?...splendid, splendid. Now look Bluffers, need a favour…"

*

The men marched forward once more walking in long straight unbroken lines, the NCOs shouting at them all the time to "keep in step, keep the formation tight." Here and there smoke was thrown to add realism and on the last walk through they had added some machine gun fire. But the experienced men knew it would be very different than this in reality. For one thing no one was firing back, and for another they were practicing in broad daylight. Regardless they marched back and forth over the same area to memorise the ditches and obstacles upon it.

Having reached the 'German' front line, the first two waves consolidated their position, spreading out and digging in before the next two waves came forward, passed through them and pushed on to the second line. Then with support from a Hampshire battalion, they were to push on to the third trench, the German reserve line and then hold it. However, the third line was not constructed as it was agreed that once they were in the German trench network, the push forward would take care of itself. Meanwhile the logistics corps were busy practicing digging the trenches that they would build during the attack, to aid the movement across No Man's Land. If successful they would effectively join the two opposing front lines up, so they became one large British network. *All very well in practice*, Will thought to himself, but he knew there were dozens of things that could go wrong.

Having said that he was particularly impressed with the work done to replicate the ground they would be crossing soon. Considering it would be dark, knowing roughly how far it was to the wire, and to each natural obstacle might be vital, despite the insistence from headquarters that the bombardment would do its work, and there would be nothing but flattened earth to cross over. The men hated the perpetual practice but Will knew that going over the same ground repeatedly would pay benefits when they had to do it for real.

Will looked behind him and saw his brother David, practicing on pretend casualties. As he watched they lifted a couple onto stretchers and set off back with them. Even here in the peaceful French countryside, in daylight, he noticed them stumble more than once. *Still practice makes perfect.* One of the medics picked a man up and placed him over his shoulder. As he had done once before with his friend Bert…Will felt a pain in his chest suddenly and stopped to rub it.

It was not dear Albert but the memory of him carrying Lieutenant Dunn on his back the last time he was in France that now pushed its way into his mind. He felt the weight on his shoulders, and now his legs began to shake and give way. There were screams now and machine gun fire, the acrid smell of smoke, and burning flesh. Men were shouting. Then the smell of gas enveloped him and Will stopped, clutching his chest as his lungs began to burn. He staggered forward a few paces before dropping to one knee.

"It's alright Sarge, I've got you."

Will looked up and for a moment saw his dad holding him up, a shadow of the hospital in Brighton looming behind him. Then it vanished and the smiling face of David was there holding some water.

"You're not supposed to be shot today Sergeant," he said, "so I assume you didn't mean to trip."

"No Private, missed my footing and fell. Thanks." He took a swig of water and noticed he was twenty paces or more behind his line of men. No one seemed to have noticed him stop. "Better get going." He looked at his older brother and saw the unspoken concern. "No offence but I'm hoping I won't need you when we do go."

"None taken." They both smiled, and Will doubled forward to catch up.

Just as he did so the CSMs called a halt in the 'German' second line and the men were told to smoke and take on water. They had been training for over four hours now, and stopped to eat cold rations in the field which didn't help morale as the sun continued to beat down relentlessly.

Will joined his company again as there was a debate going on about their tactics, and he was pleased he hadn't been missed.

"But why walk so slowly, Sergeant. Shouldn't we be charging across the ground as fast as we can?"

"Yes of course Entwhistle, and then break your legs in all the holes and such as you would in the dark. That would be clever wouldn't it you dopey Welshman?" Sergeant Picton was clearly in no mood for questions. "It's going to be pitch black, which is why we are learning the ground now, so we can move slow and steady towards the enemy. Got it?"

Owen frowned for a minute but wasn't ready to let it go. "But if a flare goes up we will be sitting ducks. What do we do then?"

"We take cover until it dies down then move on again."

"But they will know we are coming then."

"Right that's enough back chat Private. Have a rest and shut it or you will be doing this during stand down time as well. Ah Davison. Glad you're here. You can take over with this lot while I go relieve myself." He stomped off without waiting for an answer, and Will sat down with a smile at his friends.

"I still don't understand why we have to walk all together in long straight lines, Sergeant?" Owen said to Will, aware he needed to keep the formality of rank with the officers about.

"Means we can bring maximum fire power to the enemy, when we get there, rather than getting there in dribs and drabs. Didn't you read the textbooks in training Private?" He smiled to soften the jibe.

"But Sergeant Picton said Jerry was going to be smashed to pieces by our guns, so there would be no resistance," Tommy said now clearly worried.

"Well then all the more reason not to run and risk injuring yourself, and miss out on all the German souvenirs. Besides, I've seen you run Landon, and it's not a pretty sight."

"Aye, like a duck on ice," Danny chipped in and the moment passed in laughter and friendship. But inside Will shared Owen's concerns, and just hoped the information they were getting was correct. He saw the CSM approaching and stood up. Before he could speak to his friends to warn them, Tommy shouted out.

"Sergeant Major. Can't you do something about this 'eat? It's terrible 'ot out 'ere."

"I know I seem like God to you, Landon, but the weather is one thing I can't order about, much is the pity." Tommy poured some water on his face to try and cool off but it made little difference. "And I wouldn't go wasting water either. Any of you. We've a few hours left yet," Russell continued.

Will walked alongside his CSM as he continued. "They'll be alright sir, just the usual grumbling."

"Water off a duck's back to me Sergeant," Russell smiled, "they drill until they are told otherwise." But Will knew how to make a point without causing offence and pressed it now.

"Seems a bit odd though if we are to attack at night, not to do some night training too doesn't it Sergeant Major? Better for the men to make mistakes here in the dark than over there." He motioned with his thumb towards the front line. "Plus, less likely to be fatigued too, training when it's cooler."

Russell stopped and looked at Will, as always with admiration at such an old head on young shoulders. "Well officers are worried about men being injured before the off, but I've been thinking the same myself. I'll put your point to Captain Fennell and see if we can't go out tonight, especially as we have a rest day tomorrow."

Will nodded and walked back to the company.

"Good news Landon, I think I've managed to call a halt to proceedings until it cools down."

"Oh, that's champion Sarge," Tommy replied and the men all smiled now.

"Not only that but we are going to train in the shade too."

"I always said you were the best Sergeant in the Southdowns," Tommy said beaming. "You have me to thank for this lads." He looked round and was pleased to see a few men nodding in agreement for once.

"Yes, we are going to do night manoeuvres tonight instead."

Tommy opened and closed his mouth a couple of times but no words came out, and he looked like a fish out of water.

"Oh, I'll thank you alright Boyo," Owen said. "A big bloody thank you from the end of my boot." And all the men agreed now.

*

Agnes came out of the vicarage and stopped in the street to open her umbrella, then walked briskly towards St Andrews. The rain was coming down harder now, and she was pleased she had decided to prepare for it despite the bright start promising another day of sunshine. Harold was convinced the storm clouds would come in, and she never knew him to be wrong. As she walked round the church the wind changed direction and blew sheets of water straight at her, and she stopped to shelter under one of the archways for a moment. Hiding from the main spray while she waited for a lull, her thoughts turned to poor Gladys again.

She left her friend with Louise in the vicarage, the pair of them having failed to convince Gladys to eat anything. Yet despite her grief, Agnes believed in the days following the funeral, there was an acceptance within Gladys of the facts, even if there had been no emotional shift as yet. Her eyes naturally moved to the section of the churchyard where the new graves were placed, and to the modest cross adorning Bertie's resting place. There was comfort at least in the fact he had been brought home to rest.

Several feet away a much more ornate grave marked the passing of Lieutenant Commander Edward Mullings. While the Nightingale funeral had been well attended by the wider church community, the funeral of Edward had been done with full military honours and a detachment from the Naval base in Portsmouth. The church had been packed that day with many people standing at the back, and even the local press in attendance. Yet the tomb held only an empty coffin, no doubt mirroring the hole that would forever lie within the hearts of Edward's parents too. HMS Invincible had apparently broken in two and gone down in less than two minutes with the loss of over one thousand lives. Only six men were saved from that black oblivion…

Please God if one of my boys should fall, at least let him be found and brought home to me. I don't care what he looks like, just to stroke his hair and squeeze his hand once more. Please give me this.

Agnes felt bad then that she should beg for anything from the Lord, and more so in the vicinity of the Mullings' grave. She moved out into the road and began to head towards the Red Cross tent near the station to help out once again. The umbrella did little to shield her here in the open, but Agnes seemed oblivious now to the driving rain bouncing off her face.

"Not a day to be out and about Mrs Davison."

Agnes stopped as the words broke through the storm that raged within her mind. She came face to face with Walter Miller pushing his bike away from the station. His railway hat and cloak already soaking wet.

"Sorry Walter I was miles away."

"Wish I was. Somewhere sunny preferably." He raised his eyes to the heavens and the water rapped off his face. Agnes looked at his weather worn features and saw that Walter had aged much in the years since his wife passed away. She was sure that delivering the telegrams from the war office was not helping either. Where once people were excited to see him, as it meant something special was happening, now they shied away from his dark form and squeaking bike. She recalled the young couple that had moved into the station master's house many years ago, with two little lads in tow. *The smiling faces…*

"Walter, if it's ever needed, I'd be glad to help out, especially with your boys being off to the war. I'm just down by the station most days at the Red Cross tents as you know and…"

"That's very kind Agnes but I can manage the house just fine, and I've still got the lad helping at the station. I'm sure you've got enough on your plate without adding to it."

"Oh sorry Walter. I meant if ever you needed a break with the telegrams, or were too busy, I'd take some for you. I'm sure any of the ladies would if you asked us. We are looking to start a new Institute here you know, like they have in Singleton, and the ladies will be wanting ways to help the war effort." She paused aware he was staring at her now, concerned she had gone on too much.

"Agnes, that's very kind. I'd heard about the Institute in the Star. Caused quite the debate as I'm sure you'd imagine. Maybe if you set it up we can talk about it a bit more over a cup of tea. My Ethel would have rolled her sleeves up and pitched in I'm sure. Very headstrong she was." Agnes nodded knowingly. "Some of the locals might not like women being more independent but if this war goes on much longer I daresay we will need the ladies to take up the slack."

"What do you mean Walter?"

"I mean there won't be enough men left to do the work. They might not realise it yet but I have." Agnes smiled now sympathetically, the rain hitting them both without reprieve. "Eh now look. You'll catch your death. Better get off inside and get dry Mrs Davison. I appreciate the offer you know. About the telegrams."

With that he touched his hat respectfully and mounting his bike, pushed off into the storm, wobbling a bit as he did, before merging with the dark landscape. Walter's words about the men worried her now. She looked at the Red Cross tent flapping in the wind but something inside her didn't feel right and she turned round and walked back up the road towards the high street. *I want to spend time with my family today.*

*

"It's on! For this afternoon." Archie burst into the billet block beaming from ear to ear.

"What? The attack?" Will leapt up from behind the makeshift desk he was sitting at, where he was studying the layout of the German defence lines yet again.

"God no. The match. With the jocks. I've fixed it."

"Ohhh, I thought you were a bit eager," Will replied, as all the men took an interest now and began to gather round. Despite the false alarm, Will's heart was now pounding hard and he felt unexpectedly anxious. He was unnerved by how his body had reacted to the sudden prospect of 'going over the top,' and chided himself inwardly at this reaction. He breathed out hard to try and release some of the tension, then pushed his way through the assembled group to Archie to distract his thoughts, focusing now on his favourite pastime.

"How did you wangle that Bunny?"

"Well Will, er I mean Sarge, you know there's a number of regiments camped round here while they pass through on the way south?" Will nodded. "Well I was chatting to some of the Scots and they said they was

Camerons like, and I said we knew one of their Sergeants, that bloke Stewart."

"Is Maggie's husband here?" Will interrupted suddenly.

"No, these are terry torals or something they said."

"Territorials."

"Aye that's the one. Anyhow his battalion's apparently already down at that place Ced went to with the Sussexers a couple of weeks back. The Sum."

"You mean the Somme, you ignorant baboon," Owen said in his delightful Welsh lilt, from the back of the group. "I can pronounce the names better than you!"

"Oi, who you calling a baboon?" Archie continued with a mock scowl. The men grinned, enjoying the sudden ease in the tension that pervaded the room.

"Well?" Will continued.

"Well…if I can continue, without further hackles," he paused for effect looking round at the mass of expectant eyes.

"If it comes to a spelling contest with the Jerries we're screwed," Danny muttered, and the men laughed out loud now.

Archie spoke over the laughter. "Anyways, this lot are due to march down there as well tomorrow. Seems like they really are gathering the forces for a big push. Word is a massive combined front with the Frenchies and the artillery's been bombing 'em day and night for a week now. Apparently it will be a stroll in the park, from one French café to the next."

"Liberating their wine along the way no doubt," Tommy said.

"I'd like to liberate a few French girls from their virginity," Danny added, and the men cheered at that.

"Great they get all the glory while we are stuck here as a diversion like a load of dummies," David now added.

"Some of us are better at that than others boyo," Owen quipped, popping a thumb over his shoulder at Archie..

"Oi watch it carrot top," Archie retorted waving his hat in his direction.

"Besides, we have our own pubs to pillage when we attack."

"How's that Bunny?" Danny asked confused.

"I heard it in the briefing. They said the place we was attacking, Rich burger, was near the Boar's Head. If that ain't a bleedin' pub I don't know what is!"

"You bloody idiot, Bunden. That's the description our map boys gave the area we are attacking because the trenches and the geography of the area make the shape like a Boar's head. Apparently. From the air or something. Sergeant Picton said he couldn't see it on the map, looked more like a chicken to him."

"That doesn't surprise me," someone shouted from the back, and then the group descended into debate about the briefing once more. Archie began to protest vigorously about the lack of ale or incentives for the attack, and Will knew he had to step in. He stood on a chair at the edge of the men.

"Settle down!" His voice brought the crescendo of noise to an instant lull. "Never mind what's happening elsewhere." He looked at Archie. "And it's pronounced *Richebourg*." Archie shrugged as if to say '*So what*.' "Tell us about the match Archie." There were shouts of agreement.

"Alright. So some of 'em were kicking a ball about and I asked 'em how long they were here for and they said until six o'clock tonight. So, I said *you fancy a match jockos*, and they said aye, with a few other words thrown in like."

"The officers won't allow it. Got us bloody drilling day and night," Tommy moaned.

"Well that's where you're wrong Tommo. Cos I just spoke to the Sergeant Major and said it would be good for morale, and he agreed!"

"The CSM said yes?" Will asked astonished.

"Yep. And get this. He reckons old Captain Goodman's an umpire so he will ask him to ref it."

"Didn't he go with the main Sussex battalions?"

"Apparently not."

"Hang on," said Danny. "He's a cricket umpire? What good's that in a football match?"

"Listen pea brain. I've got us off training so that's all that matters. Besides if the Captain doesn't know the rules, then it will be a free for all."

Danny laughed and the rest of the men clearly liked that thought and cheered.

"You up for it then Sarge?"

Will grinned. "Of course. Who else is in?"

The men started shouting out then, hands raised. There was no shortage of takers.

"Welshy in goal obviously and me up front." The men jeered but Archie just looked at them and carried on. "Apparently young Peterson the orderly is left footed so I've already told him he's on the opposite wing to you. Tommy and Danny at the back as ever, the rest we can sort out from this mob as we go."

"Can Peterson play football," Owen asked.

"Course he can, boy's a natural," Archie lied convincingly.

“We better go and warm up then,” Will announced, grinning at the way his friend organised everybody. He patted him on the shoulder. “Well done Corporal.”

Archie smiled too now and then shouted, “And don’t forget I’m in charge.”

There were cries of dissent, and “Who made you captain?” but the men poured out of the hut towards the field beyond where the Camerons were resting.

Will pushed his notes and maps together for the Boar’s Head attack, and was about to head out when he noticed David waiting by the door.

“You alright mate?”

“Yes,” David replied appreciating the informality when they were alone. “Football’s not my thing but I will happily watch.”

“Why the frown?”

“Just thinking about what Archie said about the big push.”

“What about it?”

“Well if they really are shelling them for days before the attack, Jerry will know something’s up and be ready. It’s what we do isn’t it?”

“Yes, but with that kind of bombardment what can Jerry do? Defences will be smashed to smithereens even if they manage to sit it out. Won’t be able to stop them.”

“Let’s hope so ‘eh?”

“Yes, you miserable sod. Stop worrying so much. Besides not wanting to go over old ground but that’s the whole point of our little manoeuvre too. Keep the pointy heads distracted so they don’t know where the attacks are coming from, and then our lads will have an even easier time of it.”

“Yeh true. Sorry Will. I just overthink things don’t I?”

“I’ll say!”

“Do you think our guns will do the same before we attack?”

“Of course. Besides HQ have told us the defences are light here. We just charge through and take their lines and then draw some of their main forces away from further south. Piece of cake.”

“Yes I know, but…will they?”

“Jerry won’t know what’s hit ‘em trust me.”

“I do trust you Will. We all do.”

Will put a hand on his brother’s arm and smiled warmly.

“Thanks mate. And it’s Sergeant to you.” They laughed and walked out into the bright sunshine. Will winked at David. “Now come and cheer us on.”

Chapter 21 – Never in doubt

James stood in the doorway of the medical building watching Rose and Teresa move expertly amongst the rows of beds, treating the men. Despite all the inadequacies of their surroundings, he marvelled at the way the nurses worked tirelessly with each patient, making them feel special as if they were alone on a private ward. Above all else he smiled at the natural beauty that Rose emanated, even in the harshest of circumstances, and his heart flipped once more seeing her again.

A shadow by the door caught Rose's eye and she looked up, brushing her sweat stained hair from her face as she did. The sight of James in the doorway made her eyes instantly water and the teeth flashed white as she moved as quickly as she could towards him. Behind her Teresa smiled. She knew what Rose was feeling, and the importance of these moments. She looked for a moment longer in case Will had accompanied his brother. She knew that was daft and chided herself for feeling slightly jealous, before heading to the kitchen to make fresh tea.

"Hello Kellett. I brought you these." James produced a small bouquet of yellow roses, still yet to bloom fully, and their aroma promised new life in a sea of death.

"They are beautiful Jamie. Where did you get them?"

"Oh, I have my means." He smiled tapping his nose, and then pulled her to him and they hugged for what seemed like an eternity. Despite her grimy appearance and the smell of wounded men that hung about her like a shroud, her body felt warm and full in his arms. He ached for her now, and wished they were anywhere but here. A soldier coughed nearby. A deep raking cough that made him irritated by its intrusion into their private moment. James became aware they were in full view of the patients, and pulled her back out of sight into the entranceway.

"I'm not here for long. I'm dashing up north to see my brother, but wanted to call in and see you first."

"I'm very pleased you did. I have something very important to tell you."

James wasn't listening. He was looking around the corridor. "Isn't there a private room we can go to? You know for Generals or something with perhaps a small bed in the corner." He smiled a smile to break a thousand hearts.

She slapped his shoulder. "I can't just disappear James. I'm working and the Colonel is here. He does outrank you!"

"Pah. Do I seem concerned? Besides if you don't kiss me now it will be too late."

"Oh, so it's blackmail now is it Captain?"

"I think it goes much deeper than that nurse…" They kissed then. A deep passionate kiss that travelled through their bodies, and Rose felt herself wilting. Her mind flitted quickly around the layout of the building wondering if there was somewhere they could go. He held her tight now, guiding her back against the wall, and she felt as if she was being pulled into his very soul. She gasped as he touched her.

"Jamie, wait, not here," she heard herself whisper feebly, and then Teresa was right by their shoulders.

"The Colonel!"

Teresa pulled James back forcibly and shouted "Let me see, she needs air."

"What's going on Staff?"

"Oh, sorry Colonel. Nurse Kellett suddenly felt very faint, and the Captain here had just arrived to check on a couple of our patients. Luckily he caught her."

Colonel Hamilton looked at the face of the Guard's captain who seemed shocked, and then the clearly flushed face of his nurse who was struggling to stand.

"Well don't just stand there, get her into my office and on a chair. Captain there's a water fountain outside. Be so good as to get a cup for the nurse would you?"

"Er…I…yes of course Colonel." James looked about clearly bewildered.

"There are cups on that table over there." Teresa said, continuing to take command of the situation, as she led Rose into the office.

"Better sit down before you fall down nurse," she said with a wink.

"I didn't know we had any guardsmen here Staff?" the Colonel said, as his mind began to focus again, having stumbled on the chaotic scene.

"Captain Davison knows a number of the officers from headquarters Colonel. I think he's here to see the intelligence officer they brought in this week."

"Right well anyway carry on Staff. Nurse take your time. Maybe get some air. I can't spare anyone for long today though. You know all the preparations we have to do."

"We'll be back shortly sir," Teresa said, and smiled warmly.

The colonel walked off just as James appeared with a cup of water. Rose looked wide eyed at Teresa and let out a deep sigh.

"God, thanks T. I don't know what we would have done without you."

Teresa raised her eyes. "Well I do, but it would have got you both in trouble." She took the water and passed it to Rose. "I ought to tip this on your head Captain." The two of them laughed then but Rose looked more concerned than ever.

Teresa frowned looking at her friend. "Look I can give you two a few minutes if you want, providing you can behave yourselves? I'll go and put the kettle on."

"No, I really can't stay long," James said, stopping her with a touch of his arm. "I'll call in on the way back all being well. Got a driver outside waiting to take me up and it's important I get there. The Southdowns might be involved in the whole shebang kicking off this week."

"I see. I was hoping Will might be with you."

"Sadly not Teresa. I expect he's a little busy right now. But I can tell him I saw you. Any message?"

"Just tell him not to do anything daft and come and see me when he can. Oh and it wouldn't hurt to reply to my letters either."

James smiled. "I think I can convey that to him formally."

Teresa gave him a hug. "I'll leave you be."

She walked off and he turned to Rose. "Sorry love, bit carried away." He went to hug her but she took a little step back.

"We both were. It's fine." She made herself smile then, and said "Look Jamie I was going to write to you to come and see me so it's great you came. I wanted to tell you something…"

He looked worried then, his mind beginning to fret. "Have I done something to upset you Rose?"

"God no nothing like that. I adore you."

"Well that's a relief. You're not worrying about me in this blasted war are you?"

"I worry about you every day, though I don't know why."

He held her again now. "Look I can't say much because I don't know much, but I can tell you our regiment's not involved in the first actions. We are in reserve, and I will write and tell you any news I get."

"It's not that Jamie. Of course I want you to be safe but…" There was a knock at the door, and James saw the face of his driver standing sheepishly outside.

"Yes, what is it?"

"Sorry to disturb Captain, but I've been told Jerry has started shelling the main road north of here in the evenings and we should go now if we want to get through in time."

"Right understood. On my way." He turned to look at Rose expectantly.

"It can wait," she said.

"Are you sure?"

"Yes absolutely. Not that important really."

"It sounded important Kellett."

"Just a girl's silly worries."

He was unconvinced but decided not to push it further. "Okay then. In that case I will definitely stop in for tea on the way back. Won't be up there more than a day or so. Maybe you can convince old iron braces Hamilton to let you have a few hours off?"

"Shush the door's open. Someone might hear!" She giggled though, despite the concern and brushed some dirt off his collar. "I am due an afternoon off, so I might just use it on you. If there's no better offer."

"Oh, is that right." He pulled her in and kissed her again, and then gave her a hard slap on the bottom as he turned to go. Rose shouted and pushed him back, and they walked out into the corridor all smiles. She watched his handsome rugged frame stride down towards the exit and then for a moment he was framed in the doorway blowing her a kiss. She blew one back and he was gone.

Rose sighed and walked back into the main room, back into the crowded beds and rancid smells. She swayed for a minute wondering whether to run after him, then Teresa walked up to her and smiled.

"Well from the sound of that shriek I'd say the fresh air did you the power of good." She winked and Rose grinned childishly at her.

"I do feel much better now," she said.

"Never doubted it for a minute!"

*

As Will walked towards the field where they were going to play, he saw Joe standing amongst the gathering crowds of men and pushed his way through to get to him.

"Hey Joe. I didn't know you liked footie. Ever played before?"

"Yes, a little," Joe replied, as chatty as ever. "My father taught us the rules."

"Right," said Will, thinking it was an odd answer but smiling nonetheless. "Well hope you enjoy the show. It promises to be quite a game I think, and I wouldn't worry about the rules," he added with a grin. "We've got a cricketer for a ref anyway!"

He walked off then out into the middle of the field where the various assortment of soldiers were gathering for the kick off. Knowing how well some of the Steyning lads played, Will felt quietly confident until he was confronted with the Cameron Highlander's line up. With barely a man under six feet, the Scots looked more like a rugby pack than a football team.

Looking at the likes of Tommy and young Peterson, Will now had his doubts. Even Owen in goal, despite his Welsh courage, looked half the size of their keeper. *Thank God they're not wearing kilts,* he thought to himself, *or my lot might break and run. At least we don't have to fight 'em!* But then Sussex's answer to William Wallace strolled onto the pitch, in the shape of Archie, and with a hearty "Let's get into these Scottish bastards," Will assumed the team talk was done and dusted and there was no turning back.

"What are we going to do for goals..?" Will started to say, and then stopped mid-sentence as he noticed that wooden frames stood proudly at either end of the field. "How…?" he said, stunned at the sudden appearance of recognisable posts.

Archie motioned to the dashing figure of Captain Fennell who stood drinking a cup of tea as if he was about to watch a cricket game after all. A brightly coloured scarf hung around his shoulders and he was chatting quite amicably with the men about him. If there was a more popular officer in the Southdowns, Will would be surprised.

"The Captain snaffled up some planks from the supplies going up to the front that we use to shore up the trenches during the winter. He reckoned they could miss a few now the weather is getting better, and got a group of guys to knock them up and dig 'em in the ground. Not sure how sturdy they are but they look the part."

"Absolutely," said Will, the thrill of a game coursing through his veins once more and overriding all other emotions about the war in that moment. "All we need now is the ref…Bloody hell!"

Captain Goodman appeared wearing his cricket whites from behind the barrack blocks, and the whole crowd fell into a stunned silence. In stark contrast to the dark muddy surroundings that he now traversed, the crowd parted for this dazzling vision, as if Moses was approaching the Red Sea once more.

"Bloody Nora," was all Archie could manage and even the Camerons stood agog, mouths open as the officer strode out into the middle of the field. Despite his rank, sniggering and jibes started to break out as the men recovered from the initial shock, and it was obvious Theodore was rapidly regretting his choice of outfit.

Captain Fennell, however, didn't believe for a moment that Captain Goodman was out of place. Years of dealing with everything life could throw at him, not least from his fellow officer cadets at Sandhurst, Steven could always find the right words for any occasion.

"Bravo Captain. We want a good clean game now!"

The joke was not lost on the crowd and they laughed and cheered, and with spontaneous applause Theodore walked on, confidence restored. He called the two captains to him. Archie, and a brute of a man who unsurprisingly introduced himself as 'Jock', strolled up.

"Right, I'm not entirely sure of the rules but I'm sure you can help."

"Oh aye," Jock said and looked back at his team mates with a grin.

"Yes sir," Archie said, smiling too. "I'll keep you on the straight and narrow."

"Splendid. Well we are going to do two halves, as you say, but apparently no tea in between." He looked disappointed. "The CSM is timing us and will tell me when to blow the whistle. I want a nice fair contest now and may the best team win. Shake hands please."

Archie shook hands with his counterpart and felt the Scottish man tighten his grip and so he did likewise. They kept smiling at each other while continuing to squeeze. Just when both of their faces were turning red, Goodman stepped in.

"Well that's quite enough pleasantries. Camerons to commence. Off we go."

Archie jogged back to his team as Theodore blew his whistle with an extravagant wave. The crowd roared them all on.

"What did he say then?" Will asked.

"He said to smash their faces in. C'mon let's have it," Archie shouted, and all hell broke loose.

Within a few moments the ball had been smashed out over the crowd by one of the Camerons and it was thrown around for a while amongst his cheering companions before coming back.

"Is that six then?" Theodore asked. A number of the men looked at him, confusion etched on their faces.

"No just a throw in ref," Will said, "Ours I think."

As Peterson went to take it a Cameron ran up and grabbed it with a shout of "Get t'fack yer bloody Sassenach," and pushed him away. Peterson looked about but the throw had already been taken, and the Cameron's winger roared down the line before playing the ball inside. Their forward controlled the ball remarkably considering he was wearing army boots, and then flipped it over Danny's head and ran in the box. Tommy slipped in the mud trying to get to him and watched helplessly on the ground.

"Come out," Archie shouted, and Owen raced from his line but the man just calmly slotted it past him and the watching Scottish soldiers went wild.

"Bloody hell," Archie shouted. "Wake up at the back."

There was an exchange of expletives as the Camerons celebrated.

"Come on," Will said angrily. "We've just started."

"What happens now?" Theodore asked. "Do we change ends?"

"No, it's just our kick off," Will said moodily, and took the ball.

As the game got underway again the Sussex men tried to put some passes together but a combination of the mud and the aggressive tackling from the Scots meant they were struggling to stay in the match. There were a lot of shouts of "Ref" but every time Theodore paused and looked to the side-lines for guidance the Scots played on.

Then suddenly a great ball from Will put Archie through on goal and he lumbered forward, but just as he was about to shoot he was barged to the ground. The ball ran into the grateful arms of their keeper.

"Ref, free kick surely?" Will asked, as Archie jumped to his feet spoiling for a fight.

"Shoulder barge ref, that's all," Jock said running past, and shouted at their keeper to launch it forward quickly.

"Erm…well…I don't know," Theodore mumbled, as the men charged on.

The ball fell to the Cameron forward again and he cut inside Tommy and went to flick it over Danny again.

"Not this time you don't," Danny shouted.

"No foul Danny," Will cried out, but it was too late. Danny rugby tackled him to the ground as he went past and the man rolled over in the penalty box.

"Oh aye we're having that," Jock cried and ran forward and picked up the ball. "That's a penalty ref."

"Right," said Theodore blowing his whistle loudly and making the crowd cheer again. Will decided it was pointless to protest and stood hands on hips in midfield.

Danny walked over looking fed up, ignoring Archie's glare, and only Tommy shouted "Come on Owen," half-heartedly.

Without even waiting for the whistle Jock sent Owen the wrong way and thundered it into the net. There were chants of "Easy, easy," from the Scottish supporters and Will could see a few of their heads begin to drop.

"Come on lads, we've only just started. Let's try and keep hold of the ball for a bit, make them do the running." But he wasn't sure they were as keen as they had seemed an hour ago.

The game kicked off again, and after it was hoofed up and down the pitch a few times, Will saw Peterson free on the left and fired a perfect ball into his path.

"Yes, first time, on me 'ead," Archie screamed pounding into the middle. But Peterson took too many touches to get the ball under control and next minute with an almighty *wump*, a tackle came flying in and Peterson and the ball were dispatched into the crowd in a tangle of arms and legs. He never got up again, but simply crawled away.

The Cameron players roared with laughter as Archie looked on disgusted. "Call yerself a soldier," he muttered under his breath, then walked over to the crowd. "Right who's going to take his place then?" He looked up and down the line, but everywhere heads were bowed or people shook them and looked away. Archie cursed as Jock shouted out.

"C'mon ref get the game going. They'll have to play short if none of 'em fancies a gentle kick about."

"Throw the ball back please," Theodore called.

"Aye and chuck another pair to these Sassenachs too," one of the Camerons shouted, and there was more laughing and whistling.

Will shook his head as the ball appeared finally, and then a quiet voice said "I will play."

"Who said that?" Theodore asked, and an arm was raised in the middle of the crowd who duly parted to see who had spoken.

"You've got to be joking," Archie said looking at Will, but Will shrugged as if to say '*what choice do we have?*'

"Step forward then, look lively," Theodore demanded, and there were howls of derision from the opposition as Joe walked up to the edge of the pitch.

Captain Fennell now also stepped forward. "Perhaps a good point to call half time referee?"

"What? Oh, right yes, half time then everyone," and another shrill blast on the whistle followed.

Will called everyone together and they reluctantly came up.

"Right look, we're letting them just boss the game. We need to start controlling it more."

"Not easy on this pitch Will," Danny replied, "besides we are getting kicked up in the air and not getting any joy."

"No of course not. The Captain's not a football referee, and the plain facts are this is not a normal football game so we need to take matters into our own hands."

"You mean get stuck into 'em?" Archie asked smiling.

"Get stuck into them is it? Didn't see you do much of that boyo in the first half. You're supposed to be our leader so you are. Just running about aimlessly like a lump of lard is no good."

"Oi watch it you."

"Right look, we can't play our normal game especially on this pitch. So, any suggestions?" Will tried to calm them down knowing they had little time.

"I don't see problem," Joe said suddenly, and they all looked at him.

"Joe, no offence but you ain't been out there, and chances are you're going to end up like Peterson," Danny said.

"Yes exactly. Better just stay out wide and if the ball comes near you just hoof it up field Joe." Will smiled to reassure him, but Joe continued ignoring him.

"They are big yes but slow. Give me the ball and I will show you."

Will frowned but Owen just said, "It's your funeral boyo."

"Yeh Frosty, you get the ball out here and you might wake up in hospital. Peterson got off lightly!" They all laughed then just as Theodore blew his whistle to start again. They looked at Will now not Archie.

"Right lads, best thing is Archie stays up top and I will try and support him and whenever you get it just launch it so they don't have time to close you down. Danny, Tom keep it tight at the back and the rest of you try not to get killed."

*

They kicked off once more and immediately the Camerons charged forward. Within a few moments they were shooting again, but Owen was equal to it and punched the ball clear. Tommy hit it out wide and it fell to Joe, but the ball skipped away on the mud before he could control it and the same defender smashed it out of play and knocked Joe over in the process.

"God help us," said Archie. "We won't have a battalion to attack with at this rate. He may as well stay off too."

Will noticed Joe leap straight to his feet though and heard Captain Fennell shout "That's the spirit." CSM Russell appeared at the front of the crowd now, looking serious, but Will had no time to stop and think about that. The game was away again and he charged forward to try and halt the relentless waves of Scottish attacks.

Owen saved another cross, leaping bravely to catch it despite being battered in the process. He went to kick it to Archie but the wind blew it over to the left and the solitary figure of Joe again. This time he controlled it well, and turned to see the menacing grin of the defender bearing down on him. He stumbled losing control of the ball, and the defender dived in with both feet laughing as he did so. Will grimaced waiting for the impact.

It had been a trick. Joe suddenly straightened up and pulled the ball back with his left foot before spinning round and flipping it onto his right. The defender shot past Joe and the ball and just slid off the pitch.

Joe said "Bye, Bye" and then skipped forward ignoring the cursing behind him.

"Yes pass, pass," one of the Sussex men shouted inside him, but Joe had no intention of passing to him. Instead he hit the ball with the outside of his right boot, and it arced into the area curling away from the keeper as it did to land perfectly on the head of the onrushing Archie who powered it into the back of the net. The men exploded in cheers.

"Oh I say, well done," Theodore said, to no one in particular.

As Archie took the plaudits Will smiled at his young comrade and said, "Same again Sussex, come on."

Despite his small frame, Joe was now everywhere, and the Camerons couldn't deal with him without fouling, and their frustration grew as time went by. A particularly cynical foul on Joe as he went to play a one-two with Archie led to a free kick on the edge of the area. The Sussex men piled forward and Will offered Joe the ball.

"No. They say you do the kicks. I watch." He smiled and Will placed the ball down. Danny trotted past to add his height in the box, saying "Now or never mate."

Will kicked his boots against each other to get some of the mud off and then looked at the scene in front of him. It was just a mass of pushing and shoving. He didn't have a clear sight of the goal but with no real organised defence, decided anything could happen. Theodore shouted "Off we go," and he smashed it for all it was worth hoping for a deflection.

It didn't deflect. It didn't stop. Archie fell over taking several players with him, and a number of the Scottish defenders threw themselves at it, but the ball just seemed to evade everybody and slammed into the top corner of the net.

Now it was the Sussex men going wild and the Camerons turned on each other with accusing fingers. Russell said something in Captain Fennell's ear and he shouted to Theodore that they needed to stop in a couple of minutes.

"Do you want to stop and call it a draw?" Theodore asked.

"Oh aye, that'll be right. Not feckin' likely," Jock said brooding over the score.

"Ok," Theodore responded, taking a couple of steps back and blowing the whistle nervously again.

"Right lads. One last effort then," Will called out. "Just don't concede."

*

Another Cameron attack broke down with a great tackle from Danny and he managed to kick the ball forward to Will. As the ball bounced towards him, Will saw the CSM looking at his watch and realised time was up. Clearly something was going on, and only then did he hear the guns were going again. But not the muffled thumps that had been exploding day and night for the last few days somewhere south of them. These were their guns now. They were loud and ominous. *Our bombardment has started, time's really up.*

Despite the broken ground Will managed to control the ball and pretty much as a final gesture launched it up the pitch towards Archie. It evaded all the defenders and fell invitingly into his path and instinctively Archie caught it first time on the volley. It sailed over the despairing dive of the keeper, and smacked plumb centre on the cross bar and then flew back at almost the same speed and angle.

"Oh dammit," Captain Fennell muttered under his breath, but then breaking with protocol, Sergeant Major Russell grabbed his arm and said, "Wait."

Archie tried to get his head to it but it went beyond him and looked to be flying back to the half way line, when out of nowhere Joe appeared sprinting parallel to the goal. As the ball hit the ground and bounced up he threw himself into the air sideways and caught it with a perfect scissor kick. Like the wooden ball that flew round the pub billiards table in the Star Inn, it changed direction once more and shot back past the startled defenders who had followed the ball down the field. Back past the now prone figure of Archie who had fallen over trying to hit it. And most importantly of all back past the Cameron keeper once more before he even had time to react. Only this time it didn't hit the crossbar, but sailed unerringly into the back of the net.

"Get in you beauty!" Archie cried and Theodore blew for time. The Sussex men erupted and converged on Joe, and very soon most of the crowd did too.

"Great goal Joe."

"What a turnaround."

"What a win."

"Showed those Jocks a thing or two."

The cries came from all round as the men shouted and cheered but Will took time out to walk amongst the disconsolate Scottish players and shake their hands. Though none of the others spoke or barely caught his eye, as he came up to Jock, the huge man nodded and said "Next time laddie, we'll have you."

"Look forward to it," Will replied, and smiled even though his hand burned with the fearsome embrace.

"Right men, fall in and back to barracks. Captain Fennell has said you can have an hour in the canteen then Battalion briefing at seven pm sharp." The voice of their CSM cut through the euphoria and the men began to break up, though the chance of a drink in the canteen lifted their spirits even more.

"What about young Joe 'eh?," Will said as he and Archie walked off. "Turned the game completely on its head. Don't mind saying it now but I wasn't sure we could win at half time."

"Really?" Archie said, with a grin. "I never doubted it for a minute."

Chapter 22 – Calm before the storm

Harold walked into the Star Inn and took a few moments to let his eyes adjust in the smoke-filled bar. He nodded to a number of men there who smiled or nodded back, and walked up to the counter.

"Evenin' 'Arry, pint of the usual?"

"Yeh that'll do for starters," Harold grinned. He looked around and saw Old Gettings by the fire. He was in full flow as ever. There were a couple of the farm labourers standing nearby and what looked like a visitor to the town, salesman by the look of him, wearing a crumpled suit. *Not doing so well if the suit is anything to go by,* he thought.

"Some kitchenware bloke from Brighton, trying to flog new ideas to the haberdashers and ladies round about," the barman said, seeing where Harold was looking. "Better keep your Aggie under lock and key 'Arry, or she'll blow the allowance on new-fangled gadgets."

"That'll be the day Jim," Harold replied raising his eyes at the pot-bellied barman. Jim Hutton had worked at the Star for as long as he could remember, and he'd been coming a long time now. He was in the Navy as a lad, someone once said, but rarely spoke of it. He was one of the few people to call Harold *Harry*, rather than Hal, which he preferred, but he didn't mind. *Gettings would be loving the chance of a stranger to talk to.* He smiled seeing him shout and wave his arms about then turned back to the bar.

"I was told Roger might be here. Is he in tonight?"

Jim flicked a thumb over his shoulder towards the back of the pub. "Sat up top 'Arry. In the snug. Sad business about his lad. Wouldn't catch me back on a boat. Bad enough in the storms without people shooting at you."

Harold nodded, trying to appear interested, but then walked off round the bar and sure enough found Roger Mullings sat alone at a table, nursing a whisky. Two empty glasses sat waiting for the third to join them.

"Evening Roger."

Roger looked up, eyes failing to recognise Harold at first and then the far-off look passed and he smiled. "Oh, hello Harold. How's the farm?"

"Just grand Roger. Mind if I…?" he let the words drift motioning to the table, unsure whether to sit or not.

"Oh sure, sure." Roger pulled a chair back and Harold perched on it.

"Want another?" He drained the whisky and waved the glass at Jim who nodded back.

"No Rog. Just got here. Not staying long. Wanted to see how you're doing."

He shrugged. "See for yourself."

"It's good to see the shop open again."

"That's John's doing. If it was down to me we'd still be shut."

"Well probably good to have some normality Roger. I know everyone in town is pleased to see you open again."

"Are they? That's good." There was a hint of sarcasm in Roger's voice and as Jim approached with the drink, Harold frowned at him, and he placed it on the side of the bar and stepped back.

"Normality you say? What's normal about this bloody war? Everyone just wants to go on pretending it's not happening. As long as old Mullings is open for business, that's all that matters eh?" Roger's voice had risen and a couple of men at nearby tables turned to look.

"Come on now Rog. It's not like that. People care, you know they do. Look at how full the church was."

"Course they care. But inside they are glad it's not them. Not their sons and husbands. Listen." Harold was about to speak but paused now as Roger raised a hand. "The guns. Can you hear them? Calling to us. Warning us."

"Maybe we should call it a night 'eh? I'll walk back with you."

"Back to what? Mary's lost her mind with despair." He looked at Harold now. His eyes were full of sorrow. "I'm thinking of taking her away Hal. Away from this."

"Good idea. Have a break. Bit of time in the country or by the sea."

"No somewhere else. For good. America maybe."

"Bit drastic Roger, isn't it? What about family, and friends like?"

Roger shrugged and saw the whisky on the counter and reached up for it. Harold winced with concern. His friend pointed at him as he drank. "Got to get away from the guns Harold. You'll understand one day. They're calling our boys to their doom."

"Nonsense. We're winning this war. Besides we had a letter from David only last week. Southdowns are going to be part of a diversion manoeuvre that's all. Not even in the main attack, wherever that is."

"I hope so. For your sake. Spare you this." He tapped his chest. "Pain Hal, day and night. Inside. He was on the pride of the Navy you know. A flagship. Went down with all hands." His head drooped.

"I know mate. Can I get you home?" There was a pause and then Roger looked up.

"No, I'll be fine. Get home to your family Hal. Appreciate the concern. Not good company at the moment. See you again soon 'eh?"

"Alright Rog. Just take it easy. Aggie sends her love. To you both."

Roger nodded and waved the half empty glass at him. Harold walked back down the bar to the door. He stopped where Jim was washing some tankards belonging to regulars. "Try and keep an eye on him will you? Maybe slow down the drinks."

"I'm trying 'Arry. He's been in here a lot recently. I even watered down the whisky last time, and we stopped taking his brass. Poor bugger."

"Thanks." They shook hands and Harold stepped out into the street. It was a beautiful early summer's eve that promised another fabulous sunset. The moon was already set, waiting in the wings amongst the clear blue curtains for its nightly appearance. All should have been well. But the guns were there in the background, pounding relentlessly away like drums, day and night now.

There was a burst of raucous laughter behind him and Harold looked back at the Star. He shivered, the words of Roger ringing in his ears, and felt a chill in his spine despite the warm evening. *They don't want to think about it,* he's right, *unless it drops right in their laps.* He lit a cigarette, inhaling deeply to shake off the melancholy, and then set off purposely for home.

*

A huge cheer and some raucous laughter greeted Will as he walked into the battalion canteen where the men were gathered. Danny was standing on the bar, drinking beer out of his boot from what he could tell, while the men chanted and egged him on. Will smiled and looked around for David, making his way through the assembled troops.

"This boot on this foot," Danny shouted, waving a bare foot in the air and nearly falling in the process, "is now a famous boot." There were jeers from the friends below him. He made a mock bow and appealed for calm. "Were it not for this boot, that made the match winning tackle, that was followed by my defence splitting pass, we would not have won." He took another drink and the beer poured down his face onto his chest.

"Bollocks," Archie shouted pushing to the bar. "It was my shot that set up the goal."

"You missed Bunden," Tommy shouted, "besides it was the Sarge set up the pass. Hey there he is. Ain't I right Sarge, you set up the goal?"

"It was a team goal," Will shouted back as everyone turned to look at him. "Technically it was the wooden bar that set it up."

"Don't talk about Corporal Bunden like that," Owen said and everyone laughed.

"Enough of that Welshy. Now speaking of bars, who's for more beer?"

Men shouted as they jostled forward. Danny looked about. "Where's Joe."

"Here he is," someone shouted from the back and pushed him forward.

"He's the real hero. Come and join us Joe." Joe shook his head but was thrust forward by the crowd. Will could see he was very uncomfortable by the attention, and probably more so being expected to drink with some of these men, and so stepped into the midst of them.

"Sorry to break up the fun boys but we are due at the briefing in ten minutes. I'm here to gather everyone up and get you over there so let's get cracking. Time to get your serious faces on boys. Show's about to begin."

There was a loud outpouring of groans and boos now, but gradually the men moved off. As Joe passed Will he simply said, "Thank you Sergeant," and then carried on. Archie and Danny passed arm in arm singing some well-known tune with very alternative lyrics. Danny was still waving his boot in the air.

"Boots on Private," Will said. "Officers are at the briefing and I'd hate for you to be on punishment detail when we go on this little jaunt."

"Yes Sarge," Danny said and as they moved off he heard him mutter, "He's beginning to sound more like a Sergeant Major every day!"

"Good I hope he makes it boyo. No one deserves it more."

"Teacher's pet, that's what you are Entwhistle."

Will smiled then as his friends went off in a group. He knew this was only a minor attack they would be involved in but it gave him great pride to know so many local lads would be in it together. He looked around the empty mess hall now. *Something to talk about when we get back for sure. It will be noisy that night*, he thought, and walked out.

*

"So, to conclude, the General has decided up at HQ that the 11th and 12th battalions will lead the attack with the 13th in reserve to provide support once the forward trenches are taken, and if necessary act as stretcher bearers. Hopefully you will be idle in that regard." Captain Fennell smiled now and then paused, as the various NCOs and junior officers wrote down their notes feverishly from his briefing. He used his own cane to point to the large map spread across the boards behind him.

"First wave to take the forward trench. Second wave supports and pushes onto the German reserve trench. Waves three and four will move through the lines and consolidate our position in their third line here." He tapped the board again. "Then the two battalions should link up and push forward into the rear if they can, and hold until relieved. This is where the fresh troops from the 13th will be vital, especially in case of counter attacks which of course is partly why we are doing this. I don't think Jerry is going to just let us saunter about the countryside, helping ourselves to wine and cheese."

Someone shouted "Shame" from the assembled men and everyone laughed. "Well quite. If orders change gentlemen, and we are to hold the ground rather than just pull back in due course, then we have lots of support moving up. It all depends how well we do and if they are distracted elsewhere. But if necessary the Hampshires, and Oxs and Bucks can come forward and join us in our new position."

Fennell paused again and in the silence that followed, save for the rustle of papers and the occasional cough, the muffled staccato sound of the guns could be heard beating out their deadly rhythm.

"Zero hour will be two am the day after tomorrow. Any further questions?" The men shuffled in their seats or where they stood as the reality of the event began to sink in, but no one spoke.

"Good well then you have your orders, and a full day to go over them while we move up to the front once more. We've trained for this day for months now gentlemen, and in the last week I've seen you hone your skills ready for the off. After our guns have hammered them for two days and removed the wire and other obstacles I daresay we will be lucky to meet any resistance. But I know that if we do, you will show them what for. Good luck to all of you and I will see you at the front. Sergeant Major dismiss the men."

As the men began to file away by company, Russell walked up to Will. "Well that's upset the apple cart. Never thought we'd be in reserve. Clearly they don't know who their best men are up at HQ."

"It's a shame Sergeant Major. But I'm sure they know what they're doing. Maybe they are saving the best battalion for the last to push on through the lines to where the resistance will be tougher," Will speculated, trying to hide his disappointment.

"Perhaps." Russell clearly wasn't convinced that was true and rolled his eyes as he walked off. "You men there, stop slouching and get a move on."

Will saw Archie being shepherded out of the door and just for a moment they caught each other's eye. Will smiled and nodded to reassure his friend, but he knew that look. He had seen it up close before. Archie was terrified and the 11th were leading the attack. He was about to follow him when a hand took his arm. It was David.

"You okay?" Will said.

"Yes Will. Lots to do before the off. Won't have much time to think."

"I know. It's a funny feeling knowing you are going over," Will said. "Hard to imagine it when you are back here where it's safe and quiet."

"Not sure it's so quiet with Archie in our lines," David replied and they laughed.

"Keep an eye on him if you can Dave. He's been here before, but that's not always a good thing. Sometimes it's better not to know what it's like, if you understand that."

"I understand. I'm still your big brother and smarter than you."

Will took his brother's arm in a warm embrace, and looked about the hall. "Eerie now they have all gone."

"Nan used to have a phrase for things like this. '*Calm before the storm boys*,' that's it," he said mimicking his grandma's voice. They laughed again. The bond between them evident had anyone remained to see.

"Yes, I remember. Well let's get off then and get it done."

They walked out of the hall together and went their separate ways. Will was walking to catch up with his company when he saw Archie standing on a small mound nearby staring at something in the fading light. A few of his company stood with him. As he wondered what his friend was doing the sound of bagpipes and drums came to his ears, muffled behind the buildings. He had always been drawn to their distinctive tune at fetes as a boy, and found himself instinctively pulled to join Archie.

As he reached the top he was taken aback to see rows of men marching in a long column. The rhythmic stamping of their boots, masked a moment ago down by the mess hall, now permeated the air and he watched as the Camerons marched smartly off towards the south. Will felt a childhood pang of disappointment that he had missed the band at the front and strained his eyes in the fading light to see if he could see them. Just for a moment that little boy fought inside him to race after them, shouting and cheering in their wake, and then he pulled himself back.

"Off they go, tails between their legs," Archie said, none too quietly, and a few eyes flashed at him from the ranks. The men with Archie jeered and some called out the football score. But no retorts came.

Only the incessant beat of the boots as a thousand feet landed as one, and the quiet swish of the arms raising up and down in perfect synchronicity by their sides. Somewhere ahead a voice called out the time. *A sergeant major no doubt,* Will thought.

"Left, right, left right…" the sound getting fainter.

"Well, well, look who it isn't" Archie sneered to his mates as the unmistakable looming figure of Jock approached marching with the rest. He looked much smarter than he had done earlier in the day, though the unmistakable swelling around the right eye bore testament to the previous 'skirmish'.

"Fancy having a bloke called Jock in the Jocko regiment," Archie said, and his friends laughed.

Will could see some of the Camerons were straining at the leash to fire insults back, but was impressed with their self-discipline, especially as the officers seemed to be further forward.

"That's enough now lads," Will said and some of the men looked a bit sheepish and stepped back. Archie was about to shout something again though, but then the unmistakable sound of the guns in the distance broke out. Like a tremendous storm they could see the night clouds on the horizon illuminating with the flashes and then the rumble of death followed in their wake. Though it was possibly twenty miles away, the bombardment still sounded ferocious and the mood in the group changed in an instant.

The Camerons marched on. There was no doubt they could see the same thing but they stayed smartly in time and it seemed to Will that even the band was playing louder at the front. Jock was level with them now and Archie took a couple of steps forward. Will went to grab him worried he would push things too far, but his friend shouted out before he could.

"Give 'em hell Camerons. Show those pointy headed bastards what real fighting is."

Will stopped and nodded appreciatively, as the men round about cheered and shouted words of encouragement. Jock didn't turn his head but they could see him smile, and it seemed he grew even taller as he strode away if that was possible.

The explosion of fire from their own guns much closer made several of them jump and focused them back on their own task ahead.

"Let's go," Will said and patted Archie on the shoulder. They shook hands once more and then Will doubled quickly away to follow his own battalion.

The guns roared again. Over and over, shell after shell, and the sky flashed and cracked in its deadly rage.

Chapter 23 – Cannon Fodder

The sun was already rising steadily the following morning, as Tommy came into the dugout looking flustered and tried to stand erect. The men were busy with last minute kit checks but laughed as he banged his head, enjoying the amusing interlude from their mundane tasks. Then he blurted out "There's an officer here to see you Sergeant," and the smiles turned to frowns. Will stood up as the imposing figure of his eldest brother stooped into the confined space, and all the men were on their feet in a moment. Something about the way he carried himself meant they reacted even sharper than with their own officers.

The Guards captain surveyed the dim interior. "Not quite the Ritz is it fellers? Still less room for rats and lice if they pack you in." The men didn't know how to react to the natural ease and humour of the new officer, but one or two smiled. "At ease men. I'm Captain Davison, Coldstream Guards. For those of you that don't know, that handsome Sergeant there is my brother." The smiles turned to wide open mouths now in more than one of the inhabitants standing round about. "Just popped up to wish you boys well and brought you a present of a few machine guns, courtesy of our Corps. Might come in handy tonight 'eh if they can keep up with the advance." There were muffled "thank yous" and a few nods. "If the big brass are to be believed, apparently we could all be in Moscow by the end of the weekend."

He smiled and the men laughed now, not out of politeness but genuinely, and not for the first time Will stood in admiration of his brother. "Well anyway. If you will allow me a few moments with your Sergeant I'll leave you to your preparations."

Will walked out behind his brother and they moved a little way along the front line to a natural break in the trench where it zig zagged back and forth before continuing its journey. Then in the defensive structure designed to stop shells travelling long distances along a trench, they embraced with friendship not fear. A thought went through Will's mind how he could be hugging his brother here like this, and the following day potentially wrestling with another man of a similar size and age for his life. *This ridiculous war.*

"It's great to see you James. What are you doing here?"

"Worrying about my little brothers of course. Not that I need to really. I chatted to Harry and he said it's just a diversionary action. Apparently our planes have spotted very light troops here and I'm sure the guns will break them up nicely for you."

"I hope so."

"I don't doubt it for a moment. You know they reckon they are going to fire nearly two million shells ahead of the main attack further south? Crazy isn't it?"

"Horrible," Will replied thinking of the men underneath it. "How can you possibly live through that?"

"Quite. Anyway, they tell me your battalion is in reserve?"

"Yes, more's the pity. David's going over first but he's a medic now."

"That's right. I heard from Mum in her last letter."

"Funny how we hear the local news from back in England." They smiled together; the bond unbreakable.

"Isn't it. Anyway, I saw David last night."

"Favouritism eh? Why didn't you come along later then?"

"Well he is older Will. But seriously I came across his battalion first and then Jerry started lobbing shells over so I stayed put. Not wanting to die with an inferior regiment." Will pushed him now, and they could have been fooling around in the barns back home. "I thought our trenches were cosy but yours are even worse!"

"They do pack us in. It will be weird having my own room again when I get home. We may all have to share."

"Not bloody likely. I'm an officer now." They laughed again and James lit a cigarette. Will declined to take one. James took a deep puff on it and his face changed. "Look Will, I know you have been here before but, don't chase battles if you don't have to. It's a different kind of war now too. Just be careful 'eh?"

"Of course I will."

"Besides if your role is to draw troops away from the south before the main push, then the hard fighting might come later. So be ready."

"I'm okay James, honest."

"I know, I know…just…well you know, your mum and all."

A sentry walked past then, snapping a salute out to the unknown captain, and carried on pretending not to see anything.

"I'll see if I can stay on until tomorrow morning, so I can at least watch you kick off."

"Do you need a bunk. I'm sure we can sort something out in the Sergeant's pit."

"Much as I'm sure that's delightful little brother, and full of the comforts of home, I've already been invited to the officers' billet behind the main line. Privilege of rank and all that. I should have gone back last night that's for sure. They probably want to know what a real soldier looks like!" He grinned as Will punched his arm.

"You're asking for it James. Anyway, the toffs are probably hoping you've brought some champagne with you more like."

"No doubt. Met a Captain Fennell. Seems a decent chap. He got me squared away."

"Yes, he's a good officer. All the men like him. Just like you."

"Well can you blame them?" He affected a mock heroic stance, and Will rolled his eyes.

"Don't let me keep you from your salmon sandwiches."

"Indeed not. I'll be thinking of you though as I gorge myself." They laughed out loud together and James pulled his brown leather gloves back on. He looked immaculate, even here in the trench. The smile paused. "I *will* be thinking of you Will. Take good care of yourself."

"I will James. And you. Back there in the officers' mess." He winked. "See you later *sir*."

Conscious more men were now starting to move back and forth, James just tapped his brother on the shoulder. He wanted to hug him again, to hold him tight, and not let him go. But there was no time. *As ever in this stupid war, there's never enough time.* James walked off a few paces and then turned to look at his brother once more, but Will had already gone. Back to being a soldier.

He sighed and turned into the connecting trench to the second line and walked slowly up it, saluting several men as he did so. Behind him the sun was already at its apex.

*

Sergeant Major Russell was in a hurry. He strode along the front-line trench, barely acknowledging the men who jumped up either side of him. Finally, he came to the first of the 13th battalion's dugouts and began calling them out.

"Out of your pits and follow me. Hurry up. I want everyone to congregate in the middle." He manhandled one of the younger men emerging from the next dugout. "Private Moffatt. Shift your young legs along the line and turn out everyone, save my old boots from marching all the way. I want everyone from 13th Battalion not on posts to gather on me now. Immediately. Go!"

As Moffatt ran off sticking his head in and out of the holes, men now came up frowning with a lot of discussion about what was occurring.

"Something's up Will," Tommy said. "Maybe the attack's off lads?"

"No such luck boyo," Owen said, as pessimistic as ever.

"Doesn't matter what's up. Shift yourselves outside now, and assemble on the CSM." Will emptied his dugout in seconds and as they jogged along the line, heads bowed, he could see his sergeant major was looking serious.

As the last of the men came up Russell looked around. "Is that everyone? Right I'll keep this brief. Change of plan for tonight. General has ordered that the 12th and 13th will now lead the attack. The 11th have been moved to reserve. We will take their place on the right of the line; the attack still kicks off at two in the morning." He paused to let the news sink in and could sense the mood change in the assembled men. "We've practiced this just the same as everyone else. You know the lay out in front of you and you know the objectives. Sergeants take time now to go over it again once more with your sections, and allow the men two hourly rests by company. But I want everyone ready to go an hour before the off. Questions?"

There were none. Russell looked around at the grim faces and forced a smile. "We're the best trained men in the brigade lads. Time to put it to the test and earn that reputation. Alright?" There was a general round of nods and agreement. "Oh, and one more thing. Where's Wagner?"

"Here sir," Joe said nervously, raising a hand amidst the men.

"You're to come with me for a debrief. HQ wants you out of it ready to go back for their sniper when this show is over. No arguments. Right carry on then. Dismissed."

Will moved to speak to his sergeant major but Russell just beckoned to Joe to follow him and strode off again without waiting. Someone nearby muttered, "Keeping him out because he can't be trusted more like," and there were some murmurings of ascent. Will looked round angrily but couldn't see who it was, but managed to grab Joe as he walked away through the tide of men dispersing in each direction.

"Don't pay them any attention you're better off out of it anyway."

"Maybe they are right. They didn't keep you out of it Sergeant."

"That's because they need my experience to lead the men. You're just a kid Joe."

"There's lots of kids here."

"Yeah but they can't shoot like you." Will tried a smile to reassure him.

"Get out while you can you lucky sod, and don't mind these miserable old timers." It was Danny who now spoke up as he walked past. "They'd swap places with you in a heartbeat if they could. Not about where you're from lad. They're just jealous." He raised his voice so it could be heard for the last part. Then with a pat on the arm he strolled off.

"I like Danny."

"He's a good man. See what did I tell you. Listen..."

"Private Wagner. Today if you please." Sergeant Major Russell's voice made the whole trench look round.

"I better *jump to it,* as you say, Sergeant." Joe smiled.

"Look after yourself Joe." Will reached a hand out and Joe shook it. Will couldn't believe how delicate his hands felt, for someone who was such a deadly shot.

"Good luck Will," Joe said with a sweet smile and then turned away. Will watched him walk off then followed the tide of men to his dugout, the rumours about the sudden change now on everyone's lips.

*

James spent the rest of the day familiarising himself with the main camp. The majority of Sussex officers were busy preparing for the upcoming attack so he decided to make himself useful. He spoke to the guardsmen who had brought up the additional machine guns and helped them carry some of the ammunition and spare kit up the line, much to their astonishment. Then he went into the kitchens and spoke with the cooks before enjoying lunch chatting to a number of the logistics soldiers who were to support the attack that night. Later on, he even went into the stores looking at the supplies they needed and put in a call to Jonners to see if he could free up a few overdue items.

By the time it was dark and he noticed some of the officers coming back to their billets for dinner, James had become quite the camp celebrity. More importantly he had reassured himself that his brothers were in good hands and well supported.

The mood in the mess hall was sombre however and the officers made little conversation, eating quickly before returning to last minute tasks. Several of them wrote short notes home he noticed, which seemed probably unwarranted, but James knew nothing was certain in this war and expecting the unexpected was always best.

One officer, a captain sat with him for a few minutes and took time to discuss the plans once more. This officer was more confident, buoyed by the fact the two day bombardment had obliterated the obstacles and front line defences no doubt. As he stood to go James realised he hadn't even asked his name.

"Forgetting my manners. James Davison, Coldstream Guards."

"Any relation to a Will Davison from Steyning?" the fellow captain asked.

"Sadly yes. He's my younger brother. Got another one here too, David. Do you know them then?"

"I'll say. I'm a Steyning man myself. Have served with Will before. Good soldier. I did hear tell his brother was in the Guards. Pleasure to meet you. I'm Goodman. Theodore Goodman. I'm with the 12th battalion tonight."

"Small world Theodore. Appreciate the comments about my brothers. I'm sure it will all go smoothly tonight but good luck."

"Thanks James. Let's hope so 'eh. Bit of a hoo-hah with the General hasn't helped but that's the army for you. Anyway, must dash. Not cricket to be late for the off."

They shook hands and James sat pondering Goodman's final comments for a moment and then decided to try and find out what was going on. He went over to the officers' billet where his kit had been stowed and asked for Captain Fennell. He was told he would be along later and settled down to wait. However, when he tried to speak to any officer that dashed in and out about the upcoming attack, no one seemed keen to chat, and he became more agitated inside. *Probably briefed not to talk to strangers you fool,* James told himself.

Eventually he couldn't stand sitting about any longer and went back to the main building and tried to ring through to Jonners. But Private Irwin advised him the Major was busy so, frustrated once more, James went back out and lit up a cigarette. The night sky was clear now with only the faintest wisps of clouds drifting lazily across it. He looked at his watch illuminated brilliantly by the large crescent moon that swaggered about its kingdom behind him. *Not a great night to attack*, he mused. As he blew another waft of smoke into the cool air, he saw Captain Fennell dash into the billet ahead of him, and set off in pursuit.

"Captain Fennell. Everything ready for the off?"

James saw the captain frown at him before recognition crossed his face.

"Good Lord. Davison. Completely forgot about you. Sorry old fruit. So much to do. Are you being looked after?"

"Yes, fine really. Felt a bit of a spare part but managed to make myself useful here and there."

"Oh, you're the officer I heard was carting kit about, giving us a bad name."

James raised his hands as an apology but Steven just laughed and told him not to worry.

"Glad of those Vickers guns you brought up I can tell you. Let's hope we don't need 'em."

"Indeed. Look Steven I appreciate you're busy, but I heard there's been some issues with the General about tonight. Having a personal interest here as you know, I wondered what you could tell me?" James didn't let on what he'd heard or where and just looked as neutral as he could. But rather than confirm the previous version of events Steven first checked no one was outside and then came up close to James.

"Not great actually old boy. The 11th battalion commander, Colonel Grisewood, apparently refused to go over." James raised his eyebrows with genuine surprise but stayed silent. "Apparently told the General the attack was pointless and wasn't going to let his men be used as cannon fodder. General wasn't best pleased and relieved him of command."

"I see, and how has the Colonel reacted?"

"I'm not sure to be honest. He spoke to us very quickly and then had to leave. He was a very popular CO and it's affected the men I'm sure. Still the attack will go ahead as planned."

Fennell started to grab some things together now. Clearly keen to move on.

"What do you think about the attack? Were the Colonel's concerns justified?"

James' question clearly took Steven unawares and he paused for a moment. "Not really my place to question the bigger picture Davison old boy. I understand the concerns, but the Colonel was also feeling the strain as it was. He'd lost a brother to illness and has another due to go over with us so I don't think that helped. He was no coward, but whether we question the orders or not, we have to follow them. Too many other parts linked into this."

James nodded. "You're right of course. It's hard when you have the fate of men in your hands, and they trust you with their lives. We all react differently to that."

Fennell stopped and looked at James as if he had expressed something he had been thinking himself. "Quite. Anyway, I must leave you. You're welcome to stay here tonight as I said. If we break through to the German border I'll have a man sent back for my stuff. You can help bring it up." They laughed and shook hands. "Oh, and if you want to watch, there's an observation post about a hundred yards along to the right with views over No Man's Land. It's sunken and bagged so should be quite safe."

"Thanks Steven. Good luck."

*

The men of the Southdowns moved quietly out along the front trenches, officers and NCOs working up and down the line to get them into position. The 12th battalion were on the left and the 13th on the right facing the enemy. The forward trench was so full that the third and fourth waves had to mass in the communications trenches that ran between their front lines, waiting to file in when the first two waves went over.

The 11th battalion that would act as support was asked to move back even further to the second line and would be brought up as needed. Will saw the unmistakable shape of Archie walking off and they nodded to each other. Shortly after David appeared heading back with the rest. He wore red cross patches on his arm to denote he was a medic. *Not that Jerry would tell the difference in the dark,* Will thought. They passed within a few feet of each other but not close enough to shake hands.

"Good luck Will," David whispered, and gave his brother a thumbs up as he turned to the rear lines.

"See you later."

"Alright my lucky lads, nice and quiet now, first wave move up to the front." The relaxed voice of Sergeant Major Russell brought calm to them all. Captain Fennell appeared and nodded to Russell.

"First wave ready on the ladders if you please Sergeant Major."

"Leading companies prepare. Pass the word."

The men had drilled and drilled for this, and now moved into line. Will was in the second line and watched the men from other companies prepare on the step. He knew they would be nervous. He knew they would be scared. Just like he was. But he continued to smile at the men around him. Now his friends looked to him for leadership just like Russell said they would. Old and young alike tried to gather around the veterans to get them through the first few steps until the training kicked in. If it kicked in.

Above them the guns continued to fire. Barrage after barrage roaring overhead and landing amongst the enemy with horrific whines and bellows. Every so often screams came from the darkness ahead and men nodded with satisfaction as more of their foe were blown to bits. No longer someone's father or son. Now they were the enemy and nothing more.

One of the battalion majors appeared who would be bringing up the third and fourth waves. Major Fleming moved his lit pipe to the side of his mouth and looked at his pocket watch. He said something quietly to Captain Fennell, the words unintelligible under his thick moustache, and then replaced his watch and shook hands. Will watched him dig at his pipe now with a small metal tool and then puff on it again. He was reassured about how calm the officers were. It felt just like a training exercise and he sensed his own anxiety reduce. Appearing satisfied the major nodded and moved back into the shadows and Fennell stepped forward.

"Five minutes everyone." Will and his fellow NCOs checked their watches once more. "Bayonets please Sergeant Major," Fennell added quietly, as if chatting to a friend in the street.

"Battalion will fix bayonets by company pass the word. Fix...bayonets."

Everywhere there was the scrape of metal being drawn and clicked into place. The noise resonated in the dark, but above them the guns continued to fire. One of the soldiers was sick, heaving violently across the ladder where they were due to climb shortly, and men nearby cursed him.

"Settle down lads. Eyes front. Remember your drill. The wires are down, so focus on the crossing points. Think about the ground we practiced on. Sergeants, keep in formation, keep the men moving. We'll have engineers on our right helping with any unseen obstacles and even laying boards if we need 'em so don't get trigger happy."

Will saw the men really focus now. Some were clearly scared, especially the young ones, but all were nodding at the sergeant major's words. Captain Fennell joined in.

"Two minutes everyone, pass the word. Guns will stop shortly." He smiled in the dark, the flashing white teeth highlighting the gesture. "Right gentlemen, keep it simple, and with a bit of luck we can keep Jerry's mind away from the big push tomorrow in the south. Good luck the 13th."

A number of the men said "And you sir," and then right on cue the guns stopped. An eerie silence fell across the whole trench and Will saw the captain take his whistle out of a pocket as he looked at his watch. An orderly moved in with a lamp and Fennell checked the time and nodded. Then, smiling at the men closest to him, Will watched him put his watch in his top pocket, even pausing to do up the button. *So calm...*

Time paused.

Fennell put a hand on the nearest ladder. He looked up into the blackness and took a deep breath. Glancing back into the trench his voice suddenly roared into the silence and many men jumped.

"For King and Country then, come on!" He blew the whistle loud and long and was up the ladder in moments and gone. As the captain's blast was answered along the line, Russell shouted "Up the Southdowns!" and threw himself forwards.

There was a huge roar and the men poured up the ladders and out of the trench. Will's stomach lurched as he watched them go…and then the machine guns started.

*

Teresa took a pile of blood-soaked cloths from the trolley and walked over to where the orderlies had a boiling pan of water on the go and dropped them in. She took a large wooden ladle and stirred them for a moment before going to the sink and washing her hands. As she looked about the ward, drying her hands on a towel, she caught sight of Rose slumped down on one of the empty beds, and immediately walked quietly over.

"Are you ok Rose?"

"Oh, hello Staff. Just tired that's all. And very hot."

"Yes, we've had a run of nights 'eh. But you have been struggling of late. Spot of brandy maybe cheer you up a bit?"

"That might help." Rose managed a smile.

Teresa walked over to the large white medicine cabinet by the wall and took out a half full bottle of French brandy.

"I think the Colonel's had more of this than the patients," she said pouring Rose a shot in the metal lid it came with. She passed it over with a smile. "You know it's actually quite cool tonight. I noticed a strong breeze by the door as I went to get this just now. Do you want to go outside for a bit?"

"Yes, in a minute Staff. I just feel so hot, and a bit faint. Bit pathetic I know. Let me get my legs first."

Teresa sat down on the bed next to her friend and looked about at the men nearby. They all appeared to be asleep, which was the best thing for any of them. "How long have you felt like this?"

"Oh, just the last few minutes."

"No, I mean how many nights has it been like this?"

Rose frowned as if trying to think. "I don't know. It's been a while since I…" She paused and looked at Teresa, and now her eyes looked scared.

"How far gone are you Rose?"

"What? Oh no it's nothing like that…"

"Rose…"

"Three months I think…" the tears came now, more with relief, and Teresa gave her a hug.

"Does he know?"

Rose shook her head and pulled out a hankie to blow her nose. "I didn't know how to tell him. I tried last time he was here but…"

Teresa looked around again. "But you got swept up in the moment I know. Not for the first time."

Rose laughed a little. "How did you guess?"

"Oh please. Going off to be sick. Hot flushes when it's cool. Hamilton thinks you've lost your stomach for the work and was talking about sending you back." Rose looked terrified. "Don't worry, I told him to ignore it. Said I'd sort you out. Though frankly might not be such a daft idea to keep you safe."

"I'm not going back T. Promise me you won't send me!"

"I could order you back. But I won't, don't worry, unless things get too risky here. You need to tell him though. He has a right to know."

"I know. He's calling in on the way back. I said we could speak then." She took Teresa's hand now. "I'm scared he will run away. He will think I've done it to trap him. He's an officer and I'm just a nurse and…"

"And a very good one at that. Don't be so soft Rose. He's head over heels with you. Besides his parents are farmers not Lords and Ladies. I'll be here don't worry. I'll ensure he makes an honest woman of you." She picked up a nearby saw from a side trolley and waved it in the air. Rose laughed then, clearly feeling much better.

"I should have told you. Sorry."

"I'll forgive you. But I need some of this myself first." Teresa took a swig of the brandy from the bottle and then paused frowning.

"What is it T?"

"The guns have stopped."

*

Agnes rolled over and her arm fell across Harold's side of the bed. It didn't connect with anything and somewhere her subconscious registered the difference and she came to. The bed was uncharacteristically cold, and she looked around in the darkness struggling to focus. Harold was outlined in the window, pipe in hand, the smoke meandering towards the opening like a small summer stream. Barely moving. She watched him take another puff on the pipe and then sat up.

"What are you doing love?"

"Just listening to the night lass."

"You'll catch a chill Hal."

"I'm fine, don't worry. Go back to sleep."

She got up now ignoring his words and wrapped a shawl round her shoulders, her long nightdress trailed on the floor as she stepped tentatively towards him.

"I can't sleep if you're stood here. What is it?"

He looked down at her, features barely visible despite the bright moon outside. She felt the rich aroma of the tobacco on her face as he breathed in her direction. He put an arm round her and she was comforted by his warmth, though his heart beat quickly and seemed to leap out at her through his chest.

"The guns have stopped."

She looked up at him but he was staring out of the window now, towards the darkness beyond their farm. She felt him sigh.

"Hold me," she whispered and he pulled her in close in a tight embrace.

Chapter 24 - The first half

Will had taken a few steps forward. He was yet to take a penalty and knew he must score to keep them in the match. For him the shouts were merely a distraction. As he took the long, lonely walk forward he shut them out of his mind. He placed the ball carefully on the spot and looked up. The tall keeper seemed to fill the frame of the goal. Will weighed up his opponent - the piercing blue eyes that betrayed no sign of nerves stared back at him unflinching.

Keep focused, he told himself. Just pick a spot and go for it. His heart was pounding; so loud he felt that it must surely be heard by everyone nearby. He touched the team badge on his shirt for luck, as he always did to calm himself at the start of a game. The referee put the whistle to his lips, and Will let out a deep sigh to relax.

It began to rain hard again. Heavy drops, like falling stones, splashed and stung in equal measure, but Will wiped them from his face, knowing he must ignore everything and just focus on the ball and where he was going to shoot. He saw a drop explode in a puddle near the penalty spot, sending wet dark splashes onto the ball. Will registered the place in his mind so he didn't step there and slip.

He took a deep breath, and in the profound silence that followed he heard Danny shout, "Now or never, Will!" The voice seemed a mile away as if in a dream, and then the whistle blew and he started to stride forward, eyes fixed firmly on the ball.

There was a huge roar as if a thousand voices were unleashed at once, and everywhere the whistle seemed to echo on and on...

Will looked up. It was dark. The opposition's goalkeeper had transformed into their sergeant major who was shouting at the men to get moving. He snapped out of his memory and came back to the gruesome reality of the mud-soaked trench and lurched forward.

Will reached for the ladder pausing to wipe the rain from his eyes that seemed to be coming sideways now. He slipped in the dark and cursed as he caught his shin sharply on the bottom rung. A hand on his shoulder made him look round and Danny was there as always, face blackened for the assault. "Up you go Sarge – it's now or never!" The grinning teeth skeletal-like in the dark.

A wall of noise hit him. Shouts, screams, explosions, and the air full of a deathly buzz, as bullets and shrapnel fizzed around like the flies back home in the heat of summer. He saw men falling back left and right and shouted "Come on Sussex", at the top of his voice before hurling himself over the top.

They were just waiting for us, his mind screamed, as somewhere through this ghastly din the whistle continued to blow.

*

The soldier in front of Will stumbled and lurched back. He caught him and steadied them both. "Easy mate, watch your step." Will patted the man on the back for encouragement but as he let go, he just fell back past him and into the trench. Will was momentarily stunned and now felt a warm liquid on his hands and knew it was blood. He fought the urge to be sick. Another cry of "Come on Sussex!" made him start and he began to run blindly forward, but heard another sergeant telling them to "Keep formation, keep the line."

He slowed down again and looked around, embarrassed. But everywhere the men were the same. Confused, scared, angry; some soldiers ran, some walked, until the landscape had fractured the battalion into disparate groups of men hauling themselves forward in the mud and chaos, all their training forgotten. Then the German artillery opened up to add to their machine guns and the ground began to erupt all around them.

A shell landed nearby showering Will with mud, the clunk on his helmet heightening his senses. He decided running was the best option and made for a break in the wire where other men were now converging. Danny was ahead and to the right of him, shouting and waving his arms as if they were just mucking about on his farm back home. Will looked about but in the confusion couldn't see anyone else he knew and so made for Danny. As he closed on him another shell landed right on the wire where men were pushing through. There was a blinding flash as if he had looked directly in the sun and then complete stillness.

He shook his head and realised he was on his back and thought for one delicious moment he was home in Mill Road, lying in his attic bed on a Sunday morning. *The smell of bacon tantalisingly drifted up the stairs, seducing him and his brothers out of their warm beds for breakfast...*

Then frustratingly Peterson appeared shaking him and the noise returned, and with it more explosions and the awful buzzing in the air. His ears seemed to pop and with them the Sunday morning reverie went too. He wanted to go back there and tried to push the lawyer's son away, holding on to the side of the bed, but Peterson had a firm hold of him. The bed and bacon evaporated in the swirling deathly mist.

A tangle of thoughts hit him as his senses struggled to clear properly from the explosion. He looked about and they were in a shell hole a few yards from the wire. But which side of the wire he couldn't make out immediately. He became aware of Peterson shouting at him close by.

"Are you okay? Sarge, are you okay?"

"Where is everyone Peterson? Where's Boyd?" he replied, trying to get his bearings again in the gloomy dawn.

Despite the poor light, he could see Peterson was really scared, and mumbled almost imperceptibly: "Gone, all gone … the shell…" His voice trailed off.

Will sat up, realised his helmet was missing, and ducked down again finding it nearby. He pulled it on. *Stupid* he thought to himself, as the buzzes circled his head, knowing how many men without a helmet had been caught by flying debris or the sniper's sight. *Not that it did much,* he mused, but it gave comfort none the less. He composed himself now and then grabbed Peterson. "Where's Danny, Private?"

Peterson nodded to the wire and said: "He's gone, Will."

He was shaking, clearly close to breaking point. Will realised that using his Christian name meant Peterson was losing hold of his emotions. Will knew the officers wouldn't tolerate any sign of weakness so grabbed the boy's arm as much to steady himself as to stop Peterson running away. He could feel his own fear rising. He chanced a look over the shell hole lip to the wire and saw no one close. Further up and down men were still climbing over or through the wire. The attack was continuing and he could see the third wave preparing to come over the top some hundred yards behind them, a wall of bayonets protruding above the trench like fence posts.

"I thought the guns were supposed to kill all the Germans," Peterson stuttered.

"Well it looks like they missed a few lad," Will replied trying to get his eyes to focus in the darkness. It was impossible to get any kind of night vision with all the flashes from the guns going off, and a constant stream of enemy flares firing into the sky. Will tried to work out what was going on in a series of snapshot images in the macabre lights.

He saw a couple of his company in the next hole throw their arms up as if waving to him, and instinctively he started to wave back to usher them forward - and then watched them fall into the darkness. When the next light flashed on they were gone.

Christ.

Seeing Peterson was calmer now, Will loosened his grip on the lad to check his rifle and then looked forward. Somebody in the German lines fired a flare much further to their right and immediately machine gun fire snaked away in that direction. Will couldn't recall which of their companies was on the far side, but in the new light he saw a church steeple, ghost-like in the glare, some half a mile to the front.

Oh, there's Richebourg, he noted with a half-smile, and fixed his bearings. "Southdowns! Rally point here!" As Will shouted out he immediately heard a number of men respond and their equipment jangling as they moved towards him. Instinct told him to get going. Staying still for too long was a deadly mistake.

"Come on Peterson," he said, and dragged the lad with him as they set off again.

Something close to the wire caught his eye and he stopped to inspect it. He would recognise it anywhere. Just a couple of days ago the boot, now half buried in mud, was being paraded around the mess bar they were drinking in. It was the boot the owner claimed set up the winning goal against the Cameron Highlanders. The bright yellow laces taken from his football boots and worn for luck despite orders to the contrary were illuminated in the latest flare to be fired over the wire by the enemy, leaving no doubt in Will's anxious eyes.

It was Danny's boot.

*

James stared into the black canvas of the night from the observation post and heard the chilling sound of the whistles, that he had heard all too often before. He felt his own chest tighten as the roar of men carried to him, and then watched in horror as the flashes and explosions lit up the ground ahead of them. He recalled once seeing a revolving zoetrope in the vicarage as a small boy, during a visit with his mum. Laughing at the flickering images inside of a man riding a horse as he turned the wheel faster and faster. It had kept him transfixed for what seemed like hours, as he was transfixed now by the same ghastly images that flickered in the dark in front of him. Rifle and machine gun fire in chaotic patterns of death. Explosions throwing screaming shapes into the air. Dark lines of men appearing and disappearing moving forward.

James walked out of the back of the observation post into the trench. Around him he saw the men of the 11th battalion crammed together along the second line. He could feel their apprehension. They knew something wasn't right and he could sense their urge to get forward and help their friends. A number of them were now straining to see out in the dark until they were told to keep their heads down. Then he saw David looking straight at him. Looking to his big brother for answers. He looked around and saw a sergeant.

"Send a runner back to HQ and tell them the battalion are meeting heavy resistance. Tell them the attack may stall and need support. Go."

As a man was detailed to run back there were more explosions, more screams, and then the orders for the remaining waves to get forward could clearly be heard. It was impossible to tell from back here what was happening and James could stand it no longer. With a glance at David he pushed through the advancing men towards the front line.

*

Will lurched forward slipping on the mud but managed to hold onto the boot as he stumbled. Instinctively he dropped into another shell hole where several soldiers were sheltering from the withering fire. His eyes searched frantically for Danny, or any sign of him but there was nothing.

An officer appeared momentarily alongside him. He was covered in mud which gave him a devilish appearance as only the white eyes shone out of this dark mask wildly darting about. Without looking at who was around him the officer shouted. "Company Sergeant Major. We have to keep moving forward. Get the men through this damned wire and on. Get them moving now." Will realised it was Captain Goodman.

"Sir," came the familiar voice of the CSM who had appeared behind them unnoticed by Will. He tried to come 'to attention' instinctively while lying down, even though it was daft, but like all soldiers he was on edge in the presence of higher ranks. He didn't want to look round, just waiting for the order to move, but realised the CSM must have followed him out of the trench and wondered if he saw him go down.

"11th Division will sort out support and casualties so tell the men to push on and not stop for anything. Let's go!" the captain yelled over the noise of continued shelling.

The 11th! David was in the 11th, his brain reminded him. He risked a quick look back but it was just a sea of faces everywhere, some running, some walking blindly on, some stumbling and crying for help. Still more crowded in the holes and ruts of the unforgiving mud, waiting to bury them forever, before they darted on again like rats. Out here in this hell of no-man's land, they were all just rats fighting to survive.

"Eyes front Sergeant." The CSM's voice snapped him back from his thoughts. "No point looking back now. Only the dead and dying will be behind us lad. Got to follow the Captain." As if on cue Theodore Goodman brought his whistle to his lips and began to blow again, rising up as he did so.

"Come on Sussex!" Goodman shouted. Russell gave a roar and the men followed suit, emerging from the ground once more with shouts and cries, looking more like an army of the dead as they rose up; which to all intents and purposes they were, dancing to the whistle's macabre tune.

Will let the boot fall and watched it sink slowly into the murky water at the bottom of the hole, wrenching at his emotions as it did so. He felt like he was leaving Danny here and wanted to stay with him but knew he must push on. *Now or never lad, come on,* a voice in his head said, and he leapt forward.

They poured on through the wire and beyond, shells and bullets swatting them this way and that. Though some wooden structures had been laid across the ditches by the pioneer corps men in the first wave, they only acted to funnel the men. The fire from the Germans did not even have to be accurate to take its toll in the places where the men crowded together. It reminded Will of the sheep dips back home, the frightened creatures pushed on by Sally, funnelling them into the line where they had no choice but to go forward and be sprayed. *As the bullets sprayed them now.*

A number of men started moving away from the obvious paths and just doing anything to ignore the murderous fire. Will leapt down into one of the ditches avoiding the bridge and stumbled over a fallen officer from the first wave. He noticed it was Lieutenant Grisewood, shot through the head and lying pistol in hand. He was Colonel Grisewood's youngest brother, the colonel having been replaced of course the day before. Now his second brother was gone and Will wondered if the colonel had had a premonition. He was struck with how peaceful the young lieutenant looked. *We may all join you soon sir*, he thought seeing the hail of shells and bullets carpeting the ground ahead. He covered the officer's face with his hat, then shook his head and ran on.

*

The 13th Division came upon a sunken dyke which had not been on any map or in their training ground reconstruction. The first two waves were all mixed up now and men stumbled and fell into this man-made ditch in droves. With mounting casualties and the devastating fire from the Germans just incessant, the attack stalled here and the men's courage failed at last. Will stumbled into the dyke and sank knee deep in sucking black water. He looked to the left to see if the 12th were doing better but the smokescreen from the British guns had obscured their section completely and it was impossible to see anything from where they were.

He pushed through the black sludge pulling about his knees as he tried to reach the far side of the dyke and temporary shelter. His legs brushed against something hard, and he looked down as another flare illuminated one of the battalion lying face down dead. Will stooped to move the man away and as he did so the body rolled over and he found himself looking at Owen. He had been hit several times by the look of it and Will prayed he had died instantly. His ginger hair, shining in the phosphorous light, floated on top of the dank water, in stark contrast to its dark surroundings. "No replay this time mate," Will murmured sadly. He pushed him as gently as he could, out of the way, and then moved on to the other side of the dyke. A solitary tear slipped from the edge of his eye as he joined the sheltering men.

Everywhere the cries of the wounded and dying could be heard fuelling this morale sapping scene. It became clear to Will that few officers had made it to the dyke, adding to the chaos, and they were rapidly merging into one large pack of men trying to survive. He heard a sergeant shouting for names to count his company and Will began to do the same, as much to hear from friends as anything.

Suddenly someone shouted "Come back you fool," and Will saw 'Bod', a fishmonger from Brighton, dash to help a wounded man crawling back a few yards in front, his right leg missing below the knee. The man was moaning pitifully and Will thought he would retch at the sight. Bod was limping himself as he ran but Will knew he had always had this affliction and it just added to the piteous scene. Despite that Bod reached the man, but as he bent to pull him up, the German machine gunner reached him and its deadly snake of bullets enveloped both the soldiers.

There was an anguished cry from his right and another man raced forward and Will realised it was Herbert, Bod's younger brother. Neither would fish from Brighton pier again and Will closed his eyes as the bullets hit home. In a last grasp for life Herbert shouted "Mum," and then fell across his brother's lifeless chest in a final embrace.

Will's eyes stung from tears and the battle's smoke that also started to sweep across them now, threatening to obscure the way forward. The situation was rapidly becoming hopeless and he noticed even the CSM a few yards away had faltered at that moment. Will saw Russell's eyes waver following the desperate deaths of the Banstead brothers just now, and he was clearly searching within himself for the courage to push on.

"Everyone is scared lad," Russell had said to him just a few hours before, when moving through the companies carrying out last minute checks. "Trick is not to show it." He caught Will's eyes now and winked, as if reading his mind. And even though there was no real conviction in it, that act alone made Will glad he was here with them now.

At that moment Captain Goodman shouted out from further down the trench urging the men to push on. He scrambled out of the dyke, with half a dozen men joining him and they lurched forward, crouched low, the whole battalion seemingly mesmerised by his actions. Will saw the CSM raise up by the lip ready to go, and then a shell landed right in the middle of Goodman's party and they disappeared in an eruption of smoke and noise.

Incredibly one of them appeared out of the smoke running on but was then cut down by the guns. Will saw another dragging himself back towards the dyke but he too was shot dead. There was another shout and someone broke from the dyke and ran hell for leather to a small dip in the ground and dropped down. Will held his breath and was sure everyone was doing the same. There was a shout of "covering fire" and along the wall men opened up on the German lines. The soldier rose up once more, this time with a man on his back and ran back to the dyke. Incredibly the bullets zipped past him and he leapt back in unscathed.

"Who was that?" Russell shouted above the noise.

"Peterson, Sergeant Major," a voice shouted back. "Rescued the Captain."

"Is he alive?"

"Yes sir, but he's wounded bad."

"Right, find a medic, get him patched up."

Will was amazed that Peterson of all people would risk his life, after seeming so useless in the football match. He felt spurred on by his example but more shells landed now, some right amongst them, and more men were killed. Russell knew the attack was faltering. Without officers to push the men on it was becoming hopeless and most seemed to be missing or dead.

"Get up the line and try and find Captain Fennell, or any officer. Get them to me lad." He sent a runner off through the mud, but he had only gone a dozen paces when a bullet hit the side of the head and he fell dead. "Shit. Look lads we have to push on. We are just asking for it if we stay here. The next waves will be here soon. We have to go forward."

He tried to rally the men but their heads were down hugging the stone wall of the dyke or cowering in the mud desperate to survive. Then suddenly Russell looked up with a look of complete shock. Will followed his gaze and saw another officer heave himself out of the dyke and rise to his feet in full view of the Germans and the surviving Southdown battalion sheltering below him. Will thought it might be their colonel but then realised it was another captain and guessed it must be Captain Fennell. For a moment the whole world seemed to hold its breath, as the captain looked around him. He stood baton in hand as if on parade, oblivious to the bullets whizzing past him.

"Up, up," he shouted, while the men's legs turned cold and their heads hung, unable to go on. "Listen to the Sergeant Major. We must keep moving, get up damn you." He went to speak again but was hit in the arm and lurched forward momentarily with the force of the impact. He steadied himself on one knee before rising again and this time he roared.

"For God's sake get up now. You're the Southdown battalions. Arise sons of Sussex. Arise and do your duty. Show them what Sussex men are made of!" He was hit again now, several times it seemed and the force spun him round and he fell into a pit behind him. Will could still hear his words echo as he fell.

It didn't matter.

The effect was instantaneous and with howls, the Sussex men arose, wraith like in the thickening fog. The whole line poured forward now, all sense of fear and safety gone. They roared on unflinching into death's embrace, past the stricken captain. Will ran to where he lay and turned him over. He had been hit two or three times again and his left arm and side were a bloody mess, and he was sure to die. Even so he grabbed Will and shouted "Get on…soldier." The voice broke through the fog, as much in Will's head as on the battlefield, and he realised it was James.

"Oh God James! No, no! It's me Will," he shouted, the tears welling up, and he screamed desperately behind him, "Stretcher bearers!"

James' face flickered in recognition and he grabbed Will with his right arm, the left being shattered, and pulled him in for a moment. "Will…Forget about me now. You have to push forward and take that trench. I'll be alright…just keep the attack moving."

Will shook his head furiously and started to try and stop the bleeding. “No, I’m not leaving you here to die. I can get help. Take you back. Get you home…” His voice trailed off as he fumbled with a bandage in his pouch, overcome with the emotion of the last couple of hours. The small bandage pointless to stem the flow of blood but he had to do something.

James grabbed him again. “Now listen to me soldier. There is no going back. Do you understand? Or all this is for nothing…” He began to cough, blood appearing out of the corner of his mouth, but he lurched up again. “Now get forward and take that trench. Are you listening Sergeant? That’s an order!” He collapsed back on the ground, the effort of shouting too much for him to take.

The barked command made Will jump and he pulled back and instinctively replied, “Yes sir.”

“Good…” and then James’ face softened as the pain subsided for a moment and he spoke as if in the kitchen back home. “Will…”

Will paused, caught between his roles as a brother and serving soldier. He moved in close again.

“Yes James?”

“Look after Freddie won’t you, and…” his breath was laboured now, coming in grating rasps. Will took hold of him again, holding him up. “And…tell Mum I love her.”

The tears came again as Will nodded and mouthed “I will.” He screamed “Stretcher bearer” at the top of his voice two or three times. Bullets now zipped into the earth near where he knelt and he flinched at the sound.

James looked at him and smiled. “Go,” he said, pushing him away with his good arm. Will laid him back tenderly and with a last painful look, he was up and gone as the training taught him, charging on.

James watched him go, then his body spasmed and he turned his head back to stare up into the sky. He saw flashes in the dark and heard the roar of shells flying overhead, a long way away. An odd thought came to him. *Dad will never forgive me for not finishing that barn door.* Then the pain returned and the battle’s noise went silent, and the world went completely black for Captain James Gordon Davison of the Guards Brigade.

Chapter 25 - The Match Ball

Sally whined as Harold finished his cup of tea and started to pull his boots on, the ache in his back as constant as the routine he performed every morning.

"No thunder girl, not today," he said knowing her noises as much as anything else on the farm.

Sally hated storms, though she had worked through plenty in her time when asked to. If the lightning came though she preferred to be under the kitchen table or round their legs for reassurance. But Harold knew she was whining now because the rumbling of the last few days had stopped; always sensitive to any change in routine.

As he opened the side door she patted up by his legs and they both looked south as if for news. He noted the sun was already setting the dark clouds on fire with a deep red hue, and he should get on. *Red sky in the morning, shepherd's warning,* he thought to himself. A noise behind him made him pause and Agnes was there pulling her robe over her nightdress. Sally ran over to nuzzle her.

"Hello Aggie love," he said.

"Couldn't sleep. Have you had some tea?" she replied yawning.

"Yes. Just off to sort the cows."

They had spent much of the night on the old armchair in the bedroom wrapped in the blankets until Agnes had fallen into a fitful sleep. Then Harold had carried her back to bed and laid on top of the blankets holding her, his mind racing in the silence.

They knew that the far-off thunder they often heard were the big guns on the front firing back and forth. Old Gettings reckoned they could be heard in London before a "big push." Now the silence was even more deafening. Agnes joined Harold at the door, the smell of sleep still about her.

"Do you think our boys..." her voice broke as her deep brown eyes watered and he gave her a hug.

"Our lads can take care of themselves lass. They will be fine." He wanted to reassure himself but they had seen the lists grow on the church door. A few more names every week for local men, and indeed some women too as the bombs dropped further afield. "*No front lines anymore in this war*," Roger Mullings had said to him the last time they spoke. "*Those Zeppelins are bombing London now*."

Harold scanned the sky briefly as he broke his embrace with Agnes. He had heard the same himself but was yet to see anything to substantiate it. He made to leave and kissed the top of her head. "Stay warm lass I'll be back for my porridge."

"The guns always stop before they go over the top," she said suddenly. "You know that's what James told us when he was home at Christmas. There's going to be a big battle soon. Everyone said. Do you think that…?"

"I think we won't do ourselves any good by worrying about it. They've been shelling them for about a week if the noise is anything to go by. I can't believe any of those poor devils will be left to fight if that's the case."

"I hope they're all blown to bits."

"Hey Aggie lass come on now. That's no way to talk." He moved back and hugged her close and they listened to the silence. Sally lay across their feet in support.

"I'm sorry Hal, I just hate this stupid war and want my boys home."

"I know. Now I must get on and start the milking, and you need to sort yourself out and go and rouse Freddie for me. All this noise is making the chickens lay like crazy so that's something. He will have plenty of eggs to collect and then he can come and help me gather up the milk." He moved in front of her and took her hands in his. "We'll have a good breakfast in a while and you'll feel better being busy. It's the 1st of July. Summer's here again and the boys will all be back for a spot of leave before long. Might even make the fete 'eh?"

He kissed her on the cheek and pulled away. Agnes smiled at his words, but they did nothing to warm her. She watched Harold go with Sally running alongside him, her keen eyes watching his movements; and then she shivered and went back inside and closed the door, needing the security of the old house.

As Harold reached the shed the old barn door banged on its rusting hinges. *Might have a look at that later*, he thought to himself. The echo from the door continued and he paused, milking stool in hand, frowning at the sound. Then he realised what was different. The shelling had started again.

*

They were scythed down together as they threw themselves forward. Brother alongside brother, fathers sheltering sons, friend falling upon friend. Those not hit by the hail of bullets were flung into the air by the shrieking shells in a twisting dance of death.

Yet forwards they went, spurred by anguish and grief, on and on towards the German line. Desperate to reach the foe, they found some inner strength to carry them over the sucking mud, until they reached the trench at last, and with bomb and bayonet the men of Sussex swarmed in.

Will reached the trench rim a couple of minutes behind the first men and the sight that greeted him was nothing more than sheer madness. Everywhere soldiers were locked in duels, fighting in groups or one to one, like a writhing mass of enraged ants, all order seemingly gone. Will didn't hesitate and jumped in; all sense of reason now lost as the grief of seeing his brother lying stricken overwhelmed him.

He came face to face with a large German using an entrenching tool to strike out at the tide of Sussex men, his weapon clearly lost. As the man saw Will he lurched forward, but he dodged the blow and hit him in turn with his rifle butt in the side causing him to stagger backwards. In one swift movement Will brought his rifle round and punched forward with the bayonet into the German's stomach. Thrust. Twist. Remove. Just as he had practiced many times in camp.

The man cried out and collapsed, and as he did so Will saw another German aiming at him, and dropped to one knee and fired instinctively. His opponent was momentarily thrown by his stricken comrade slipping back, and that split second cost the German his life. Will's unerring marksmanship hit him dead centre in the chest killing him instantly. An eerie calm now came over Will as he mechanically fought in the German trench. There was no emotion; only a cold emptiness inside him driving him on.

He looked to his right and saw Tommy wrestling with a German of similar stature both holding onto each other's rifles and pushing back and forth against the trench wall. Will shot the German through the back, pushing him aside as the man groaned and fell dead. He grabbed Tommy and pulled him up.

"Okay?"

"Thanks, Sarge," Tommy nodded, clearly anything but okay, but then none of them were had they stopped to think about it. Tommy looked at Will now and saw a wildness in his eyes that he'd never seen before.

"You okay Will?" He asked taking his friend's arm momentarily. Will spun round but checked himself and for a moment there was recognition in his eyes as he nodded at Tommy.

"Yes. Keep fighting. Clear this trench."

Just then from somewhere ahead of them a grenade exploded and through the smoke the CSM appeared like a magician on stage, barking orders, restoring order.

"Get this trench clear for the third and fourth waves. Barker, get some bloody fire down on that German support trench. Keep them pinned down instead of us." He turned and sent a flare up and then shouted "Job's far from done boys." Will watched him pause, aim forward and fire out into the ground between the German first and second trenches, and saw a fleeing enemy soldier throw his hand up and fall silently out of sight. Will stared at the piles of German bodies around the trench and realised not all of them were from their attack. While a lot of the defences had not been damaged, their artillery had clearly collected a bloody harvest amongst the German lines at least. Here and there fires were raging which added to the whole grisly scene. *Like being in hell itself.*

"Davison, stop bloody gawping and help Dunsford with that Jerry machine gun. Get it turned around and put it into the bastards."

"How do we work it Sergeant Major?" Dunsford asked automatically, the former stable hand shaking as he helped Will lift the gun.

"Jesus Dunsford, should have sent the horses here and left you behind. You will never make Corporal at this rate. About as much use as a chocolate teapot in my army. Just help the Sergeant here. If Davison can work it out anyone can. Point and bloody shoot. How hard can it…" Russell suddenly stopped speaking and screamed "Get down!"

Will had learned a long time ago to do things without question and dropped into the bloodied waters of the trench floor instantly. He found himself staring at the glazed eyes of the German he had bayoneted earlier, his mouth still open as if in protest. He looked beyond the accusing stare of the dead man from his place on the floor and saw a group of Germans massing by the dog leg in the trench. Before he could react a grenade whistled past him and Will marvelled at the actions of the CSM who was already firing before the grenade had even hit home.

The Germans had also started to fire and Dunsford, who had paused to look before reacting, had been hit in the throat and now fell across Will's legs clutching fruitlessly at his neck and making wretched gurgling noises. Then the grenade exploded and two Germans catapulted out of the trench like gymnasts in a display, and when the smoke cleared they were all gone.

Will realised then his hearing had been affected by the blast as he found the CSM hauling him to his feet and shouting but the sound was gone. With a rush it came roaring back. "…and get that bloody gun working Sergeant. Break's over!" He nodded at the sergeant major but was a bit unsteady still on his feet so Russell took hold of him for a moment.

"You hang in there lad, you're doing great. Just keep a handle on your emotions." There was a gentleness to Russell's voice that belied the horror of their predicament but seemed to break through Will's locked emotions.

Will looked at his sergeant major and struggled to hold back the tears.

"My brother, he…"

"I saw lad. No idea what he was doing here but brave bastard that's for sure. Got us all going again."

"I had to leave him."

"We've left half the battalion back there, so don't let it all be for nothing now."

Will nodded as Russell added "Carry on," and strode off down the trench firing as he did.

Soldiers ran past Will as he steadied himself, and he grabbed hold of one and gestured at him to help him with the machine gun. It only occurred to him as they frantically manhandled the gun to face the German support trench that he had no idea of the rank of the man he grabbed! He was relieved to see it was Private Abbott, the tobacconist's son from Grist Lane and not someone higher ranked. They set the gun up and Abbott cocked it and held the bullet belt out for Will to feed it in as he fired.

"My brother's dead," Abbott said matter of factly, "Shot in the face." Then added "Action clear," and as Will stared at him the man started firing with a fixed expression at the German trench.

"I'm sorry Abbott," was all he could say but the words were lost in the chatter of the gun. Abbott's young brother had played cricket for Steyning and he knew their Mums were in the choir together. *He couldn't think about that though. Couldn't think about any of it. Except what they were doing right here and now.*

"Empty!" Abbott shouted, and Will rapidly changed the belts over and tapped him on the helmet to tell him to commence firing again.

Just then the third and fourth waves poured into the trench, in response to the 'all clear' flare. They were depleted from the shelling, but with far fewer casualties than the first two waves as the German guns had been all but silenced in this forward trench.

Major Fleming appeared with the third wave.

"Any officers here CSM?"

"No sir, not in my sector."

The major nodded to the sergeant major. A brief shared moment of the grim toll already taken. Looking at him more closely now, Will could see in the light of the fires that besides the trademark moustache favoured by all officers, he also bore the same signs of rapid ageing thrust on all the men in this war that made it very hard to determine how old anyone was. Something that seemed so simple back home. He was covered in mud and had not only ignored the directive from head office to carry his baton but was also holding a rifle instead of his pistol. *Now here was an officer who understood this whole bloody mess,* thought Will, as he changed the machine gun belt again and slapped Abbott on the helmet.

Above the noise of firing and explosions the major shouted. "I've got Captain Fennell with me and a couple more officers. They were pinned down for a while but can help now. No sign of the Colonel?" Russell shook his head. "Look CSM, the momentum's with us. I want to have a crack at that second trench before the Hun can regroup and it will start getting light soon, which won't help us once the German guns get a proper view of what's going on. The Captain will take the fourth wave forward." Will saw the CSM visibly exhale and look at the men around him, then his training kicked in and he simply said "Yes sir, of course."

"Well done Geoff." The major followed up his moment of rare intimacy, by patting the CSM on the arm, further breaking down social and military boundaries in this hellish meeting point.

"No idea what's happening with the 12th at the moment. Smoke has completely obscured their section and we can't even be sure they've made the trench let alone taken it." The major turned to Captain Fennell now. "I'll hold here with half the men reinforced by the third wave. You take the rest of these men with the fourth wave and push forward while we provide cover. If we can take that second trench and hold it I will signal the 11th Battalion to come forward and reinforce us here and then send fresh troops to you. Understood?"

"Yes sir," the captain replied and they exchanged salutes.

The major moved up the line and Captain Fennell stepped forward, smiling as ever. His face was a patchwork of mud and blood Will noted, although he was unharmed himself.

"Right Sussex, Companies A, B and E prepare to move forward, C and D will remain here to hold the trench under Major Fleming. CSM get the men ready." The voice of the captain reassured the men. They liked order being restored and everywhere half dead souls roused themselves to fight once more. Rifles were loaded, bayonets checked, and bombs handed out by those staying behind.

They massed against the trench wall again, although it was a German trench this time, which seemed slightly odd. Captain Fennell caught Will's eye, his face a canvas of blood and dirt. "Hello Davison. Good to see you alive lad. Leave the gun now and grab your rifle. You'll need that famous speed of yours for this one."

As Will did so, Tommy Landon appeared and spoke to the captain. "Sir, I've been detailed to stay behind but I'd like permission to go forward with me mates."

"Hasn't got any mates the bloody liar," an anonymous voice shouted from somewhere and some of the men nearby laughed. Smiling too, the captain replied, "I appreciate that Private but you stay with your own company and make sure you keep their heads down."

"Understood sir," Tommy replied and exchanged a disappointed glance at Will.

"Yeh and you better shoot straighter than you do on the pitch you short sighted sod," another voice called out, and Will smiled.

The moon cast a deathly pall over the scene now as Fennell looked up and down the trench at the rows of men, breathing hard. Their precious breath rose in icy clouds past their bayonets, gleaming still in the burning glare. The captain still cut a dashing figure despite his hideous face paint, and for a fleeting moment Will thought of Alice, and the beautiful looks she had inherited from her parents. *Would she be thinking of him now?* It was a bizarre thought to have at a time like this and the memory unsettled him and he shook his head to try and lose the image. Then he saw his captain raise the dreaded whistle to his lips and blow it. *Alice be damned*, he thought.

Someone shouted "For Steyning," this time and here and there shouts for local towns went up. Another man shouted "Up the Lambs!" referring to the nickname they were given of *Lowther's Lambs* after Lord Lowther, who had raised the Southdown battalions.

"Come on then you lambs," Fennell shouted, picking up on the theme, and once more hurled himself over the top. Will felt a surge of pride in his captain and fresh reserves of energy flowed through him. The CSM followed in moments and then the next wave of men were up once more with a roar.

As Will went to climb a hand held him back and a voice said "Look out Will." He turned and saw Tommy pulling a football from his back pack.

"What the devil?" he began, but before he could say anymore Tommy launched the ball forward with an almighty kick towards the second German line. Will watched it bounce forward incredulously and it disappeared from view just as Tommy clambered over the trench past him.

"Come on mate," he shouted.

"Tommy wait, where the hell are you going?"

"To get my ball back of course," and with a flash of a smile he ran off.

Chapter 26 - The Second Half

David stood with the men of the 11th battalion in the forward trench, watching the horrors unfold in front of them. By the time they were moved forward ready to support the other two battalions, wounded men were already coming back. Some dragging themselves unsupported while others were carried back by friends who then turned and ran back into the melee. Many of the men waiting here recoiled at the wounds of their comrades, and looked away as their own fear grew. David immediately moved forward to help one of the injured men and slowly some of the others did the same.

"They are all pinned down up ahead," the wounded man said through fevered gasps. His eyes were wide open in terror. "No cover, it's chaos. All the officers are dead."

"Alright son, settle down," a veteran sergeant said behind David. He beckoned to a couple of men to carry him back down the line, aware the man's words were further unsettling his own company. The officers of the 11th moved up and down the line trying to steady the men and then further down the trench one of their companies was ordered forward. David heard them go over the top with shouts and cries. But no cheers now.

"We need to get out there. They need us Sergeant." It was Archie Bunden now who called out. Inside he was truly terrified. His legs ice cold with fear. So he shouted to mask it from himself. Other men took up the cry, desperate to do anything other than stand here and listen to the night destroy their friends. An officer told them to be quiet and wait for the order, and they shuffled about once more.

The Germans were shelling the area of No Man's Land relentlessly and they saw numerous men blown apart trying desperately to get back to the safety of their trenches. It was horrific watching men they knew, who only hours before had sung and drunk alongside them, now dying in the dark crying out to mothers and sweethearts.

David suddenly saw George Miller, the station master's son, appear from the black void staggering back towards them carrying a man over his back. As he got closer he realised George was carrying his brother, Ben, who was groaning with every step.

"This way George, not far now," he called out, not caring about the sergeant standing nearby. George nodded, staggering on. A shell landed nearby and he stumbled and fell, then rose once more and bent down to pick his brother up. One of the men in the trench climbed out and ran the few yards to help him, and together they lifted Ben between them and moved forward.

Another shell landed and there was a bright flash, and mud and smoke covered the trench wall. When it cleared the three men had gone. Only a helmet remained where they had been standing.

"Where are they," someone shouted.

"They must have been blown somewhere, we need to look," David answered.

"They're gone lads," the sergeant said behind them without moving. "You won't find anything but death."

"Gone? They can't be gone…I know the Miller boys," a blackened face said in the gloom.

"Then say a prayer for them," the sergeant answered.

Archie stared transfixed at the helmet. It seemed to glow in the dark, and he realised something was burning inside it. He turned to the side and vomited as his legs began to shake.

An officer appeared then moving down the line giving out further instructions. Archie felt ashamed and pushed himself against the blackness of the rear wall. As he did so a face appeared over the parapet to their left. Some of the younger men raised their rifles, their nerves betraying them.

"Hold fast it's the Sergeant Major," the officer shouted.

Sergeant Major Carter jumped down into the trench and gratefully accepted a water bottle, taking a long drink before removing his helmet and pouring some over his head. He nodded to the officer, aware even in the dark that saluting in the front trench was never wise. Archie realised close up that the officer was the replacement colonel who had taken over the 11th from Grisewood, and gave a silent prayer that he hadn't spotted him being sick.

"What's the update Sergeant Major?"

"It's not good sir," Carter said struggling for breath. "The wires for the 12th were completely untouched. We managed to get through in places but then our own smoke from the shells drifted back onto us and it became impossible to see. The Colonel has been wounded along with a number of officers and our attacks became uncoordinated and broke up."

"Christ. Any news on the 13th?"

"None sir. I thought you might know more here. Major Forbes asked me to come back and try and find out what's going on."

The colonel shook his head and looked about him at the sea of anxious faces.

"Has anyone made the trenches?"

"There might be some groups that have sir. Hard to tell. I was in the fourth wave so by the time I got through the wire, I met the Colonel being brought back and was asked to get a handle on the situation by the Major, and try and regroup with the 13th."

"How's the Colonel?"

"Not good sir. I told some men to take him to an aid station."

"Ok what do you need?"

"There's a particularly nasty machine gun emplacement over on the right of our sector that's sweeping across both fronts. I'd like to take a section and try and clear it. Then we just need support with the wounded to save sending our own men back. If the 13th have had any success I suggest we send reserves in there and that might draw some of our Jerries away and allow us to push forward. But it's hard to tell friend from foe out there sir, so I can't give you any clear idea."

The colonel let out a deep sigh. "So much for light resistance. Right take your men Sergeant and I'll mobilise the rest of my battalion in support."

Archie stepped forward. "I'd like to volunteer my section Sergeant Major." He had no idea what made him speak up, but knew if he didn't go forward now, he might never move again.

As the men in his section stared at him, Carter stepped forward. "Corporal Bunden isn't it?"

"Sir."

"Ok follow me. Let's go."

"Good man," the colonel called after them as Archie and his team scrambled over the top behind the CSM, and began the deadly game of cat and mouse with the incoming shells as they raced forward into the dark.

David watched them go and then joined the dozens of heads that now turned to their commanding officer.

"Right then company commanders. Some of you heard most of that exchange I'm sure. I'll keep two companies here in reserve, the rest of the battalion to split in two and move forward to help with casualties and if possible push onto their front line and support our troops. Pass the word to prepare."

*

As the 13th battalion poured forward towards the second trench, Will heard someone shout "Come on Sussex" repeatedly as if in the distance. He could see Tommy racing ahead kicking the ball in front of him. It was an extraordinary sight and one he was sure would confuse the hell out of the Germans. But already the first men with the captain were nearing the second trench and were throwing bombs as they did so. As the major had predicted, the Germans seemed to be in a state of confusion, and resistance was much more sporadic here. Despite this, men continued to fall ahead of him, some thrown back with desperate cries; others silently, collapsing slowly, as if lying down to sleep.

A few moments later though the Sussex men were in the next trench and bitter fighting commenced again. The Germans regrouped to repel the British soldiers once more, and seemed to have an endless supply of reserves. Will's stomach tightened as he approached this carnage, and as the cry of 'Come on Sussex' came forth again, he realised the man shouting it was in fact himself. Then he jumped down into the trench, firing as he did so.

Captain Fennell was trying to organise a defence with his troops now pressed on both sides of the trench they were in, and also taking fire from the front. Behind them the shelling intensified between the German lines effectively hemming them in. While they had gained a foothold in the second trench, without reinforcements they were unlikely to be able to hold, and Fennell knew the chances of more men getting to him unless they attacked in strength would be slim. He calculated they had less than a hundred men here now.

"Sergeant Major!"

"Sir?"

"Take a third of the men and try and break through on our left towards the 12th. With a bit of luck if they are having the same issues as us they may try the same thing. Judging by the amount of Jerries here, I doubt they have made the third line so let's try and consolidate here. I'll try and widen our position and if the 11th can support in strength, we may be able to push on."

Fennell didn't believe his own rhetoric but tried to stick to the plan, and he could tell by the look on Russell's face that his sergeant major shared his doubts. But he took thirty of the nearest men and moved left, firing as they went.

"Sergeant Davison."

"Sir."

"Take two sections and push along the trench to the right. Don't get strung out though."

Will took twenty men and immediately ordered them forward and they moved steadily along the trench. As they advanced however, they met with fierce resistance including machine gun fire raking across the top of the trench so the progress became quickly bogged down. Twice Will ordered them to throw grenades and charge ahead and despite inflicting a number of casualties more German troops just poured forward in their place. Behind him Will heard a roar in the darkness and orders shouted in German, and became worried any counter attack in strength might cut them off from the main group. As if to push home the point, the enemy now massed in the trench ahead. It was clearly a coordinated push on all fronts to dislodge them and Will ordered a fighting withdrawal.

"Pull back by pairs, fire and retreat. Cover each other and make our way back to the Captain."

However, they had barely gone ten yards when the enemy charged and now they were hand to hand fighting again in the trench. Will saw a number of his men fall, wounded or dead, and several more were surrounded and dropped their weapons and surrendered. *He couldn't blame them. What would he do? Fight to the death? He would know soon enough,* he thought, and pushed a couple of his men back down the line.

"Get back to the Captain, and tell him we can't hold here."

"Look out Will!" A cry from the left made him duck but someone pulled him back as a man lunged at him with a bayonet. There was a shot right by his ear and the pain in his head was intense for a moment, and in the dark void Will heard the assailant scream and fall away. He looked round to see who had grabbed him. It was Tommy.

"Owed you that one Sarge." Will nodded as Tommy dragged them both up. He looked round and saw they were the last two left.

"Time to go." Will reached in his ammunition pouch and found one remaining grenade. Without hesitation he pulled the pin and lobbed it forward a short distance.

"Go!" He pushed Tommy ahead of him and they ran down the line. At such a short distance and in the confined space the grenade was devastating. Will shivered at the awful sounds behind him as it took its deadly toll, but didn't dare pause to look back.

As they rounded a corner in the German trench they saw a number of rifles pointed at them. "Sussex," Will shouted and the men eased their weapons down. He found Captain Fennell still walking up and down the dwindling group, encouraging the men and trying to hold out.

"Couldn't get anywhere sir, there are too many."

"I know. There's no sign of reinforcements and we're desperately low on ammunition." Will could see the normally relaxed officer struggling to remain calm and knew he should say something. Just then Peterson came running along the trench from the direction of Russell's party, clearly terrified.

"Captain Fennell...Sir. Sergeant Major sent me…"

"Calm down son, what's the situation?"

"Germans counterattacked sir. Got in behind us too. We lost a number of men and some were taken prisoner. I was at the back. CSM shouted at me to get out and tell you."

"Where is the Sergeant Major?"

"Last I saw he was surrounded sir."

"Right we've got to try and get through to them. Davison…"

There were shots from the left and Peterson screamed and fell against the wall. As Will stared in shock a number of Germans appeared.

"To the left watch out," Fennell called out.

"We're trapped," one of the men shouted as they now fired at the new threat.

"Hold your ground," Fennell snapped. "Keep firing." In his mind however he knew the position was hopeless, and to fight on would just throw needless lives away. The Germans had now cut off the communication trenches too, either side of them, so to get back to the forward trench they would have to climb out and run over the open ground. He looked behind them and saw the shells and machine gun fire lighting up the ground. *Suicide.* He sighed and saw Will looking at him. *There was no choice but to surrender.*

He was about to speak when the shelling noticeably shifted. The guns had clearly been ordered to reduce their range and now the shells began firing on their second line where the fighting raged.

"Look out, get down," he called, but the shells blanketed the area and he heard more of his men cry out. However, as the small group of Sussex men huddled together, Fennell realised that the Germans were now shelling their own troops in the dark. Clearly in the confusion they must have thought the second trench was lost too, and now the enemy ran for cover either side of them but not before losing a number of their own men. Fennell quickly appraised the situation.

"The left line is open. Everyone, make for the connecting trench and pull back to the Jerry forward line and re-join the rest of the battalion before they figure out what's going on."

The men needed no second invitation and ran like the wind up the line, some stumbling and falling in the darkness but everywhere hands pulled them up. Will and the captain were the last to go but as they made for the gap, a group of soldiers rushed towards them from the left.

"Look out sir," Will said, but then a voice shouted "Sussex," and Sergeant Major Russell and half a dozen men ran up.

"Sergeant Major! Am I glad to see you."

"Not as much as I am to see you sir. Thought we were for the chop, then the Jerry guns landed right amongst us and we made a dash for it in the chaos before they recovered."

"So did we, right let's get going. Back to the main battalion. Move them out S'arnt Major."

"You heard the Captain. Move."

*

Private Irwin knocked on the door and waited to be called in. He had been on duty since eight o'clock the previous morning and barring a couple of hours rest last night, he had remained at his post to support the major with the constant stream of information coming into HQ. He yawned and immediately his eyes began to droop. A muffled voice brought him back from the warm embrace of sleep.

"Come in Irwin."

Irwin blushed as he shuffled in, despite knowing the major couldn't possibly know he was struggling to stay awake. *But he seemed to be able to read minds,* Irwin thought.

"Anything?"

Irwin forced himself to focus. "It's very hard to get a clear picture sir. I've been unable to contact any of the senior officers at the front. But one of the signals men said they had got into the forward trenches."

Harry Johnson frowned, taking a long drag on his cigarette while he pondered the scant news. "Any word back from Captain Davison?"

"Nothing more sir. I've tried the line since he left the message but, after the orderly said he wasn't there, the last couple of times no one even answered."

"Well he'll either call again or turn up for tea I have no doubt. I'm sure he's busy watching things unfold. If the Southdowns are in Jerry's trenches they will need support to hold on. Try once more, and if you can't get through, send runners to the supporting brigade and tell them they must move forward and relieve the Sussex if they haven't already done so."

"Beggin' pardon sir but it will take someone a couple hours to get there. Shall I keep calling in the meantime?"

"No Private. You look done in." Irwin blushed again now. "Get those orders out and then turn in for a few hours. Ask the runner to report back to me direct with any updates from the front. Anything at all."

"Yes sir. Thank you sir. Do you want some fresh tea before I turn in?"

Harry paused about to say yes, then saw his orderly was barely able to stand up. He smiled. "No that's alright lad. I can sort myself out. Public school training and all that. Off you go."

Irwin snapped up a salute and walked out. As he picked up the phone to carry out the major's orders he felt guilty for leaving him, but the pull of his bed was much stronger.

Inside the room Harry looked again at the map of the *Boar's Head* salient and the marked plan of attack. The news they were in the forward trenches was good. He frowned as he hadn't asked if there were any casualties. He doubted there would be many and all seemed to be going to plan. But he knew they would need reinforcements especially for the rest of today, as the big push went in. Jerry would throw everything at them to dislodge them, and the sun would be up soon. He hoped James' brothers were okay and would feel better once he had a clear report.

Harry cleared a space on his desk and then leaned back in his chair, lifting his feet up to perch on the desk edge. He inhaled deeply on his cigarette and allowed his eyes to lightly close.

*

Sergeant Major Nelson led his small party through the smoldering wire once more. They ran half crouched from shell hole to shell hole, as bombs and bullets searched for them in the dark. As before they came across another group of casualties, but here only one of them still moved. Carter instructed two of his group to take the wounded man back which left him with just three soldiers. Archie was one. The smoke was so thick ahead it was impossible to see where the German front line was, or indeed locate any of the 12th.

He had tried to move in a straight line along the right of their sector hoping to come across the last known place where he had seen a company moving in strength. But they had found only groups of corpses lying together as if in sleep, or hung like gruesome gargoyles on the wire. Those men that were moving were wounded, crying out in the night, which brought further bullets upon them. Any that still had rational thoughts were crawling back to their own lines in silent agony, and one by one Carter had detailed his small detachment to help them back.

Corporal Bunden had impressed him. Twice he had gone back, once carrying a man on his back and twice he had somehow found them again. The second time he said two of their own party had been hit and killed and that thought made Carter realise their role was now futile. *He was wasting more lives trying to save dying men.* He hated pulling back but without any clear orders and unable to see, it was impossible to push on. He motioned to them to gather round, and then a machine gun's chatter nearby made them all duck down. The flashes from the gun lit up its position and they could see several Germans silhouetted in the glare. They were not firing in their direction though but away from them into the darkness.

"They must be firing on the 13th," he hissed quietly to the men. "We must be nearer their sector than I thought. You three aim your rifles on the emplacement and when I shout, fire as fast as you can. I will get round behind them with a grenade and then hopefully finish them off. If you aim at the flashes you should hit something. Just make sure it's not me." He saw their teeth show white in the gloom.

"Shall I come with you Sergeant Major?" Archie whispered.

"No Corporal, stay here and make sure these two get back safely if I don't. We don't know how many are down there and it might be like hitting a bee hive. I'll need a minute to move round and find their line to the gun. If I don't shout get out anyway."

He moved off then and the three remaining soldiers watched their NCO disappear. Archie nudged them and they raised their rifles together, watching the machine gun flash away as it continued to fire.

"You aim to the right. Evan you aim left. I'll aim at the gun. That way we might get more than one. Get ready."

In the moments that followed a number of noises forced their way into Archie's head. Groans from dying men; shouts in the dark from friend or foe; the scream of the shells still pounding the area around them; the machine gun's constant rapid rattle. He blanked it all out honing his senses into the space ahead of him. Then the sound that mattered carried to them.

"Open fire!" and the men began shooting without a pause.

There were cries of alarm and a scream, as Archie nodded satisfied they were hitting something or someone. Then an explosion rocked the scene followed by more screams, piercing this time, and Archie told his comrades to hold fire. They saw the image of their sergeant major pass through the flames, and then heard several shots, and a further solitary shout, and then silence. Now the sound of German voices somewhere nearby came forth and a second machine gun opened up nearby firing wildly at them. Carter's voice shouted above the noise.

"Corporal get the men out of here on the double. Get back to the trench and report to any officer you find. I will be right behind you. Go."

Archie was torn but knew he had to do as he was told and tapped the men on the shoulder. The three of them set off back at a fast, low run, the sound of firing increasing behind them.

Chapter 27 - All for nothing

"We can't hold. Without reinforcements the position is hopeless." Major Fleming spoke quietly so as not to be overheard.

Captain Fennell looked about him at the remaining body of men, a number of whom were carrying wounds. The shelling continued unabated and now the Germans had regained their second line they were pushing forward up the communications trenches towards their old forward trench. Although a party of the 11th had reinforced them, they were hopelessly outnumbered and stretched too thin. *The major was right. Just a complete cock-up from start to finish. So much for all their planning.*

Fennell sighed. "I agree sir. The lads have done incredibly well given all the obstacles we have encountered, but to try and hold out longer will just waste more lives needlessly, and none of us may get back. Anything from the 12th at all?"

"No Captain. Except one of the young lieutenants from the 11th said there was a report they had not even made the forward trench. Our own damned smoke worked against us." Fennell looked at his senior officer and saw only a resignation in his face. He was worried despair might overtake them all.

"If we are going it has to be now sir."

"Yes. Pass the word. We will go in sections and try and cover the retreat for as long as we can. Head for the sunken dyke and from there back through the wire. God save us all."

"Sergeant Major. Organise the men to go ten at a time. We will try and coordinate, but in the dark with this shelling it's going to be everyman for himself frankly. Just try and get back as many as we can."

The Southdowns abandoned the trenches they had fought so hard for, and ran for their lives back towards the safety of their own lines. Some carrying colleagues, still more fell unable to move on, and had to be left. As Will sprinted towards the dyke he was aware of fighting in the dark behind him; not everyone had got out in time.

He slid into the sunken dyke and came face to face with David working on a wounded soldier. They shook hands and looked at each other with relief and sadness.

"James is gone." Will said.

"What? Where?"

"He's back there somewhere behind us. I need to get his body."

"Oh God." David slumped forward, head down. Then he continued binding the wound of the man next to him for a moment as if trying to ignore what had just been said. When he looked at Will again, tears were running down his face. "I saw him go forward. I should have known he would go over."

Will squeezed his brother's shoulder hard. There was no time for grieving though, as the firing now intensified on their line and the shelling began to move forward.

"Load up who you can and follow me," the Major was shouting. "We will go in two waves. When I get back I'll get as much cover fire as I can bring down on the bastards. Captain hold as long as you can and then pull out. Come on then let's go."

He leapt out of the trench with the first few men and the machine guns opened up to their left. Fleming was hit several times and fell dead on the lip and the men with him were killed or wounded.

"Jesus Christ," Russell said and then went to help the captain pull the major's body in. The bullets hammered the edges of the dyke and another man was shot through the head and fell silently.

Fennell cried out, hit in the arm as he tried to retrieve the major's body. He slumped back against the side of their temporary shelter. They were pinned down in the same place as they had been a couple of hours before. In far fewer numbers. The position was hopeless. Will looked out into the night behind them.

"Don't do it Will. You'll die trying."

"He would have come for me."

"Yes, and he would also have bollocked you for it. We have to live now. For mum and dad and…"

Just then there was an explosion to their left and the machine gun went silent. There were shouts and more shots and then after a short pause, the gun began firing again but this time in a different direction.

"What's going on, Sergeant Major," Fennell asked weakly, clearly losing blood.

"Jerry seems to be shooting at something else. Not sure if they are mistaking each other for us."

"Maybe the 12th. Perhaps we should hold in case they break through to us."

Russell looked around. "We can't hold sir. I think we should go. Now, while there's a chance."

"Give the order."

"Davison! Sergeant Davison."

Will ran over. "Sergeant Major?"

"We're all going to go. Get the men ready to go in one rush. I'll help the Captain here. Try and get anyone out that's still alive."

"What about the Major sir, and…"

"We leave the dead. Save the living. Get ready."

In the dark the remaining men massed against the far wall of the dyke ready to sprint back for their own lines. Will realised Tommy was no longer with him. He called to the men roundabout but there was no recognition amongst the blackened faces. He tried to recall when he had last seen him, but it was back in the German rear lines.

Russell helped up his captain. "Ok sir?"

"Yes indeed…" Fennell winced for a moment with the pain and then forced a smile again. "All for one and one for all 'eh Sergeant Major?"

"I just hope it ain't all for nothing sir. Right let's go."

As the men now climbed up and out there was a groan near where Will was, and he paused for a moment.

"Come on Will," David said, "we have to go now."

Will crouched down and in the dark saw a wounded officer lying half submerged in the water. He pulled him up to a sitting position. It was Captain Goodman.

"God sir we nearly left you."

"Go…" he said feebly, "save yourself."

"Give me a hand David, quick."

David lifted the stricken captain onto Will's back and together they scrambled out of the dyke and began running forward. Will fell more than once but each time David was there to help him up. Bullets now flew amongst them, and flares went up lighting up the ghastly scene. As they passed the wire there was a soldier crawling on all fours, his eyes covered in blood. David stooped to pick him up.

"Get going, get going," he shouted and Will staggered on bent low, unable to turn round anyway. Miraculously he made it to their trench where willing arms were waiting to help them in. Will looked about, breathing heavily, relieved to be back, the enormity of the situation not yet having sunk in.

"Captain here needs attention," he shouted, but there were no medics free and he realised now the trench was full of men lying injured or dead.

In fact, there were far more men not moving than those who were trying to help their comrades. He laid his captain down against the trench wall as carefully as he could and checked to see he was still breathing. He sank to the floor as someone gave him water, pouring some over his head.

Most of the living were simply collapsed against the safety of the walls like himself. He recalled only a few hours ago the lines of men standing here chatting, waiting to go over the top. The men's mood buoyant and eager to get going. Now there was nothing but the silent stares of those that survived, eyes searching the dark interior for answers. The cries of their wounded friends punctuating the night.

Russell saw Will kneeling on the floor and came over. As he came closer he saw Will was trying to help Captain Goodman. Luckily the captain had passed out from the pain and lay half submerged in the bloody waters of the trench.

"Dammit, I've just sent our last medic back with the stretcher party carrying Captain Fennell and another wounded officer."

"My brother's a medic sir. He should be here somewhere."

Russell walked up and down the line in each direction calling for David, but shells now began to land on their own front line and he shouted for the men to take cover. He doubled back to Will crouched low.

"I can't see him so you'll have to take the Captain."

"My brothers are out there…" Will said looking desperately at Russell, who knelt down by him now speaking softly.

"Look Will, you need to get him back or he won't make it. Get someone to help you and get going to the forward aid station." Will nodded and picked himself up. "You there, Private Duncan is it? Help the Sergeant here with the wounded officer. Get going."

They lifted Goodman up between them. He moaned pitifully. Russell took Will's arm. "Get yourself a spot of brandy while you're there lad."

*

The scene in the trench was nothing compared to the sight that hit Will as he carried his injured captain into the dressing post with Private Duncan. At least the night had blinded him to some of the horrors at the front but here, amongst the lamp lit beds, the rows of injured men attacked his senses and almost overwhelmed him.

They spoke to a nurse who scanned the crowded tents looking for space and then shouted something to an orderly nearby, and Will watched him lift someone off a bed to make room for the new arrival.

"Please don't make a fuss…" Goodman muttered weakly. Will wasn't aware his captain had regained consciousness.

"You're safe now sir," he said, "you'll be taken care of here."

Goodman's blackened eyes looked at him. "Davison?"

"Yes sir."

"Was the attack successful?"

Will didn't know what to say. In truth he wasn't entirely sure, but he knew they had made good progress, though at what cost he couldn't answer. He looked at the lines of wounded men lying here. Luckily at that point the nurse returned with help to carry the captain away.

"The battalions did themselves proud sir," he replied, and Goodman smiled and nodded as he was taken from them. Turning to Duncan, Will said, "I need to check the casualty lists here. I will see you back at the front. Be careful Private."

"Yes, Sergeant," Duncan said, but as Will watched him leave the tent he saw him lurch to one side suddenly and throw up. He looked away. It was not surprising, the stench of festering wounds and waste from the men was unbearable here. He was amazed at how the nurses worked on in these conditions with barely a flicker of emotion as each new horror was brought in. *What must they be keeping inside*? he thought. Then for a moment his mind turned to Teresa and he felt an incredible surge of emotion. *What I would give for a cup of tea and a smile right now.*

Another nurse appeared now, older than the first, the sleeves on her tunic covered in dried blood. "Can I help you soldier?"

"I wondered if you had any lists yet of the men brought in?"

She looked at Will for a moment then waved a hand behind her. "As you can see its chaos here and we have barely had time to record anything yet. We will get the paperwork to HQ in a couple of days."

"A name then," he said, "Please. You may have heard something."

"Look it's impossible to know all the names here now, apart from senior officers…" She was getting impatient but Will persisted, interrupting her.

"My brothers. I'm trying to find news. Anything."

The nurse stared hard at the weary soldier in front of her.

"Over there on my desk. There's a list. It's only the dead mind. Names scribbled down. And not all of them have been identified yet. It's very rough. Some of the names have just been given to us, their bodies are not here. I just thought it would help to write it down…" She paused and for a second there was a glimpse of emotion, then a shout behind them made her change. “You can have a look. Just be quick and put it back where you found it.”

Will raised his eyes at the last comment, then looked about the room.

“Thank you. In that case can I look over the beds too?” The nurse was already walking away and paused briefly throwing her arms wide again.

“There’s not much space here and we can’t have every man and his dog wandering about either. Infection is bad enough as it is. But…go on. And no talking.”

Will realised he hadn’t even got her name but she was gone now so he walked as discreetly as he could around the lines of wounded men. He saw faces of men he knew, and he saw things he wished he hadn’t seen and would struggle to forget. But he didn’t see his brothers or any of his friends. With a sigh he walked over to the desk and picked up the list of names, holding it to a nearby candle that flickered in the dawn breeze. He gasped at the number of entries scribbled down. *So many.*

He went down them with his finger, then turned the page and continued. Names that conjured faces in his mind jumped out at him now. Abbott, Miller, Peterson. He went down the list again and saw that there were two Millers not one. A name caught his eye. Entwhistle, Owen. He struggled with his emotions now, and tapped the paper while he thought about the young Welshman, before his eyes moved on down. But there were no Davisons.

*

The sun was in full ascent when Will got back to the forward lines. Everywhere there were reminders of the night’s attack. The floor was littered with spent cartridges, and every few yards there was a piece of discarded equipment and even the occasional weapon. Worse were the bloodied bandages that seemed to line the trench floor like some macabre mosaic.

Will didn’t look too closely at the sludge around his feet. He didn’t want to see any more blood and gore. The most heart-breaking thing as he walked along the line were the number of letters home stuck into trench walls, sandbags and dugout doorways, pinned by knives or bayonets. All of them never to be reclaimed by their owners. Last lines of hope; regrets and fears; or love for countless families and friends back at home.

He stopped by one that had a beautifully ornate crucifix hanging on the bayonet next to the letter. The body of Jesus glinted in the morning sun as it spun slowly on its silver chain. Will saw a young wife’s picture holding a baby on her knee placed in the top of the letter. *A young widow now, or else destined to live on a meagre army pension with a crippled husband...* He looked at the religious artefact again. *Where were you?*

He couldn't cry, as much as he wanted to the tears just wouldn't come, and all he felt was anger and an overwhelming fatigue. The shells came again, as they had been doing since the attack. Unceasing. He didn't care in that moment whether they hit him or not. Then the face of his brother James suddenly came into his mind and he ducked down instinctively. A shell landed on the lip just a few yards away and white-hot shrapnel tore into the sandbags above his head. He looked up at the crucifix still swinging on the long knife. *Ok, ok* he thought, and then saw a familiar figure coming along the trench towards him.

"Archie! Thank God!"

Archie walked up to his friend and smiled, though the usual bravado was gone. They shook hands and stood for a moment. Archie's face reflected Will's own weariness, and he realised they were both filthy almost beyond recognition.

"Am I glad to see you Will. I can't find anyone we know."

"James is dead."

The formalities of rank had gone in that moment and something snapped between and they just hugged. They clung onto each other as if their lives depended on it, and then both men wept. After what seemed like an eternity, Will tried to focus on the here and now and answer Archie's concern about their friends.

"Owen is gone. I saw him. Danny was lost at the start. I never found anything of him…" His voice trailed off. "We lost so many men, officers too."

"Some diversion. They were just waiting for us. It was chaos on our side, I don't even know what we achieved."

"Jerry was out in force. I can only hope it's done what it was meant to."

"The CSM is dead," Archie said suddenly.

"What Russell?"

"No. I don't know about him. The CSM from the 12th, Carter. He was a bloody hero. Captured a machine gun single handed and used it to cover the retreat."

Will nodded now, remembering the sudden change in fortunes as they struggled to get back.

"Did you see him get shot?"

"No. He came and asked some of us to help him, and he was definitely back in the trench at the end of the attack. Then word got round there were lots of wounded men in No Man's Land so a number of us went out to get them. But the shelling got worse and worse, and once the sun came up Jerry started shooting at anyone from the forward trench too. Even the medics. So, they told us to sit tight and not go out again. But I heard Carter just kept going back, and then someone said he'd been shot and killed. They got his body I think."

He shook his head and went to take out a cigarette but his packet was crumpled and empty. "Jerry even counter attacked at first light but we had support from the Oxs and Bucks and drove them off. I'm told they took a lot of our lads prisoner too."

Will was only half listening as Archie went on, focused on something he had said. "You said they were shooting medics?"

"Yes." Archie paused, then realised the implications. "Where's David?"

"I don't know. He was with me on the run back then we got separated carrying men back. I need to find him."

"I'll come with you. I'm sure he'll be alright."

*

Sergeant Major Billings stepped out of the NCO's dugout and began organising the men nearest him to start clearing up the trench. He sent sections off to gather personal effects and others to pick up discarded kit. Another group were dispatched to slowly walk the trench floors in their section ensuring there were no unexploded bombs lying embedded anywhere within sight. Now the roll call had been completed they had to get the men busy with basic soldiering tasks until they were formally relieved.

At least there were companies from the Northants, and Oxs and Bucks to take over sentry work and give them a rest from the intensity in that regard. Not that they could effectively manage much today. Billings mused on the lists he had left with his opposite number, Russell, and struggled to comprehend the numbers. There was hardly an officer left unharmed and they needed to draw on all their experience now to lead the men until someone took control again. He saw Will and Archie approaching up the line.

"Corporal Bunden. Good timing. You're with me. We're going back to get fresh supplies for the men and sort out the relief we were promised. I heard you did the battalion proud out there last night, bringing in wounded men. It will be in my dispatches." He looked at Will as Archie stood awkwardly not knowing what to say. "Sergeant Davison isn't it?"

"Yes, Sergeant Major."

"Your CSM wants to see you inside. Were you wounded lad? I was told you were at the aid post."

"I took one of our Captains back there sir."

"What's it like there?"

"Just utter chaos Sergeant Major. I saw two pages of names of men we've lost."

Billings looked at them with desperately sad eyes. "I think they are going to need extra paper."

As the two men walked off with Archie frowning over his shoulder, Will stepped into the gloom of the NCO dug out. He took a moment to adjust his eyes from the bright glare outside and then saw Russell sitting on a bunk, wearing just a shirt and trousers. He couldn't recall ever seeing him without a tunic on. Even when he had come out to his home last year to ask him to join the Southdowns, he was dressed in a suit and tie.

"You asked for me Sergeant Major?"

Russell was holding a pile of papers and kept moving them from front to back looking at them. Finally, he looked up. "Yes. Yes, I did. How is Captain Goodman?"

"He's going to be okay I think sir."

"That's a relief. I had similar news about Captain Fennell too. They may be the lucky ones."

"Sir?"

"We lost a lot of officers last night. Still trying to get a full picture. Do you want a coffee?" Will shook his head. "Something stronger then." He nodded to a bottle of half empty whisky with a couple of rusty beakers next to it.

"No thank you Sergeant Major. Do you know if anyone found my brother James' body sir?" Russell looked at him blankly for a moment. "Captain James Davison of the Guards? He fell during the attack."

"Oh yes. Sorry Will, not as yet. But as I said the lists are still being made up. We've had half a dozen men crawl in from No Man's Land in the last hour. Miraculous. Though I doubt there will be many more…"

Will saw him stare at the papers again and thought he should go, but hadn't found out why he was here yet.

"Sergeant Major. Did David report in?"

"No. That's why I sent for you. But he's listed here as wounded, and according to the reports it's not good. He's been taken straight to the main hospital at Béthune I'm told." He looked up now. "Some news at least in this whole confounded mess."

"How bad sir?"

"I'm not sure lad. So many details coming in." He threw the papers down and walked over to the small table with the whisky on. Pouring himself another drink he gestured with the bottle to Will. This time Will nodded and Russell poured another large shot.

Will took a swig from the cup and grimaced as it burnt the back of his throat. His mind raced as his mouth struggled to recover and he looked at the sergeant major siting back on his bunk. "Do you know if the attack was a success Sergeant Major?" Russell looked up with world weary eyes.

"I don't even know what constitutes a success back in HQ Will. But here at the front it's measured in casualties not yards. And I hope to God this so-called big push in the Somme was worth the sacrifices." Will saw his grip tighten on the papers he was holding until his knuckles went white. Then he looked at Will and saw the anxiety in his face. His old persona kicked in and he attempted a smile.

"Off you go lad. You won't be missed for a day or so here while we sort ourselves out. If anything changes I'll send a runner to the hospital. But if he's not there, straight back yes?"

"Yes sir. Thank you."

*

Harry Johnson paced up and down the room waiting for Irwin's return. The sun broke through the slatted shutters to make sparkling squares of light on the floor, which twinkled from the millions of dust specks that flew about in his wake as he walked back again. There was a knock at the door and he made himself sit at the desk before answering. Irwin entered.

Harry looked at the private trying to gauge the news to come.

"Have you heard from the Somme?"

"Yes sir. Initial reports are very mixed though. I have been told the attacks in the south with the French have gone better than expected with large gains made already. Some beyond initial targets."

"Excellent. Excellent. And the north?"

"That's been a lot harder to clarify sir. There are some reports of successes but others are…"

"What? Spit it out man."

"Well sir, I've been told some regiments have not made any progress at all. Resistance has been severe."

"What? After a seven day bombardment?"

"I know sir. I've asked for clarification. But I spoke to a Canadian major who said some of the German defences were untouched, and that blowing up the mines tipped them off to the attack time. He said casualties were…well as I said it's unconfirmed sir." Irwin couldn't look at his officer now and Harry became worried.

"Casualties were what Private?"

"Over seventy percent in his sector. Unconfirmed sir. "

"Well that's ridiculous. I will go down there myself if I have to and get a clear picture. I can't go to the General with that." He looked at Irwin now and could tell there was more. He felt a chill creep up his back and became unusually anxious. "What else?"

"I caught a runner from the Scottish regiments. He said some of them had been wiped out without even making the wire. He was crying sir."

Harry stared out of the window for a while and then turned back to look at Irwin hovering in the twinkling dust. When he spoke his voice was quiet and unassuming as if speaking to a small child.

"Did you get an update on the Southdowns?" Irwin nodded. "Let's have it."

Irwin spoke as if reading from a history book. "The 13th got as far as the reserve lines but were then driven out. The fighting was too severe and with heavy shelling reinforcements couldn't reach them. The 12th were hampered by smoke and the attack became disjointed. They did make the front line though as well and engaged the enemy for several hours too before being driven back. The 11th tried to support but suffered similar problems."

"Casualties?"

Irwin didn't speak, but simply stepped forward and handed Harry a sheet of paper. He looked at the paper, then stared at Irwin as if for confirmation, then looked at it again. The paper told him that out of eighteen hundred men who had gone over the top, over three hundred were confirmed dead, and potentially as many as a thousand more were wounded or missing.

"So, it's all for nothing then," he said without looking up. Irwin maintained his silence. In truth he was in shock himself and could barely comprehend the things he had been told on the telephone.

"There's a list of officers confirmed killed on the back sir."

Harry nodded. "Leave me." He heard the door close after a few seconds and turned the sheet over with trembling hands. The list of names of officers alone was bad enough. But the one thing he kept telling himself could never happen; the one thing he dreaded above all else, was there in black and white. He looked at the typed letters and the tears burst forward in large drops onto the paper, rebounding onto the desk as Harry Johnson's heart broke.

Davison, J.G. Captain, Coldstream Guards. Killed in Action.

Chapter 28 - Now or never

Will walked into the main camp at Béthune and was struck by all the additional tents that were now set up around the main hospital buildings. As he walked through them to the central structure he realised they were all full of wounded soldiers. His pace slowed as he looked into each one as he passed and struggled to comprehend the sheer numbers of men being treated here.

He paused at the entrance to the brick building looking back. *A dozen large tents or more*, he thought. Knowing the layout from his last visit, he avoided the frantic activity in the main entrance and slipped quietly round the side to where he knew the staff kitchen was. The noise inside stopped Will in his tracks. Cries and screams came from every corner of the main room, and he had to work hard to block the images from the night from his thoughts. He didn't see Teresa approach until she stood next to him and he jumped slightly as she said "Hello."

Will didn't reply he just hugged her and she held him tight stroking the back of his head. She looked at his face and clothing covered in mud and blood.

"Are you injured?" she asked pulling back slightly from him.

He shook his head, then looked beyond her… "All these tents…"

"I know, it's awful. Most are from the Somme region. They are coming in faster than we can deal with them and we are just one of a dozen hospitals in the region."

"How bad is it?"

"They are not telling us a lot about numbers but some of the men coming in said whole regiments were lost, and that there's been no progress. They say we have lost thousands, but am sure that's exaggerated. That can't be true can it?"

"I don't know. Jerry's a lot tougher than they think at the top brass. If all the hospitals are like this, and these are just the wounded then…" His voice trailed off and he looked directly at her. "You have Southdown men here I was told."

"We have a few yes, I can check records to narrow it down but you may have to check some of the tents. How bad was it Will?"

"It was carnage. They were waiting for us. Not weak at all. Wires weren't cut. There was this trench and…" he started to cry and she moved in, her own tears mingling with his.

"Oh my love."

"My brother David's missing," he said looking up, wet grimy streaks criss crossing his face.

She wiped them away tenderly, and then a small frown crossed her head. "There is a Davison. Here in the main building. He is David I think. In all the chaos I didn't put two and two together. Come on." She took his hand and led him inside, stopping by a small white table to check a ledger. Yes D. Davison, row fifteen." She frowned again reading some hastily scribbled note by his entry. "Will, it says he's in a bad way, perhaps you should wait…"

"Where is he?"

"Over there by the middle arch, but Will do you need…"

"I'll be fine."

Teresa watched him walk slowly through the mass of beds, head slightly bowed as if approaching a church alter. She felt he had aged ten years since she last saw him, and her eyes watered again. Teresa tried clearing up a number of used implements and pans from the last operations but found herself moving back to watch him again.

Will checked the boards on the ends of the beds in row fifteen, and then two from the end saw the hand written scrawl of his brother's name. He knew there could easily be other Davisons in the British army, even David Davisons, but when he saw his brother's greatcoat draped across a stool between two beds, his fears were confirmed. His brother lay on his side facing away from him, and Will's initial emotion was one of relief that at least he was here. He picked up the coat and ran his thumb over the name tag lovingly stitched inside by his mother and her face appeared to him then, smiling as she sewed at the kitchen table.

Her smile faded as Will realised only one leg lay stretched out in front of his brother, and now as he focused he saw the head covered in bandages, and the fingers missing on the left hand. As his senses honed in more, he blocked out all the other cries and groans around him; the shouts and clangs of metal as nurses and doctors worked relentlessly to help these pitiful men. He focused on his brother's breath, coming in long slow rasps. His throat tightened.

Will dropped the coat on the bed and took the stool to move round and sit facing David. He looked at his face, half covered, and after a moment the unbandaged eye opened. Recognition flitted into it.

"Hello Sergeant." There was an attempt at a smile followed by a long wince of pain, and another hard-drawn breath. But the voice was not David's, it was Danny Boyd.

"Danny!"

"The very same…still as…dashing…as ever." The words were clearly a struggle but despite his injuries there was still a sparkle in his one good eye which scanned Will's face now. "Were you looking for…someone else?"

"My brother. They said he was, well you."

"Sorry to…disappoint…" he smiled again, and once more the face contorted with pain at the action.

"Hey it's fine. I thought we had lost you Danny. It's great to see you."

"Excuse me for …not getting up." He nodded down the bed and Will looked at him taking in the extent of his injuries. He was in a ghastly way, and it took real control not to show that in his face when he looked back.

Will smiled instead. "I'll let you off Private."

"Did we win?"

"I think a score draw would be more appropriate."

Danny closed his eye for a moment, as if acknowledging the fact then said, "We'll beat them…back at our place." He coughed now, and it didn't seem to stop and Teresa appeared by Will's side as if by magic.

"He needs rest Will."

"This is Danny Boyd, not David," Will told her.

"Oh?" Teresa said while wiping Danny's face with a cold compress.

"He carried me," Danny murmured from behind Teresa.

"What?" they answered in unison.

"Found me…wrapped me in his coat…carried me back."

"Ah that explains the identification mix up then," Teresa said, sounding every bit like the army nurse then, as she fussed over him.

Will just nodded and smiled again and patted Danny's wounded arm. He tried not to focus on the missing fingers, or the burns he saw now travelling up under the bandages. Teresa moved to the end of the bed, taking out a pen, and changing the name.

"Is this the nurse…you are sweet on…Sergeant?"

"What? Who told you that?" Will was thrown by the sudden change in direction.

"Everyone." He smiled then and Will blushed and looked at Teresa, who gave him a wink.

"I see…well this is Teresa, yes."

"You need to…snap her up. Before someone else…does. Like me…"

"Oh, is that right. I think you need to focus on getting better first Private," Will said, only half joking.

"I might stay here…a while…if she's looking after me." He winked then but very slowly. The mind was still sharp, like the Danny of old, but the body was not working with him.

"I might get you transferred too, so behave."

"Listen to you two fighting over me. I'm standing here you know." Teresa pretended to be offended. "Perhaps I don't want either of you. Thought about that? I fancy myself a nice rich Colonel or a General. Be a lady of leisure." She began pretending to fuss over the bed now, but Will knew she secretly loved the attention.

"See what I mean Will…Don't leave it too long…Now or never mate…"

He smiled again and his breathing eased.

Teresa frowned and moved in, and picked up his arm. She felt his pulse, and then put her head on his chest suddenly. Danny continued to look at him with his one sparkling blue eye, the smile still on his burnt face, as she checked him over. Then she turned and put a hand on Will's shoulder.

"He's gone Will."

Will looked at Teresa then back at Danny. She reached in and closed his eye, then pulled the cover gently over his head.

"Alright Danny, I hear you," Will said, then stood up and moved away. Teresa wrote something on Danny's board and then spoke briefly to an orderly. She followed Will to the doorway.

"I'm sorry Will."

"Probably for the best," he replied without looking at her. "Keen sportsman. Football, cricket. Would have hated being crippled." He shook his head, then turned to her. The eyes were red again, and her heart lurched. "I have orders to get back if I didn't find David."

"Of course. I'm sorry your brother is still missing. If I hear anything I will let you know. Can you ask Jonners for help? Ask around different hospitals." Will nodded. "You know the Guards have a number of hospitals down the road, maybe he was taken to them. It's chaos at the moment and men are being moved anywhere there is space. James is due to call in here when he's heading back to his sector. I could…"

"James is dead."

"What?" Teresa's face went white, and she just said quietly, "How?"

"He came to watch the attack, but went over the top with us…he was killed urging the men on, when the attack stalled."

"Oh god Will, I'm so sorry." She took him in her arms now, and hugged him, kissing the top of his head, and then stepped back and kissed his hands. "Why don't you stay with me a while?"

"James is dead?" The female voice came out of nowhere before Will answered. Their heads spun round together and there was Rose, standing arms by her side. Will looked at her and just nodded. Teresa let go of Will's hands and made to comfort her.

"I saw you…came to say hello…" she said pointlessly, her mind scrabbling to process the words. She dropped a towel she was holding and it fell, lifeless to the floor.

"We didn't mean for you to hear that."

"I have a right to know. He's my boyfriend. I'm carrying his baby." She began to shout now, the emotion welling up.

"Of course you did Rose, I'm so, so sorry."

"Now what will happen to me?"

"Let's go inside Rose."

Rose jerked back now, anger rising inside her. "Get away from me… I knew this would happen. Too good to be true. This shitty stinking war. I hate it." She looked at Will. "I hate soldiers." She ran off into the building sobbing, and Teresa turned to Will.

"She doesn't mean it, it's the shock."

"She's pregnant?" Teresa nodded and Will took a couple of steps away looking up into the sky. The clouds obscured the sun casting a gloomy haze across the camp. "Christ, what a mess," he said, his head dropping down again.

"I'm sorry, I need to go after her. Please stay. Wait until I have calmed her down."

"I have to go, report back."

"You need to rest Will. You can come in my office and have a cuppa while you wait. I have a bunk at the back there now. We often grab a few minutes when working back to back. Why not lie down for a bit?"

"If I lie down Teresa I may never get up again. I have to go. Tell her I'm sorry. I'll find a way to let you know what we are doing."

"She'll be sorry for you too. I know she will. She was fond of you. I know I can't force you to stay." She took him in her arms then not caring who was about and kissed him on the lips. Then she kissed his cheek and his eyes and stroked his face as she held him to her. "Just know I am here for you anytime."

"I know T. I love you."

"I love you too." They kissed again now, passionately, and for a moment he took her hands and kissed them softly. Then he pulled away and marched off. Teresa watched him go for a few steps and then turned and walked quickly after Rose.

*

Rose blundered through the main building and went out of the open side doors. The shouts of "Nurse" from the beds as she passed by, nothing more than background noise to her now. Her head spun with the trauma of the news and she felt overwhelmingly sick. She stumbled on into the ground beyond the buildings and propped herself for a moment by a wall and then threw up over it.

Her stomach ached with the retching and with the agony of the news, and she found herself apologising to her unborn baby. She patted her stomach trying to soothe it but the emotion welled up and she was unable to stop the sobbing. Her mind whirred with thoughts. *Why James? Why him?* She held onto the wall to stop herself collapsing and looked about at the crowded hospital camp. *Why am I here? So far from home and everything I love. What was I thinking? I need to get away, back to England. Back to the museum and forget nursing and this stupid war for ever. Yes that's it. Dead artists are a lot less painful than dead soldiers.* As if on cue the baby kicked inside her.

Who are you fooling Rose? That life is gone for good. They won't take you back with a baby. You've messed it up good and proper this time girl. She felt like she was going to be sick again and sank to her knees, and closed her eyes for a moment. Tears ran freely down her cheeks. When she opened them, she frowned for a moment, not sure what she was looking at. Then she realised. Behind the wall were piles of equipment stacked up out of the way, all belonging to the men that had died there no doubt. Or those being sent home who might never fight again. She sat back on her haunches and looked at the massed piles of bags and canteens, webbing and equipment, and despair at the waste flooded her every pore.

Then just as the sun peered out again from its gloomy repose, something glinted in its gaze, and caught her attention. She reached out and the coldness she felt transferred itself to her and she knew what to do.

*

Teresa searched frantically for her friend. She couldn't shout inside for fear of upsetting the patients and more so because she didn't want to cause a scene, but she moved as swiftly as she could; reassuring grasping hands as she passed the beds. A flash of colour through one of the side windows caught her eye, and to her relief she spotted Rose a little way off standing by one of the rear yards.

She walked out slowly so as not to startle her friend who was looking out towards the far landscape. The greenery that surrounded them bringing a temporary illusion that all was still well in this part of the world.

"Rose," she called softly as she walked across the hard ground, feet crunching despite her careful tread. Rose turned to face her and smiled, and Teresa smiled back, and then paused realising something was wrong with the image in front of her.

Her neck went cold as she saw the revolver that Rose now held in her right hand, clearly missed in the chaos of sorting out the pile of discarded equipment that lay behind her.

"Hey," Rose said, as if meeting casually in the town.

Teresa worked hard to control her voice. "Rose, I am very sorry about James. It was an awful way to find out, but everything will be okay you know. Let's go inside and chat. Let me help you."

"It's not your fault. I'm sorry for Will and his family you know. I didn't mean to shout at him. I was a cow wasn't I?" Teresa knew she had to keep Rose talking while she thought of something.

"He knows you were just upset. No one blames you for how you reacted, it's perfectly understandable."

"How is he?"

"Very sad of course, we all are. He had to go back." Rose nodded but didn't speak again. Teresa had slowly moved forward and could see tears running down her cheeks. "Rosie love. Don't do anything daft. You have to live for both of you now. James would have wanted that. If he had known about the baby…"

"It would have just added to his worries. Probably got him killed anyway thinking about silly old me instead of his job. Better this way." She smiled, her face a mask of sadness.

"Let me take that Rose. That's not the solution. Come and have a cup of tea and let's talk about the future. You're not alone you know. You've got me, I'm not going anywhere. James' family will help, and I'm sure Will would make a great uncle."

"All very twee," Rose suddenly said, anger flashing across her face, "but I'm the one left holding the baby. Literally." She raised the gun towards her head and terror leapt inside Teresa's chest.

"Please Rose no!" She lurched forward, not caring now about being cautious but Rose was already pulling the trigger back as she placed the revolver to her head. Teresa cried out, knowing she was five yards short and just reached out with her hands.

Time slowed down.

There was a blur of movement, and a bang as the gun went off and Rose collapsed to the ground. Teresa screamed and the world span casting her to her knees. For a moment she couldn't look, eyes closed against the image that would scar her for life. Then the sound of crying made her open them.

Rose was half sitting, resting against the wall, long silent sobs wracking her body. The gun, still smoking, lay several yards away on the ground. Teresa realised then that Rose's head was cradled in the arms of another person. Her mind cleared from the nightmarish fog and she focused on the scene in front of her.

Will held Rose in his arms. He looked at Teresa whose face went through a myriad of emotions from confusion to relief. She went to speak but her mouth uttered no sound.

"I thought I'd take you up on your offer of a cuppa after all," he said matter of factly, in answer to her questioning eyes. "Took the short cut round the side to your kitchen and saw you both here. Thought you needed a hand." He looked down at Rose then.

"Lost enough people I love today thanks very much. You leave the shooting to me Rose."

Teresa felt her chest would burst for this young man crouched in front of her. She crawled forward on her hands and knees, and embraced them both. Then she cried and cupped his face in her hands.

"Thank you" she whispered, finding her voice again.

Chapter 29 - The Post

Will waved 'thanks' to the driver who he had hitched a lift with, back to the front lines, and walked wearily back up the communication trench. The progress was slow with men moving back and forward here in large numbers. He wasn't even sure if the Southdowns were still at the front judging by the chaos he had seen as he travelled back. It looked like battalions were being moved around like pieces on a chess board with much less strategy. What was certain now however, was that the 1st of July was being talked of as one of the worst days in the history of the British Army for losses. It was being discussed openly too. The more people he passed, or spoke to, the more the horror and the carnage was revealed. Not just hundreds, but thousands of casualties. And one officer had said *tens of thousands. In one day.*

He paused trying to understand the implications of that. Will wondered about the Sussex who had marched down there only a few days ago. And Ced. And the Camerons they had played against.

"Keep moving if you please."

A fresh-faced Lieutenant gave Will a nudge in the back and he turned, seeing a line of new recruits in smart uniforms all bunched up behind him. Their clean faces peering forward, nervously. The lieutenant looked at Will's appearance and wrinkled his nose. *I probably do smell,* he thought.

"Sorry sir," he said and turned to carry on. The young officer realised he was a veteran of the recent action and seeing his stripes on the tunic softened his tone.

"That's alright Sergeant. When you're ready. Tough time what?"

"You could say that sir," Will replied and strode on without looking back.

As he reached the forward trench he looked left and right, recognising the layout but not the men moving about here. They were Oxs and Bucks he noted from the badge. The Oxfordshire and Buckinghamshire Light Infantry had been due in behind them he recalled, to potentially reinforce their capture of the German trenches. Soldiers passed him, some nodding, others averting their eyes. He saw the new recruits now start to file into the trench and the officer asking for directions as if he was in the street back home. Then a voice boomed out and they all jumped and the chaotic jumble of men began to flatten out either side. Will grinned as the shouting continued.

"…and keep your bleedin' heads down if you don't want to waste your time wandering up here just to get 'em shot off in the first five minutes. Can't spare the men to get you carried back neither."

The lieutenant looked at Sergeant Major Russell like a frightened rabbit, but then began to reassert himself and asked where they should go.

"I'll get you squared away sir. Follow me if you please."

"Shouldn't you salute me Sergeant Major?"

Russell paused and came back to the officer, holding his gaze for a moment. "Apologies sir but we have snipers all over this area and if I salute you, it will mark you out to them to be shot." The lieutenant looked about quickly then and even ducked lower than he already was. Russell turned with a satisfied look on his face and then saw the smiling figure of Will nearby. "Just a moment sir."

He walked up to Will and shook his hand. "Decided to re-join us have you? Thought you might stay away from this madness actually. Any joy?"

"No nothing," Will replied. "A mix up with identification. Danny Boyd was in David's coat. He died while I was there."

Russell looked around sadly. "Barely enough left standing to put two companies in the field." Then, looking at the replacements standing by, he added "God help us if Jerry counterattacks in strength."

"They say we lost thousands yesterday in the attacks Sergeant Major. Is that true?" Russell nodded.

"I fear the worst lad. The word is the Southdowns are being moved down there to bolster the ranks. Our battalions are so decimated we are being put into other regiments and not necessarily the Sussex." Will took a moment to process this then looked at Russell.

"Where do I report?"

"To me for now, in the absence of any senior officers. If you go a hundred yards that way you will find some of the 11th skulking about. Let me get the newbies squared away and then I'll come and find you. I'm told we have a Major due up the line to collect us and pass on any further information."

"Any news on Captain Fennell sir?"

Russell looked at his favourite sergeant. "Liked him didn't you. We all did. Well safe to say he's going to be okay lad, and has been shipped back to England I'm told. If he's any sense he'll get himself a desk job."

Will smiled at this and they shook hands again and went their separate ways. Will worked his way slowly down the line, amongst a sea of strange faces. He felt lost suddenly, and struggled to make his legs keep moving forward as the enormity of the last couple of days weighed on him. Now he had time to think, the personal losses and the lack of any real success made him feel a real sense of despair inside. Will felt faint, and swayed for a moment putting a hand out to steady himself against the mud wall. Its cold touch only seemed to exacerbate his inner turmoil and the darkness of the past battered at him internally.

"Aye Aye. Stand by your beds lads! Here he is." The familiar shout broke through the black mists and he looked up to see Archie standing a few yards away, smiling warmly. It was not the first time Archie had brought light to the darkness and Will ignored protocol and gave his friend a hug. In truth they were good for each other, and had been for a long time.

"Sergeant must have heard the brew boiling. Come and join us for a cuppa." Then he lowered his voice and just for Will's ears added "Anything?" Will shook his head. Archie gave a sympathetic look and then said, "Have you heard we are being broken up? Scattered across the front."

"Yes, I just saw the Sergeant Major. Do you know where yet? Or who?"

"Course not Will. This is the bleedin' army after all. The people at the front are always the last to know." Will tried a smile, then Archie paused at the entrance to the dugout.

"I'm sure David will turn up. You know there have been stragglers coming in over the last twenty-four hours."

"I hope so." In a rare moment of tenderness Archie placed a hand on his friend's shoulder and patted it. It didn't need to be more than that. The unspoken bond between the two friends ran far deeper than words or actions.

"Well one thing's for sure," Archie replied, "Jerry's gonna pay for this, the next time we get the chance." Then his serious face dispersed and the old persona returned as he ducked through the wooden doorway. "Oi Hursty. Shift your arse off the bunk. Make room for the Sarge."

*

Over a week had passed since the fateful action of the Southdowns, when Agnes bustled into the railway station humming one of her favourite hymns. She found Walter Miller knelt in front of an old stove adding a log. It was very warm outside but she knew he liked to keep it going all the time. "*For comfort*," he once told her.

"Hello Walter."

He looked round, closing the fire grate before getting up. "Oh, hello Mrs Davison. Someone sounds happy."

"It's a lovely day outside and I'm off home now, but we had a few cakes left over from the church sale, and I thought you and young Charlie would like them."

"Very kind. Very kind indeed," he repeated, nodding at her and walking over to take the small bag of treats. He placed them carefully on the office table. "Everything go well at the sale?"

"Yes, thank you. We made a nice little profit for the church funds. I believe we have nearly got enough for the replacement bibles and the two new pews we wanted."

"Oh, that's splendid. Those rickety old chairs in the side aisle have certainly seen better days. Will be lovely to have the pews back."

"Yes. Well I must be off." Agnes turned to go and then saw a handful of small mail sacks tucked under the table. "Somebody's birthday Walter?" she joked.

Walter's mood changed in a moment and he looked uncomfortable. "I'm sorry I didn't mean to pry," she said, realising at once that she had made a mistake.

"It's ok Mrs Davison. Just a bit unsettling is all. Those sacks were dropped off up at Crawley by one of the Brighton fliers, and have come down here from Horsham. Driver said the delivery man told him there were dozens like it at the Crawley depot being sent on in all directions from London. I've got to sort them out and get them on the right trains."

"What are they? Letters? There seems a lot."

"Worse, they're telegrams." He looked at the floor and shuffled about with his feet. "From the war office." Agnes knew what he meant straight away but he added the dreaded words regardless.

"Are they…for here?" She stuttered with the question. Her upbeat mood of a few moments ago, now shattered in that moment.

"No, thankfully. I'm told they are all coming out of the 'Big Push' on the Somme. They say the casualties are in the thousands."

"That's just so terrible," Agnes replied. She felt a mixture of relief and guilt at the same time for the fact it was somewhere, anywhere, that her boys were not involved. "My Harold said he'd heard rumours about this down the Star, but I just thought it was, you know, Mr Gettings and the like, full of stories on a few ales."

Walter smiled. "Well old Gettings does like a skin full as you know Mrs Davison. No disputing that. And a good yarn to go with it. But I think there's a lot more truth here than even he knows. More's the pity."

"Have you heard anything about the Southdowns and our local men?"

"No more than you. Just what I said at church last week about my George's latest letter home, saying about being involved in something further north but nothing major. I expect we will hear from them eventually."

"My boys are not the best at letters Walter, but if I do hear anything I will tell you. I best be getting along. Hal will be wanting his tea."

"Thank you Mrs Davison. And likewise, I'll do the same. Good day to you."

Agnes walked out of the office and quickened her step along the platform to the entrance. She would be late home now, and knew he would wonder where she was without explanation especially with an empty stove. But Harold was not one to shout and fuss, like some of the men she heard about. If anything, it was her own pride in timekeeping that was bothering her. But the sense of relief helped lift her mood again, and Agnes began to hum another hymn as she walked up the road to the high street. As 'All things Bright and Beautiful' tunefully echoed her steps, behind her a whistle signalled the arrival of the five twenty evening train from Horsham. But the shrill call passed her by as she pressed on deep in thought.

*

Walter Miller went back to stoking the fire, and then glanced sideways at the bags lurking like a naughty dog under his table. He sighed, remaining crouched by the small grate and held his hands out to feel the warmth, despite the high temperatures outside. He clung onto the feeling for reassurance but the whistle of the incoming train broke the spell, and he hauled himself to his feet, muttering at the same old aches and pains that plagued his joints.

Picking up his flag that lay next to the sweet-smelling cakes from the WI ladies, Walter pottered outside as the evening train huffed and puffed its way into the platform in sympathy to his own predicament. He nodded at the driver's face as it passed, barely visible in the steam. The express drivers rarely chatted to the local men.

The Garretts from Upper Beeding got off. They had been down to Shoreham for the day looking at lace for their daughter's wedding dress. He tipped his hat to them as they passed, showing their ticket even though he didn't ask for it. *No need.* Jacob King stumbled out of the rear carriage. A sheep farmer from Wiston, he had gone early to visit his ailing mother near Coombes. But by the look of the way he stumbled along the platform, he had called in at a couple of other places along the way!

"Evening Jacob. How was your mother?"

Jacob paused for a moment while he tracked down the source of the voice, then his face broke into a smile. "Ah Walter." He touched his hat respectfully and nearly lost his balance. "She's not so bad thanks. Old age you know. Just have to be there as a support."

Walter smiled sympathetically. He watched Jacob fumble with his bike left behind the sheds, before he mounted unsteadily and slowly pushed off. *He can barely support himself,* he thought with a smile. *No doubt he will stop off in Steyning for some more 'support' on the way home.*

"Evening Walt."

The new voice made Walter turn round, and he saw the solemn face of Stanley Kerr looking at him from the guard's wagon.

"No one getting on?"

"Not tonight Stan." Stanley nodded and immediately waved the flag to the driver ahead; aware he was a stickler for timings.

"All okay?" Walter asked.

"Can't grumble. As long as I keep the boss happy." He gestured towards the engine where the blackened face of the driver waved back once. "Yourself?"

"Oh, you know. Same as ever." Walter replied smiling. The train started to move and Stanley had to hold the door handle to stop himself falling forward with the jolt.

"Oh, nearly forgot. Got a mail bag for you that ended up in Shoreham by mistake. These young 'uns these days working the lines with the regulars away, always making mistakes." He raised his eyes as he reached behind and grabbed the small sack. "I'll be glad to get back to normality when this is over."

He threw the bag onto the platform as the train pulled away, moving inside and closing the door to the carriage with a last wave. Walter nodded back, and stared at the bag. He had known Stanley for many years on the railway, and also knew he remained unmarried. Too old to fight and with no sons to send, to him this war was just an inconvenience. He moved closer to the bag and saw the label was facing upwards. It simply said *Steyning Region; Sender - War Office.* It mirrored its friends waiting inside under the table. Like them, it was full to the brim.

*

An hour later, Agnes was setting the table for dinner. Harold had been caught repairing one of the top fences anyway so hadn't even realised she was late home. By the time he came down to the house to wash up, the aroma from the pie and vegetables wafting deliciously out of the open kitchen door negated the need to ask what time dinner would be, and he pottered past with a simple greeting and peck on the cheek.

Agnes smiled at the simplicity of her husband. Although sometimes the monotony of her day did get to her, she also enjoyed the familiarity of their routine and took comfort from it. Besides now she was involved in her other work, and with the Women's Institute movement continuing to inspire her, she had plenty to occupy her thoughts to counteract the dullness of her chores.

Warm food on the table and a warm embrace at night, and they will never do wrong by you. Her mother's words the day before she was married suddenly popped into her head and made her smile. She paused, plates in hand, as her mind drifted back. Though Agnes knew there was a lot more to her relationship than food and sex, and felt her marriage was much happier than her mother's had been, the advice hadn't been entirely wrong.

She put the plates down for the three of them and called to Freddie to wash for supper. Her thoughts now were on her mother, whose early death still brought sadness to her heart, especially as her father only increased his drinking after her passing and joined her within the year…

Fred bounded into the kitchen.

"Cor that smells delicious. What's for tea mum?"

"Rabbit pie and veggies," she said being dragged back to the present.

"Mmm pie, I'm starving."

Agnes smiled at her son and began to serve up their food. Keeping busy held the sad thoughts of her parents at bay, and she chatted casually to Freddie about his butcher's work until Harold appeared. She had been so focused on staying in the moment that it was only when Harold nodded towards the town and mentioned the bells that she realised they were ringing.

"Bit odd for a Friday night. You missing a choir practice love?" He sat down and smelt the pie. "Rabbit. Lovely."

"I don't think so. Maybe the ringers are just practicing. Something coming up I haven't heard of perhaps. Help yourself to the vegetables." She noticed Freddie become suddenly deaf at the words, having just grabbed a couple of potatoes, and she heaped some carrots and beans onto his plate. He pulled a face.

"Get them down you, they will…"

"Make me big and strong…yes I know Mum." He ignored them and tucked into the pie. The bells seemed to grow louder in the room and it was clear all eight were now being used.

"Not like you to miss an event in the diary though lass. Any gravy?"

"Hmmm?" she replied only half concentrating now. "Oh yes sorry." She took the jug warming on the top of the stove and poured some liberally over Harold's food before doing likewise to Fred.

"Doesn't make them any better," he grumbled.

"Do as your Mum says and eat up lad."

Agnes put the jug down, leaving her own food uncovered. She suddenly had an image of the mail bags at the station flash into her head and shivered. She looked at Harold.

"Something's not right."

He popped another piece of pie in his mouth, his plate already half empty and looked at her. He saw the concern.

"Alright lass. Why don't you put my plate to warm and I'll pop over there."

"I want to come with you Hal."

"There's no need. I'm sure it's nothing."

"Please."

"Ok, come on. Let's take a stroll."

Agnes took their plates and put them in the top oven to stay warm.

"Freddie you can finish your food, and then wash those pots for me."

"Oh what? Why me?"

"Because your mother told you to, that's why lad. And they better be done when we get back."

Fred nodded sullenly and watched them go out of the door, totally disinterested in why the bells were ringing. He waited until he heard the gate click, and then lifted the cloth off the pie on the stove and cut another piece for himself and scooped it onto his plate. The plate was now full to the edges but he grinned and pushed his vegetables onto the floor to make room, where Sally gratefully pounced and licked them up in seconds.

"Our secret 'eh Sal."

*

Harold and Agnes made their way up the High street and soon found themselves following a stream of equally curious residents responding to the unusual sound as the bells of St. Andrew's called out to the parish on this warm July evening. As people saw friends and neighbours walking past, they came out of shops and cottages and very soon the trickle of people became a crowd who wound their way towards the church; rumour and speculation rife amongst them.

Overhead a flock of Canada Geese in a perfect V formation followed their path, crying out noisily to each other. As they veered off towards the fields near Eastwood farm, where they gathered every year before Autumn called them south, Harold took comfort in the predictable routines of the season. He paused to watch their flight and dwelt for a moment on how fast the year was passing by once more. Then someone bumped into his back, having failed to notice him stopping, and with a muttered apology he strode on to catch up with Agnes.

The first sign that anything was seriously wrong however, came with the sight of Walter Miller slumped on a bench by the church wall, a large group of people standing round him. Harold steered Agnes towards him and had to use his strength to get close to where the man was now sitting, head bowed, while people fired questions at him.

"How many were there?"

"When did you find out?"

"Is my husband safe Walter?"

"Did you see our Bill's name?"

"Why haven't you got the post Mr Miller?"

Caroline Landon looked up from where she was sitting arm round the besieged station master. "The names are all inside. The vicar's going to read them out. It's the best way. Go in the church. Leave him be now."

People turned and began to push back towards the church gates. Someone stumbled by Harold and fell over his leg, and he bent down and hauled her up before she was trampled on. It was Constance Purfield from the flower shop. She looked at him, eyes wide with terror, and pushed on without a word.

Agnes glanced at Harold. She was frightened now and gripped his arm. She tried to call Caroline's name but with all the hubbub surrounding them the words were lost. Caroline was crying too. Suddenly there was a terrible scream from the churchyard and women nearby screamed too in reaction and now everyone started to run towards the church. Harold dug his feet into the ground and wrapped his arms round Agnes as men and women bounced off him.

"Watch it you idiots," he shouted angrily, not caring who was there. Faces flashed in front of them and then were gone. Friends, strangers, workers. Rich and poor alike.

Suddenly they found themselves alone except for Walter and Caroline. Harold led Agnes forward, her feet faltering on the cobbles.

"What gives Walter?"

Walter seemed to take an age to look up.

"They're gone Harold. My boys. Both of them gone."

"Oh god," Agnes said. A terrible feeling of dread biting into her stomach. She moved forward to comfort him.

"Walter thinks my Tommy too," Caroline added softly. Agnes felt sick, and fought against the overwhelming feeling of dread that rose within her. She placed an arm on the shoulders of her friends. Walter continued to speak as if to himself.

"I stopped looking after a while. The names…they just kept coming." He stared at them, a look of utter disbelief on his face. And shock. Pure cold hard shock wracked his face to ruin.

"How many?" Harold asked.

"Vicar's got the list. He's going to read it. Thought best to tell people in church. Not that he cares," he added with an angry jerk of his thumb towards the church.

"I'm sure the Reverend cares deeply Walter," Caroline said. But she was sobbing now, and without another word stood and made her way slowly to the church gates too, where more and more people were arriving. Agnes watched her go, eyes wet with fear.

"Not him," Walter mumbled. "God. Where was he 'eh?"

Harold was lost for words and simply shrugged.

"Did you see our boys' names Walter?" Agnes asked, her voice so quiet it was barely a whisper. He shook his head.

"You said a *list*…" Harold added. "How many names?"

Walter stood up now and sighed. He looked at them as if debating whether to betray a secret or not, and then said "Too many to count. There was an official letter with the telegrams, detailing the casualties."

"Are you coming in?" Harold asked.

"No point. *He* caused it…" he nodded at the church again, "…let *Him* sort it out." With that Walter walked away towards the station.

"I'll come and see you after," Harold shouted to him, without response, then saw Agnes already stepping quickly towards the church path and set off after her. His chest thumped and his hands were trembling, but he made himself follow his wife up the path. Near the entrance a lady had fainted and one of the church wardens was helping two men lift her onto a flat weathered gravestone, for want of anywhere better to help her. Where once they would have stopped to help without question, the Davisons now strode past with barely a glance.

*

As they went inside, Harold and Agnes had to pause as the church was packed. Many people were standing, calling out. Others were kneeling in prayer. Harold was surprised to see the Squire and Celia Goodman here, and not at the front in their usual pew, but standing off to one side amongst the common folk. The noise was suffocating, but as the Reverend Arthur Congreve-Pridgeon took the slow winding stairs to the pulpit, a hush blew across the people gathered there in moments. All eyes fixed on the papers he held in his hand.

"Let us pray." Two hundred heads bowed as the Reverend gave a short prayer of praise to God, and then led everyone in the regular *Lord's Prayer* which crackled with emotion. Harold could barely say the words but noticed Agnes spoke fervently. Again, a hush descended as all eyes raised once more to the ornate wooden pulpit in the corner of the church.

Arthur looked out at the massed faces of his congregation. He had faced many challenges in his role as reverend to this parish, and indeed prior to that, but nothing like this. Difficult confessions, local tragedies, the death of an infant...all paled into insignificance alongside this moment. He took a deep breath and began to speak.

"I have here a notification from the War Office advising us that the Southdown Battalions took part in a local raid on June 30th. It was addressed to our own Squire, Sir Francis Goodman, whose brother as you all know was an officer in the Southdowns. With his kind permission I can read it to you now."

Harold looked over at the squire and saw Celia grip his arm, head bowed. She was clearly struggling not to cry, and the squire patted her hand twice and then looked round to see if anyone was watching. He met Harold's eyes and for a second all status vanished and he simply nodded at him. Harold nodded back but for others the strain was too much and people began to shout their questions again.

Arthur raised his hands for quiet, and several of the churchwardens moved amongst the people asking them to settle down. It wasn't easy to do, and the reverend knew he must press on quickly.

"In the early hours of the 30th June, three battalions of the 39th Division of the 116th Brigade, known locally as the Southdown battalions, went over the top in order to create a diversion to the enemy prior to the main attacks to the south on the 1st July. Despite strong opposition they succeeded in capturing the enemy front-line trench, and also were able to move into the German support trenches..."

At this news many of the men shouted out in encouragement and some even cheered. Arthur waited a moment and then continued.

"They held out until forced to retire due to overwhelming odds. In doing so they prevented the enemy from sending additional troops and supplies to other areas where our main forces were attacking. But in achieving their objective of drawing enemy forces to them, the Southdowns sustained a large number of casualties..."

At this the noise broke again, and numerous women shouted out or began to cry, but many more simply hung their heads to pray. Some began demanding to know how many were lost.

"Our senior churchwarden Harry Best has the list of casualties for this region. We have been advised of those killed in action, or those who are listed as missing in action. I am at pains to advise you that those who are listed as missing may already have been accounted for by now. It takes time for details to reach us. Do not presume they are dead. They may be safe and well or in hospitals somewhere yet to be identified, or could of course be prisoners of war. I can only tell you what I know from previous communications and with the Squire's own feedback."

He looked at the Squire now in desperate need of support, and many people turned to look at their local landowner too. But the Squire simply turned and guided Celia away towards the side door. She was slumped against him and could barely stand, and Harold knew that could only mean things were very bad. The congregation turned towards Arthur again, and some began to push forward towards the alter, and the sidesmen had to step in to stop them.

"How many men have been killed?" someone shouted out.

Harry was frightened by the crowd in front of him and looked at Arthur.

"Give me the lists," Arthur said to him quietly reaching down from the pulpit. He realised only he could do this now or there would be chaos. He straightened up in the pulpit and spoke out slowly and firmly.

"I am told thirty five men have been killed from the town, and in total eighty seven in the region. A significant number more are posted as missing..." There was a gasp from the crowd and unexpectedly silence descended as the shock hit home.

"How many in total?" a strong voice called from the back.

Arthur looked up to see Harold Davison looking at him, and all eyes moved first to Harold and then to the Reverend.

"The official communication cites the Battalions lost over half their number, or to be precise over twelve hundred officers and men have been listed as killed, wounded or missing in action."

There was a communal groan across the church as the number registered with the congregation. One woman at the front began to sob and slowly her cries increased into a terrible wailing and everywhere men and women began to cry. Agnes grabbed a pillar next to her to prevent herself from falling and Harold moved in and put his hands on her shoulders. He heard her muttering over and over, "It's not them, it's not them."

Arthur called out over the noise. "I will read out the names of all those listed from this region as killed or missing, and Harry and his team will hand out the telegrams for anyone who wants to collect them now. Then I will stay here and lead us in prayer for as long as anyone wants to be here. The church will remain open day and night from now on if needed."

It was almost impossible to make himself heard above the noise now, and Harold was angry he couldn't hear what was being said. He looked round and then picked up a chair propped near the door and stood on it.

"Silence! Let the vicar speak." People nearby jumped at this sudden yell, and the noise began to recede. "Read the names please," he called to the reverend, and then climbed down a little embarrassed by his actions. He walked back to Agnes and she smiled at him briefly. They held hands and waited.

"Private Abbott G. Killed in action.

Private Abbott W. Killed in action."

There were several exclamations at the death of the brothers, and Harold now took Agnes in his arms.

"Sergeant Alsopp G. W. Missing in action, presumed dead.

Lieutenant Anderson R. Died of wounds received..."

Each name brought a cry, or a shout. Punctuating a constant murmuring that filled the church pews like angry bees.

"Lance Corporal Blizedale, Killed in action.

Private Boyd D. Killed in action." Harold shook his head at the name.

"Private Brandon T. F. Missing in action, presumed dead..."

Agnes glanced briefly at Harold as the dreaded alphabet moved on...her eyes wild and desperate.

"Corporal Chase T. M. Killed in action

Lieutenant Cullings F. W. Killed in action.

The reverend continued in the same solemn tone.

Davison D. M. Missing in action, presumed dead…"

The words hung in the air, and several people nearby now turned to look at Harold and his wife. For a moment she stood staring at the vicar. Then her arms slipped from Harold and she collapsed to the floor.

Harold dropped down immediately and scooped her up in his arms. Time seemed to stand still then. He was trying to hear if Will's name had been called next but heard nothing. The alphabet moved on. Someone appeared with water but he waved them away and stood up, Agnes' prone body in his arms. His mind registered the voice of his friend, Alfie Entwhistle, crying out behind him.

"No. Please God no." But Harold couldn't stop and made his way slowly to the exit. As he carried Agnes through the great oak doors the names continued to be read out and there was an audible gasp as the list reached G.

"Captain Goodman T. S. E. Wounded…"

As they walked down the path, Agnes stirred murmuring in his arms. Harold spoke soothingly to her as he had done to the boys in the middle of the night when they were little, and nightmares broke their sleep. Now the nightmares were here and he may never be able to wake them. Behind them the voice of the vicar continued his terrible sermon.

"Private Peterson D. Killed in action…"

"Lance Corporal Purfield, T.S. Missing presumed dead…"

Agnes looked up at him, confused. "What? What's happening?"

"It's alright lass I've got you. You fainted. We're going home."

Her mind exploded back into the present, and she shouted out. "David! My boys…"

"Hey now. There, there. It's just David they called and he's only missing. He'll come right."

"He's dead, I know it. Our boy Harold. Our little boy."

Harold walked on carrying her up the street, as people stopped and dropped their heads sadly. News roared through the town like a raging fire, and in a few minutes the light of Steyning had gone out.

Harold stopped for a moment on the corner of the high street, and set his wife back on her feet. They hugged for a long time and then he kissed her tenderly on the top of her head, and brought his mouth close to her ear.

"I'll find him. Dead or alive. If I have to go over there myself. I'll find him. We'll get him home to us."

Chapter 30 – The Day Sussex Died

Will sat at the table in the sergeant's dugout in their front-line trench. Sergeant Major Russell walked over with two hot mugs of tea and leaned against the wall next to him.

"Writing home?"

Will nodded. "Will it be censored do you think?"

Russell raised his eyes. "I think most of the lads that did the censoring are lying out there in the mud so am not sure anyone cares currently. Think the news is out now lad. Besides with the disasters down south, what we did here is probably the least of anyone's worries."

"All for nothing you mean."

"Yes. Colonel Grisewood was right in that regard, poor bastard."

"You mean losing his brothers?"

"Well that, yes. But more the fact he said we would just be cannon fodder. Awful way to say *I told you so*." Russell lit a cigar but didn't offer one to Will, knowing the young sergeant still refused to seek comfort in beer or smokes. "What are you going to tell them?"

"The truth as much as I can. About James, David and the whole bloody mess. I doubt they will hear much officially."

"You're right there lad. The new CO who came up from HQ said all news was being diluted and any incidents like ours were being swept under the carpet."

Will gave a wry smile. "Incident? Is that what it was? Funny that. I thought it was a diversionary attack where we got well and truly caned. Not an incident. Sounds like we got caught cheating at cards."

Russell laughed. "You're starting to sound like an old hen now Davison. Better get you some leave soon or you will end up like me." Will smiled back and Russell popped a spot of rum in both their teas and handed one to his favourite sergeant. "Medicinal purposes Will. Keep out the night chills." He winked.

Will nodded and they clinked mugs. He picked up his pen again.

"I'll try and put a positive spin on it then."

"That's the spirit lad. Can't have too much bad news back home. Upsets the toffs over breakfast." He gave Will a pat on the back and took another puff on his cigar.

"Yes, I guess sixty thousand casualties in one day would make their milk turn, without mentioning the poor old Southdowns."

Russell gave Will a sympathetic look. He decided to change tack. "What's happening to the nurse that you spoke about? Your brother's lass."

"Rose? Oh, her Staff Sergeant is going to try and get her sent back to England. Archie, I mean Corporal Bunden, has written to his girl in Brighton, you know the Sister in the hospital, to see if she can work there. I think Teresa's going to see if Colonel Hamilton will sign it off."

"Teresa being the Staff Sergeant?"

"Yes." He realised he had broken formality.

"And your sweetheart?"

Will blushed at the frankness of the remark and looked questioningly at the sergeant major.

"Oh don't worry, it's not common knowledge. But I don't get where I am without keeping two ears to the ground and my nose in the wind laddie. She's a looker too I'm told."

Will nodded. "I feel so sorry for Rose, but I'm going to tell my mum too. She'll know what to do."

"They always do. Besides if the baby survives all this trauma she'll be a grandma and will want to be involved. Make you an uncle too lad, at nineteen. Fancy that."

"I hadn't thought about that," Will said sitting back for a moment. "It will do mum some good to have something to hold onto though. Something positive you know?"

"Amen to that lad."

The door to the dugout flew open and a private popped his head in.

"Beggin' your pardon Sergeant Major. The CO is asking for you up at company quarters. Orders to move on are through."

"I see lad. Anything else?" he asked as the young replacement soldier hesitated. The lad nodded.

"Sergeant Davison is requested to report back to the main camp. He's to resume his former duties."

"Very good, carry on. Tell them I will be there directly."

The soldier in the smart new uniform nodded and disappeared.

Russell shook his head and muttered to himself. "Sending us children now. All children. Not soldiering this." He looked at Will. "Finish your letter and then get back to base. Should be able to find a courier there to get it away. Sounds like its back to sniping for you lad." He held out a hand and Will stood up. "I'll see you around."

They shook hands and then Russell picked up his helmet and stepped out into the bright light of the day. Will watched him go, then sat down and continued to write. It would be the third time he'd started this letter, and he decided it was easier to just discuss the attack and leave out news of Rose for now. *That was too much to take in at once.*

*

Later that day Will walked down the line to the rear camp, everything of value to him pushed into the large bag on his back, which clunked with every step against his rifle and webbing. As he walked into the open yards near the supply depot he saw Joe for the first time in several days, and the smile that greeted him brought a warmth to his heart.

"Hello Wagner."

"Hello Sergeant. How are you?"

"Surviving," Will replied with a raise of his eyes.

"I am so sorry about the regiment," Joe said. "So much loss."

"Yes, you were better off here Joe, that's for sure."

"I wanted to fight. I am not afraid."

"I know that Joe. Though it's okay to be scared too. We all were that day." He paused for a moment and Joe looked around unsure what to say. "So, what gives?"

"Oh, the top brassers have ordered us to carry on as before. To find the ghost."

Will smiled at the boy's attempts to copy the local chat. "Suits me. Here or somewhere else?"

"I think we move. They asked for you inside." He handed him an envelope with what Will presumed were their orders. He reached inside his tunic.

"Right-O. Do me a favour Joe and get this letter over to the couriers for me. Its urgent tell them. Then I will meet you back here after."

As Joe nodded and walked off, Will saw a large body of soldiers forming up nearby ready to march, and realised they were Southdowns. He looked towards the building nearby and decided it could wait a few minutes longer. As he approached the men, the familiar tones of Sergeant Major Russell barked forth from the front of the line and the group snapped to attention. Then with little fuss they broke into their marching pattern and moved off. After everything they had been through, they walked with dignity and precision, and Will felt an overwhelming sense of pride watching them go. *If I wasn't so tired I'd give them a cheer and no mistake,* he thought to himself.

Towards the back of the line he saw the unmistakable bulk of his friend Archie and jogged over to walk alongside him for a moment.

"Hello Bunny. Going anywhere nice?"

"Hello Sarge," he replied as cheerily as ever. "Off on our holidays to some little place called *the Somme*." He raised his eyes at his friend. "Sunshine, vineyards, cafés with gorgeous serving girls. You know, everything we was promised when we signed up." The men round about laughed.

"Should be lovely then."

"Walk in the park. Care to join us?"

"Love to, but got my own orders."

"Oh I see, special privileges? Well watch out for that. You know where that can lead you." Will nodded, recalling their first ever casualty in 1914, who had been assigned to tend to the Colonel's horses and was killed when the stables were bombed.

"Indeed. What's happening to the battalions?"

"12th and 13th are being merged to other regiments. Some with the Royal Sussex already down there. Us boys of the 11th are staying together as no one else wants us." There was more laughter now. "Still got the spy with you I see."

Will looked back in the direction Joe had gone. "He's no spy Archie. Glad he's on my side truth be told. We're off after the 'Ghost' again."

"Just joking Sarge. He still looks out of place though."

"So do a lot of us."

"Ain't that the truth? Watch he don't get spooked 'eh?" Archie winked and smiled at his own joke. Will raised his eyes and then patted him on the arm.

"Well I best be off Bunny. You watch that thick head of yours won't you?"

"I will Sarge. And you. Don't get shot 'eh?"

"Do my best," he smiled and then called out "Good luck Southdowns!"

There was a crescendo of shouts and then the men fell silent, and the sound of stamping boots carried them away. As they reached the crest of the first rise in the road south, they broke into song. Will watched them go with tear filled eyes, and then turned to walk back to the offices. He took the orders out of the envelope as he went to report in. Scanning the document, he could see they were being posted south to a new sector. He scrunched the paper in his hand as he walked on determinedly. *Time to settle the score.*

*

Less than a mile away Hans Liebsteiner stood in a small farm building, surrounded by a number of German officers and other ranks. Most of them were studying a map of the front lines spread across a redundant kitchen table. Part of the wall behind them was missing and the rest were showing signs of decay from previous fighting; but they were well back from the front line, and reasonably shaded by the surrounding orchard, from prying eyes above.

Even so there was clearly an urgency to the briefing as soldiers were dispatched regularly with new orders for the regiments based here. The officers glanced up nervously at any fresh sounds of fighting, only too aware this had been a front line setting not that long ago. One of the officers broke off and stepped over to Hans, and passed him an envelope.

"Sorry to keep you waiting Leibsteiner. Here are you new orders. You are to stay working alone as requested but we have a new sector for you now." He gestured to the table and Hans followed him over to look at the map. Hans felt uncomfortable amidst so many senior ranks but focussed on the task in hand. The German Major continued. "There are reports of a number of high ranking British officers seen regularly near here. Probably inspecting the front, and no doubt stopping for tea."

Hans smiled politely as a couple of the other officers laughed. He looked more closely at the area. *It would take time to learn*, he thought.

"The fighting has been intense there for days now, so there is a lot of fluidity in the front. You can take advantage of the chaos no doubt?" He raised an eye at the young sniper but Hans simply nodded briefly before looking at the map once more. He began to take in roads, rivers, buildings…

Irritated that the young soldier didn't offer any conversation the major decided to get him on his way. *This unteroffizier was useful but expendable, and hardly a key player in the conflict.* He deliberately placed his gloves on the map Hans was looking at, causing him to glance up.

"You have a copy of the sector in the file I have given you. There's a driver outside Liebsteiner. He will take you part of the way. Use your orders to report to the 121st Division, and from there you are on your own. You can file reports in the usual way. Any questions?"

"None sir."

"Excellent. Dismissed."

Hans saluted and tucked the orders in his jacket, picking up his kit bag by the door as he went out to find his driver. He looked forward to testing himself in this new sector near *the Somme.*

*

Harold came into the kitchen with a paper under his arm. He had walked into town with Fred to the butcher's where he worked, in the hope of seeing Roger Mullings. But there was no answer in the house, and he wondered if they were away again. The Mullings had scarce been seen since news of their son's death broke, and were it not for John the shop might have stopped trading altogether. Walking back from town, he wondered if they were inside and just refusing to greet the outside world, but on questioning the staff they denied any knowledge of where they were. *Well briefed by John no doubt,* he concluded as he walked back up Mill Lane. *Still it keeps our Fred occupied with everything going on and the town needing its meat.*

Agnes had got some home-made mushroom soup on the stove, and smiled briefly as Harold came in, and then continued to get their lunch ready.

"What's that you have there?"

"Newspaper from town."

"Not like you to get a paper."

"Aye well the headline caught my eye. Local reporter has written something about our David's battle."

Agnes stopped what she was doing and came straight over to the table, wiping the food stains from her hands on her pinny as she did so. Harold opened it up for her to see.

The Day Sussex Died was emblazoned across the top of the paper in bold letters. Agnes put a hand to her mouth as her breath caught momentarily.

"Have you read it?"

"Aye I have. Doesn't say a lot more than we know. Reporter says it was almost impossible to find anything out. All hushed up of course. Typical of the top hat brigade."

Agnes ignored him and read it anyway, perching on the side of one of the kitchen chairs almost subconsciously as she took in every word. The estimated losses were at the bottom, which could not be 'formally confirmed' and it invited the reader to look inside for a list of names for the Sussex men.

"He says hardly a town or village isn't affected by this?"

"Yes, I know, not surprising given the numbers." Harold picked up a spoon and tested the soup and nodded appreciatively.

"He says there are a couple of hundred men missing. Either prisoners or…"

"Yes lass. Look why don't we have some soup 'eh? It's nothing we haven't heard and until we get something official then it's all just rumours. We'll go up to Crawley at the weekend as we said, and speak to the local ministry. Mum and Dad will look after Freddie so we can take as long as we need."

Agnes nodded and patted the paper a couple of times, and then stood up and moved back to the stove. "Can you get the bowls for me Hal?"

He folded up the paper and put it on the side dresser, and then reached down a couple of bowls and placed them where the paper had been. "You know I'm sure Will is going to write too as soon as he's allowed, and he will tell us what he can."

"I hope so," she said and began ladling soup into the bowls. It smelt delicious and Harold's stomach grumbled in anticipation. He was about to sit down when a shadow moved slowly past the kitchen window. It made Agnes jump and Harold stepped quickly to the door. He opened it and found the stooping form of Walter Miller standing there.

Harold felt his stomach turn cold and automatically looked down at the station master's hands and saw the dreaded post clutched there. Walter followed his eyes and immediately passed a letter up.

"This came from your Will. I took it off the post boy save him coming up. It's dated after the attacks so he must be okay." He tried a smile but his face seemed to hold back the happiness.

Harold looked at the letter then turned to look at Agnes. "See love, what did I say? I told you Will would write. Bit spooky that mind you, when I was just talking about it. Here have a look lass." He realised he was talking quickly and made himself take a breath as he handed over the letter. *Nerves, calm down,* he told himself. "I was worried there Walter, I thought…"

"I also have this," Walter said, cutting him off. He spoke without emotion and his face remained impassive this time.

Harold stared at the telegram. He didn't want to take it, but eventually his large trembling hand took the fragile note and he stepped inside without speaking.

Agnes held Will's letter tightly to her stomach now. Her other hand gripping the chair in front. "Who is it?" Harold slowly turned over the brown envelope and began to tear at the edge as his wife began speaking rapidly as if to herself. "Have they found David? Is it Will? Did he write this letter on the day of the attack? Gwen got a letter a week after her telegram. Is it Will, Hal?" Her knuckle turned white on the chair back as she begged him with wild eyes to put her out of her misery.

As Harold slipped out the card, Walter pulled the kitchen door to and walked quietly away. He knew they would not be replying, and he made his way down to the gate where his faithful bike waited by the old stone wall.

Harold looked at Agnes and quietly announced, "No, not Will. It's our James lass. Our boy is dead."

Walter heard the cry from Mill Farm as he cycled off. He had heard many cries like that since the war started, and more than ever this year. They haunted him day and night, and especially in his dreams when his sons would often appear as little boys shouting to their daddy for help. The pain grew inside him like a cancer that could not be cured as did his hatred for this war, and this world. He turned the corner to the high street and the bike creaked mournfully away as he went.

*

Agnes did not cry. She looked at the note and then handed it back to Hal. He came to embrace her now but she turned her back on him, and saw she had scrunched up her son's letter. She tutted and then straightened it out on the table several times. Harold was speaking in the background but her mind had gone blank. Her senses closed down to protect her from the pain and shock that now pressed in on all sides.

She walked slowly upstairs to her bedroom and knelt by the large bed that had been their wedding present. Underneath it she pulled out a small trunk full of clothes and carefully began to place them on the bed. At the bottom wrapped in brown paper she found the long woollen black dress she had worn for her parent's funerals. It had not been out since that day, but now she took it out and carefully laid it on her dressing chair, before replacing the other items and returning the case to its original resting place.

A short while later Harold ventured upstairs, and with a delicate knock on the door, walked in. Agnes was sitting on the chair by the window looking across the fields to the Downs at the top of their farm. A fresh wind made the lush meadows sway back and forth and shadow clouds were chased across the slopes as the sun played hide and seek. She was all in black from neck to toe, and her face was ashen pale. Yet she held her poise with a regality that made Harold feel proud and distraught at the same time.

"I brought Will's letter up Aggie. It's sensitively written as you'd expect from the lad. Talks a lot about what happened, and some news for other folks too." There was no reaction from Agnes so he continued. "I thought you might like to read it; help make sense of some of this…" She turned now and there was a flash of anger in her eyes, but she didn't speak and turned back to the window. "They were real heroes lass. All three of them. James was there. Led the attack…" At these words he began to cry, and Agnes turned frowning and saw her husband's crumpling face. She stood up and grabbed his arm tightly with both hands and pulled him in.

"He wasn't there," she began. "He wasn't on the lists. A different regiment. Doesn't make sense."

Harold took a breath and forced himself to speak. "Wanted to be there for his brothers. Came to watch them and give his support." He wafted the letter as if quoting it. "They went over together our lads. Real brothers…" His head dropped and she took the letter now and placed it by her side. Then she embraced him tightly, but still her tears didn't come. Something in her subconscious told her if she didn't mourn them they weren't really gone, but in truth the shock was too great to comprehend and she dabbed at his eyes with her sleeve, refusing to accept it.

"Why don't you go and put the kettle on and forget the farm today?"

"Shall I shut the curtains downstairs?"

"Not now Hal, not yet. I've got beds to make and rooms to tidy. I'll be down in a bit."

He kissed the top of her head and walked slowly away, every ache and pain of his forty odd years of farming now bearing down on his shoulders with a sudden weight. Agnes walked into the blue room that James and David had shared as boys. She wasn't going to cast their home into pitiful darkness so tied back the curtains and opened the window allowing the summer breeze to come in and charge about. She puffed up the pillows on both beds and then straightened one of the quilts. As she turned to go she saw two wooden hobby horses stood in a corner, next to the wardrobe.

For a moment the young lads charged round her feet shouting and laughing, swords held high, as she chastised them for being so noisy, only half meaning it. Then they collapsed, felled by some unseen enemy and she stooped to help bring them back to life for another go. But there was only the old rug in her hands, and the dust on the floor that swirled as she grabbed it.

She sank to her knees. And sobbed.

Chapter 31 – Light at the end of the tunnel

The death of Walter Miller plunged the town of Steyning deeper into darkness. Already there wasn't a street in the town that didn't have a house with curtains drawn, or a shop with blinds at half-mast. The battle of the Boar's Head had destroyed the flower of Sussex and not just in France. The emotional impact on relatives and friends back home grew with every month that passed, and with each new telegram that arrived. Worse were the wounded men returning from the front, crippled or broken, who were a constant reminder in every town and village of the horrors of this conflict.

Walter had unfairly been tarnished for being the bearer of bad news as the war dragged on; for the simple reason that the telegram office was based in his station. Where once he had taken pride in having two such responsible roles, the telegrams became a stone around his neck, and eventually it had pulled him under. Though the residents had rallied round on the death of his boys, with many like the Reverend Arthur calling in several times a week, it was all too little too late.

When the panic-stricken young Dempsey arrived at the vicarage to say the points had jammed, and Walter had not been back for a couple of hours, the alarm was raised. First men rushed to free the points before the express train came through, and then as time went on Sergeant Legg and his constables organised searches of the neighbouring area, and began to track his last movements. The search had barely begun when the driver of the express train appeared in Steyning to tell them the train had halted near Turner's gap; because someone had jumped off the lip of the tunnel in front of them as they came out.

Walter's bike was found on the grass mound above the entrance to the tunnel, with his beloved station master's cap and tunic folded nearby. A photo of his wife and children lay in the breast pocket. When the train finally came into Steyning, many of the passengers had to alight to get some tea and air due to the shocking news. It was left to the police and some hardened helpers to go and recover the grisly remains of the former station master.

There were two ceremonies at St Andrew's that week. First for the poor unfortunate Walter, that drew in crowds and former colleagues from across the region. There was a guard of honour for the coffin of train drivers and signal men, with flags raised high above the pall bearers and a single whistle being blown. For a number of the mourners there, the sound of the whistle caused them to break down in tears, and not just for Walter.

The following day James Davison's memory was celebrated. Agnes said they would celebrate his life, not mourn his death and was insistent there was to be no empty coffin, like there had been for Edward Mullings. If James' body was ever found they would bury him then, but regardless of that she had already expressed a strong desire to go to France after the war, and see the place where he had fallen. "That is where they would have their marker," she had told Harold.

Harold took it upon himself to write to Will to ask him to have it recorded somewhere so they could find it again, and when he told Agnes about this, she simply said, "And that is why I married you Hal."

However, Agnes knew in God's eyes he must be remembered and agreed with the Reverend to still hold a service of thanksgiving for his life, and to mark a plot where she could sit and think about him. *Where they all could if they wanted.*

The church was packed again. There were few people in Steyning and the surrounding villages that didn't know the Davisons or like the boys. Many were touched by the kindness of Agnes, and Harold's constant willingness to help over the years and they all came now to pay their respects.

Fred had not spoken two words since the news of his brothers broke. In the butchers he was left well alone. John Mullings knew all too well the effects of grief on the family. Harold's parents worried about the effect on the young lad and tried to encourage them to engage with him. But Harold was as stoical as ever and had simply said, "He'll chat when he has something to say."

When the Davisons arrived with Fred in tow, their close friends had to work hard to make a path through the mourners, who filled every inch of space inside the church. Agnes automatically went to sit in their usual pew near the back of the church, but was guided forward to some spaces saved near the front by Harry Best. But as they went to sit an extraordinary thing happened.

Celia Goodman, who had been sitting on the front row in the Squire's stalls, came back to Agnes and took her arm.

"We've saved you seats at the front. You will come and sit with us." Harold went to decline respectfully, regardless of the occasion, feeling this was not their place to be. But then he saw the Squire beckoning them towards him with a smile, and they all moved forward. Celia sat next to Agnes and turned to her as the congregation began to settle down.

"I had a letter from my Teddy this week." Agnes frowned trying to focus. "You know Theodore. He said your Will saved his life at the Boar's Head battle. Carried him home and got him to an aid station. He would have died or been captured otherwise. I will never forget this."

Agnes didn't know what to say, but simply smiled and said "I'm sure they all helped each other. They were all brave men."

Celia began to cry unexpectedly, and the Squire frowned at her but then continued to speak to one of the sidesmen about some matter on his estate. Harold put an arm round Fred to stop him staring, and pointed out some of the decorations around the church.

"Are you okay Celia?"

"You ask me that Agnes? At a time like this?" She took out a delicate white handkerchief and dabbed her eyes. "I've been such a beast to you at times, I know I have."

"Oh look, forget about it Celia, it's all in the past."

"No. I know I have. I've been jealous of you having children, and being so content. It's ridiculous isn't it? And what with the pressures of the estate, and then this war, it's been hard." She blew her nose and Agnes patted her arm. "And now you have to suffer this. Can you forgive me?"

"Of course."

"You are welcome anytime at the Manor." She looked along the pew. "All of you. And you can always sit here. I will make changes."

"Celia. You are who you are, and we are who we are. This war is terrible but when it ends a lot of things will just carry on as before. You will have your life and we will have ours. But I am grateful for your words."

Celia looked at the farmer's wife sat next to her, and saw such wisdom in her face. "Perhaps," she said nodding. "But your family will always be welcome at Goodman manor, and if Will comes home safe, God willing, Teddy will want to thank him I know. Am I right?" She looked at the Squire then and he turned for a moment and fixed the Davisons with a firm stare before smiling briefly and nodding.

"Indebted to your family," was all he said, and then gestured to the Reverend Arthur to start the ceremony.

"You're very kind Celia," Agnes whispered and the two women linked arms while Harold looked on, unsure what to make of what had just happened. A cacophony of notes from the back made everyone suddenly turn round, and several people jumped at the sound. Unbeknownst to the

Davisons, the Squire had sent out a message to the local military camp and two buglers attended resplendent in dress uniforms to play the Last Post during the prayers. Their 'réveille' brought the entire building to silence in seconds.

The Reverend Arthur Congreve-Pridgeon, wore the dark robes befitting the occasion, but as he stood in front of the packed congregation he smiled warmly and raised his arms high.

"I welcome you all into God's house. Once more we find ourselves here not through joy but through circumstance, and yet I know God's love shines down on all who enter *His* home, whatever the reason. At the behest of the Davisons, there will be no burial ceremony after our service. While we mourn the loss of another of our wonderful community, taken early unto God, we gather today in celebration of the life of Captain James Davison of the Coldstream Guards. It is the family wish that your prayers and thoughts remember this man when he was alive, and give thanks to Our Lord for his time here on Earth."

Somewhere from amongst the congregation there was a call of "Here, here," and Agnes moved now to hold onto Harold and Fred. The reverend continued.

"In our thoughts and prayers today too, we reach out to David Davison and all the men of Sussex currently listed as missing, and ask our Lord to guide them home." Arthur paused as his words echoed across the crowded church, where many now nodded in assent, or simply stood looking on sympathetically with tear filled eyes. He smiled again now and nodded to his wife at the piano. "We start by singing the hymn *All Things Bright and Beautiful*, which I believe was a particular favourite of James." The people rose as one and the uplifting sound carried across the town for all to hear.

*

It was late evening when Harold and Agnes walked back into Mill Farm. Harold's parents had taken Fred back with them for a couple of days to allow the couple some time alone to reflect on the events of these past weeks. They were surprised to find a letter on the mat when they got home, a second letter from Will in as many weeks. Harold went to check on the livestock, Sally by his side as ever, while Agnes revived the stove and made some tea for them.

They came together as a fabulous sunset turned the top fields golden in its splendid hue. Harold sat by the fire, cradling a large mug of tea and

Agnes came over and stood for a while watching the flames lick around the grate, her hand resting on her husband's shoulder.

"It was a lovely service today," she murmured, still transfixed by the glow.

"That is was lass. A fitting send off for sure."

"I don't believe they have gone." Harold looked at her concerned. "Oh I know they are both probably dead Hal. I just don't think our boys have gone far."

"What, you mean Heaven?"

"Well maybe some part of them rests there. But I think their spirits will always be here, in their home, with us."

"That's a lovely way of looking at it."

Agnes took Will's latest letter out of her apron pocket and then sat on Harold's lap. He didn't say anything but just adjusted his position to allow them to be comfortable and put his tea down on the floor. "Will you read it to me Hal?"

"Of course lass." He kissed her tenderly on the cheek and then took it out, eyes squinting slightly in the fading light. It was a short note really, and clearly written in haste, but Harold read slowly so that Agnes could savour every word.

Mum and Dad,

I hope this letter finds you well and that our Freddie is doing alright too. I am fine and still plodding on as ever. The Southdowns are being moved to a new region soon and the battalions are being split up. I am to be given new orders as well. I can't say more really, you know how it is.

I have continued to ask for any news about my brothers but with no success. There have been several raids by our other regiments in that sector and I have spoken to some of them on their return, but no more bodies have been found. It is some time now since the last survivors of the attack made it back. Our sergeant major who you met, Russell, has been a great comfort and support to me and all the men these last few weeks. He even interrogated some German prisoners about our missing, but there was little they could tell us. I feel for all the families at home whose loved ones are missing or gone.

I miss home. But I am well and safe. Try not to be too sad. We are all doing our duty and know that one day we will succeed. James and David did our family proud.

I needed to tell you some more news that I left out last time. But it's important and may be a bit of a shock. James had a girlfriend over here, a nurse. Did he tell you? They had been together for a while. She is a lovely girl called Rose and worked in a museum I think before the war. Anyway, she is pregnant! There it is. I know James was going to marry her. Least he probably was. She worked with a friend of mine, Teresa, at the main hospital. She said they were very much in love! Rose took the news of James very badly, so I think they are going to try and send her home but not sure when. But Teresa says the doctors think mum and baby are well.

Thought you should know though. James has a baby on the way.

That's all I have time for. Sorry if it's a shock. Will write again.

Will x

Agnes stood up and took the letter from Harold. She read the last lines again.

Harold reached forward and took a box of matches from the fireplace and lit a cigarette. "Grandparents? Now that is a shock. He's right there."

"That poor girl," Agnes said now. "I must write back at once. Find out more details. Trust your sons never to tell us anything."

"He is in a war lass."

"Never mind that now." She got a pen and some paper and sat down. Then sprang up again and looked about the kitchen. "We'll need to get some things in and I will prepare one of the rooms upstairs."

"Eh?" Harold stood up.

"The blue room would be lovely but it will need new paint Hal, and the curtains need washing."

"Why?" Harold said, confused. "Whatever for lass?"

"So, she can live with us of course. We need to find where she is and bring her here."

Harold looked about him, as his wife paced back and forth ticking off lists in her head. Then finally she sat down and began to write feverishly. There would be no arguing with her on this point. But in truth he didn't want to. For once there was some good news to think on, and regardless of what that meant, right here and now that was all that mattered. He walked into the parlour and took two bottles of ale out.

Agnes paused for a moment, pen on her lips as she thought about what to say. Then she looked up as he came back in the room and smiled.

"Thought we could celebrate," he said.

Chapter 32 - Animal behaviour

Agnes finished the food parcel she was working on and passed it across to Caroline Landon to label it ready for delivery to France. It was particularly glorious for early September and the sun twinkled through the awnings, tempting them to leave the Red Cross tent and come outside. She took a sip of the cool lemonade that one of the ladies had provided, and stood up to get some air. Stretching her aching back, the long black dress that was her constant companion now, caught on the table leg and ripped slightly.

"Oh bother," she muttered, lifting the hem to examine the damage. "Oh well, no use worrying about it now. I'll sort it out later."

"You talking to yourself again Aggie?" Caroline said, who was sitting at the next table, scribbling down notes about the parcels they were creating. She was also dressed in a long black dress of a similar shape and pattern. In fact, all but two of the ladies working here today were wearing black, Agnes noted. *The whole town was in mourning.*

"I need a break Carrie," Agnes said without looking round. "Our Freddie will be here soon from work, scrounging for some cake no doubt. So, I'll go outside to get some air and wait."

"Good idea. Might join you in a bit. We've done enough today I think."

"I'm not sure we can ever do enough," Agnes replied as much to herself as anyone in the tent.

"Gwen's going to the talk about the new women's association this weekend with Lady Denman. Are you going to go Aggie?"

"The Women's Institute you mean? Yes, I hope to."

"Will Harold let you? Gwen said she might not tell her Alf. Just say it's a girls' night out."

"Really?" Agnes turned round now and looked at Caroline, but her mind seemed miles away. "I'm not sure Hal understands yet, but he's not stopped me going to the first couple of meetings. Besides I hear Madge Watt is going to be speaking at this one. She was instrumental in bringing the WI over here from Canada you know. I think she's coming all the way over from Wales where they've already set something up, to help us here."

"I'm not sure it's my thing Aggie," Caroline said a little nervously. "I'm happy to do my bit of course, but not sure they will let us set up a women only society. Can't see what good it will do."

Agnes looked intently at her friend now. "I think it's important we go Carrie. We have to change the order of things or this war will be for nothing."

"I don't think this war will ever end," Caroline said, "Not for some of us." Her eyes were full of tears now, and Agnes walked back to her and placed a tender hand on her shoulder.

"It will end one day. It has to. And when it does we have to do everything we can to make sure we don't have another one like it."

"What can we do Aggie? It's the men that make all the decisions, especially the big fat politicians sat up in London. What we do out here in the countryside doesn't matter to them, except when they want a vote, and we can't even do that."

"We will. One day. Things are changing."

"Pah! If you mean those suffragette women, chaining themselves to buildings and throwing themselves under horses, that's no Christian way to behave. I heard all about that before the war and it hasn't changed anything for us has it."

"Deeds not words," Agnes said quietly, quoting the Suffragette slogan.

"What did you say?"

"Nothing Carrie. I just think time will tell that's all. So, does that mean you won't come with us to the meeting?"

"I didn't say that Aggie," Caroline said a little indignantly. "Just don't expect me to chain myself to the vicarage." They both laughed then but the sound of raised voices from outside made Aggie pause and raise a hand.

"Quiet please ladies," she said and the women working in the tent all stopped. It was much clearer then, and the sound of angry voices carried to them across the bright lawns outside. "It's coming from the cattle market I think," she added.

"Probably Old Gettings arguing over the price of lambs again," one of the ladies said and they all laughed in agreement. Agnes stood by the flaps to the tent and looked towards the Mart.

"No, it's over by the station it looks like," she said over her shoulder. "There's a crowd gathering. I'll go and ask someone."

"Be careful Aggie," Caroline shouted after her, and as she walked forward Agnes began to wonder if she was doing the right thing. She could hear a lot of angry men now, and this wasn't the usual arguments over beef and pork. They were moving as a mob towards the station, where she could see the smoke from a train rising and she began to feel scared. *It would be the four o'clock,* she thought trying to calm herself with some normality. *But why would the men be so angry?*

Agnes looked back to the Red Cross tents and saw Caroline and a couple of ladies standing watching her. Then a shot rang out and they all screamed as her body jolted automatically.

Agnes looked round terrified, unable to comprehend what was happening. But something still made her walk towards the crowd, despite the shouts from her friends behind her to stay back. She saw one of the Mart auctioneers standing on a box looking towards the station and went over to speak to him.

"Can you tell me what's going on?"

"I'd stay out of it, if I was you love."

"But why are the men so angry. Was that a gunshot?"

The man looked at Agnes with a frustrated shake of the head. His fatty jowls quivering as he did so. "There's a trainload of German prisoners stopped in the station. Some idiot decided they could get off for a bit so the men are going up there to move 'em on like."

"Oh no. Will there be trouble?" As if to answer there was a fresh outburst of angry jeers and obscenities, clearly heard now, from the crowd ahead.

"I'd say that's obvious wouldn't you love. Now why don't you get off home where you belong and let us farmers give 'em a Sussex welcome." He gave her a wink and she recoiled with disgust at the fat, sweating auctioneer leering at her.

"My husband's a farmer too I'll have you know. Is Harold Davison with them?"

"No idea and I ain't got time to chat no more either. Look if you're wearing black 'cos you lost somebody then you'll understand that those bastards deserve what's coming to them."

Agnes looked down at her dress automatically and felt her grief forcing itself to the surface. She took a moment to compose herself and then tried again. "Someone has to stop this. It's not Christian."

"No? Well maybe God made 'em stop here so we could have a reckoning? Thought about that love? Now as I said you best get out of the way; this is men's business."

Despite her fear, Agnes was angry now and her body trembled in acknowledgement of both senses. She wasn't going to be scared off though, and was about to challenge the red-faced auctioneer further when Fred appeared on his bike.

"Hey Mum what's going on?"

Agnes looked at him and Freddie was a little startled by the wild look in his mum's eyes and took a step back. "You alright Mum?"

"Oh Freddie. Yes. Come here." She pulled him to her and noticed the man step off the box now and waddle up the road towards the back of the crowd. She was aware she was feeling angry again and softened her look for her son. "You need to stay away from here. Those men are upset that there are Germans at the station and…"

"Germans here? Cor that's amazing. Can I see?"

"No!" She surprised herself with her sharp retort but still had to hold Fred to stop him shooting off towards the station. "Was your Dad at the Mart today?"

"Hmm?" he said straining to see what was going on.

"Fred. It's important. Where is your Dad today?"

"He's with Mr Mullings. I just left him. Remember he said he was going to help him shift some of the furniture about now they are renting out some space?"

"Oh thank God yes. Look Freddie I need you to cycle back there as fast as you can and tell your Dad there's trouble at the station and your Mum needs him."

"What go back? Do I have to?" he whined.

"Yes Fred. Go now. It's very important. Ride as fast as you can do you hear?"

"Alright Mum," he said reluctantly.

"And Freddie, tell your Dad I need him urgently."

*

Simpson Reilly stood inside the station office watching events unfold around him. The train heading up to London had stopped while the engine took on more water, and at first Simpson had thought it was a freight train, with the carriages closed up except for small windows at the top. But then soldiers had slid open the doors on the first truck and a number of prisoners had been allowed to get off for a smoke and stretch their legs. They looked to be emptying one carriage at a time but in the end they got the guard to open all of them to save time and the Germans poured onto the platform.

There was only a military police sergeant and eight soldiers for the entire train of over a hundred prisoners. But in truth the risks were not high. The soldiers were armed and kept a distance between themselves and the prisoners, and also Simpson noticed that many of the Germans were either old men or young boys, and not at all intent on escaping. Even the more able-bodied men amongst them that might have caused trouble seemed to be quite happy to be out of the war. Their eyes all carried the same haunting look Simpson had seen on some of their own men when they were home on leave.

As the soldiers started to order them back onto the trains, one of the Germans had noticed the cattle market, and pointed it out to a couple of his friends. They had stood transfixed and then, ignoring the commands from the military policemen, they wandered across the platform for a closer look. *Most likely famers themselves,* Simpson thought, *or just enjoying seeing something normal again.* The shouts from the sergeant to get back to the train had been loud enough to carry to the farmers over the noise of the animals and the auction, and that was when the trouble started.

Within moments dozens of angry locals had come up to the station fence shouting abuse and threats. The sergeant did his best to calm them down but after recent events they were in no mood to listen and began climbing the fence. As the prisoners bolted for the safety of the train, stones began to rain down on them, and then a warning shot was fired. Simpson could see the engine wasn't ready to leave. They were still trying to get the fire stoked up enough to get a fresh head of steam on, and as one or two of the Germans were hit, others began to turn back and confront the farmers.

There were not enough soldiers to control the prisoners now that things had become ugly. Simpson sent the young station hand Charlie to fetch Sergeant Legg from the police station, but he was damned if he was going to do more than that. He was only here as temporary cover from Horsham, helping out due to the shortages, and he was promised a quiet couple of weeks before his long overdue retirement. So the last thing he needed was to get involved in some *argy bargy*.

"Mr Reilly. What's going on? I heard a gunshot." The voice of Agnes made him spin round startled and he looked at her wondering what to say for the best. "Can't you do anything? You have to stop this before something bad happens."

"Stop it? Why? I'm not risking my neck for a few Jerries. They started the bloody war."

"Mr Reilly, people could get seriously hurt. You have to go out there and speak to them."

"No. Not my job. It's Mrs Davison isn't it? Best you go home miss and let the soldiers deal with it."

"Why does everyone keep telling me to go home? You're the station master. This is *your* station."

"It's only a temporary posting while they find you a permanent replacement. I'm due to retire you know. Overdue. Only helping out because…"

"Because there's a war on, and just because you're not sitting in a trench doesn't mean you can stay out of it."

"Now wait a minute. You can't speak to me like that. I'm the station master."

"Oh, so you *are* the station master." Simpson began to squirm in his seat. "It's Simpson isn't it?" He nodded. "I know you Mr Reilly. I remember a few years ago when those gypsies came down to cause trouble at the Mart you were here visiting the fete with your family. You stepped in with my Hal and stopped them. Remember?"

"That was your husband?"

"Yes. Harold Davison."

Simpson was conflicted now. He had felt like a God that day and had really taken to the farmer who had fought back to back with him. They had even had a write up in the local press. He looked outside as the shouting intensified and his courage faded again.

"Was a long time ago," he muttered now looking at the floor, "before the war. It's all different now."

"We were proud of you that day. All of us. Your Lettie especially. She'd want you to help now Simpson."

"She's not here though is she?" He looked straight at her now. "She's dead, like our boy is in France. Like a lot of your boys here too. Thanks to that lot."

He gestured his thumb over his shoulder towards the platform where the soldiers had now formed a line between the farmers and the prisoners. Their sergeant could be heard shouting at the engine driver to get moving. He gestured back to him with a shrug, as if it was hopeless. The shouting intensified and someone threw a bottle that smashed against the train carriage and caused a number of prisoners to scatter.

Agnes watched Simpson slump in a chair as the emotion overtook him now and she felt pity for him. Then she took a deep breath and stepped out onto the platform.

She walked in amongst the prisoners, several of whom looked at her with open mouths. As she approached the soldiers the sergeant came running over.

"Miss better wait inside until your train arrives. It ain't safe 'ere miss."

"It's *Mrs* actually, and I'm not here for a train. I'm here to put a stop to this."

Agnes ignored his protests and looked round. She saw an older German soldier crouched over, protecting a younger one who had been hit by one of the flying objects. They both looked very scared but the young one had striking blonde hair and her heart lurched. She went to help him now, and there were angry shouts behind her.

"Get out of there."

"Bloody German sympathiser."

"Let him bleed."

Trying to protect Agnes now, the sergeant ordered his men to push the farmers back and now a full-scale scuffle broke out. Several of the men were clubbed to the ground and at least one soldier was knocked over. Then someone threw a stone at the sergeant who ducked at the last second, and it hit Agnes on the side of the head. She swayed for a moment, and then collapsed onto all fours, her head throbbing like mad. She felt like she was going to be sick, and then a hand gently took hold of her to help her up and she saw it was the older German soldier. She smiled but as he went to speak, Simpson ran up and pushed him back roughly.

"Get away from her!" He knelt down over Agnes. "Mrs Davison what were you thinking? Come on we have to get you out of here. The police will be here soon."

"He was only trying to help," she murmured. "Can you help me up Mr Reilly?"

As Simpson gently lifted her to her feet, Agnes felt the side of her head and blood was running freely down it. She struggled to stay upright now as more stones came and Simpson deflected one with his arm. As it ricocheted across the platform, the sergeant turned and saw Agnes and the anger grew in his face. He stepped back from the throng of struggling men and fired another shot in the air.

There was a momentary lull in the fighting and then a voice shouted out, "Why are you protecting them? They're the enemy ain't they?"

"These men are prisoners of war and as such they are under my protection."

"They're bloody Jerries," someone said.

"Stand back all of you and let this train depart."

"Murderers. Killed my Jack," a faceless man shouted out.

"Stay away from this station," Simpson added, being emboldened once more, and the sergeant stood next to him now and glared at the men.

The men started to push again but Agnes stepped forward. She swayed unsteadily on her feet for a moment, and Simpson moved to catch her, then her eyes focused in and she stood tall and looked about. The sight of the lady standing there blood running down her face caused the mob of men to pause. All eyes turned to her now as she scanned them.

"I know you Bill Cartwight. And you Michael Filbert. Does Izzy know you're here?" The man went to answer then looked down. "Mr Abbott, I'm ashamed of you. What are you doing here?"

"They killed my lads, Mrs Davison. It ain't right this lot come and stay here. Eating our grub. I'm too old and gammy to carry a gun they say but I can still fight."

There were shouts of assent and the crowd stirred again.

"Get out of there lady. They deserve what's coming to 'em."

"Agnes, we're sorry you got hit," Cartwight said, who seemed to be leading them. "You know we didn't mean it." The men nodded and a few looked at their boots ashamed to catch her eye. "But you should know this is right, as much as anyone. You've lost your lads."

She nodded slowly and turned, and for a moment it looked like she was going to walk away. Some of the men looked at each other and smiled.

"Get ready," the sergeant said quietly to his men behind her.

Then she took a few steps back and pushed between the soldiers, but instead of walking off she took hold of the young blond German prisoner. He resisted at first, the fear rooting him to the spot, and he shook his head feverishly as his colleagues protested.

"Mrs Davison! What are you doing?" Simpson protested.

She ignored him and smiled at the soldier. "It's okay, let me help you." She looked at the other prisoners staring at her now. "I'm not going to harm him." The tall German clearly spoke English as he said something to his comrades and they stepped back.

"She's gonna wallop him," a voice from the crowd said.

"Knew she'd be on our side."

"Ma'am?" the sergeant said, confused as to what was happening.

Agnes turned round with her arm round the German. She looked at the crowd.

Eyes ringed with blood glowered at them.

"One of my boys is dead. That's true. Another is missing, presumed dead I'm told. Along with many others. For all I know my Will might be lying dead somewhere as I speak."

"Shame!" someone shouted.

"Make 'em pay".

"But maybe one of them is standing in Germany right now. In a prisoner of war camp. Or maybe travelling to one, and right now somewhere in Germany an angry mob of men are throwing stones at my boy. At our boys.

At young lads like this one here." She pushed back his hair to show his youthful face. He can't have been more than sixteen. "Somewhere out there your sons and fathers, uncles and brothers, might be standing miles from home, alone and scared. Is this what you want to happen to them?"

"For all we know it could be," Cartwight shouted taking a step forward.

"And does that make it right? Do we want to be the same as them? Is that what God would want Bill?"

"An eye for an eye isn't it Mrs Davison?"

Some of the men agreed but far fewer than before now.

"We want to be better than that don't we? Do unto others as you would have them do to you, that's what the Lord said. Let these men go, and maybe our boys will be treated the same."

"It's not right Agnes."

"None of this is right. This whole mess," she shouted suddenly, causing several of them to move back startled. "But if we just keep fighting back and forth and taking revenge, there will be no end to it and no one will come home. I just want my boys back…" her voice broke and Simpson stepped forward.

"You heard the lady, that's enough of this now. Let 'em go lads."

Just as the tension started to ease, there was a loud whistle from the train, signalling it was ready to depart.

"Get the prisoners on the train Sergeant, quickly," Simpson said and the soldier nodded.

The whistle served to make the more militant ones flare up again though and they would have rushed forward in a last attempt to get the prisoners, who were now rapidly getting on the train, had two events not happened simultaneously. First, there was a commotion at the back of the crowd as the portly Police Sergeant Legg arrived with two constables.

"What's going on 'ere then?" he shouted, and immediately some men at the back broke away.

At the very same moment in front of them, the sound of a squeaking bike and ringing bell could be heard as Harold Davison rode onto the platform on Freddie's bike. At any other time and place the huge frame of Harold wobbling about on the small bike, legs up by his chest, would have looked comical; and the men might have laughed…

But most of them knew Harold Davison, by reputation if not personally, and they knew his temper. Although Agnes kept him in check most of the time he was not a man to be riled. He threw the bike down on the platform and strode over to his wife's side. He took one look at her blood streaked face and span with the grace of a ballet dancer before walking right up to the crowd.

"Which of you cowardly bastards has done this to my lass? I'll bloody murder the lot of you!" He pushed his face into several of the front row, and they shrank from him, including Cartwight.

"Harold, it's fine now. It's over," Agnes said quietly.

He looked at her and she managed a smile, and he looked at the soldiers and then at Simpson appraising the situation.

"Men tried to have a go at the prisoners, Mr Davison. Your missus stopped 'em." Simpson looked at the floor more worried now than ever.

"I see, and where were you?"

"I was just one man; besides they are Germans…"

"I know you," Harold said.

"Yes, I'm Reilly. Simpson Reilly, the temporary station master."

"From Horsham?" Simpson nodded. "Well you've softened and no mistake. As for this lot," Harold continued pointing at the prisoners pushing onto the train, "all I can see here are a bunch of scared, injured men. And this is your station. While they are here they should be in your care."

Simpson nodded but couldn't speak.

"Its fine Hal, it's over as I said," Agnes repeated touching his arm now.

"Is it?" he spat at Cartwight, challenging him to disagree.

The policemen got to the front then just as Harold squared up to the last few remaining men from the Mart, and with a last look at the train, they just turned away.

"Get this train out of here Mr Reilly," Legg ordered, taking charge belatedly. "I'll leave one of my lads at the station for the rest of the shift just in case."

Simpson nodded at the burly policeman who was sweating noticeably now after hurrying from the station, no doubt, which he was not accustomed to doing often. With a wave of the flag and a whistle he got the train inching forward at last. But just as it did so one of the prisoners shouted from the open train door window. It was the tall German who had tried to help Agnes.

"Your name is Fräu Davison I think?"

"I'm Mrs Davison, yes," she said, slightly taken aback.

"I met a Davison in France. A British soldier."

"That's nice feller. Common name. Good luck to you," Harold shouted as the train began to move away. *Last thing he wanted was some Jerry upsetting Agnes even more.*

"He was an officer," the man shouted above the noise of the train. "James he said his name was."

"What?" the Davisons said simultaneously.

Agnes broke her husband's hold and moved forward quickly.

"Where was this? When did you speak to him?"

"Can you stop the train?" Harold said turning to Simpson.

"Sorry Mr Davison, driver won't see me now, he's already turning the corner ahead. Hey careful there!" he shouted over Harold's shoulder.

Agnes was running alongside the train now, and she spontaneously leapt onto the running board of the train door, as Harold set off after her along the platform. The German looked startled, then held her arm for safety.

"Careful Fraulein."

"When did you see him?"

"At Christmas in 1914. We exchanged gifts. He is with the Guards you call it, yes?"

"Yes," she replied, then her head drooped. "I thought you meant recently."

"No, I am sorry. I have been a prisoner for three months now. How is he?"

"He's dead," she said, her eyes full of tears once more, and the man's face frowned seeing her pain.

"I am sorry Fräulein. My brother also died this year. A terrible war for us all is it not?" She nodded as he continued. "My father is in charge of a prisoner of war camp in Belgium. That is, as you English say, ironic yes?"

"Yes," she smiled briefly, then the train rattled as it began to accelerate and she almost slipped. He held her tighter.

"You must get down now please."

"I have another son missing, and a third over there somewhere," she blurted out. "They were in the Southdowns. Our local regiments. Sussex men." He frowned struggling with the words against the noise of the train and how quickly she spoke. Agnes had no idea why she was telling a stranger this now but she wanted to share it.

"I pray for you," he said. "Maybe they will find your missing boy."

"Thank you."

Then she was lifted into the air suddenly as Harold pulled her back just before the last carriage reached the end of the platform.

"What were you thinking lass? You could have been hurt!"

She wasn't listening. She just watched the receding face of the German looking at her as the train pulled away.

"I didn't get your name?" she shouted now.

"Meyer. Heinrich Meyer." He called back, and waved before the carriage pulled round the bend and disappeared in a cloud of smoke.

She waved after him anyway despite the fact the train was gone, and then turned to Harold.

"He knew our James. Said they met at Christmas in 1914. Exchanged presents…" She turned and looked back up the empty track now where the sound of the train could still be heard in the distance. Faint wisps of engine smoke clung to the track like reluctant souls from the departing men.

"Always had a heart of gold our James." He touched her bloodied face gently now and kissed the top of her head. Agnes' eyes looked at him without seeing. He knew she was miles away in her thoughts.

Harold's mind whirred about the day's events, especially his wife's actions. She had always been strong, and he was proud of her bravery, but what she did today had shocked him; and not just because she was almost seriously hurt. He felt fear again, and he realised it wasn't just about the events at the station. It was change that scared him.

The change in Agnes since news of their sons broke added to a growing feeling of unease. Harold closed his eyes for a moment and gave a silent prayer. He didn't know if it would do any good but right now he needed all the help he could get in his life. When he opened his eyes again Agnes was looking at him. She smiled and squeezed his hand, back in the here and now.

"C'mon, let's go home lass, and get you cleaned up."

Chapter 33 - A shot in the dark

Will and Joe moved slowly forward through the shallow copse towards the outbuildings of a small hamlet in an area close to the German front line. They were technically in No Man's Land but the lines here had moved back and forth almost daily and only last week the British front line was right where they now stood. It had since been pushed back to its original location prior to the Somme offensive on the 1st July. Now they worked through a small wooded section that neither side currently occupied but which had seen some bloody fighting at the beginning of July for the sake of a few hundred yards of ground.

Miraculously at least half the trees here still stood reasonably intact, despite the intense shelling, while in patches others were no more than charred roots where their former owners once existed. It was difficult and dangerous terrain to pass through, but they had no choice in the matter now. More than one report had placed a sniper working in this sector, with an unacceptable level of casualties resulting from it. A British team sent to flush him out had both been killed. So, within a few days of Will and Joe arriving here, they were dispatched to find him and kill him, "at all costs."

Everywhere they walked there were signs of the bitter struggle for this pitiful section of woodland. Equipment, spent cartridges and even the occasional unexploded shell littered the ground, and the two men moved forward very slowly. More than once they came upon a corpse that had not been recovered, often rotting or missing limbs, and both of them recoiled at the sights and smells. Although the weather was still very humid, the men wore scarves for just such an occasion and both pulled them up over their noses to bring some respite to the senses.

As they reached the edge of the wood, the sun was beginning to set behind them, and Will became aware their shadows may give them away. He motioned to Joe to follow him further to the north, to get an advantage, and his young comrade nodded and fell in behind him. Progress was painstaking but necessary. They had covered only eight hundred yards since their last set up point, where they spent the previous twenty-four hours observing the trees for movement. Will knew their enemy, if it was the so-called *Ghost*, could be just as good as them. He would probably lie still for the same length of time trying to flush them out. It was a deadly game of *cat and mouse*, with both relying on the other blinking first. Eventually they had to move, but so far had found no sign of anyone having passed through these woods recently. *No one alive at any rate.*

He paused noticing a wire in the failing light, and followed its course to a tree where an improvised booby trap could clearly be seen still poking out of the ground. It may be useless now of course but he was taking no chances and pointed to it as he stepped over the wire. Once Joe was safely through, he took out a small pot of white paint he carried in his back pack, and marked the tree to the side so that if they came back this way, they would hopefully see it. Will made a mental note of each marker he left as far as possible for it was not unknown for enemy teams to move marker stones or tags to fool them into taking a different way back, where fresh traps awaited.

Joe had taken advantage of the pause to drink some water and passed his canteen now to Will who smiled gratefully, and took it. He saw the mental strain of this work on the young sniper's face, and felt sorry once more he was caught up in this conflict when he should be swimming in a lake somewhere or fishing with his father.

Where would he have been now? And with who? Not Alice Pevensey he was sure. She wouldn't have chatted to him more than once were it not for him joining up. He pushed away the childish anger he felt. *But if he hadn't joined up he wouldn't have met Teresa either. So, in a way Alice goading him to join, led him to Teresa. Strange how these things work out. Had he really told her he loved her?* He smiled. *He was sure he did, and she clearly felt the same...*

Joe nudged him to break his thoughts and put a finger to his lips. There were voices ahead from a group of buildings, and as they watched, a lamp was lit in the upstairs window of the nearest one. Will gave the canteen slowly back to Joe and pulled his rifle forward. Scanning the other buildings nearby he beckoned for them to make for a small haystack to the side of the occupied building.

*

Hans Liebsteiner adjusted his legs once more from where he lay prone in the upper loft of the barn. The cramp had got worse over the last couple of hours and he would have to move soon. The light was going fast and he cursed his German colleagues who moved noisily back and forth in the buildings nearby. Soon the lamps would be on and his night vision would be distorted. But he knew the more normal their activity was, the more the enemy would not suspect he was there.

It was a change of tactic for Hans. Not to be out deep in No Man's Land but to work amongst his own lines. *Hiding in plain sight* in effect. It had worked so far, but he knew he must still keep moving regularly or risk becoming complacent. The British team sent to find him had been amateurish and easily disposed of. But all his senses warned him of a new threat. A more significant and dangerous threat in the shadows and it put him on edge. He was aware of another team that was causing fear amongst his own troops even if the officers didn't care. *They should. One day it would be their heads exploding over their maps, while drinking schnapps. No more jokes about tea then.*

Part of him wished his British counterparts were successful; he found many of his senior officers detestable, but there was still a job to be done. Before the war he had been on hunting parties with his father in the mountains, and often English gentlemen had come along to shoot with them. He had never thought then that one day they might hunt each other, and he wondered if even now, one of those 'Lords' was out there crawling through the mud. The image made him smile, but then just for a moment he caught sight of movement ahead of him and his senses snapped back and the tension returned.

Now as his eyes adjusted he could clearly see two men moving slowly from left to right in front of him. He calculated the distance to be no more than eight hundred yards and adjusted the sight on his rifle accordingly. He checked his rifle slowly and made sure the firing mechanism was working smoothly, then took out two more bullets and stood them next to his right hand. He could fire three shots within a few seconds of each other and more than once had hit two targets before the first even realised he was shot. He watched and waited.

They were moving cautiously but not low enough to be safe. The sun was behind them, lighting up their shapes as they moved from one wooden section to the next. He watched as the men paused now to share a drink. They were clearly nervous, keeping low and making it very difficult to get a clean shot away, but in drinking they relaxed a little and just for a moment allowed more of themselves to be seen.

It was a perfect killing opportunity. Two hits and then back to a large rum and a warm bed. He saw one of the Englishmen pass his bottle to the other. As they went to move off, Hans fired, taking up the second cartridge as he did so and with a half breath firing again. The third cartridge was in the chamber of his trusted rifle as the initial one found its mark. As the first soldier fell the second cartridge hit his colleague, but off centre taking him through the shoulder and throwing him backwards where he bounced off something behind him. Unlike his companion, this soldier cried out as the pain took hold, but before his brain could register a warning, the third cartridge arrived, impacting just above his left ear and he fell without further noise.

Lieutenants Orville and Huntingdon had both graduated with first class honours from Cambridge in 1912. One in Classics, and one in English. They had been friends since *Fresher's Week* and both joined their local regiment. The esteemed university and its community would mourn the loss of two more of its brightest generation.

*

At the sound of the first crack Will had reacted faster than Huntingdon ever could have, leaping forward and pulling Joe to the ground regardless of the noise. His time in France and his work as a sniper giving him reactions few others shared amongst the regular rank and file, especially with so many new troops. Will also knew if the first shot was aimed at them, one of them would be dead, but he was still pleased that before the second crack sounded they were both flat out in the dirt. The third shot coming a few seconds later, allowed him a brief moment to look where the sound came from; and the barn to the left of the hamlet betrayed its occupant with the slightest of flashes. *Got you, you bastard.*

They crawled on their hands and knees now round the side of the front building to the haystack Will had spotted. A couple of the soldiers had emerged on the far side of the house to investigate the shooting. They called out in German and then obviously must have had a reply as they walked back inside. Will looked at Joe and raised an eyebrow questioningly.

"They were just checking in," Joe whispered.

"Right, follow me."

They moved like shadows now, flitting across behind the haystack and ducking over a low wall behind the first house. To Will's delight they found themselves in a small walled garden that ran parallel behind the buildings. Will checked to see if anyone was nearby but the area was clear, so he gestured to continue silently forward and they doubled along behind the wall to a point close to the barn.

An old water butt stood here in the angle of the walls, and Will removed his helmet and decided to risk a look. He pointed to Joe to watch behind them for movement, and then slowly climbed up. The barn was quiet but he noticed a door at the back facing them and nodded to himself. *That's our way in.* Voices to his right made him duck below the wall again and they increased in volume as orders were now clearly being given. He saw Joe was alert too, and tapped his ear to signal his comrade to listen to what was being said.

After what seemed like an age he risked another look, and saw a dozen Germans lined up facing away from them. As he watched, they marched off down the road, and in the twilight sky they quickly became distorted shapes. Will noticed a large number of lights flickering some distance away and estimated that was their main lines. Another solitary voice made him look back, and he saw a soldier walk back into the house. For a moment through the open door he could see perhaps one or two more men sat by a table but no more. The door shut, and darkness crept across the scene. Will dropped down and moved in close to Joe.

"We're in luck. Most of them seem to have scarpered for the night. Just a handful of men left in the house. I can't see any sentries anywhere. Must be a forward observation point."

"Yes, I heard one of them say not to fall asleep, and something about relief times but could not make it all out. They are a listening post for night time I think."

"I agree, but our man is in the barn opposite so now's our chance. There's a door twenty yards away. It's on two floors so we go in there nice and slow, and you take the ground floor and I will go up. But watch for traps. All being well he won't be expecting anyone coming behind him except with his supper, so we will serve him up a different delight."

The joke was lost on Joe, so Will just told him to get ready and climbed on the water butt again. With a nod to his colleague he was over the wall and landed softly on the other side. Seconds later Joe landed next to him. They listened for a few moments and then ran crouched low to the door. Joe peered in a window next to it and shook his head to say he couldn't see anything.

Will opened the door an inch at a time. Partly in case of any kind of trap, but more so knowing the slightest squeak would give them away. He let his eyes adjust again for a moment and peered around. The inside of the barn was full of all sorts of machinery, and two empty stables were by the front wall, where double doors were closed and locked on the inside. *Just in case,* he thought. As they moved forward a couple of paces, they could see a small lamp flickering upstairs through the floorboards and they both froze. Will nodded to his friend to check the stables at the front and pointed with his rifle to the stairs on one side to indicate he was going to go up.

The stairs went to the back of the building over his head, and he knew he would be exposed as he went up.

Will moved as slowly as he dared in the dim light, anxious not to knock anything over as he moved forward. As he began to take the stairs one at a time, sweat ran freely down his head as he expected each step to betray him to its master with a creak.

None came, and three steps from the top he was able to raise his head slowly above the opening in the floor. There was nothing but darkness ahead of him but he paused anyway, every muscle straining to be unleashed at the slightest sound. Then he turned completely round on the step he was on, scanning the dark corners until he faced the front of the barn. The lamp burned faithfully away here, its candle half spent, illuminating a small area in front of an open window. Will took a fraction of a second to take in the scene.

A blanket lay on the floor with some old sacking nearby that may have served as a pillow. The table with the lamp contained a jug and a plate with some bread and a knife, but nothing else of substance. A glint drew his eye to the cartridges on the floor. Two lying close together, their work done. A third lay under the table where it had spun away no doubt. The barn was empty. He had gone.

Of course he would. He had fired. What was he thinking? Why would he stay here in an obvious location where they could be shelled? You idiot Will. Must have moved as soon as he fired while we scrabbled about behind the buildings. For all I know he could have marched off back to camp with his chums. He heard Joe still creeping about downstairs and felt stupid now. He considered their options further. *Would he be in the main house? No. Not this one. Clearly preferred his own company. Could I have shot him from the woods? Maybe. Too clever by half I think.*

Dammit. Need to go.

Will turned to walk down the stairs and as he did so a flash of movement caught his eye. There was a rustle from behind some old boxes and then one of them was pushed forward. His brain screamed out. *It's a Trap! Still here! Move!* And he threw himself down the stairs, not caring for noise now. Below him Joe saw the shadow, heard the noise and fired through the floorboards as Will came tumbling down on him, knocking them both to the ground. There was a strangled cry and then silence.

Joe pushed Will off and sprang up the stairs, two at a time, reloading as he went. Will was up in a moment and after him.

"Joe wait, be careful."

But Joe stopped at the top of the stairs and then let out a small laugh, which made Will pause, confused.

"We got him," he said smiling. "Behold the dark assassin." With that he held up a cat and tossed the lifeless body down the stairs at Will.

"Christ almighty," Will said. "I lost one of my nine lives just then."

Joe frowned at the remark, but then both men smiled at each other, and Will spoke up. "He's gone and we need to go too. That shot is bound to spark interest over the road. C'mon."

Both men moved quickly to the door but as they reached it, there was a shout from the house. Someone was calling to Hans to check he was okay. Will peered through the crack in the door and saw a German approaching carrying a mug, the contents of which gave off steam into the night sky. The soldier called again, clearly more concerned this time.

"Dammit. Company," he said raising his rifle.

Joe placed a hand on it to tell him to back down and wrapped his scarf round his face. Then he shouted something muffled in German back, and the man laughed relaxing once more and came on casually. Will gave his friend a 'thumbs up' and beckoned him to stand behind the door. As the German entered calling up the stairs, Will hit him hard on the back of the head with his rifle and he fell down unconscious.

Joe checked he was out cold and then asked, "Shall we tie him up?"

"No forget it. Let's go before his mates come looking for him. We'll go right out of here and move diagonally away from the house and then cut across to the woods." He glanced out of the door at the house. It was all quiet. "Let's go."

They moved fast, eyes darting left and right. Will's mind was whirring about the sniper; half of him wondering if he might be watching them as they ran. But the most important thing was to get out undetected. As they ran round the last wall they passed two small sheds that clearly served as the toilets for these men. The stench in the night humidity was rancid and they increased their pace past it, not worrying about the noise now they were already a couple of hundred yards from the house.

But as they passed by, the end door opened and a German soldier came out still adjusting himself, trousers only half pulled up. Even in the dim light they saw his face register in shock and for a moment he just stood there, mouth open. Will ran to the door and kicked it sending him sprawling. He got up but immediately tripped over his trousers and fell again, and the friends started laughing as they ran.

He began to call out for help though and then grabbed his rifle and fired wildly into the dark, still kneeling on the ground, so they sprinted off and were swallowed up in the woods in moments. Later on, Hoffmann, a new recruit, would find himself in trouble for causing an alarm, and suffer endless jokes at the hands of his colleagues for making up a crazy story about seeing British soldiers in the toilet.

All but one. Hans Liebsteiner would listen to the story in the sergeant's canteen, where he was celebrating his latest triumphs and a promotion, and know his hunch was right. *He was being hunted.*

*

Will and Joe reached a clearing in a small wood and he called a rest. He looked about trying to control his breathing and listen, but there were no sounds above a night time barrage some miles distant, the skies illuminating like lightning with each fresh explosion.

He took out his canteen and spoke to Joe. "Should be fine here for a few minutes. We're some distance from the buildings and I doubt they will follow us in this, especially as they won't be sure which way we went. Besides by the time they call up for support we will be home for tea. Even so best wait a couple minutes to be sure before we push on." He turned smiling, and saw Joe sitting on the floor already. "Water?"

Joe didn't answer and he went over and knelt next to him. He was breathing hard. "You ok? Need to exercise more mate. Too much fine dining in the trenches."

Joe nodded and then looked at Will. "I've been shot."

"What? Don't be daft. Where?"

"Here under my left shoulder. Crazy German must have got lucky."

Will touched his friend's side and he winced in pain. The uniform was wet, and he knew it wasn't sweat. "Shit. Silly sod why didn't you say something? How bad is it, can you tell?"

Joe shook his head and said "I knew we had to get away. Thought it was just a graze at first, even that I'd caught myself on a tree, then pain got worse." He slumped back. "It hurts Will."

Will looked back the way they had come but there was no sign or sound of any pursuit. "Right we have to get you patched up, then back to the lines pronto." He removed his pack and took out a small dust sheet they used for camouflage sometimes, and a torch. "You hold this over us and I will take a look." He took out a first aid kit too and set to work, with Joe struggling to hold the sheet with one arm.

"I need to cut your tunic, Joe. The wound's too deep for me to see and I have to get some pressure on it. It's bleeding freely and you will weaken fast if I don't."

Joe nodded and Will cut through the fabric and then pulled open the shirt below. Joe was wearing some kind of padded top under his shirt, which was also soaked in blood now. "Crikey mate no wonder you're struggling. You must be boiling in all this gear." He went to cut the under garment and Joe grabbed his hand. "Just patch it up until we get back. We haven't time."

"Look mate I once carried a man back without stopping to check him, and he died. That isn't happening again. It will only take a minute." He took a roll of bandage out of his pack and some tape, and then cut the garment. The wound was bad but looked to have passed through the side, and Will was relieved the bullet was not inside his friend.

"Its fine honest Will, just put a pad on it and…"

"Jesus Christ." Will exclaimed loudly pulling back, and stared at Joe. He knelt pointing at Joe, and the wound began to bleed freely again.

"Oh no," Joe muttered.

"You're a…but you've got…" He stared, uncomprehending for a moment.

"I'm a girl Will. Josephine."

"Jesus Christ," Will said again. Joe gave a groan now as the pain increased, and Will made himself reach down to stop the bleeding. "I have to...you know…touch you."

"It's fine," she replied. "Just stop the pain Will."

Luckily Joe closed her eyes and Will worked quickly pouring water to wash the area and then placing bandages at the front and back of her to try and pressure the wound. He tied it off round her middle and was embarrassed when he touched her exposed breasts on more than one occasion but it couldn't be helped, and the more she cried out in pain, the less he worried. Saving his friend was all that mattered.

"That will have to do until I get back. Is it okay?"

She smiled at him and nodded weakly, clearly in discomfort. Will did his best to cover her up again, and then had a thought and took off his own tunic. "Here put this on. The buttons aren't ripped on mine." He helped her into his tunic, discarding her own torn and bloody one in the process.

"Right come on Joe."

He lifted her up, but despite her groans, she still gave him a pat on the shoulder and said "Thanks Sarge."

"No worries, let's get home," Will said as he hoisted her onto his back. *This feels familiar* he thought to himself as he staggered back to the edge of the wood. *Seem to make a habit of carrying folk out here.* The last four hundred yards were straight across the exposed mud of No Man's Land. Going out they had crawled from shell hole to shell hole, but he didn't have the time or energy for that.

"We're going straight over Joe and no stopping. If you get killed tell me and I can lighten my load."

She laughed, which was a good sign and then said "Go for it."

The moon was behind thick cloud and once more their luck held as they moved slowly across the ground to the known gap in their own wire, and then pushed on to the trench. Twenty yards out they were challenged by the sentries and Will called a password and pressed on. At the trench friendly hands helped Joe down and then Will jumped in behind her.

"Almost shot you then mate," one of the sentries said. "What you doing out there?"

"Not going to let anyone else shoot us today feller," Will replied. "We're a sniper team. And it's Sergeant to you. He's wearing my jacket." Joe looked at Will as he said that, her face showing gratitude he kept up her pretence.

"Oh sorry, Sergeant," the young soldier said embarrassed. "I will fetch the Lieutenant to get this man some help."

"No time. I'll take him myself to the aid post. Get him up on my back."

As they pressed on, Joe spoke up. "Thanks for not giving me away."

"Don't worry. Haven't quite figured it all out yet, but it explains why I never saw you showering with the lads! First things first though, let's get you to the hospital, which won't be easy."

At the aid post the doctors were busy with other patients, so Will persuaded an orderly that the wound was urgent and got Joe transferred to the rear hospital, where he knew Teresa worked. There was a hospital truck leaving shortly and they got her on it, and then he climbed in with her. A medic climbed in too, sent by the doctor with an apology as they had been too busy to look at her, but Will didn't mind. This would be easier to deal with.

As the truck bounced along Joe seemed to cry out with every jolt but Will did his best to keep her stable, as the other man looked at the wound. As he pulled back her clothing the medic said "Jesus Christ, he's a woman."

"My thoughts entirely. Now shut your mouth and get on with treating her or you'll be swapping places." The medic went to speak again, but saw the deadly look on Will's face and so continued to work on the wound the best he could.

Joe seemed to have calmed down by the time they reached the main camp, and as soon as Will made himself known to the nurses there, Teresa appeared with a team of helpers and whisked her into a side room. Will took Teresa to one side.

"Hello handsome," she said and gave his hands a squeeze.

"Hello you. No time for that mind." She pulled a mock sulky face. "That's my sniping colleague there. Got shot as we made good our escape."

"Yes, looks nasty, but clean though. He should be fine."

"That's just it Teresa. *He* is a she."

"What?" she exclaimed, being genuinely shocked for one of the few times in her life. "But how?"

"Don't know exactly, but I guess the short hair and young looks, she passed herself off as a boy. And a damn good shot to boot, so no one looked too carefully. In all this chaos, no one looks too much at anything."

"Crikey," Teresa said.

"So I want it hushed up. It can't get out T."

"Leave it with me. I'll make sure the orderlies are kept out. Hamilton may want a look but he's as good as gold on secrets trust me. Especially for me." She winked.

"Oi. Look I'm serious."

"I know. God knows how she hasn't been found out before now. Must have been a shock for you eh?" She squeezed his arm.

"You have no idea!"

Teresa laughed. "I better go. Anyone else know about this?"

"Just the medic we came in with. Couldn't help that."

"You leave him to me. What's his, I mean her name?"

"Joe. Short for Josephine."

"Sweet. Brave girl too. Will you stay this time?"

"Yes please."

"Good. I was hoping you might. Go and get a drink in the kitchen and there's a bath down the corridor there if you want to wash up a bit. You could do with it." She smiled. "The bed in my room is still vacant. If you can stand more than one woman in a night I could join you later." She gave a mischievous grin and walked off.

Will watched her go. Teresa grabbed one of the male orderlies heading to the room and pushed him away, taking the trolley from his hands, and then went in the room and shut the door. His emotions of the last few hours were a complete jumble and he felt physically drained now he was able to relax. But inside he felt very much alive.

*

A couple of hours later with a hot drink and some food inside him, and having cleaned up some of the last twenty-four hours of mud and filth, Will began to feel human again. Instead of getting some sleep though, he had sat on the steps outside the main hospital building waiting for the doctor to finish looking after Joe. He walked along the corridor now to see how things were going and found the room empty bar the patient. A small candle flickering in one corner by the bed, cast a subdued shadow across the room.

He crept quietly in and looked at Joe who now rested quite peacefully away from everything. She opened her eyes.

"Hello Sergeant. Still being my guardian angel?"

"Hey Joe. Did I wake you? How are you feeling?"

"Much better. I wasn't asleep. Thought you may have gone back by now."

"No, I thought I'd stick around and check on your first."

She smiled and winced slightly as she shuffled in the bed. "I'm sure there are worse places to be than among all these pretty nurses."

Will felt himself blush a little but was sure the dim light saved him.

"Try not to move too much. Let the nurses look after you. I'll keep a track of how you are doing don't worry."

"Thank you. Think you can manage without me?"

"Oh, I'll try Joe." He smiled now and patted her shoulder. "Do you still want me to call you Joe?"

"Yes, I prefer it. Josephine is too formal."

"Ok then." He went to leave. "Oh, and just for the record, you scored a terrific goal in that match. You're a natural."

"Thanks Sarge. You didn't do so bad either." She smiled and closed her eyes again, and Will slipped out closing the door with a light click.

*

Teresa was finishing some soup in the kitchen with her colleagues when she saw the medic that had come in with Will smoking a cigarette nearby, waiting to return to the front. She walked over.

"Hello there," she said with a dazzling smile. "You brought in the young sniper with the Sergeant didn't you?"

“That’s right nurse yes. Bit of a shocker ‘eh?” He grinned cheekily.

“Yes quite, and it’s Staff Sergeant by the way.”

He straightened up now, suddenly on edge. “Sorry Staff. No offence like.”

“That’s alright, none taken. Look there’s some hot soup in there if you fancy a bit before you head back. Few minutes won’t make a difference I’m sure.” The same disarming smile as before made him resume his previous demeanour.

“Don’t mind if I do. Will be quite the story when I get back won’t it?”

“Not if you don’t want to end up here.” Her face became very severe.

“What?” he said, now very confused.

“Let me put it in small words that you understand Private. If I hear any talk of this anywhere in the camp or on the front lines, even if it didn’t come from you, I’ll chop your balls off. Is that clear?”

The man went bright red and stuttered wildly.

“Good. Enjoy your soup soldier.”

She saw Will come out of Joe’s room and walked off then smiling to herself as the medic ran out to the truck to get away as fast as possible. All thoughts of soup forgotten.

“You should be resting,” she said to Will, the caring voice back once more.

“I was going to. Wanted to check on Joe first. She going to be okay?”

“Yes. Hamilton says she was very lucky. Missed all her main organs and arteries. Lost a lot of blood though, so needs a few days’ rest of course.”

“What did the Colonel say?”

“Nothing. That’s why we all love working with him. He just treated her the same as everyone else in here.”

“I wish everyone would, but at least she’s safe now. Will she get put back on the front?”

“Course not. It’s me you’re talking to. I’ll pop her off to Brighton with everyone else. I think between us we are keeping that hospital fully staffed don’t you?”

Will laughed. “Not sure that’s a good thing T. Then again knowing Joe, she may want to come back.” Teresa frowned. “I think she’s on a mission. Trying to prove something to someone. Just a feeling I had before I knew she was a girl. Better warn Sister Dent over there. She will know what to do.”

Teresa gave a mock salute and then smiled. “More tea?”

Will shook his head. “What’s the latest with Rose?”

"I got a lovely letter from your Sister Dent. Elsie I think she said her name was?"

"That's right. That's Archie's lass. She looked after us both."

"Rose is in good hands then. Her note said Rose has arrived safely and is already helping out. Just like her. The doctor says the baby sounds healthy and has survived the trauma."

"Good. I'm glad. I'll write to Mum again and tell her she's there, and let Archie know too. He will want to take the credit." Teresa laughed and Will took her head in his hands then and kissed her tenderly on the lips.

"Where did that come from?"

"Just wanted to say thanks. For everything."

"Well it takes more than that to get round me," she teased, though inside her heart was thumping wildly. "Anyway, off you go and get some rest while I finish my work."

"Aren't you going to tuck me in?" He winked and she raised an eye.

"I can see you are going to be a troublesome patient." She took his hand. "Come on then soldier."

Chapter 34 – Peace at last

Harold paused against the wall and relit his cigarette. The biting wind signalled that winter's harsh grip was not far away, and he pulled the jacket collar up around his neck. There was a cry from up above, and he looked up to see the local Heron moving slowly overhead. He recalled a time last Christmas when he had seen the bird while sitting with Will. *It would be Christmas again soon. How the time flew. All my sons were alive then...*

He pushed off back down to the house, satisfied the sheep were fed, unwilling to let the dark thoughts flood his mind in the day as they did at night. *Keep busy Harold*, he told himself, and focused on Sally running back and forth as they strolled back down the hill. He noticed her limp was a little more pronounced recently but she was as game as ever. "Getting old like me lass," he said to her, rewarded with a wag of her tail as always when she heard her master's voice. *Might need to get a new pup in the spring and get it trained up*, Harold thought to himself.

He was still thinking about whether Tulip Farm would be breeding more collies next year as he walked in the door, and didn't immediately see the notes on the table. Fred was there eating a sandwich in front of the fire.

"You're home bright and early lad," he said.

"Half day closing Wednesdays," his son replied through a mouthful of crumbs, "and John let me off mopping."

"Mouth closed when eating. You know what your Mum would say lad." Fred scowled into his sandwich, irked he was simply answering a question, but thought better than to argue the point. "Soft spot for you that John has," Harold continued, washing his hands at the sink. "You've fallen on your feet there." He noticed the notes as he turned round rubbing his hands briskly with a towel. "What's all this?"

Fred made a point of finishing what he was eating and Harold raised an eyebrow at him.

"Mum's gone out. She's left some instructions for you she said."

"Gone out? Where?" His mind went through her weekly diary and didn't alight on any particular event. "She shopping in town?"

"To the station," Fred replied. The words made Harold tense for a moment, recalling the incident at the station last month, but he convinced himself all was well and carried on.

"Oh right, she's at the Red Cross tent is she? What's for lunch then?" He walked into the parlour but saw nothing prepared. Fred found himself facing more than one question at once and decided just to focus on the last one.

"Mum's left us a sandwich. It's on the side over there under a cloth. She's made tea too. It's ready by the stove for later."

Harold stopped by the sandwiches and turned round. "Tea? How long is she out for then? Is she going to one of those Institute meetings?"

Fred shrugged and popped the last piece of ham and bread in his mouth. Then he remembered something else and added, "Oh there was a letter from Will. Mr Reilly brought it. He's delivering post and telegrams now too, since the postman got called up. Said he's staying here longer or something." Seeing his dad frown he just pointed to the notes. "It's on the table. I think that had something to do with her trip."

"Trip? I thought you said she was at the Red Cross tent?" Fred began to mutter he hadn't said that, but Harold ignored him and sat down with the food at the table. He picked up the notes and was relieved to see no telegram in the pile and glanced briefly at the first piece of paper with some scribbled instructions about their food. He looked at Fred. "Wouldn't do you any harm to listen properly once in a while. You can get yourself out and fill up the log basket for me while I find out what's actually going on."

Fred continued to mutter as he picked up the empty basket and stomped outside but Harold paid him no attention. He looked at Will's letter and placed it carefully to one side, before opening Agnes' second note.

Hal,

Letter from Will for you to read. It's taken nearly a month to get here! Rose is in Brighton. I'm going there straight away to see her. Have left food for you and will be back tonight or tomorrow if I have to stay somewhere. I will work it out. I know you understand. The baby needs a proper home.

Look after Freddie for me. Love you.

Aggie xx

Harold rocked back in his chair and stared at the note. "Oh lass," was all he said to himself and then with a sigh, he opened Will's letter and began to read.

*

Rose walked along the corridor carrying a pile of towels and headed to the laundry.

"And what do you think you are doing Rose?" The voice of Sister Elsie Dent rebounded off the brightly polished floors and stopped her in her tracks.

"I'm just helping out with the washing," she replied, as the Sister clipped up the corridor to her.

"You're not here in an official capacity my dear." She took the towels off her. "You may be a nurse, and a very good one by all accounts, but I have my orders. *Some light duties* are what the Colonel's instructions said, *at our discretion.* Which Dr Harrison has left up to me."

"But Sister I'm fine. I want to help. It passes the time."

"That may be, but you are our guest, and I will decide what's best for you." She leaned in closely. "You have a precious gift there Rose. And I happen to be quite fond of the family connections too. Besides my Archie would have me on punishment duties if he knew I was making you work."

Rose smiled. "I wouldn't say anything Sister. Let me do something please."

Elsie went to reply but just then Rose jumped and clutched her stomach. "Ohhh," she cried out.

"What is it my dear? Do you need the Doctor?"

"No. No. It's just the baby kicking is all. He's very active, like his father."

Elsie smiled. "Hmm, well that's as may be. But that proves my point. It's rest for you. And anyway, for all you know, it might be a girl. You're hardly a shrinking violet are you?"

They laughed then, and Elsie touched Rose tenderly on the arm.

"Can I at least make tea then Sister?"

"Now that I do approve of. That is a light duty. And as I said before, it's Elsie when we are alone ok?"

Rose nodded and turned back in the direction of the kitchen as Elsie marched off to the laundry. The baby turned again and Rose paused in the hallway. She smiled at the intricate carvings on the Georgian staircase, and wondered for a moment about their designer, and who may have originally owned this marvellous building. "Those were the days Rose," she said to herself, reflecting on her past work in the museum, and her love for the arts. She imagined some well-known writer or philosopher throwing grand parties here, and ladies sweeping down the stairs in expensively layered gowns that glittered off the gold inlaid bannisters.

There was a shout from one of the wards down the hallway, followed by the sound of hurried footsteps, and then more urgent voices. Rose raised her eyes as the regal image disappeared in a moment like her old life had, and carried on walking. "Strong tea I think is required," she said to no one in particular.

"That's always a good suggestion I find."

The lady's voice made her turn and she saw a middle-aged woman in a long black dress and dark hat standing in the main entrance. She looked tired, but Rose couldn't help noticing how pretty her eyes were.

"Oh sorry," Rose said smiling politely, "I was thinking out loud. Can I help you?" The lady took off her hat and gloves.

"I'm Agnes Davison. I'm here looking for a Rose Kellett."

Rose's heart lurched and she automatically put her hand to her stomach as the baby turned again. Agnes followed Rose's hand and saw the swollen belly. She burst into tears, and moved forward instantly and the two ladies hugged.

Elsie came out of the laundry at the sound of the patient shouting and saw the two ladies embracing at the main entrance. As she moved forward discreetly, she recognised Agnes immediately despite the dark attire, from when she had visited before while they were treating Will. Inside she felt a warmth she had not felt since the last time Archie was home. Some peace at last.

*

Will sat in the sergeant's mess in base camp cleaning his rifle. Unable to find out where to report to on his return, he had been instructed to stay in camp and wait. His hands worked automatically as his thoughts were still back in the hospital and the delicious hours he had spent there with Teresa. He smiled and closed his eyes, and for a moment she was there once more smiling back at him, the eyes sparkling like jewels in the dark. She had stroked his back until he fell asleep, the safest sleep he had experienced in months. The dawn's light had found him reluctant to leave, and Teresa happy to delay their parting…

"Ah there you are Davison. There was a rumour you were back."

The voice of Sergeant Major Russell brought Will back into the cold unfeeling walls of the hut, and he stood up as Russell entered.

"I thought you were at the front Sergeant Major. I've been waiting for orders," he added, worried he should have reported somewhere by now.

"I was, but I'm back here for a couple of days overseeing supplies. I've got someone here who is keen to see you," Russell continued, and as he spoke Captain Fennell walked into the door behind him. His right arm was in a sling but otherwise there was no evidence to suggest the horror they had all been through, or the circumstances of his wound. Fennell appeared immaculate as always. The new uniform highlighting his handsome features even more, and the charming smile was there as ever.

"At ease Davison." Fennell put his hat under his arm and perched on a nearby crate. "How are you feeling?"

"I'm fine sir, how are you now?"

Steven Fennell looked at the young sergeant standing opposite him with admiration. He nodded to him as they shared a connection that can only be passed between men that have stared into the abyss and survived. "I'm good now thank you. Arm's still a bit stiff but should be out of this sling in a week or so. Luckily I can drink gin with my other one!" Will smiled.

"That's good sir. The Sergeant Major said you wanted to see me?"

"Indeed. I hear you had a run in with our resident ghost a few days ago. Young Wagner was injured too?"

"Yes sir. We missed him I'm afraid and Private Wagner was shot as we made our way back."

"Is he going to be okay?"

Will nodded. "The doctor said he would make a full recovery, although I believe he may be shipped to England for a while." Will lied smoothly to protect Joe's real identity.

"Well at least we know he's not a spy now 'eh?" Fennell said, looking at Russell who smiled politely.

"Never in doubt in my mind sir. Will I be getting a new partner?"

"No. At least not for the foreseeable future. Winter is just round the corner so the campaigning will be pulled up for a few months no doubt. I'm taking you out of the field Davison and putting you back in the line with the rest of the troops." Will nodded as the captain continued. "We are going to be rotating for Christmas leave too. Try and get as many of the Sussex men home as we can after what they have been through. The Southdowns have been decimated this year, and being on the Somme hasn't helped. Morale is low. But of course, every regiment has been hit hard so we can't all go."

"No sir, I understand." He felt conflicted about going home, especially with Teresa here, but knew his parents would love to see him, so he waited while Fennell continued.

"The thing is Will, I'd like to get the Sergeant Major here home to his family. The 11th are still pretty much intact but need experienced heads. We thought about moving Geoff over but he's still tied up with the other battalions that are patched together." Will thought it odd to be called by his Christian name by an officer, but knew now he had to let Russell go before him.

"The Sergeant Major has been here since we sailed sir. It's only right he gets some time off. I'm sure there are other CSMs available that can help us out for a few days. I will pick up what I can sir."

"I know that. You've not been home yourself either, and the Sergeant Major thinks with your recent losses you should have a break."

"I don't have any children though sir. I can go next time perhaps."

"Are you sure lad? Are you ok?" Russell had a look of genuine concern and Will moved to reassure him.

"I'm fine Sergeant Major. Honestly."

"It will be more than a few days though. We are giving men a month at home over Christmas. Proper break. I will make sure you get back in the New Year though. I promise that."

"Thank you sir."

"Well that's settled then Sergeant Major." They exchanged a look and Will frowned not understanding.

"Yes sir. Give him time to settle into his new role anyway." Russell smiled now.

"I don't think I've been away long enough to forget how to stand guard sir," Will said joking, and the other men laughed but he still felt as if he was missing something. The captain walked up to Will and patted him on the arm.

"Will you've been given the 11th. You're to be their new CSM. It's all approved. I suggest you spend a couple of days with your opposite number here and learn what you can. Big shoes to fill, but I'm assured by Geoff you're the man to fill them." He shook Will's hand then, while Will stood in shocked silence looking at them.

"I thought the 11th had a new CSM?"

"He was killed fighting at Beaumont Hamel."

"I didn't know. Sorry." Will paused for a moment then continued. "But sir, there are much older men than me with more experience."

"Davison there are Captains in my mess that would still be at university if they were back home. And Lieutenants that can't shave."

"If you're good enough, you're old enough," Russell added.

"Quite right."

"I don't know what to say sir."

"Good. That means you're the right choice. Right I must get on. Best of luck Sergeant Major Davison." They exchanged salutes and he walked out.

Will looked at Russell and then said, "What now?"

"Well lad. First we get your new tunic sorted out. Then we go and have a drink. You're not due to the front until the weekend so time for the shock to wear off." He laughed and slapped Will on the shoulder and then added, "I can't wait to see Bunden's face."

Chapter 35 - On a wing and a prayer

"Run that past me again, Private."

Private Irwin flushed with embarrassment now, knowing exactly how this would be received. He couldn't meet his officer's eyes and mumbled the message again.

"HQ have been approached for a prisoner exchange sir. They want you to oversee it. Something about Christmas spirit."

"Right." Harry Johnson stood up and walked round the desk. He poured himself a Brandy and then perched on the table edge. Taking a swig, he stared at his orderly looking sheepish by the door. "And Jerry just waved a white flag and walked over did he with a note, and knocked on our door?"

"Not exactly sir. Apparently they did try that, but the Northumberlands shot the flag off the stick."

Harry smiled. *Cheeky bastards. Good for them.* "So, what then? They rang up and made a dinner reservation?"

"No sir, they sent a Pigeon."

Harry splurted his Brandy onto his sleeve. "Damn and blast." He fixed the private with a firm stare. "You're kidding right?"

Irwin shook his head and braced for the next outburst. The major had lost much of his joviality since news of his friend's death in July. Which was compounded by the casualties of his beloved Guards in the Somme offensive.

"A bloody Pigeon brought the request." Irwin didn't reply, deciding discretion was the better part of valour. "And I suppose we sent a winged messenger back did we?" Irwin's eyes betrayed the answer. "Un-bloody-believable. This war becomes more insane by the day." He dabbed at his sleeve with his handkerchief and then topped up his drink. "And when, pray tell, do they want this *exchange* to take place?"

"First week of December sir. They thought it would be good for morale with Christmas and all that."

"Ding Dong merrily on high," Harry muttered sarcastically. "And do I walk over there, or are they going to fly me with a couple of eagles?"

"Sir?"

"Never mind. What are the details?"

Irwin handed the major the orders. “Shall I wait sir?”

“No go on. Rustle me up some food if you can.”

“Anything particular sir?”

“Well a spot of Pigeon pie would go down great.”

Irwin smiled unsure whether he was joking and hesitated.

“Just get me the usual hash and find me some wine if you can. Dismissed.”

As Irwin left Harry opened the orders and scanned the details. There was to be an exchange near the Amity Bridge…First week of December… It was a special request so they wanted twenty officers in exchange for ten British troops… *What? Damned if they will.* He was to oversee it personally…General’s orders. *General be damned.*

He looked at the list of ranks offered for exchange. *Not an officer amongst them. Do they think we were born yesterday? No Sussex men. No Coldstream Guards either, his mind registered sadly. He’s not coming back...Post Office Rifles, Cheshires, Welsh Regiment. Even a bloody Indian soldier. Doesn’t make sense.*

Harry threw the paper down on the table and strode to the window. He lit a cigar and looked out at the swarms of men moving back and forth below like ants on an endless quest to please the Queen. Except in this case it was King and Country. As he watched the men however his anger dissipated. They were just ordinary people, doing what they were told. The rankers had just as much right to be freed as the officers. More perhaps, as they had no say in any of this madness. Here was a chance to bring a few of them home to their families. Send Jerry back to his. *Who knows, one of these German officers might see sense and call the whole thing off. Not that he cared for any of the Hun.*

He watched as some men struggled to control two mules that bucked and kicked out against their load. *I know just how they feel. Probably going to get my head shot off though. Dammit.* He stubbed his cigar in a saucer on the desk and picked up his hat and gloves. *Oh well. Can’t live forever. Time to see the General old boy.*

*

The low morning mist swirled eerily across the bridge. Major Harry Johnson stood in the middle of it and shivered. He was not sure if it was the cold or the atmosphere that made his skin prickle, but he stood peering forward all his senses on high alert.

If they are going to shoot me it's going to be now. Knowing my luck, they will miss and I'll fall into the river and drown. He gave a small prayer but felt his body tense in the silence.

"Any sign sir?" The voice close by made Harry jump, and he looked round to see his sergeant major standing a few paces behind him. "Didn't mean to startle you sir. Men are all in position."

"It's ok. Impossible to see anything in this fog. Are the prisoners ready?"

"Sergeant Green has unloaded the trucks and got them lined up under guard, as you said sir."

"Very good. Any issues at all and you get 'em loaded back up and out of here. And if any of them make a break for it then you know what to do."

Sergeant Major Thomas moved alongside his former CO and nodded. He was glad to have the major back with them if only for a few hours, and the men felt the same. "We're well dug in sir. If they try and rush the bridge then we will…"

Harry raised his hand and Thomas went silent immediately, and brought up his shotgun that he favoured for close quarter fighting. It was a personal weapon he had carried since the start of the war, and had come in handy more than once. He aimed it down the bridge as the sound of footsteps could clearly be heard.

"Go and get ready Sergeant Major."

"I'd rather stay and cover you sir."

Harry looked round at the experienced soldier standing next to him. He missed the buzz of the front line and the camaraderie of the men. Despite the danger, he longed to be free of the endless paperwork demands from HQ that now blighted his daily life. Although he had major misgivings about this event, he welcomed the chance to be back at the sharp edge once more.

"I'll be fine. Wait for my signal."

Thomas nodded and walked away and as he did so, a solitary German officer walked slowly towards them, appearing out of the swirling mist like the ghost of some former soldier. He appeared unarmed like Harry, as per the terms of the exchange, and as he came closer it was obvious he was much older too. Grey hair sprouted from beneath a sharp peaked cap, that glistened with moisture from the air. A few steps away he came to attention and offered a sharp salute.

"Oberst Freidrich Meyer, Herr Major. You are Johnson I believe, yes?"

"Major Harry Johnson at your service sir. Sent by Headquarters." He returned the salute.

"I am the camp commandant from Cambrai." Meyer sniffed the air disdainfully.

"A miserable morning Colonel."

The colonel raised his eyes. "Is there ever a good one in this war?"

Harry smiled sympathetically. "Shall we get on with it sir. I believe the ceasefire only allows us one hour."

"Yes indeed Major. One hour's break from the madness." He turned and waved into the fog behind him. "I will send your men over."

Harry pulled his coat tightly about his shoulders. Behind him the sergeant major signalled the men to lower their weapons. The prearranged signal that 'all was well' as he adjusted his coat, led to a collective sigh of relief on the British side.

"Have the prisoners brought up Sergeant," Thomas called back.

There was the sound of movement from both sides of the bridge and then men began to appear, in a variety of uniforms. Some were still in good condition, others less so, and appeared to be a collection of borrowed items. There was no talking and they crossed the bridge silently towards the middle. Sergeant Green led the German officers forward and stopped when he reached Harry.

"I've got the list of our men to check off sir."

"Jolly good."

The prisoners passed each other with barely a sideways glance although Harry noted several of the Germans nodded to the colonel as they passed by. Behind him the sergeant checked off the names of their own troops. Harry felt on edge. Something just seemed off about this whole event and he wanted it done as soon as possible. As the last of the British troops passed by, who he noted was the Indian soldier, he turned to his counterpart. Meyer was standing silently with his hands on the side of the bridge, watching the river pass peacefully beneath them.

"Hardly seems fair you getting two men to every one of ours. At this rate we'll be outnumbered two to one." He attempted a laugh to put himself at ease as much as anything.

"Special request," the colonel replied without turning round.

Harry frowned. "I don't understand."

Meyer turned round now and smiled. "I don't think any of us understand anymore Major. So, we must focus on the little details and try to keep a sense of reality no?"

Harry didn't follow the colonel's comments and became more uneasy as a result. He took a cigarette out and lit it, and then offered one to Meyer.

Meyer shook his head. "I prefer to have a cigar back in the camp when this is done."

"Left my cigars behind sadly."

Behind them Sergeant Major Thomas saw the lit cigarette and sprang into action. "Something's not right. Stand by." The men immediately returned to their defensive positions as the first returning prisoners were ushered off the bridge. Everywhere the sound of weapons being readied could be heard.

"Are you Mathur, Garwhal rifles?" Sergeant Green's voice echoed off the bridge.

The Indian Soldier nodded. "Rajiv Mathur, Sergeant Sahib. But I am not infantry now. They made us cavalry when our regiment was broken up. But I am not for horse riding and my horse did not approve of me on its back." He smiled at the sergeant. "It relieved me itself of my presence. Hence here I am." He shrugged his shoulders and raised his arms as if chatting to an old friend.

"Never mind that now you bloody Hindu. Get going. That's the last of them sir."

"Jolly good. Thank you Sergeant," Harry said, feeling the tension ease a little.

"But I am not being the last sirs," Mathur said stepping back towards Green, "there is one more."

"What?" Harry said, looking from Meyer to his sergeant and back.

"That's all ten sir, I promise." Green double checked the list just to be sure even though he knew he was right. "What are you talking about man?" He looked angrily at Guptha who recoiled a few steps.

"Sirs, I am not for intruding but there is another man over there. Quite the extraordinary thing Sahib. I know his brother."

Harry turned to the German officer. "What's all this? Is this a trick?"

Meyer waved into the mist behind him. "No trick Major I assure you. You can stand your men down. As I said it's a special request."

Behind them Guptha had continued to chat. He was very scared so spoke rapidly. "I met his brother last year during fighting. He carried wounded friend from woods but he died. Was most sad. Most unusual to meet his brother and…"

"Shut up blathering and get off the bridge. Now!" Sergeant Green stepped towards Guptha who nodded, saluted and bowed in the space of a few seconds and walked very quickly away.

"Request from who Colonel?"

"My son is a prisoner in England. I got a letter from him telling me that a lady had shown tremendous kindness to him and some of his men, when they were threatened by local people. He mentioned her name and asked me to look into it, in case any of her sons were in my camp." Harry stared intently now at the tall soldier who limped out of the mist. "As incredible as it may seem, we had one with that name. I knew we couldn't release one man so I arranged this exchange to try and repay a debt. The little things, as I said Major."

"What name?" Harry asked without looking at the colonel. But as the soldier came up, he recognised the family resemblance and his eyes widened. "Good God."

*

The first scream when it came made them all jump. Joan cried out involuntarily, while Arthur and Harold leapt to their feet and began pacing. Freddie looked up at the ceiling from the book he was reading.

"Crikey is she dying?"

"Don't be daft Fred," Harold scolded, but as another scream echoed round the house he walked over to the larder and got two beers for him and his Dad.

"That's just the baby on its way," Joan said to Fred, "and the doctor's with her so no need to worry." Joan continued to knit feverishly in the rocking chair they had bought for Rose at the auction a month ago. She rocked back and forth as she did with increasing speed, her agitation clearly evident despite any words to the contrary.

"Well don't sound good," Fred mumbled, and Joan gave him a look and glared at Harold as if to say *"Don't say anything else."*

"Spot of Brandy would be good too if you men are helping yourselves," Joan added, after a pause, and Harold poured a glass without speaking.

Suddenly the kitchen door to the hall opened and Agnes came in. They all froze and looked at her which made her stop short. She scowled at them and then tested the water warming on the stove with her finger, nodding satisfied.

"Hal, get another of these ready for me will you. Where are the other towels?"

"Oh, I put them in the parlour, on the table."

"Right." Agnes picked up the bucket of hot water and went to leave, and then turned to Freddie. "You alright love?"

"Yeh we heard the shouting."

"Everything all right Agnes?" Joan asked.

"Yes, won't be long now." She smiled and looked at Harold, who took comfort in it. He'd paced this floor more than once with Agnes upstairs so he knew now all would be well.

"I'll get the water on," he said with a nod.

*

Polly Jenkins blew warm air into her hands as she came back into the hospital after overseeing the arrival of the latest batch of patients. She handed the list to one of the senior nurses, and then went to find Sister Dent who she knew would be discussing the allocation of beds. She found her in conversation with Dr Harrison in ward three and waited discreetly by the door.

The Sister made a couple of notes on a chart hanging by poor Lance Corporal Etheridge's bed and then, seeing Polly, she said something to the Doctor and came over. "How many today Nurse?"

"Twenty-four Sister. Six more than expected. Eleven wounds, five gas, eight limbs," she reported, as she had been trained, checking the maths in her head as she did.

"Hmm," Elsie said. "We will be four beds short. Though Etheridge has just passed poor man. Any walking wounded?"

"Two, and their wounds are not too bad on first checks Sister."

"Right well get the orderlies to move Etheridge to the mortuary and then ask Sister Clarke in ward five to have Burton and Mickle moved to the day room, so we can use the beds. Put up the temporary beds and add our walkers to it." She frowned as her mind clearly raced through all the men in her care. "The Colonel will be going home soon but I can't move him from a bed, much as I need it. That'll have to do while we assess them. I will come now."

Polly nodded but then paused. She waited a moment until Dr Harrison had moved further down the ward. "We've had another special in from the nurse in France." She lowered her voice conspiratorially while pulling a note out of her coat pocket.

Elsie raised an eyebrow. "Not another nurse pregnant by the Davisons?"

Polly shook her head, missing the humour in her senior colleague's remark. "No, it's a girl who was wounded in France. Josephine Wagner. She was shot. But she's in civilian clothes."

"Then what is she doing in a military hospital? That's one less bed to find straight away." Polly looked concerned at the comment. "I know it's hard but there are civilian hospitals for civilians. We are stretched thin as you well know. I don't know who this Staff nurse thinks she is but this is not a charity home for waifs and strays. Show me the note."

Elsie read the scribbled details from Teresa. Her frown grew as the story of Joe's background unfurled across the page. She put the note away and looked up.

"Where is she now?"

"Still outside in one of the ambulances that brought them in. Shall I have them drive her to Shoreham?"

"Don't be ridiculous nurse. She's military personnel from one of our allies. She belongs here. Let's get them all in." Polly looked even more confused but was used to orders being changed every hour, so just fell in behind the sister as they strode out of the ward. "Oh, and don't mention anything about the note to anyone else. She's military personnel and I will think of something before I go off shift. I will probably work my day off tomorrow."

"Yes Sister, though you might rather not."

"I beg your pardon." Elsie stopped dead and Polly almost walked into the back of her.

"You might prefer to have the day off." She pointed out of the front window. "He came in with the wounded. Hitched a lift, he said." She grinned widely and then added, "I'll help get the patients in while you catch up."

Elsie didn't reply. She had already quickened her step to walk outside and now stood staring at the looming frame of Archie. Emotion broke through all rules and regulations and she whooped as she ran down the stairs to greet him.

*

At that moment shouts broke out in Mill Farm too, as the news that Rose had given birth was announced by Doctor Corbett as he came downstairs to clean up, and join Joan in a large brandy. Joan then chastised the men for shouting and Harold and Arthur decided to go to the Star straight away.

Agnes remained upstairs ensuring Rose was comfortable. She held the baby close to her, and the years rolled away to when Fred had been there. Rose stirred in her half drowsy state.

"She's in good hands I can see," she smiled.

Agnes beamed back. “A little girl. About time in this family. She’s a beautiful little angel. We must think of a name for her of course.”

“I already have. My mother was Victoria. I want her to have that.”

“That’s very pretty Rose.”

“Yes, I thought Victoria Agnes sounded just right.”

Agnes’ eyes filled up once again. The emotion had been coursing through her since the baby was born alive and well. “Victoria Agnes Kellett,” she said softly.

“Victoria Agnes Davison,” Rose replied. “It’s what he would have wanted.”

A tear dropped from Agnes’ cheek onto the forehead of the baby, and it screwed its nose up and twitched momentarily before settling again with a yawn. Agnes rocked the baby back and forth and made soothing noises as Rose looked on contentedly.

“Thank you,” Agnes whispered.

Chapter 36 – Chocolate

It would be another cold, frost laden start to the day. Will bent low and stamped his feet and bashed his arms as best he could, trying to get warm. He was acutely aware how far sound travelled when the lines were quiet, and was keen to ensure the noise didn't bring the shells in earlier than anticipated.

His clothes were still damp from the night before, despite his best efforts to stay warm. His body shivered automatically, like a dog throwing water from its fur, trying to shake the very chill from his bones. He longed for the sun's warming touch, to bring some respite from the cold at least, and looked to the East for signs of its arrival.

Already the sun was rising, peering slowly and cautiously over the dark landscape as if to mirror the very actions of the people it was soon to shine upon. But this winter sun seemed different to back home. It shone like a giant torch that gave no warmth; bright but cold, as if it had the very life sucked out of it like everything else.

Will looked out over the front line through his trench periscope. He could see ice lining the edges of the nearest shell holes and wondered where the year had gone. Certainly summer had gone in the blink of an eye, like a Mayfly's dance.

A starling called across the field in front, heralding the moment with a shrill reveille. A second answered it and for a moment it reminded Will of his early days on the farm, helping his dad milk the cows before most children his age were even out of bed. He briefly recalled the sights and smells of that time, though it seemed so long ago now, and the feeling of fresh warm milk splashing on his hands and face as he struggled to handle the large cows under his dad's stern gaze. What he would give for a glass of that milk now to warm him through!

"The post came up with the morning relief S'arnt Major. Package for you."

Private Duncan interrupted Will's thoughts of home and he noticed now up and down the line, men were appearing from their holes to start another day.

"Thank you Private. Who's in the forward posts today?"

"Royal Sussex S'arnt Major. 1st Battalion. I'm on my way up to relieve them."

"My old mob. That's interesting. I wonder if I will recognise any of them anymore."

Duncan remained silent. Since half the remaining Southdowns had been posted home for Christmas, Will was the only one he still knew. Everywhere battalions and regiments had been patched up and pieced together since the awful Somme campaign. Any single company could have a dozen different cap badges in it, and it sapped at his morale.

A small group of men assembled near the slim trench running out into No Man's Land to the listening posts. Will guessed their ages to be anything from eighteen to thirty-five, but they all treated him with the same respect.

"Alright lads. All set?" The men nodded, and one or two automatically checked their equipment again.

"Keep your eyes sharp and your heads down. It may be nearly Christmas but that doesn't mean we can relax and enjoy our turkey roast just yet." He smiled and the men smiled back, fully aware the food wouldn't be any different to any other day, save for what they got from home. He watched them file away and then spotted a raised piece of mud cut into the side of the wall as a makeshift seat. He looked about and found a small length of broken wood frozen into the floor where it had come away from the walkway. With some difficulty he prised it free, and laid it on the dank throne and perched there.

News from home replaced the sun's warmth in his heart. His mother gushed with news of the baby, and how busy they were looking after her. Will smiled hearing how grumpy his dad was about the broken nights' sleep. *I know how that feels though I'd rather be awake in a bed than a trench.* He made a mental note to write to Teresa and let her know about Rose, and then daydreamed for a moment about his love. It had been some time since he had a picture from Fred but there was a homemade Christmas card in this one with a kind of nativity scene with Rose's baby marked as Jesus and Will in uniform standing guard. He laughed but then wished it had been James standing there instead, and the smile faded.

"Well stone the crows. If it isn't the young sniper come to grace us with his presence. Miserable as ever I see, even at Christmas."

Will looked up to see the smiling face of Ced, under a mud-covered steel helmet. One of the many newly issued headgear which looked like it had seen plenty of service already. The large moustache was still as prominent as ever and twitched now as Ced laughed.

Will stood up and the Sussex men with Ced now looked nervous as they saw the sergeant major's flashes on his tunic.

"Bloody Nora. A Sergeant Major now? How the hell did you manage that? I might have known you'd out do me," he added pointing to his sergeant's stripes.

Will saw the other men noticeably shrink back expecting the usual explosion from an NCO being addressed so informally, but he just smiled broadly and stepped forward to shake Ced's hand.

"Hello Ced, you old bugger. I might have known Jerry wouldn't get you either. Not worth the bullet."

They held the embrace for a long moment, memories and nightmares shared passing between them in their ancient eyes. Then Will broke the moment and reached for his package.

"You're just in time. Jam from home," he said, holding up some blackberry jam that had survived the journey. "And chocolate."

"Now we're talking. Just like the old days. You lot can hop it to your bunks. This is Sergeant's business."

The men began to trudge away disappointed and then Will called after them.

"Here, I got some biscuits too. There's plenty around at the moment so have these with your brew up." He tossed the homemade treats to the last man and they all called out a cheery thanks.

"You're too soft to be a CSM," Ced teased. Will gave him a look that made Ced think otherwise, though inside he was proud as punch of the young lad's progress. He'd liked him from the first moment they met in the trenches in 1914, and knew all the men would too.

"Let's go and get a brew on and tell me all the news," Will said, and they walked off together once more.

*

"The Pastor got it at Thiepval."

"What Lifton?"

"Yes, and Corporal Swift too."

"I liked the pastor, that's sad."

"You know that Major that ran the hearing at Estaires? Some posh name or other?"

"Major D'Arcy?"

"That's the feller. He got chopped defending captured trenches against Jerry counterattacks at Beaumont-Hamel. He got the VC for his actions, and one of his officers was wounded and got the MC. Wittering I think."

"I knew them both yes. They were good officers."

"I think Wittering is going to be okay. He was sent home along with Sergeant Picton, who lost his leg there. But they didn't think he'd make it."

"If he got to Brighton there's a chance. They saved Archie there."

"Yes, and sorted you out, I was told."

Will nodded and looked down for a moment, until the memory passed.

"Anyone else I know?" Ced shook his head.

"I heard about your brothers Will. I'm sorry so I am."

"Thanks Ced. Still hasn't really sunken in. I keep expecting them to walk round the corner every day." He looked to the doorway and the room turned dark.

"Archie also tells me he's going to marry the nurse that saved him," Ced continued, knowing he needed to change the subject. Will smiled.

"Is he indeed? Well I know he's smitten with one of the Sisters there. A right dragon, but heart of gold."

"Just what the bugger needs. Keep him in check."

"Well if anyone can, she can."

"Archie also told me one of our Sergeant Major's was in love with a nurse too…" He winked at Will now and took another bite of the bread and jam they were enjoying.

"Corporal Bunden needs to learn to keep his mouth shut, or he'll be on latrine duty for a month." Will laughed and swigged the last of his tea. "I should be off and check the men. Let you get some rest."

Ced stood up. "It's great to see you again Will. I heard on the grapevine you've been out there looking for snipers for weeks." He gestured with his thumb to No Man's Land where the light was becoming brighter by the second.

"Yes, it's good to be back on the line for a while truth be told. Though I have unfinished business come the New Year." Ced nodded, understanding.

"Well I have *unfinished business* with my bunk so I will see you later *Sergeant Major.* No doubt you will be a general by the time I wake up."

"Who knows Sergeant!" They laughed as they teased each other.

"Here, you nearly forgot your chocolate." Ced tossed it to him. "I bet you still have your sweet tooth. Try and focus on the here and now Will. It's all we can do. Besides it's nearly Christmas." He smiled again as Will turned and walked out of the dugout.

As he left Ced, to walk to the listening post, the Starling swooped and swirled away from the trench ridge, knowing by now not to linger too long. Will popped a piece of chocolate in his mouth, savouring the delicious moment of luxury it brought him before he shuddered again with the dawn's embrace and pulled his greatcoat about him more tightly. Keeping low he moved out into the advanced post in No Man's Land and nodded to Duncan and the men on duty there. He took one of the scopes from them and crept to the rim at the front.

Cautiously, slowly, mimicking the sun's silent almost imperceptible rise above him, he looked into the telescope for movement - signs of another attack that would make this day like any other. Nothing stirred.

The bird made one more pass flitting over their heads, and then flew low towards the German lines. Will watched him go, envious of the starling's freedom to just fly away. Then he looked in the scope once more. There was a glint near the bird, just for a moment, and Will stared intently at the area. But there was nothing but the cold silence out there. *Sun on the frost no doubt,* he told himself, though his senses were always alert. He sat down on the floor of the post and watched the clouds racing overhead. For a moment he was a little boy again, wishing the day away, so he could scan the night skies for any sign of Santa's sleigh.

His thoughts wandered then to home and hearth and he closed his eyes. James' handsome face smiled at him in the dark, and David's kind eyes sparkled still, and he sighed as the loss weighed on his soul. He thought then of Teresa and her warm red lips, and Archie shouting and laughing with his mates, and the moment passed. *"Cheer up Will, you miserable sod."* Ced's voice rang in his ears and he opened his eyes. Private Duncan glanced at him wondering perhaps if he was asleep. *Had he been? He was very tired.* He stood up.

"Right lads I'm off back down the line. Any sign of movement at all and you come and find me."

"Yes sir."

"Soon be Christmas sir."

Will looked at them. "Yes lads, it will. God bless us 'eh? Everyone."

"Thank you sir."

*

Hans let his finger ease on the trigger. He didn't know why. Perhaps he couldn't find it in himself to shoot someone on Christmas Eve. He'd had enough of this year, of the killings, that much was certain. Just for a moment there had been a chance, when the soldier raised his head to watch the bird, but something stopped him.

As the bird flew over him now, he eased the rifle back, and slid down into his hole. He would make his way back and try and find some peace somewhere in this cursed place. He glanced back towards the British lines.

"Merry Christmas Tommy," he murmured, and moved silently away.

*

Sally heard it before the rest. Her low growl alerting Harold to the sound of the gate closing. Although the house was quieter this Christmas Day than in previous years, with only Fred home now, the presence of Rose and her baby brought a lightness to the room. The chatter between the family gathered around the dinner table as they fussed over the baby, meant no one else picked up on the noise straight away.

Harold stood and walked to the door, and Sally instinctively crouch crawled rapidly to his side across the floor in the way only collies can, from hundreds of years of controlling herds. Her movement from the fire caught Agnes' eye and she stopped serving the vegetables and looked at Harold, reaching for a luke-warm cup of tea.

They had seen their friends at church that morning. Checked the lists on the door they had checked a hundred times already that month, without any word on Will; trusting his ad hoc letters to mean he was still well. As Freddie set off back to their home with his parents, Agnes had stopped Harold and told him that she would know if Will was gone, she would feel it; and he had truly believed her.

Having spoken to all their neighbours, they were not expecting any visitors. In fact, only once on a special day like this had anyone turned up unexpectedly when Harold's friend Jeff Arnold slipped and broke his hip on ice in the yard at Tulip farm. Their young son had run a mile to tell them, unsure what to do because the doctor was out. That was a Christmas day some ten years hence, and Jeff had succumbed to TB over three years past, so Harold knew this was no ordinary visit.

Sally growled again. The hair rose on her neck and Harold made soothing noises as he opened the door. Arthur stood up behind him now and as the shadow of the visitor crossed the kitchen window Joan reached over and held Fred. They recognised the hat and cloak form of Simpson Reilly and Agnes gripped the sink with her free hand, the other squeezing the handle of her tea cup so tightly her knuckles turned white. Victoria cried out suddenly making them all jump, and Rose rocked back and forth making soothing noises and patting her back.

Harold stepped out of the door and there was silence at first and then a few murmured words that no one inside could make out. Agnes saw her husband reach out his hand to take the dreaded telegram, news that Will was gone, confirming her darkest fears that she spoke out so loudly against. She could see her husband's hand shaking with uncontrolled emotion and felt the lump in her throat. Even the old clock in the hall seemed to pause, respectful of the moment.

But no paper appeared and instead Agnes saw Harold's hand filled with the hand of another in an unbreakable embrace. He turned and pushed the door wide open and stepped inside. A tall bearded man stooped in under the door frame in a borrowed coat and hat that were really too big for him. As he straightened up they all saw the uniform flash under the coat.

"Aggie dear," Harold said in a voice choked with emotion. "Your son is home."

"Merry Christmas Mum."

David's voice once more echoed off the walls of Mill Farm as his tear-filled eyes looked at everyone gathered there.

The tea cup smashed on the floor and Agnes let out a cry that was neither a scream nor a cheer, but something that only a mother that has lived with bereavement can conceive from the depths of her soul. The kitchen erupted in noise as the family surged forward with a roar, Sally spinning as she barked, understanding the occasion.

Old Gettings reckoned you could hear the shouts from Mill Farm that day up on the Iron Age hill fort at Chanctonbury Ring. He was probably right for once.

***

Author's historical notes

Claude Lowther

Claude Lowther was a Conservative Politician and owner and resident of Herstmonceux Castle in 1914. At the outbreak of war he raised 'The Southdowns': the 11th, 12th, and 13th Battalions of the Royal Sussex Regiment.

Lowther was a recognised and respected figure in the community and was able to receive permission from Lord Kitchener to raise his battalions. He did not just rely on posters however. He sought out other men well regarded in the community such as Neville Lytton and empowered them to raise men too. Lytton travelled the county in a car, often accompanied by a doctor, and went house to house in his search for men willing to join the army. At the end of this process, Lytton arrived in Eastbourne with 150 men destined for the battalions.

Whilst Lowther temporarily held the rank of Lieutenant-Colonel, like many others who had raised battalions in this manner, he did not lead them to France himself. He returned to Herstmonceux Castle once his work was completed.

The battalions he had raised bore the unofficial title of 'Lowther's Lambs', men of the Southdowns who had joined up together to fight together and became part of the wider Royal Sussex Regiment. In time they would be deployed to the Western Front and Lowther's Lambs saw their first sustained action on June 30 1916, the day before the Somme. Many of them would not return home.

The South Down Battalions: *The Day Sussex Died*

The sound of artillery at the outbreak of the Battle of the Somme could be clearly heard on the Sussex coast. The noise of the guns routinely drifted across the channel and could be heard as far inland as London on some days. The sounds of fighting were particularly loud on 1 July 1916 as men rose from trenches to face the single worst day in the history of the British

Army. By sunset, 57,470 men had become casualties, of which 19,240 were dead.

Sussex's worst day had, however, taken place 24 hours earlier.

Hiding such a large-scale offensive from the German army was not a simple task but British high command was keen to try and draw away as many of the German defenders as possible by launching diversionary attacks elsewhere along the front.

The battle at Ferme du Bois near Richebourg has largely passed out of popular memory. It is not mentioned in the Official History of the War for Britain and, coming a day before the infantry attack on the Somme has become heavily overshadowed by the fighting there. The men of the 11th, 12th and 13th Southdowns Battalions that would lead the fighting were unaware that their assault was a diversionary raid. Their objective was the nearby salient, a bulge in the line, known as 'The Boar's Head' and it was to be 'bitten out'.

Before the attack could even be launched problems were afflicting it. The Southdowns had been taken to a constructed replica of the battlefield from which to train on. This 'fake' battlefield also drew attention to the numerous drainage ditches in the area, including one immediately beyond the British trenches. It may also have neglected to include a large dyke running through the centre of no man's land. This training lasted only a few days.

Upon learning of the plans for battle, Colonel Grisewood, commander of the 11th Battalion, famously declared that 'I am not sacrificing my men as cannon-fodder'. Grisewood was promptly relieved of his post. Grisewood had already lost one brother during the war to illness. He would lose another at the Boar's Head.

Attack on the Boar's Head

The 12th and 13th Battalions were given the responsibility to lead the attack with the 11th Battalion, having had their role reduced following Grisewood's dismissal, tasked with providing carrying parties. At 3:05am on 30 June 1916, the Southdowns went over the top.

The Germans had known they were coming for several days and, as would be discovered in 24 hours at the Somme, the artillery bombardment at Richebourg had had little effect on the German wire. As a result, the attack was a disaster.

Whilst bridges had been laid out to aid in crossing the drainage ditches, it also meant that crossing this obstacle meant that even German guns firing blind could catch men in the open. Those men who managed to clear No Man's Land soon found themselves caught in the smokescreen that was supposed to blind the Germans and were unable to see where they were going. The war poet, Edmund Blunden, who witnessed the attack also reported that men had become trapped in the hitherto unnoticed dyke. As British soldiers reached the German trenches the fighting descended into brutal pitched hand to hand fighting until the British were eventually driven out.

Company Sergeant Major Nelson Carter single-handedly captured a German machine gun post and used the weapon to cover the retreat of his fellows before fleeing German trenches himself. He then repeatedly re-entered No Man's Land to rescue wounded men and carry them to safety. On his final trip he was shot through the chest and killed. He was posthumously rewarded the Victoria Cross for his bravery.

Other awards for the Southdowns included twenty Military Medals, eight Distinguished Conduct Medals, four military crosses and a Distinguished Service Order.

These awards were not greeted with much enthusiasm. Blunden, who had volunteered for service with the 11th Battalion of the Southdowns at the outbreak of the war, declared that upon hearing of the real reason for the attack that 'the explanations were almost as infuriating to the troops as the attack itself'.

Aftermath

When the time came to take stock, the casualty numbers were tremendous. The 11th Battalion had sustained 116 casualties whilst supporting the attack. The 12th Battalion lost 429 men either killed or wounded. The 13th Battalion, however, had been almost entirely destroyed with over 800 men being killed, wounded or captured. In total, the three Southdowns

Battalions suffered 366 killed and over 1000 wounded or taken prisoner. The majority of officers and Non-Commissioned Officers (NCOs) in these positions were among the casualties. Around 70% of those that died came from Sussex with estimates including up to 12 sets of brothers.

The Women's Institute

The first Women's Institute was formed in Stoney Creek, Ontario, Canada in1897. Inspired by a talk given by Adelaide Hoodless at a meeting of the Farmer's Institute, local farmers Erland and Janet Lee were instrumental in setting up the new organisation. They were supported by the Ontario government who appointed Laura Rose to be the first organiser in 1899.

The movement brought women from isolated communities together and offered training in home economics, child care and those aspects of farming that were traditionally done by women, such as poultry keeping and small farm animal husbandry. WIs quickly spread throughout Ontario and Canada, with 130 branches launched by 1905 in Ontario alone, and the groups flourish in their home province today. The Federated Women's Institutes of Ontario (FWIO) has more than 300 branches today with over 4,500 members.

Madge Watt, a founder member of the first WI in British Columbia, organised the first WI meeting in Great Britain, which took place on 16 September 1915 at Llanfairpwll on Anglesey, Wales. The first WI in Britain was formed under the auspices of the Agricultural Organisation Society (AOS). AOS Secretary, John Nugent Harris, appointed Canadian Madge Watt to set up WIs across the UK. and the first WI in England was Singleton WI in Sussex.

The AOS set up a Women's Institute sub committee to oversee the work and Lady Denman was appointed Chairman. The organisation had two aims: to revitalise rural communities and to encourage women to become more involved in producing food during the First World War.

After the end of the First World War, the Board of Agriculture withdrew its sponsorship, although the Development Commission financially supported the work of the forming of new WIs and gave core funding to the National Federation until it could become financially independent. By

1926 the Women's Institutes were fully independent and rapidly became an essential part of rural life.

Since then the organisation's aims have broadened and it is now the largest women's voluntary organisation in the UK. The organisation celebrated its 100th anniversary in 2015 and as of 2018 had approximately 220,000 members in 6,300 WIs. Today it plays a unique role in enabling women to gain new skills, take part in wide-ranging activities, and campaign on issues that matter to them and their communities. The WI is a diverse organisation open to all women, and there are now WIs in towns and cities as well as villages.

Suggested Non – Fictional Further Reading

The Day Sussex Died, by John A. Baines. (This remains the only definitive book written on the history of Lowther's Lambs by the late John Baines. Offical accounts at the National Archives in Kew remain scant and restricted 100 years on).

Undertones of War, by Edmund Blunden. (Incredible eye witness account from one of the great war poets of the First World War).

Somme – Into The Breach, by Hugh Sebag-Montefiore

The WI – A Centenary History, by Mavis Curtis

Centenary History of the Royal Army Medical Corps, 1898 -1998, by J.S.G.Blair

The Royal Army Medical Corps in the Great War: Images of War, by Timothy McCraken. (Wonderful pictorial glimpse into the conditions in the Great War from a fellow Lancaster University Historian).

Dunant's Dream: War, Switzerland and the History of the Red Cross, by Caroline Moorehead

Also do listen to 'In A South Downs Way' – a beautifully composed album by Damian Montagu about the Southdown battalions composed in 2018 to mark the centenary of the end of the First World War. With narration by Hugh Bonneville and Christopher Timothy.

Acknowledgements

Yet again I find myself indebted to a number of people for their time and assistance in writing this book. Without doubt my wife and sons must be first for cheering me on from the sidelines.

A number of my fellow students from my writing course gave support and critique in equal measure, of whom the authors Anna Hansell and Graham Bullen are always inspiring. Anne Macdonald and Jo Learmonth helped with specific farming input to bring necessary realism to my fiction, and Annie kept my local Scottish references firmly in hand. But special praise must be given to Anne Duncan, my proof reader and copy editor of the early clunky drafts, without whose time I may not have caught the eye of a number of publishers.

Special mention to the ladies of the Federated Institutes of Ontario, Canada, and in particular Kristy Van Hoven and Alyssa Gomori at the Erland Lee Museum and the Stoney Creek branch, who contributed a number of excellent historical documents for my research. Ably supported by WI members in Sussex, England and the Isle of Wight!

Johnson's Butcher's in Thirsk, North Yorkshire, was my first job as a young apprentice working in the shadow of the legendary Alf Wight Vetinary Practice (who wrote as James Herriot), and perhaps something of that magic rubbed off as I too slipped and slithered back and forth amongst those old meat houses. While the events here are fictitious, I am grateful to those days that provided an insight and detail for the job, and indeed where some of my old colleagues work still…

In addition I have received wonderful input from a number of historical societies, and staff at the National Archives in Kew; as well as the British Red Cross, National Farmers' Union and Young Farmers; and former serving soldiers of the RAMC. Too many to mention but all in their own way have helped the construction of this series to date, and continue to help as I move forward with book three! (Hint).

Family and friends of course have all helped to keep me going during the difficult periods, and especially recently when the pandemic put paid to not one but two publishers! *To lose one 'publisher' may be seen as a misfortune, Mr Sowerby, to lose both looks like carelessness* (Apologies to Oscar Wilde for manipulating a line*)*.

But from the ashes of despair and all that... so grateful thanks to my publishers New Generation for stepping so nobly into the breach (I'm off again), and to David and Saskia in particular, at a time when things looked bleak.

A number of places helped me launch 'The Whistle,' and special mention should go to the staff of Steyning Museum; the chairman and staff and players of Steyning Football club; Father mark Heather of St Andrew and St Cuthman Parish church in Steyning; the staff of Dimbola Lodge on the Isle of Wight, where many ideas of the books were sketched as well as launched; and last and certainly not least White Rose Book Café in Thirsk in North Yorkshire where I grew up and where I held my first book signing event. A wonderfully inspiring setting.

And on the back of the success of my first novel, it would be remiss not to thank you, the readers, for your patronage and humbling praise of my efforts. To receive glowing feedback from North America to New Zealand, and from Scandinavia to Scarborough makes it all feel more worthwhile.

Though at the end of the day it was the Davisons that made it all come together of course….

Lilly Louise Allen is a Watercolour Artist and Illustrator based on the Isle of Wight in England. Lilly specialises in editorial food illustration and art for food establishments and events. However her portfolio extends far beyond these interests and she is a highly talented artist that I have been fortunate enough to work with on both my novels.

She has once again captured the heart of the story through her work in a brilliantly emotive design. I would highly recommend her to anyone looking for inspiring ideas and gifts.

https://www.lillylouiseallen.com